CHAOS RISING

BOOKS BY PERRY MORRIS

THE LEMURIAN CHRONICLES
Book I: Children of the Blessing
Book II: Chaos Rising

LEGENDS OF LEMURIA
Novellas based on adventures from various heroes
of the Lemurian Chronicles
Renn and the Bounty Hunters
Shamael and the Battle at the Well of Sacrifice

To get a **free copy** of *Renn and the Bounty Hunters*,
subscribe at www.perrymorris.net/free.
You can unsubscribe at any time.

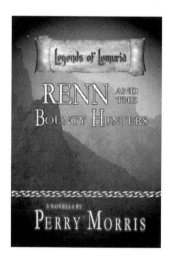

BOOK II OF THE LEMURIAN CHRONICLES

CHAOS RISING

PERRY MORRIS

TABLE OF CONTENTS

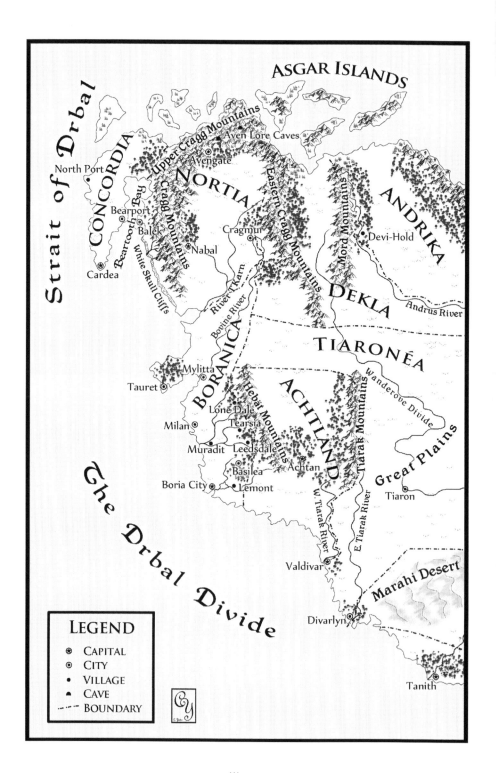

The Lands and Seas of

Lemuria

Pitané

ELDER ISLAND

The School

Sentry Cliffs

Aanith

Andrika Mountains

Port Andrus

Andrus Fens

Andrus Lake

BREMENON

Ava River

Bremenon View

Great Plains

North Port

AVALIAN

Kuri-Kula Mountains

Kurulan

Kanoi

Ksarral

KAHAAL

Rakanin

Kah-Tarku

TIARONÉA

Elahnas Gorge

Blaylin

Kiran

Menet

Anytos

Alfheina

Devlyn

Dyndara

Quarnon

Lemurian Sea

Marahi Desert

The Necro-Sea

Gray Mire Marshes

N
W E
S

SARUNDRA

DOMERIA

LEAGUES

0   50   100   150   200   250

ACHTAN

ANYTOS

AVALIAN

AVEN CITY

BASILEA

BORANICA

DOMERIA

ELDER ISLAND

FORVENDALE

KAHAAL

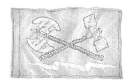

KURULAN

MENET

MORDRAHN

NORTIA

TIARON

VALDIVAR

BANNERS OF LEMURIA

PROLOGUE

"What are you doing, number five?"

Ignoring the question, Cremin pulled dark cotton trousers over his loincloth, opened the gilded trunk at the foot of his bed, and tucked the map of the palace into his loose sleeve, before removing his arm from the trunk so no one would see the map.

He wished he had privacy in Page Hall—that's what the king's servants called this room. Sometimes they called it the King's Candy Room, because they secretly referred to the five pages as the King's Candy.

Soft pillowed beds and lavish furnishings ornamented the large room. Beautiful tapestries and paintings of feasts and lovers embracing adorned the walls. The soft gurgle of running water from the ornate fountain located in the rear of the chamber helped create a serene atmosphere. A table of fresh breads, fruits, and wine stood on either side of the water feature. The aroma of the warm bread overpowered the scented oils the pages lavishly applied to themselves. Even at his father's mansion in Divarlyn, Cremin had never dreamed of such excess.

"The name is Cremin," he said, finally responding to the other page's question. "And my free time is not your concern, *number one.*" Cremin openly mocked the pecking order of these playthings. True, he was one of them in the eyes of everybody here at King Reollyn's palace in Valdivar, but he wasn't anything like the others. They embraced their lives as the king's personal pages. It probably didn't occur to them that once they no longer interested the king, he would send them away.

So far, Cremin had been able to avoid the king's private chambers, but he didn't think that would last much longer. After all, he'd been here six weeks now. His black skin was probably the only thing keeping him from the king's bed. Cremin was a novelty for sure, that's why the king wanted him for a page, but he guessed the king didn't favor the physical characteristics of *the people*. Or perhaps the king didn't want to offend Caloth, Cremin's father, who was the Raji Matla of *the people*, by taking his son to his bed. Truth be told, his father wouldn't care, so long as his going to the king's chamber helped Cremin learn more about this strange people and thereby secure a good trade agreement with King Reollyn.

"Have it your way, *number five*," the other page emphasized his number in order of seniority, "but if you're gone for long, you'll miss massages."

Cremin shrugged, pulled the silk curtain aside and walked to the antechamber. Those soft fools were almost as bad as the king. If *the people* were greater in number, he would simply advise his father to bring an army, take the city by force, and dedicate the victory to Solra, may his name be blessed. Then there would be no need for a trade agreement giving them preferred treatment in the glass trade in Valdivar. But *the people* didn't even number a thousand yet. It had been fifty years since his great-grandfather's ship brought them to this land—blown off course for weeks by a terrible storm. They had sent an expedition a few years later to find the homeland, but it returned with no success. Every expedition afterward either returned with no news or never returned. So *the people* made a small district in the southern city of Divarlyn their new home.

Cremin flashed a toothy smile at the two men guarding the door as he left the room. There were sections of the palace he wouldn't be allowed to wander, but so far no one had stopped him as he explored each evening. The guards always watched him as he went from place to place, but they never questioned him.

The map tucked in his sleeve had been purchased by his father at a great price. He had acquired it from a man who claimed to have been a former captain of the house guard here at the palace who had been wronged by King Reollyn. The man had fallen on hard times and sold what state secrets he knew to Cremin's father—the gods would punish such disloyalty to an anointed king, but it was not forbidden for *the people* to use whatever means necessary to acquire the wish of the Raji Matla. In fact, Cremin believed Solra, may his name be blessed, guided this disgraceful man to his father—just for this purpose.

This map wasn't an ordinary guide to the castle; it plotted the secret entrances and exits, as well as the hidden passageways below and through the castle. The man who had sold Cremin's father the map boasted that even the king didn't know every passageway on it.

Cremin had studied the map many times. He looked at it so often he sometimes saw it in his dreams. He brought it with him because he worried the other pages might go through his things while he was away and find it.

At the end of the long hall, he entered a side staircase that the pages used to get to the throne room several floors below. But rather than go down, he climbed toward the upper floor. There would be guards at the top of this set of stairs—it was the king's private floor. Only three stairways accessed this level: this private staircase, the grand staircase, and a circular stairway in the back corner of Page Hall that led directly to the king's rooms. All entrances were guarded.

But Cremin didn't go to the top of the stairs. Instead, he stopped on the first landing and pulled on an iron sconce next to a large tapestry. He cringed at the sound of stone grating against stone and held his breath as he looked over his shoulder and up the next flight of steps. He listened for a shout of alarm or any evidence somebody noticed the sound. He heard nothing, so he slipped behind the tapestry and through the opening in the wall that led to the hidden passageway beyond. He cringed again as he pulled the sconce in the hidden corridor that moved the secret door back into place.

He stood in complete darkness and listened. Without windows to let in the cool evening breeze from the ocean, the cloying heat made the dust in the air stick to his nostrils. It smelled like dried wood and tasted like dirty sawdust.

Satisfied he was alone, Cremin took a bit of slow burn from his pocket and two small stones. It only took a couple of scratches from the stones to light the slow-burning tinder, which had been treated with a special pitch that easily caught fire and smoldered. Only *the people* knew the formula for slow burn. Some families in their community made a handsome living selling slow burn to the native inhabitants of Lemuria. By the light of the slow burn, Cremin could just make out his surroundings and walk without tripping. Good thing he'd memorized the map because there wasn't enough light to read by.

Somebody had recently used this passageway. A fresh set of prints on the dusty floor testified of that. Cremin thought that to be a good thing—his extra set of prints wouldn't draw attention.

A circular, steel ladder rose from the corridor, and Cremin climbed to get to the king's floor. A quick investigation at the top revealed that the other set of prints ended here as well. He wasn't the only person spying on the king then—not surprising. Again, he looked down the corridor in both directions and down the circular ladder to the level below. His heart pounded in his chest, and he had to concentrate to slow his breathing. He didn't know what would happen if anybody caught him here, and he didn't want to find out. But his duty to his father, the Raji Matla of *the people*, took precedence over his own safety. One had to be faithful to one's ruler—even if Caloth was his father. In fact, it was even more important for Cremin to be obedient *because* Caloth was his father. Solra, may his name be blessed, required obedience to one's father.

A small shaft of light cut through the darkness, illuminating dust motes in the passageway. The light came from a pinhole in the wall. Cremin could hear muffled voices on the other side, coming from the king's bedchamber. He pressed his cheek against the wall and peered through the hole.

The luxurious furnishings of Page Hall didn't prepare him for the lavish excess of the king's personal chamber. A grand, unlit fireplace gilded with gold filigree had its mantel adorned with two marble statues, a large gold-framed mirror, and beautiful flowering plants. Shiny purple material, enhanced by beautiful tapestries and paintings, covered the walls. A plush divan sat in front of a window where the silk curtains were drawn, allowing a person to view the lights of the city below. Two servants stood, waiting to satisfy the king's every whim—one near the door and the other at the head of the king's bed, next to the miniature cushioned litter where the king's favorite white-haired cat groomed itself.

The king lounged on a bed with a canopy of heavy purple and gold material tied open with gold tasseled ropes. His cream-colored silk robe fell open so Cremin could see the king's chest, and he was flirting with number three. Cremin thought the young page's name was Brekia or Brokia. The other pages just called him number three. He had been in Page Hall when Cremin left there a few minutes ago, so he must've just arrived. *Praise Solra, may his name be blessed,* Cremin thought, *that the king didn't ask for me.*

King Reollyn had blond hair that fell in loose ringlets to the nape of his neck and was tucked behind his ears. He looked better without one of the colored, powdered wigs he normally wore. Sometimes, the king wore a heavy crown, but not often. The heavy crown rested on a skillfully carved, ivory table next to the bed, but there was no sign of a wig. The king's narrow face and high cheekbones helped draw attention to the subtle cleft that marked the center of his chin. He wasn't unattractive, if one was inclined to favor men. Solra, may his name be blessed, didn't forbid such attractions, but being with a man didn't appeal to Cremin.

Number three sat down on the bed next to the king, and Cremin turned away. It wasn't right to spy on people's intimate moments, and this was definitely a moment he would rather not watch.

No matter, this network of passageways led to plenty of other places. He would just wander and see what he could find. *Information is power,* his father would say. And you never knew where powerful information would come from. A quick prayer of safety to Solra, may his name be blessed, and then Cremin went back down the circular ladder—silent and listening intently with each step.

For the next two hours, Cremin investigated various passageways. He listened to a conversation between servants behind the wall of their eating room. He was amazed by how free they were with their opinions when they thought no one listened. He made a mental note to return here often. He learned a lot about the workings of the palace, the quirks of dignitaries, and conversations the servants eavesdropped on during the day. *Shameless people,* he thought, although he would never speak openly of his leaders this way—even if it were true.

The servant's quarters were located in the basement, but a set of stone stairs led to more passageways below. These, he knew from his study of the map, led to three secret entrances outside the palace grounds.

Cremin heard distant voices below, so he crouched in a corner at the top of the steps and smothered his slow burn. After it cooled, he wrapped it in the piece of leather he'd kept in the palm of his hand to keep from being burned. Then he placed it into his pocket next to the striking stones. He felt his way to the bottom of the rock-hewn steps and followed the voices. His heart pounded beneath his shirt, but he'd trained many years for moments like this. It's why he came to Valdivar and submitted himself to the humiliation of becoming one of the king's pages. This is how he best served his father, the Raji Matla.

The voices grew louder as he walked, careful to make no sound. His dark skin and clothing made him nearly invisible, but noise would give him away just as easily as being seen. A dim glow spilled into the corridor from a side room. Cremin didn't dare look through the door, but he didn't need to.

"The king doesn't listen to me, priest."

Cremin recognized the voice of Lord Steward Halbert.

"I've tried to get him to grant you an audience, but you know how he is. He is not a religious man; however, I think he's considering making the worship of Lunaryn the state religion. And he's much more concerned about his next ball than the plight of the poor."

"Lunaryn! Doesn't he . . . Are you . . . But . . ."

Cremin could hear the contempt in the priest's voice.

"*By Turoth's black heart,* the good citizens of Valdivar wouldn't stand for it. El Azur is the god of our city and has been since its founding!"

"So I've warned him," Halbert reassured the priest, "and I think I may have forestalled him on this."

This was very curious. Cremin had stood near the king in the throne room for nearly ten hours a day for the past six weeks. He had never heard the king mention religion, and he'd certainly never heard Halbert discuss any of this—the cult of Lunaryn had, perhaps, been discussed in passing, but nothing about state religions or Halbert pleading on behalf of poor citizens.

"Why do you think I brought you to this hidden room?" Halbert said. "If word got back to the king that I gave money to the priests of Azur, he'd lock me in the dungeon and then I could do nothing for the citizens of our great city."

"But we use the money to help the poor," the priest said. "Surely he must understand that a starving and desperate populace creates instability. The temple of Azur is filled with the homeless and hungry."

"I sympathize with your plight, Priest Chalmer, I truly do."

"Azur bless you, Halbert," the priest said and sighed. "I fear you and General Prothus are the only remaining men of influence who truly love the people. And with the general off fighting the war, your efforts are our only hope."

"I appreciate that." Halbert sounded sincere, but Cremin didn't believe it. He'd seen the man's arrogance on a daily basis. Halbert was a politician first and foremost. He was up to something. Cremin heard a clinking thud, and Halbert said, "This is all I can spare for now, Chalmer. I'm afraid if I take more it will be noticed."

"Thank you, my lord," the priest said. "Your patronage will not go unnoticed. I will make sure the people know they have a true friend in you."

VITIATE

Shamael stared into the dark liquid of the scrying pool, rubbed the smooth skin on his head, and narrowed his eyes. The girl Kahn had kept in his study was with two escaped slaves and a boy who looked similar enough to be her brother. Was it possible? Had the girl's brother, the Child of the Blessing whom Kahn had so desperately wanted for his pet, come to the caves and rescued his sister? It didn't seem likely, but who else would attempt such a thing? It *had* to be her brother, Avaris.

Kintara had sent a team to Kahn's study to retrieve the grimoire during the battle at the well. Her team had killed the defenders Shamael sent to protect the Grand Warlock's chambers. After Kintara's team left with the book, these three boys probably just walked in and freed the girl. Had Kintara not done this, he would still have the girl as his prisoner. Another reason to kill Kintara the next time their paths crossed.

He leaned forward and looked again at the images in the shadowy waters—three dark-haired, dark-skinned Devi teens and a white teenage boy with reddish hair. They looked tired and anxious. He shifted his view to the mountains surrounding the teens and then traced backward from their position to the east entrance of the caves. It had been two weeks since he had fought and defeated Kintara at the well of sacrifice, and he assumed these three had escaped during the pandemonium of the battle. But they were less than twenty leagues away—they were traveling slowly.

He rubbed his head, stood straight, and considered the best course of action. He didn't have time to go after them, but he hated to let them escape. At least Kintara wasn't with them. The last thing he needed was for her to have control of a Child of the Blessing.

His new council would be waiting for him in the Grand Warlock's study—his study—so he dispelled the images with a wave of his hand, left the scrying room, and headed down the narrow stairs that led to the main corridor several hundred steps below.

As he made his way down the seemingly endless rock-hewn steps, he wondered if it would be possible to build a scrying pool in his chambers. This location was extremely inconvenient and time consuming.

Transformation had always been easy for Shamael. With the added power he possessed as Grand Warlock, it took little more than a thought. Still, he touched the hawk-shaped pendant under his shirt to help focus his mind on the shape of the animal he wanted to assume.

In mere seconds, his body shrank and transformed from skin to feathers, and from arms to wings. Shamael hopped into the air and dove down the narrow stairwell toward the corridor, relishing the intoxicating freedom that accompanied flight. A group of off-duty soldiers covered their heads and scattered as he flew into the main passageway with a screech. Everybody in the caves knew that animals this deep under the mountain were Shapeshifters or Warlocks, so they quickly gave way anytime such a creature was present.

Only ten minutes later, Shamael fluidly resumed his human form as he landed outside the closed door to his study. He brushed his long black cloak, straightened his burgundy silk shirt and made sure his pendants were tucked underneath. He walked forward, held up his right hand, and with a thought caused the newly replaced iron-studded door to swing open.

Fortunately for his council, they were all waiting patiently around the large antique wooden table in his study—except for Jenot, who stood at a bookshelf. The table had belonged to a king of Concordia more than three hundred years ago and had been seized during a raid. It had been collecting dust in one of the storage chambers since that time. Shamael had his servants scrub the study and remove the cage the Devi girl had been held prisoner in and used the space for this table instead. He needed a place to sit with his council and lay out his strategy—something Kahn would never have done.

Shamael's guests stood as he entered. The hook-nosed Jenot, with long greasy hair, set a book he'd been perusing back on the bookshelf in the wall near Shamael's desk. Shamael motioned for them to sit. Jenot smiled his wry grin and walked to his seat. Shamael noticed the bags beneath Jenot's snakelike green eyes were darker than normal.

Shamael looked down and gave Shadin Dorid a cold smile. Shadin was a pudgy man who wore the green robe of the order of Witches. "Are you feeling well, Shadin?" the Grand Warlock asked.

"Yes, milord." Shadin wiped a bead of sweat from his forehead with his sleeve. "Just a bit warm."

Shamael poured himself a goblet of Boranica red and stared at Shadin as he swirled the wine. The liquid clung to the sides of the goblet and released a sweet fruity aroma.

Shadin shifted in his seat. His eyes darted from Shamael to General Nishkral, who was sitting next to Shadin, and back to Shamael. Nishkral was larger and more muscular than most Kirocs, and his wings were folded against his back, which caused him to sit forward in his chair to avoid the backrest.

Shadin wrung his hands. His graying, ruddy brown hair was matted against his forehead. His beard still had color next to his round cheeks, but his whiskers faded to gray as they grew outward.

Shamael sat in the cushioned throne-like chair at the head of the table. "I didn't see you at the battle, Shadin." The Grand Warlock set his wine down, took a clam from a pewter tray, and cracked open the shell with a thought. The corner of his mouth turned up. The added power that came with the mantle of Grand Warlock was obvious, even in a simple task such as splitting clam shells. Shadin squirmed in his chair as the slippery meat with a hint of salt slid down Shamael's throat. "I do hope you weren't fighting alongside Kintara. I'm told you are quite fond of her."

"Of course not, milord." Shadin's hand shook as he wiped at his forehead. "I was trying to maintain order among the Demonologists."

Shamael took a sip of wine. He found silence was more effective than words in circumstances like this.

Shadin's eyes darted at the others seated around the table. He wiped his head again and said, "May the demons feast upon my soul if I'm not speaking the truth, Lord Daro. I am loyal to you!"

That was about as serious an oath as one could make, and Shadin's assertion that he was carrying out his duty with the Demonologists during the battle could be easily verified.

"And what of your feelings for Kintara?"

"I have no feelings for her. She is an outcast and a tramp!"

Shamael raised an eyebrow. The others at the table chuckled, but Grilic, a purple-skinned Kiroc who sat at the head of the table opposite Shamael, boomed with laughter.

"We've all seen you grovel and drool over Kintara." Grilic's rotting teeth showed through his snarling grin, and he narrowed his beady yellow eyes and leaned forward. "Are we really to believe you have no loyalty to her?"

Grilic was a Kiroc magic user with a wild shock of black hair the texture of straw and a single curved horn protruding from the right side of his forehead. The left horn had been cut off after he passed out during a brawl at a tavern. He found the man who cut it off and killed him for it. That horn now hung proudly at his neck from a thick gold chain on top of his red Necromancer robes. Grilic was responsible for overseeing the training of Witches.

"I swear *by the dark of K'Thrak*, I am loyal to Shamael." Shadin hit his fist against his chest. "Kintara is like any other woman. If she can't be a useful tool, she should be sent to the well of sacrifice—she has no hold upon me!"

"That's all women are good for, is it?" Ancilia Biment had been silent throughout the exchange. She was a patient old woman, but the tone in her question made it clear she wasn't impressed. She sat to the left of Shamael, just opposite of Shadin.

Shadin's eyes now darted from Ancilia back to Shamael. "What I mean is that we all must be useful to the cause of Ba Aven, or we are fit only to be sacrificed at the well."

Ancilia peered down her nose at him. Her long gray hair fell in waves over her black dress. She had been a friend to Shamael since he had been a boy, struggling to survive on the streets of Valdivar. She was a Shapeshifter who had been sent to spy in Valdivar by Kahn Devin, though the other thieves didn't know that. She became one of the best thieves in the guild. She also recognized the gift of power in Shamael. After he became the guild's thief master, she persuaded him to go to the caves and study Aven-Lore. She probably possessed enough power to become a Warlock, but Shamael suspected she didn't have the stomach to kill a fellow Shapeshifter in order to advance. Some people had silly qualms like that.

"You are dismissed, Shadin." Shamael waved his hand. He would let the man retain his position over the Demonologists—for now, at least. "Return to your duties."

"Thank you, Lord Daro." Shadin's face flushed, and in his rush to leave, he bumped the table as he stood, causing the books stacked in front of Clenmon Mishlok to topple.

Clenmon blinked and looked around the room like he just realized he wasn't alone. He scowled at the fallen books and muttered as he restacked them. He was the official archivist. He'd held that position since before Kahn Devin came to the caves. The contrast between Clenmon and the Kirocs couldn't have been starker. He was a frail old man with long, thinning white hair that hadn't likely been washed or combed in years. His face had nicks from the dull razor he used to keep his face shaved. Shamael thought it strange the man bothered with shaving when he neglected all other personal hygiene, until Shamael learned that Clenmon's beard at one time had been so long he tripped over it and fell into a desk stacked with books and a full inkwell. Two ancient manuscripts were damaged during that episode, and since that time the old man shaved every day.

Shadin muttered an apology to the archivist, bowed to Shamael, and made for the door.

"And Shadin," Shamael said. The Witch, halfway out the door, turned and wrung his hands. "Don't disappoint me or I will take you up on your oath and *you* will become a sacrifice at the well."

The portly Witch bowed again, wiped a bead of sweat from his face, and ran out the door.

A deep, grating chuckle escaped from Grilic. "I don't think you need worry about that one." He fingered the horn hanging from the chain on his neck. "He doesn't have the courage to defy you."

"True," Shamael said. "But I'm not ready to give him a seat in my inner circle. The five of you are here because you have earned my trust. Unlike my predecessor, I want advisors who understand and contribute to my strategies." He took another sip of wine as he let his words sink in. Grand Warlocks historically had been secretive, only divulging pieces of their plans here and there when they deemed it necessary. That, in Shamael's opinion, was why the Aven-Lore hadn't increased in influence for the past millennium.

He surveyed the eclectic group gathered around the table. Ancilia was noticeably proud of him. Her faith in him all these years had finally paid off. The Kirocs and Jenot watched him with curiosity, and the archivist nodded his head and rubbed at his chin.

"Jenot, what word have you from the three?" Shamael didn't need to elaborate on who the three were. That was a common reference among Aven-Lore users for the high priests and priestesses to the gods K'Thrak, Danisyr, and Necrosys.

"They will be here for the ceremony, my lord. Siersha and Hodran have confirmed they will travel through the eternal wayfires from their temples on the night of the new moon in two days' time. Torin will be here tomorrow and has requested an audience with you."

"Very good. I have another task for you, my friend."

Jenot gave a wry smile that caused his thin lips to look like a crooked line beneath his beak like nose and nodded in deference to Shamael.

"The girl Kahn held prisoner in this room has escaped with her brother and two runaway slaves—"

"Her brother?" Ancilia interrupted. "The Child of the Blessing?"

"The very one," Shamael said. "I have seen them in the scrying pool. They are still close by, about twenty leagues south east of the east entrance. I want you to take Demon Dogs and their trainers to intercept them."

"Am I to kill them, milord?" Jenot asked.

"The slaves are to be returned so they can serve as an example for other slaves who might consider escape—they will be sacrificed. The girl is also to be returned to be used as a sacrifice."

"And the Child of the Blessing?" Jenot rubbed his hands together.

"Kill him."

Jenot Lexton's eyes lit up, and Shamael knew what the man was thinking. The boy's bones would make powerful magical implements.

Shamael scowled. "Bring his remains to me."

Jenot's expression darkened, but he bowed his head in acquiescence.

"Lord Daro," Ancilia said. "Perhaps we can convince him to join us. He would be a powerful ally."

The archivist nodded in agreement but was then distracted by a bug crawling down a white strand of hair hanging in front of his right eye.

Shamael shook his head. "Kahn believed that, too. He implemented elaborate plans to bring Avaris to our side. But Kahn failed. The boy will never join us." He said that last with a note of finality and looked from face to face, waiting for any other objections.

"Take a dozen Demon Dogs with trainers who can work magic, Jenot. You can't afford to fail."

"He is a mere boy," Jenot spat with contempt but changed his tone when Shamael's eyes narrowed. "I won't fail, milord."

"He may be a *mere boy*," Shamael said, "but he escaped Kahn Devin. It wouldn't be wise to underestimate him."

Jenot's thin lips curled in an apparent attempt to smile, but it looked more like a grimace, and he tilted his head in deference to Shamael's wishes.

"Clenmon," Shamael said, and the archivist looked up from studying the bug he held between his fingertips. "I see you brought the tomes I asked for. What have you learned about the source of Nefarion Drakkas's great power?"

The two Kirocs and Ancilia's eyes grew wide at the mere mention of the ancient, traitorous Grand Warlock's name. Shamael smiled inwardly but pretended not to notice their discomfort. Jenot leaned forward and rubbed his hands together as he stared at the dusty tomes. Clenmon cleared his throat and rested a hand on the volumes stacked on the table next to him.

"Nefarion is the most powerful Warlock on record," the archivist said in a dry voice, "but he greatly enhanced his power through the use of vitiate."

"Has your research uncovered how a vitiate is created?"

"Vitiate?" Ancilia voice carried a note of alarm. "Lord Shamael, Nefarion was cast out and hunted by Monguinir. In his wrath, the demon lord swore he would never allow a Grand Warlock to create vitiate minions again. It took five centuries for us to regain our numbers after that battle."

"I thought you might know about the vitiate, Ancilia," Shamael said. "Like me, you are a student of history. I'd wager most in these caves have never even heard the term."

"As a student of history," Ancilia said, "I needn't remind you that Nefarion Drakkas also had the dragon Roskva and her children on his side, and he *still* lost his battle with our master."

"You are correct, which is why I will present my plan to Lord Monguinir before I carry it out."

"Excuse me, Shamael." General Nishkral's voice boomed in comparison to Clenmon's and Ancilia's. His bat-like wings and skeletal face with a row of small spiked horns circling his head made him appear fierce.

As Shamael looked at him, he noticed Nishkral's jawline was angular, and his eyes were a magnificent shade of violet—he wondered if perhaps, somewhere in his distant past, the Kiroc general had Avuman blood running in his veins. That would be a strange combination. He made a mental note to ask Clenmon if such a thing was even possible—that could wait until later. Shamael nodded for him to continue.

"What is a vash . . . vosh—"

"Vitiate," Shamael said. "They are soldiers of sorts, but their weapon is a particular set of magical abilities."

"They were much more than that." Clenmon grew lucid as he discussed ancient history. He leaned forward, and his voice dropped conspiratorially. "They were more . . . *and* they were less. The vitiate have a direct connection with the Warlock who creates them. He can see what they see and speak to their minds. Distance is no hindrance to this ability. Their strength in the lore is increased because of this connection to the Warlock, but the cost . . . diminishes them."

"What, exactly, is the cost?" Jenot asked. His green eyes gleamed as he was sucked into Clenmon's tale. Shamael thought the old archivist a bit overly dramatic, but this was exactly the kind of information he needed. This was why the archivist would be a part of his inner circle.

"They give their agency entirely to their master," Ancilia replied mat-ter-of-factly, earning her an irritated look from Clenmon, who was obviously enjoying the rapt attention from the others. "The cost is their soul."

"That's not entirely accurate, Ancilia," Clenmon countered and smiled as everyone's attention focused back to him. "It's true they lose their agency and even their soul in this life, but once they die, their soul is released and travels to Valhasgar, the same as everybody else. They are released from the control of their master, but they retain the knowledge they gained as a vitiate."

"Interesting," Jenot said. "For somebody weak in the lore, becoming a vitiate would be a shortcut to greater power in their next life."

"Very good, umm—"

"Jenot," the small Warlock in tight brown leather supplied to the archi-vist who looked at him like they'd just met. They may well have, Shamael supposed—he didn't think Jenot spent much time down in the archives.

"Very good, Jenot," Clenmon said. "There hasn't been any vitiate since Nefarion's betrayal, but the histories speculate the vitiate gained power equivalent to three lifetimes' worth of normal advancement from their connection with the Grand Warlock's power."

"This is all good, Clenmon," Shamael said, "but does the record say *how* to create a vitiate?"

Everyone in the room looked expectantly at the wizened old archivist, who grimaced. He shook his head and rested his hand on the stack of old books. "I've read them all several times, but Monguinir demanded that that particular knowledge be removed from all records after Nefarion's betrayal."

Everyone looked at Shamael. He wanted to slam his fist on the table and curse, but that would appear as though his plan had failed before he even began. Was that relief on Ancilia's face? Probably. Shamael swirled the last bit of red wine in his goblet as he considered the archivist's words, then drained the cup. He reached up to rub his head but stopped himself. He didn't want to appear indecisive. Instead, he stood, locked his hands behind his back, and smiled as though he hadn't a care in the world.

"Then I will ask Lord Monguinir how it is done."

The Kirocs looked impressed with his declaration, Jenot and the archivist nodded in agreement, but Ancilia's eyes bulged, and her mouth dropped open.

"Ancilia, I want you to work with Shadin to identify fifty candidates from among the Demonologists and Magicians."

"Fifty?" Her voice rose in pitch, and she shot to her feet. "What if Lord Monguinir won't allow it? Even if he does, we won't find that many among the Demonologists and Magicians. We'll need to draw from the ranks of Witches as well."

Shamael nodded. "Grilic, see if you can convince a few Witches to become vitiate." Truth be told, Shamael would be happy with thirty, but if they found fifty, it would be all the better.

The color drained from Ancilia's face. "My lord, Nefarion had only twelve vitiate. What do you intend to do with fifty?"

"Chaos," he said. "We will create chaos in all nations of Lemuria."

THE HUNT

Kintara perched high in a sturdy pine tree perhaps a quarter mile above the east entrance to the caves. She had flown up here this morning, resumed her human form, and watched the Kiroc guards below for the past three hours. The smell of the meat they cooked over an open fire for their lunch wafted up the mountain and mixed with the crisp scent of pine sap by the time it reached her nose. She pulled a stray strand of black hair away from her face and tucked it behind her ear as she considered her options.

Two weeks ago she'd fought Shamael at the well of sacrifice for the ultimate prize—she'd lost. Instinct and the will to survive screamed at her to flee as far from the seat of Shamael's power as possible. But that's exactly what he would expect her to do. He'd probably completed the ritual at the well of sacrifice several days ago, so he would be much stronger in the lore now. She couldn't hope to win a battle against him. She would have to bide her time and watch for an opportunity to kill him by surprise. Somehow she would find a way to eliminate him.

But for now, he was the new Grand Warlock, and she was an outcast. She would be hunted and possibly killed. She'd gambled and lost.

The Kirocs' standing guard turned and looked into the mouth of the cave. Kintara heard the bone-chilling howl of Demon Dogs reverberate off the rock walls of the corridors. They were coming for her. At least she'd had time to recover—she wouldn't go down without a fight. It surprised her they hadn't come before now. Her trail was more than a week old, and she'd covered scores of miles—most in the air. Even Demon Dogs wouldn't be able to track her now.

A dozen massive, pitch-black beasts burst out of the maw of the cave, rabid with the excitement of the hunt. She didn't think they could smell or sense her from this distance, but she reverted to the form of a hawk anyway. On the heels of the Dogs came ravens, wolves, and other animals—handlers for the Demon Dogs. So, Shamael didn't send regular Demon Dogs—he had sent Dogs with handlers who were Shapeshifters. The new Grand Warlock wasn't taking any chances. At least he had enough respect for Kintara to send a formidable force to track her down.

The Demon Dogs howled and barked—anxious to run and hunt. Their handlers transformed into their human forms and each brought their Dog to heel. With her hawk eyes, Kintara could see that they each wore the red robes and black sash of Shapeshifters; Warlocks had better things to do. But then a Warlock with long black greasy hair, wearing tight brown leather clothes, sauntered out of the caves. With a single word, he commanded the attention of the handlers and massive black beasts. She didn't need superior hawk sight to recognize Jenot Lexton. Of course that slimy little Warlock would support Shamael. She never bothered to hide her revulsion for the man. He probably asked for the assignment to kill Kintara because she'd rebuffed his unwanted advances so many times.

Jenot held a piece of leather material out for the Dogs to smell. Kintara didn't recognize the object; it didn't belong to her. The howling of the Dogs echoed across the mountains and they barked with hunger and anticipation of a kill. When the handlers released them, the Demon Dogs searched for the scent for mere moments before they bayed and charged southeast up the mountain opposite Kintara's position.

Curious. They had clearly caught the scent they were looking for, but Kintara hadn't gone in that direction. And the leather scrap wasn't hers. Maybe they weren't hunting her after all. If not her, then who? If she were in human form, she'd twist her hair as she watched them run up the mountain. But in this form, she just cocked her head a little to one side. She should fly as far as she could in the opposite direction. Oh well, what did she have to lose now anyway? She hopped off the branch and soared into the sky, circling higher and higher so the vicious group below wouldn't see her.

Jenot and the handlers transformed back into their chosen animal forms so they could keep pace with the Dogs. They were already cresting the first mountain peak and heading down the next, barely stopping to make sure they were still following the scent. Whomever they were chasing wasn't doing a good job of hiding their trail. Of course, hiding your trail from Demon Dogs was nearly impossible.

Kintara followed the group for several hours before she took a short side excursion at one of the mountain meadows to capture and consume a field mouse and then transformed to her human form to drink from a cold spring. She filled her pewter cup with water and forced a bit of the aeon myriad to heat it so she could steep the leaves of her special brew. She forced the bitter, warm liquid down—she should've been accustomed to the flavor after doing this twice a day for the past twenty years, but it was as nasty as ever—and then took another drink from the fresh spring to wash the flavor from her tongue.

It didn't take long to relocate Jenot and the others after her brief stop; the Demon Dogs barked and bayed like ravenous monsters. They obviously weren't concerned about letting their prey hear them approach. In fact, just the opposite was probably true; they wanted whomever they were chasing to hear them. It would cause fear, and Demon Dogs fed on fear like starving wolves fed on fresh rabbit.

At dusk, Kintara located the target of Jenot's chase. There were four of them—three boys and a girl. They were still a couple of miles ahead of their pursuers, but at this pace, they would be overtaken within the hour. Why was Shamael interested in these four? Kintara flew a short way ahead of the small group and found a perch where she could get a better look at them. They charged into view, and everything made perfect sense.

Two of the boys bore the markings of runaway slaves, but they didn't matter. The girl was the child Kahn Devin had been holding prisoner in his study, which meant the other boy was most likely her brother—the Child of the Blessing, Avaris Mordrahn. He was the same boy she saw with her new recruits just before the well of sacrifice went dark, she was certain of it.

Shamael must have somehow figured out the Child of the Blessing had rescued his sister and escaped the caves. Given Shamael's gift with scrying, he'd probably seen them and their location before he summoned Jenot and the others to hunt them down. The only remaining question was what Shamael planned to do with them. Well, the pursuing group wasn't an envoy on a diplomatic mission—they were hunters and killers.

The four kids stopped running, and Kintara cocked her hawk head to one side. Why would they stop with killers on their trail? The Devi tribe slave boy—probably from Avaris's own tribe—spoke to the others and pointed out defensive positions to them. He held the girl's hand and tenderly led her to a large rock protruding from the mountain with thick bushes covering one side. He pulled one of the bushes back and helped her get into a well-hidden cavity between the stone and the mountain. Once he released the bush, the girl was invisible, even to Kintara's hawk sight.

Incredible, she thought. These three boys intended to make a stand against a dozen Demon Dogs, Shapeshifters, and a Warlock. Kintara admired their bravery. And perhaps it was the smart thing as well—at least this way they got to choose the battlefield. It would still be a slaughter, and the bushes and stone wouldn't hide the girl from Demon Dogs. In the least, it would be entertaining to watch.

Renaul stared dumbfounded at Avaris and Lekiah. They *actually* wanted to turn and fight! Renaul didn't know how many were chasing them, but it sounded like an entire pack of Demon Dogs. And Demon Dogs never came alone; they always had their handlers with them. Early in his captivity under the Cragg Mountains, he'd been assigned to the kennels. He'd had to feed the Dogs, clean their cages, and carry out any other task the handlers dreamed up for him. He once saw a large man torn apart in mere seconds by a single Demon Dog. Sure, Renaul and his new friends had defeated a witch and a few soldiers in the cave mines to free some slaves, and they'd killed a couple necromancers to rescue Kalisha from the Grand Warlock's study, but they wouldn't wouldn't defeat what hunted them now.

Avaris gestured to give him instructions. They didn't speak the same language, but during their escape from the caves they had learned to communicate in other ways. But all Renaul could do now was stare. Maybe it was time for him to leave his companions. He had helped rescue Lekiah and Kalisha, and they'd helped him escape—he owed them nothing. The girl had slowed them down and now they were all going to die because of it. If he went out on his own now, maybe he could escape. But, that would only happen if his friends drew all the attention of the Demon Dogs. They would die so he could *maybe* escape.

Avaris was like Renn—a Child of the Blessing. The gods had plans for people like Renn and Avaris, didn't they? And even though Renaul couldn't talk to these savages, they were two of the best friends he'd ever had. That settled it. Their fate would be his fate.

"I don't understand. Start over." Renaul's gestures and tone were enough to cause Avaris to stop talking and try again. Using hand gestures and sticks as props, Renaul finally understood that Avaris wanted him to search for animal bones, especially skull and thighbones.

Renaul jogged in increasingly larger circles around their current position, looking for animal carcasses. He chuckled sardonically and kicked at a pile of sparrow bones—he felt almost as though they were mocking him. They were bones, just what he needed, but they were worthless to an Aven-Lore user—even Renaul knew that much. At this rate their hunters would be on top of them long before he found anything useful.

He looked to the sky and bit his lip. The sun would soon drop behind the mountain to the west. Renaul saw two vultures silhouetted against the darkening sky, circling not far from him. Vultures circling? That could only mean one thing. He ran as fast as he could, stumbling over loose rocks and a stump as he rushed to the location under the birds. He burst into a small clearing and found himself staring at the glowing eyes of a mountain lion just finishing its meal—a large stag.

The cat was as startled as Renaul. It jumped to its feet and made a sound like a woman screaming. Renaul drew his sword, shouted, and charged. If he couldn't face down a lone mountain lion, he'd have no chance against Demon Dogs. The animal decided the remainder of the carcass wasn't worth fighting over, and it turned and disappeared into the trees.

Renaul hurried to the stag, the smell of blood and deer hide causing him to cringe. He watched the spot where the mountain lion had retreated into the forest while he hacked off the head and two front legs of the stag with his sword. The kill was still warm and bloody, but Renaul didn't have time to clean it. He re-sheathed his sword, wrapped the head and legs in his cloak, and retraced his steps.

Avaris and Lekiah had erected a crude wall of stones four steps wide and waist high, and now Lekiah was climbing a nearby tree to a thick branch twelve feet above the ground—this would give him an advantage with his bow, but Renaul knew the Devi warrior only had a handful of arrows, so he wouldn't be in that position for long.

Renaul dropped the cloak, now soaked in deer blood, in front of Avaris. The long-haired Devi boy stared at it then looked at Renaul and raised his hands, palms upward, as he gestured at the skull and bones that still had meat clinging to them. Renaul shrugged and gave him an apologetic smile. Both boys turned toward the north and stared with wide eyes and rigid jaws down the hillside—those last howls sounded close.

Avaris turned back to the bloody pile at his feet, pursed his lips, and narrowed his eyes. He bent down and picked up the deer's head by an antler. Avaris's body emitted a faint white glow. With a swooshing sound, the white energy surrounding him surged into a single focal point and rushed through his hand and into the animal's head. The hair and meat on the skull sizzled and smoked and Renaul scrunched his nose against the fetid odor. The entire thing burst into flames so intense that Renaul had to step back, but Avaris appeared unharmed and unconcerned. He just continued to push white energy into the skull. Renaul shielded his eyes against the bright glow. He'd never seen white power before—only red or green.

The white fire died as fast as it began, and all that remained was the clean, dry skull of a stag. Avaris then took a thighbone in each hand and repeated the process. The boy was visibly tired after he finished, and Renaul gave him a drink from the waterskin and a piece of dried meat. Before Avaris took a bite of his food, the piercing bay of Demon Dogs and the crack of dead wood announced the arrival of their pursuers.

Renaul heard the twang of a bow and the rush of an arrow fly overhead, and then a thud and a yelp. He squinted to make out the shadows in the distance. His heart pounded, and it felt like his stomach had climbed into his chest. He drew his sword, preparing for an attack he couldn't see.

A streak of red energy blazed out of the eye sockets of the deer skull in Avaris's outstretched hand and lit up the clearing. This time, Renaul both heard the pained yelp *and* saw the Demon Dog reduced to ashes by the attack. He also saw another Dog lying on the ground with an arrow protruding from its eye. But the red light showed him something else: they were all going to die.

A line of massive Demon Dogs snarled and foamed at the mouth a mere twenty paces away. Their black fur was tinged with a hint of red cast by the dull light that surrounded the bones in Avaris's hands. Out of the sky birds and a bat dropped to the ground and transformed into human lore users. A wolf, a mountain lion, and two coyotes walked through the line of Dogs and also transformed into humans.

Avaris shot another beam of crimson energy at the group, but before it made contact a red shield appeared and absorbed the attack.

"There is no need for your sister and friends to be hurt, Avaris." The man who spoke had transformed from a fox and wore tight brown leather. He had long greasy hair and rubbed his hands together and licked his lips.

"You'll have to speak the Devi tongue," Renaul called out—a spark of hope entered his mind at the man's pronouncement that no one needed to be hurt. "Avaris doesn't speak common." And how did the man know

Kalisha was with them? Renaul stole a glance to where she was hiding, but he couldn't see her.

The man called out again, but this time Renaul couldn't understand him. Avaris shouted something in reply. This exchange occurred a few more times, before Avaris looked at Renaul and Lekiah as though considering his options. Lekiah shouted angrily and shook his head—obviously, he wasn't happy about whatever bargain the greasy-haired man tried to strike. Avaris argued with his Devi friend. Renaul looked to the line of assailants and noticed half of the Demon Dogs were gone. He scanned the forest but saw nothing. Still, he knew they were out there, probably surrounding them.

Avaris dropped his bone implements and came out from behind the rock wall. Renaul saw the greasy-haired man in tight brown leather grin. The man pulled out a skull and held it forward. How had he hidden that in his tight leather? The eyes of the skull glowed, and Renaul knew what would follow; he'd seen it several times over the past few years.

But before the man released the attack, Lekiah rolled out from behind the rock barrier and fired an arrow as he came up on one knee. The skull flew from the man's grasp, and he looked at his impaled hand in disbelief—then he shrieked with pain and cried out, "Kill them all!"

Avaris and Renaul dove for the cover of the rocks as red energy shot from skulls and thighbones of half a dozen lore users. Demon Dogs howled and rushed forward in anticipation of a swift kill. Lekiah rolled and loosed another arrow, felling another black furry beast with a bolt through its right eye. Lekiah dove to a different spot as a red blast of power exploded at the place he'd just occupied.

Avaris grabbed the two thighbones he'd dropped moments before, and they sprung to life with barely contained red fury. He rose above the small rock barricade and shot streams of angry power at the attackers. A red shield materialized and absorbed one of his streams of power, but the energy from his second stream broke through and obliterated two of the Demon Dog handlers who were helping maintain the shield.

Renaul heard a crashing sound from behind and held his sword in front of him with both hands as he turned to see what it was. He glimpsed a massive black beast flying toward him, then felt the weight of it crush him to the ground.

Kintara's golden hawk eyes stared at the battle scene unfolding in the clearing below. Three Demon Dogs were dead, and Avaris had killed four Shapeshifters—she knew Warlocks who would already be dead if pitted against these odds. The red-haired teen struggled to push the Demon Dog off him—his had been a lucky kill. The Demon Dog had been impaled by the sword the boy held when it landed on him.

However, the Devi boy with the bow leaped, rolled, and fired his arrows with deadly accuracy. So far, he'd been able to evade the magical attacks, but he would be killed the moment one of the lore user's blasts hit him. Kintara chuckled as she watched Jenot hold his hand in pain while trying to remove the arrow, but in her hawk body, it came out as a clucking sound.

The teens were doing well, but it wouldn't be enough. The boys would die and so would the girl. The ring of Demon Dogs and Aven-Lore users continued to tighten around them like a hangman's noose. Another Dog fell to an arrow, and two more Shapeshifters were incinerated by Avaris, but the noose was getting tighter.

The remaining lore users—there were seven, including Jenot—were stronger than the six Avaris had already killed. Still, six dead in less than two minutes was remarkable. If she'd had him during the battle with Shamael, she would've won.

The boy with the bow ran out of arrows and cast it aside in favor of a sword, then stood beside Avaris. The red-haired slave managed to shove the dead Demon Dog off him and stood on the other side. In this defensive position, they continued to fight. Demon Dogs circled and lunged, just outside the reach of the swords, sizing up their opponents. It didn't take long before the Dogs attacked—two Dogs leaping toward each boy at the same time. The boys swung and fought bravely, but they were about to collapse under the assault.

The remaining magic users sent bolts of red power toward Avaris—their combined streams created a massive river of power. This would be the end. Kintara was surprised to realize she felt a twinge of regret. She would have liked to work with this so-called Child of the Blessing. With her mentoring him, they could accomplish great things. Maybe even supplant Shamael. But Avaris was as good as dead. Even a well-constructed energy shield couldn't stand against this onslaught—and since the boy hadn't created a shield yet, Kintara doubted he knew how to make one.

Just before the massive surge of red power crashed into the boys, Avaris shot his own bolt of energy, and it collided with the blast from the Aven-Lore users. The boy's attack should have dissipated like wax under intense flame. Instead, there was a loud crack like two lightning bolts colliding in the sky as the streams of energy met in midair—battling for supremacy.

The stream of power from Jenot and the other lore users slowly advanced. Avaris dropped to one knee, his teeth clenched and his brows furrowed, but he didn't give up. Still, he was losing. Kintara wouldn't have believed this if she hadn't witnessed it with her own eyes. The amount of energy Avaris channeled through these two bones was staggering—and they were just common animal bones. Even with bones from a powerful Warlock's body, she wouldn't be able to summon this much strength.

The two boys next to Avaris were on the ground now, struggling and thrusting with their swords, but both were losing. It was just a matter of time—very little time. Unless . . .

Kintara made a rash decision—she had much to gain and nothing to lose. She launched into the air and flew behind Jenot and the handlers. She shimmered into her human form as she landed, pulled out a skull, and summoned enough power to create a shield between Avaris and his attackers.

With a shield protecting the young Devi boy, his stream of power surged to a raging river of crimson energy that sliced through the ranks of lore users like hot coal through snow. Surprised screams were silenced almost as fast as they sounded. The lore users burned and dropped lifeless to the ground—all except Jenot, who'd always been a snake. He must have maintained a shield around his own body during the battle rather than expend his complete energy on Avaris. Jenot always made sure he had a way out, regardless of the cost to others. Still, Avaris's attack sent him reeling head over heels across the clearing and into the forest.

Kintara turned her attention to the Demon Dogs, whistled, and issued a loud command that she amplified using the power still surging through her. The Dogs snapped to attention, listened to her orders, then charged down the mountain to run back to their kennels in the caves.

"You'll die for this, you traitorous bitch!" Jenot cried out from somewhere behind the trees.

"I'm here now, you slimy lizard," she said. "Crawl out of your hole and fight."

Kintara waited for him to speak again so she could determine his location, but Jenot didn't reply. He had probably changed into a fox and was running for his life.

She turned to the three boys, blew a strand of hair off her face, and sauntered toward them.

VISIONS AND LOCKETS

L umornel, the Elder Seeress of the Avumen, pulled away from the scrying pedestal in the center of her flower garden, pushed a thick strand of green hair behind her ear, and took a step back. As the cool white mists receded into the bowl, the aroma of daisies, tulips, and roses returned to her nostrils. She folded her arms across her chest and tapped a long finger against her cheek. The goddess Lunaryn hadn't shown her anything new, but there was plenty to try to piece together.

She wished she had an apprentice—she frequently wished for that. Raevil, the Elder Bard of the Avumen, had Arthlynian to talk things over with—well, they were both hermits, so maybe they didn't collaborate much. Still, it would be nice to have somebody who understood the nature of visions and prophecy to discuss things with. However, the goddess hadn't deemed it necessary to reveal an apprentice to her yet, so she was left to her own musings.

The humans in the world appeared determined to make a mess of things. Every time she viewed the happenings in Lemuria, matters grew worse. Armies were laying siege to Tiaron, but the king of Valdivar continued to feast and live a life of extravagant excess. The battle in the caves of the followers of Ba Aven had ended a few weeks ago, but the Warlock who'd won the battle had once been a ruthless thief master in Valdivar— he'd likely be worse than Kahn Devin.

When Camden—no, Raven as he preferred to be called now—returned to Forvendale with his soul partner, Aleah, it sent a shock through the Avuman nation. Not just because he had violated tradition by bringing another human into their society—who could potentially reveal the secret to the rest of the world that the Avuman were alive and well in Bremenon—but because Lumornel, long ago, saw visions of a time when her people would return to fight side by side with humans. The Elder Magi, Gwaeben, made it clear that as long as he was alive, this vision would never be fulfilled.

Perhaps the time wasn't now for her vision to be fulfilled. But events in the world of humans seemed to be leading that direction. Raven's father, Lord Drake of Basilea, still wasn't aware Kahn Devin had died, but he suspected something was wrong. Lumornel couldn't hear what he said to his eccentric counselor, the Mage Ishtar, but Drake was visibly upset and nervous.

When she'd scried for the city of Tanith in Domeria and Achtan in Achtland, darkness clouded her vision. Then the darkness faded, and she saw Aleah, by herself, fighting back the darkness. Raven wasn't by her side, which was worrisome. When she'd attempted to look into Raven's future, all she could see was his half brother, Danu, in need of help. She saw fighting in Raven's future. More fighting than one man could do in a lifetime—even an Avuman warrior who lived seven hundred years wouldn't see as much battle as the scrying pool showed around Raven. The implications were obvious, but she couldn't say specifically what the future held by these visions.

Lumornel placed her hands on the small of her back and leaned back—her joints ached. She'd been standing still for several hours, considering the things she observed from the milky liquid in the ornate bowl. The sun was closer to the horizon, but she was no closer to understanding exactly what the future would bring.

She picked up a pewter cup of warm goat's milk and took a sip—well, it had been warm when she'd entered the garden many hours ago. She drew energy from the aeon myriad, warmed the liquid to her liking, and took another sip. Perfect. She walked through the intricate stone arch that led into her small home. Her visitors would be arriving soon.

Raven and Aleah had been enjoying a few weeks of peace after their wedding ceremony, and it was, unfortunately, time for Lumornel to interrupt their bliss. The darkness over Tanith and Achtan grew more intense each time she viewed the cities. The young couple needed to leave, and soon. She didn't consult with Gwaeben on these particular visions or her decision—he'd probably never let them leave if she did.

Lumornel's musings were interrupted by a knock at her door. She set down her goat's milk, pushed a stray lock of green hair behind her ear, sat in the red cushioned chair—leaving the divan on the opposite side of the sitting room open for Raven and Aleah—then motioned toward the door for her porter to let them in.

"Welcome to my home," she said as the young couple entered. "Please, sit down. Would you care for tea?" They smiled, thanked her, and sat where she directed. Lumornel could tell by the way they squeezed each other's hands that Aleah and Raven were nervous. To be fair, almost everyone who visited her was nervous. Her milky white eyes looked like the full moon and caused many to believe she was blind. Most were uncomfortable looking at them, so they fidgeted and tried to look elsewhere. At least these two looked directly at her as they waited.

"I trust you've had a pleasant stay in Forvendale," Lumornel said to Aleah, as the servant poured tea.

"Very much, thank you."

Lumornel didn't know Aleah well, but she was impressed with the young woman's courage. She could see why Raven was attracted to her. Aleah had olive skin that tanned easily and blended nicely with her long brown hair and brown eyes. She was slender and athletic, but also feminine enough to be considered pretty. From her father, she had inherited an angular jaw line and slightly arched eyebrows. From her mother, she had inherited her skin color and height, although she wasn't quite as tall as most Domerian women—another gift from her father's side.

"I won't insult you by pretending I didn't have a specific purpose for inviting you here." Lumornel decided it would be best to forgo further pleasantries and jump straight to the crux of the matter. At this, they both visibly relaxed. An unusual reaction, but then, they were warriors. They would rather know what they faced than pretend a problem didn't exist.

"As Seeress of the goddess, I see many things." She took another sip of her goat's milk while she chose her next words. "Kahn Devin is no more, but that doesn't mean the danger is over—it is growing. The new Grand Warlock seeks chaos in the land, and he is not as cautious as Kahn was."

"No offense, Elder Seeress," Aleah said, "but Kahn was *not* cautious. He killed innocent people trying to get at Renn. In the end, he attacked him on the very doorstep of the lore masters' school. He was killed by Renn because he ignored caution."

"Yes," Lumornel agreed. "You are correct. And as I said, compared to the new Grand Warlock, Kahn was cautious."

Aleah and Raven frowned and glanced at each other. Raven set his tea on the dark walnut end table next to the divan. With his black hair and penchant for wearing black clothes, it was no wonder they gave him the nickname Raven.

"I assume you tell us this because it has something to do with us," he said.

"I tell you this because your futures are still intertwined with the power struggle to come."

Aleah shook her head. "I fulfilled the promise my mother made to the oracle. I helped get the Child of the Blessing to Elder Island. I spent my entire life preparing for that mission and I completed it!"

Lumornel couldn't blame Aleah for being upset. Humans lived such a short time, and Aleah had spent what little life she had doing things others told her to do.

"I'm going to do what *I* want to do for a change," Aleah said. "I refuse to continue being led around this continent by prophecies and visions."

"I don't want my life to be dictated by visions, either," Raven said. "However, if it's truly necessary, then I'll do it so long as I am with Aleah."

The girl gave him a shy smile and squeezed his hand. Lumornel smiled wanly at seeing Raven interact with a woman this way. He'd always been so independent.

"You have free will. That is a gift from El Azur," Lumornel said. "You are free to choose how to act on the information I am about to give you. However, you are not free to choose the consequences of your decisions."

"What if I refuse to hear these prophecies from the goddess?" Aleah said. "What if I get up and walk out of this forest and turn my back on the Avuman people, just like you've turned your back on us for the past millennium?"

Raven looked taken aback that his wife would address one of the elders in this fashion, and Lumornel had to take another sip of her goat's milk to keep from rebuking the girl for insolence. Perhaps, if she were in Aleah's position, she would feel the same way.

"As I said before"—Lumornel set down her cup, leaned forward, and met Aleah's determined eyes with a gaze that caused strong men to wilt—"you have the gift of free will so you are free to take that course of action if you wish, but you are not free to choose the consequences."

Lumornel was impressed at how long Aleah held her gaze before relaxing her shoulders and dropping her head in defeat.

"I'm sorry," Aleah said. "These past few weeks of having Raven to myself have been so wonderful. I began to believe we could start a normal life together—just the two of us." She took a deep breath, raised her head, and squared her shoulders. "But like Raven said, as long as I'm with him, I can do what is necessary."

Lumornel blinked to keep a tear from falling down her cheek. At times like these, she wished somebody else could be the messenger for the goddess.

"I see a great darkness over Tanith and Achtan," Lumornel said. "Aleah's face appears, and the darkness dissipates in Tanith but then grows in Achtan. Her face then appears in the darkness of Achtan with a myriad of others, including beasts, and the darkness is held at bay."

"What does it mean?" Raven and Aleah asked at the same time.

"I believe both cities are now, or soon will be, in grave danger, and

Aleah must intervene, or both will be lost to great evil. You must first go to Domeria and fight the darkness in Tanith. Once your mother's land is secure, you must take an army to Achtan to fight the darkness there."

Aleah's mouth opened and closed a few times as she tried to speak. She held out her hands and shook her head. "I can't just ask my mother to send an army to Achtan. Even if she agreed to such a request, I wouldn't be the one to lead our army. Leandaria is the high general of our armies, not me."

"Who is Leandaria?" Raven asked.

"She's my eldest sister."

"The visions don't show me why you will lead, only that you must."

Many emotions crossed Aleah's face as she considered the implications of what Lumornel said. The Seeress watched them play out and wished she had better answers to give Raven's new wife.

"I know little about your mother and sisters"—Raven took Aleah's hand—"but I'll help you anyway I can."

Aleah smiled at him, and once again, Lumornel struggled to stop her tears. She took a deep breath and steeled herself for what she had to say next.

"Raven, I see no end to your path. But I see Lord Danu and battles—many, many battles."

"Okay. After I help Aleah, we will go to Danu."

Lumornel shook her head as the words left his mouth, and the young couple grew stiff.

"I'm sorry, but your brother's need is immediate. Danu will die, and darkness will spread across Boranica if you are not by his side."

"No, please!" Aleah's voice cracked, and Lumornel could no longer restrain her tears as Aleah cried. "Please, there must be some other way. There must be something you can do."

"I can't leave Aleah, Lumornel," Raven said. "I can't just let her go into danger alone. I know she's a great warrior, but . . . she's my soul partner."

Lumornel sat a little straighter and prepared to give them a platitude like, *I'm sorry, but it is the will of the goddess.* Instead, she tapped her chin as a thought occurred to her.

"I can't change what the goddess has shown me." She quit tapping and held up her hand to stop them from protesting. "However, there *is* something I can do. Wait here, please."

Lumornel went to her private chambers. At the foot of her bed sat an ancient brass chest. The lock snapped open when Lumornel blew on it. The box opened of its own accord, slowly, controlled by special hinges that managed the movement of the lid. She removed some old clothing, a few books she'd saved from when she was a small girl, and two blankets. She ran her finger along the beaded base of the chest until she found the latch that opened a hidden compartment. She smiled wistfully as she removed the contents and considered them. The human Wizard who had made these two pendants died before Lumornel's time, but judging by the craftsmanship, he had been extremely skilled in the Azur-Lore.

The pendants were simple in design—a matching pair of wooden lockets inlaid with strange brass runes. Though the lockets were more than a thousand years old, the wood felt as strong as if it were carved last week.

Raven and Aleah rose when Lumornel returned and looked at her expectantly. The Seeress smiled and bade them to sit.

"These lockets don't look special or costly," she said as she held one up for them to see, "but they are unique and priceless."

"What are they?" Aleah asked.

"Legend has it that these pendants were worn by the Wizard Greyfel and his lover, Elahna. It is said he spent two years crafting these."

"What do they do?" Raven rose and walked closer for a better look.

"Greyfel had a lot of enemies," Lumornel said. "He worried they would take Elahna when he was away. These lockets allowed them to sense each other, like a piece of fine steel drawn to a lodestone." Lumornel handed one of the lockets to Raven. She could see the reflection of the brass runes in his black pupils as he studied it.

"You can't communicate through these," Lumornel said, "but you will know where to find each other, should the need arise."

Aleah tilted her head as she took the other necklace and ran her fingers over the brass symbols. "So I just put this on and I can sense the other necklace?" she asked.

"No, we need to prepare them first. I will need hair from each of you and a drop of blood."

"That sounds like something Cole's grandmother would ask for," Raven said.

"Who is Cole?"

"One of Danu's men," Aleah said with a smile. "It's not important."

Raven returned the locket to Lumornel, winced as he pulled out a piece of hair, and gave it to Lumornel. Aleah raised an eyebrow but handed her necklace back and followed his lead. Lumornel took one locket, cupped it in her hands, and chanted softly. She blew on the rune, and the locket snapped open. She took Raven's hair, twisted it into a small circle, and placed it inside the locket. It made a soft click as she snapped it shut.

"Now I need a drop of your blood."

Raven pulled a knife from his boot and pressed it against his arm until a bright red bead of blood appeared on the end of the blade.

"Let the blood drip onto the rune."

When his blood touched the brass, a gleam of light raced around the rune, and the blood sucked into the brooch with a metallic ringing sound.

Lumornel handed the locket to Aleah, and she placed it around her neck beside a protection rune necklace. The Seeress knew Raven gave her that necklace before they came to Bremenon to protect her from the magic the Avuman used to scare off intruders. Then Lumornel prepared the other locket with Aleah's hair and blood the same way she did with the first. Raven placed that second locket around his neck—also next to a protection rune necklace.

"I wish I could do more," Lumornel said, and she truly did.

Aleah smiled and said, "This will be enough. I can feel Raven next to my chest, tugging on me." She wiped a tear from her cheek. "Thank you, Elder Seeress." Aleah pulled Lumornel into a tight embrace.

Lumornel was taken aback at being touched this way, but she relaxed and hugged the girl in return.

APPRENTICE FOR A WARLOCK

"**S**tay back," Avaris shouted at Kintara.

She would've given him a mocking smile if she hadn't just witnessed his power. The deer bones he held in front of him still glowed with faint red energy—enough that Kintara could see his long black hair matted with sweat against his brown skin. He rested with one knee on the ground. She couldn't believe he hadn't toppled over with exhaustion already.

"If I wanted to hurt you, you'd already be dead," she said.

She shook her head and walked forward. Deer bones? He'd held off nearly a dozen magic users with simple deer bones he'd dried himself only moments before. What a ridiculous notion. She wouldn't have believed it possible if she hadn't watched him do it.

The two slave boys struggled to their feet. Both were covered with deep cuts, their clothing ripped and wet with blood, but they would live. That is, if they let Kintara help them.

"You can tell your sister to come out," Kintara said. "She's no longer in danger."

The Andrikan Devi slave boy stumbled forward, positioning himself between Kintara and Avaris. The redheaded slave's arm shook, but he lifted his sword toward Kintara and assumed a fighting stance. Avaris studied her through narrowed eyes. Kintara could almost see him weighing her words as he stared at her.

"Kalisha, you can come out." Avaris pushed himself to his feet.

The dark-haired slave kept his sword leveled at Kintara, but whipped his head around and glowered at Avaris. "She's one of *them*!" he hissed. "She can't be trusted."

"Then trust *me*." Avaris reached out and pushed down the sword arm of the redheaded slave boy.

"If you harm her, I'll kill you." The dark-haired slave threatened Kintara. Leaves rustled and rocks scraped as the girl crawled out from behind the bushes.

"What is your name, slave?" Kintara asked the fool boy who threatened her.

He glared at her. He *actually* glared at her. He was trying her patience. But she wanted to earn the trust of Avaris and he was obviously a close friend to the slave boy, so she smiled and repeated, "Your name?"

"Lekiah, warrior of the Andrikan Devi."

"Ah," she said. No wonder he bore the brands of a runaway slave. The proud warriors never lasted long in the mines. They ended up as sacrifices at the well because they refused to be domesticated.

"Well, Lekiah," she said with just a hint of condescension. "I just risked my standing with the entire Aven collective to save you and your precious Kalisha from certain death. Logic should tell you I have no intention of harming her or any of you for that matter."

"Why *did* you save us?" Avaris asked, releasing his hold on the Aven power, which caused the clearing to turn dark.

Kintara drew power into the skull in her hand, causing it to emit a steady flow of red light. She set it on the crude stone barricade next to the boys so they would have enough light to see one another.

"Because I want something in return."

"I'm done being used by your kind." Lekiah's voice dripped with anger. The girl steadied the young warrior, who was clearly exhausted from the battle. She refused, however, to look Kintara in the eye. Lekiah's face and arms seeped blood. "Kalisha and I are going to choose our own path."

Kintara laughed harder at this than she had laughed at anything in a long time. It probably wasn't the best way to win favor with this group based on the rage in their mutual expressions.

"You are not only young and naïve but foolish, too," she said, which made them angrier. She wouldn't have pushed them so hard, except she knew they were too injured and tired to walk away. They had no choice but to listen.

"This world is filled with people who are going to do exactly that—use and manipulate you." She looked down her nose and pointed at Lekiah's forehead. "You and your friend are runaway slaves—anybody can see that by your brands. How well is that going to work for you as you attempt to live a normal life?" Lekiah didn't respond, but he continued to glare at her.

"However," Kintara continued, "if Avaris and I strike a bargain, I will remove your brands and help you. And just maybe I can give you a chance at a free life together with your precious Kalisha." Kintara placed her hands on her hips and blew a strand of hair off her face. "I doubt you'll receive such an offer from Shamael Daro."

"What do you want with me?" Avaris's eyes narrowed once more.

"I will tell you in a moment," Kintara said. "But first, it's getting cold, and I'd like a fire. Slave, fetch some wood." That last she said to the red-headed teen.

"He can't understand you," Avaris said. "He doesn't speak normal language."

Kintara laughed again, harder than before.

"It is you, young Avaris, who doesn't speak normal. He likely speaks the common tongue of Lemuria. Most of the continent speaks his language. You, on the other hand, speak the language of the barbaric tribes." She probably shouldn't be this blunt with him, but she wanted him to know she wouldn't coddle him. If he chose her bargain, he needed to understand how things stood between them.

"What is your name, slave?" she said to the fair-skinned teenager in common tongue.

He hesitated, looking to Avaris for direction. Avaris just shrugged since he couldn't understand what she'd asked. The redheaded boy squared his shoulders. "Renaul," he said.

"Why have you tied your fate together with these barbarians?"

"Because this one is a Child of the Blessing."

This took Kintara by surprise. She assumed the boy had simply been caught up in events and was a bit unlucky, but maybe he was more than that.

"How do you know he is a Child of the Blessing, Renaul?"

The boy looked at Avaris. "It's obvious. His age, his power. He reminds me of Renn."

"How do you know Renn?" She kept the surprise out of her voice.

"I grew up next to him. He is my friend."

"How did you come to be a slave . . ." And then she remembered that Kahn had an operative named Raul who ran a farm next to the Child of the Blessing who lived in Leedsdale, Boranica. When Raul failed to deliver the boy named Renn to Kahn, Raul brought his wife and son to the caves instead, hoping the Grand Warlock would show mercy. And Kahn did—a little anyway. He made the son a slave—presumably this boy—sacrificed the wife, and sent Raul to be an indentured servant to the high priest, Hodran.

Renaul didn't reply to her question regarding how he became a slave, but the coloring in his face, which was already red due to the crimson light from her skull, grew redder and he clenched his teeth.

"It was your father, Raul, who did this to you," she said. "And you hate him for that."

"I'm going to kill him. That's the only thing that matters anymore," Renaul said.

"I can help you with that goal . . . if your new friend, Avaris, agrees to my bargain." A spark of hope appeared in Renaul's eyes and he looked at Avaris with hope.

"What did you say to him?" Avaris asked.

"Same thing I told Lekiah. If you agree to my bargain, I will help him get what he wants."

"And what is your bargain?"

"I want you to become my Apprentice."

"That's it?" Avaris asked. "Become your Apprentice? Why?"

"You need me."

Avaris didn't look convinced by this declaration, so she reluctantly added, "And I need you."

"I don't need anybody, and I don't trust you," Avaris said. "You helped us win this fight, but only because you wanted something from me, not because you're a good person."

"You're right. *Everything* I do is because I want something." Kintara knew this wasn't what Avaris expected her to say. He would expect her to lie and try to persuade him with false reassurances, but he'd been lied to his entire life. He wouldn't trust her unless she was brutally honest. And even then he might not trust her.

"But that doesn't mean we don't *need* each other," Kintara said. "Now that Shamael knows who you are and that you aren't likely to become his disciple, he will send others to kill you. Next time, he'll send twice or three times as many."

"I can hide," Avaris said. "This is a big land."

Kintara harrumphed and blew an unruly strand of hair of her face. "You can hide? You don't even speak common tongue. Where will you go? Shamael is the Grand Warlock now. He has ways of finding you. How do you think your attackers found you so easily? I can protect you. I can teach you the language. I know the secrets to keep you and your friends invisible to Shamael. I can teach you how to use your power so you can protect yourself."

Avaris folded his arms and pursed his lips.

"Maybe she's right, Avaris," Lekiah said. "Maybe she can help all of us."

"I'm not convinced." Avaris rubbed his hands together and sat down on the cold ground.

"Why haven't you gathered wood as I asked?" Kintara snapped at Renaul.

The boy glared but then averted his eyes and limped to the edge of the clearing to search for dead sticks and logs. At least he knew to obey a Warlock.

"The last time I saw you was in the caves before the fighting began." Avaris watched Renaul limp away as he spoke to Kintara. When his eyes turned back to her they were sharp with accusation. "You had many children chained together and led them into the caves against their will."

Kintara placed her hands on her hips but didn't reply.

"For all I know," Avaris said, "you made similar promises to them before you locked iron links around their necks and ankles."

"True," she admitted. "I have done that many times. And most of the children I forced to the caves became powerful disciples of Ba Aven—Witches, Necromancers, Shapeshifters, and even Warlocks."

Renaul returned with an armful of wood that he dropped to the ground. Kintara picked up the glowing red skull, redirected the energy to the wood, and it burst into flame.

"Some of those children, I will admit, became slaves or sacrifices, but only because they didn't show the aptitude for greatness. I think that question has been answered in your case." Kintara sat on the ground near the fire, opposite from Avaris. The others also moved near the warmth of the flames.

"And what's in it for you?" Avaris's brows furrowed. "You said everything you do is for you."

Kintara nodded. "I lost my bid to become the Grand Warlock, and Shamael is too powerful for me to defeat. I am an outcast to be hunted and killed." She waited and watched his reaction. The boy was good—he waited her out. "You will become the greatest lore user in history, and I will be at your side. I will protect you now and give you the training you need, so you may one day protect me and restore me to my place of prominence in the Aven-Lore."

She stretched her hands to the fire and rubbed them together. She hadn't softened the truth, and when she looked up, she could see in his eyes that he knew what she said was true. She thought he'd argue more and demand promises or say something like *I need time to consider it*, but he surprised her again when he nodded and said, "When do we begin?"

Kintara smiled. He would be great, indeed.

"Right now," she answered. "Lekiah, come here." She stood, and the young Devi warrior limped to her. She picked up the skull, drew energy into it, and then held it against the scars on his forehead. She muttered the words: "*Kram vomer Aven.*" The boy screamed in pain as the power rushed from the skull into his skin. Avaris jumped to his feet, and Renaul drew his sword when Lekiah fell to the ground.

"Look at him!" Kintara commanded before the two boys did something foolish.

"His slave marks are gone!" Renaul said with wide eyes.

"Yes, your friend Avaris has decided to accept my bargain."

"Can you remove mine, too?"

"Yes, and I will tell you where your father is so you can get your revenge . . . if that is truly what you want."

The redheaded boy from Boranica smiled and nodded. After removing his marks, Kintara said, "I suppose we'd better clean and dress your wounds. I didn't save you just to let you die from infection. But first, there is another reason I made this fire—"

"Why can't you just heal their wounds," Avaris interrupted her, "like you did with the slave brands?"

"This is your first lesson, Avaris," Kintara said with a wry smile. "The Aven-Lore is not the power of *healing*. It is the power of *power*. If you want to be a healer, then you'll have to learn the Azur-Lore. Or at least you will need to learn about potions and such. Since we don't have the supplies or time for a healing draft, we'll have to settle for cleaning and bandaging."

"But you healed their slave brands," Avaris said.

"I didn't *heal* them; I *reversed* them. Those brands weren't burned into them like cattle brands. They were placed there by use of the Aven magic. But these wounds are actual, physical wounds made by claws and teeth. I can't reverse them. I can only heal them with traditional methods."

Kintara's waterskin was nearly empty, and what remained she used to wet a piece of cloth she took from one of the dead Shapeshifter's robes—it looked relatively clean, so it would have to do. She tossed the empty skin to Avaris's sister, Kalisha. Lekiah snatched it out of the air before it hit the girl.

"There's a spring several hundred paces in that direction," she said pointing straight down the mountain. "Fill that up and bring it back."

The girl looked toward the dark tree line in the direction Kintara pointed and back to her. She didn't move.

"There's nothing to be afraid of," Kintara assured both her and Lekiah who looked dubious about sending the girl out into a dark forest by herself. "We've killed all the magic users, and every animal ran off the moment they smelled the Demon Dogs. There's nothing dangerous within miles of us right now."

Lekiah bit his lip and studied the tree line before gently handing the waterskin to Kalisha and giving the girl a reassuring smile.

"How do you know there is a spring down there?" Avaris asked.

"I may look young, but I've been alive a long time. This isn't my first time in these mountains."

Kintara used the wet rag to wash the worst of the blood and dirt from the boy's wounds.

"Avaris, I want you to find four oblong stones." She pulled the leather thong from underneath her dark wool shirt where she hung her pendants, and held out the protection stone she always kept next to her animal familiars. "About this size. The darker the better—black onyx is best, but shards of shale will work if necessary."

The boy nodded once and left to carry out the task. He would make a good Apprentice, she decided. Maybe Myrrah hadn't been a complete failure in his early training.

Kalisha returned with a full skin of water shortly after Avaris left on his task. By the time the boy returned with the stones, Kintara had cleaned the wounds and tied off the last cloth bandage around Renaul's thigh. Fortunately, she had plenty of material to use since the dead Shapeshifters—at least those who hadn't been entirely incinerated—wouldn't need their robes any longer.

Kintara put the black stones close to the fire. She pulled in aeon myriad and forced a tight stream of energy at the rocks. First, she smoothed the edges and then bored a small hole through each stone. Dust and smoke rose from them, filling the air with an odor that smelled like burning dirt.

"Okay, I'll need a few drops of blood from each of you," Kintara repeated the instruction in common tongue for Renaul's benefit.

"What for?" Lekiah pursed his lips and drew down his eyes. Kintara supposed he would be suspicious of everyone until he was far away from the caves and back in the Andrikan plains.

"You want to be free from the Grand Warlock and his friends, don't you?" Kintara asked and pushed an irritating strand of black hair from her eye. The boys both nodded—Renaul didn't understand anything they were saying, but he hadn't objected to her instruction. "These stones, once infused with your blood, will hide you from his scrying as long as you wear them next to your skin." They furrowed their brows and glanced at each other.

"Scrying is a way to view things from great distances," Kintara explained. "Shamael is particularly talented and practiced in this art. It's how he knew exactly where to send Jenot—the Warlock who just tried to kill you."

"How do they work?" Avaris asked.

"When you scry for a person, it's easiest to locate them if you have a piece of hair, fingernails, blood—something from their body. It acts as a sort of lodestone. We are creating the reverse of that with these stones, and it will repel his attempts to scry for you."

Their faces were blank as they stared at the stones. They obviously didn't comprehend. "Have you ever held two lodestones side by side in such a way that they push against each other? That's what we are doing."

Avaris nodded, held out his arm, took a bone-handled knife from Kintara, and cut into his skin. His blood sizzled as Kintara dripped it over the smooth, dark rock. She murmured the necessary words and enveloped the hot stone in power to force the blood to penetrate deep into the amulet. Once this was done, she poured water on the rock to cool it and picked it up. She held out the knife Avaris used a moment ago, infused red energy into the blade, and scratched a rune into the rock. The ancient protection rune reminded her of a diamond with the lines that formed the top continuing upward to make a V shape on top of the diamond.

"Keep this on you at all times. The blood infusion will hide you from scrying. This rune will protect you from magic attacks, at least a little."

"I've seen that mark before," Renaul said, looking curiously at the stone as she handed it to Avaris. "A soldier in Lord Danu's army had one, I think."

"In Concordia, parts of Nortia, and even Boranica, you can find merchants selling trinkets bearing this rune in street markets," Kintara said. "But it's associated with the pagan gods of Concordia, so it has lost favor with most people."

The other teens followed Avaris's lead, and Kintara finished the stones in a matter of minutes. It helped that Lekiah and Renaul were still bleeding a little; she didn't need to cut them again.

"We shouldn't stay here long," Kintara said when she had finished the last amulet. "But I think we're okay for one night. It will take Jenot some time to reach the Grand Warlock's study, tell Shamael the story of what happened, and then return with reinforcements." She laughed at the thought of that slimy snake of a Warlock wringing his hands in front of Shamael as he related to him how he failed at his first assigned task. If they were lucky, Jenot might be too afraid to return to Shamael.

"What's so funny?" Lekiah raised a single brow.

"Nothing you need to concern yourself with. I'm certain we will be safe here tonight," she said. "But we leave at first light."

THE CATACOMBS

Renn held his fur-lined cloak closed with his left hand and the staff of Greyfel in his right. He shivered—not from cold but because the ground beneath him was dead. The meadow in front of the school had vibrantly awakened from its winter slumber. Streams with cold runoff snaked their way down the mountains and through the meadow, bringing life to everything in their path—except for the large circle of dead ground where Renn stood.

Demaris, he reminded himself. Renn was the boy who couldn't protect himself. Renn was the weakling who couldn't defend those he loved.

But Demaris had killed this large circle of ground, rendering it void of life. He felt nothing in the earth as he bent down and plunged his left hand into the muddy soil. No life at all. Using the staff to amplify the reach of his probe only confirmed his fears: this spot of ground was completely dead as far below the surface as he could penetrate, which was at least as deep as a tall tree.

"Do you think it can be healed, Genea?" Demaris asked without looking up. The last thing he wanted was Genea to see his eyes rimmed with tears. She'd probably try to hug him or something else equally as awkward.

"I don't know, Renn." She laid a hand on his shoulder. Well, at least it wasn't a hug. "Perhaps Lady Daria would know."

Demaris shook his head. "I already asked her. She said I transferred the intelligences of life into Raven."

"What does that mean?"

"Usually, when somebody draws on the intelligences within the aeon myriad, they use the life power and then release it; it goes back to where it originally came from." He shook his head and let out a deep breath. "I never released the aeon myriad. I transformed it and locked it inside Raven's body."

"What about the staff?" Genea asked. "After all, it is *the* staff of Greyfel. Certainly, he would've known what to do."

"I've tried, Genea. The staff has no memory of anything like this."

His irritation with this line of questioning helped him blink the tears away. At least enough that he didn't think his eyes would betray that he'd been on the verge of crying. He smelled the soil. He didn't expect to smell the freshness of life—and he didn't, just dirt—but it gave him a few more moments for his eyes to dry. He stood, wiped his muddy hand on his cloak, and turned toward the school gates.

"Come on. Lunch is nearly over. We'd better get back." He started walking without her, not really caring if she followed.

"You did save Raven, you know." Genea hurried to catch up. "And saving him brought love to Aleah—something she may have never discovered otherwise."

"Was it worth the cost?"

Genea stepped in front of him and slapped him as hard as she could. It nearly knocked him over, so he assumed it was as hard as she could hit.

"Oww! Why did you do that?"

"How dare you say such a thing, Renn Demaris!" She had one hand on her hip and the other pointing in his face. "Raven and Aleah saved all of us countless times. You and I would be dead long ago if it wasn't for their sacrifice. He deserves to live and experience love and so does Aleah. If the patch of dead earth were *twice* this size, it still would have been worth the cost!"

Demaris rubbed his cheek and watched her stomp away. Her thick, wavy, brown hair bounced as she walked, and he stared longer than he should have at the way her hips moved. Well, Genea always had an opinion about things, and usually a strong one at that. He wished he could be as certain as her that what he did was right. But who was he to judge what life to destroy and what life to save? He dropped his hand and followed her to the gates.

Everybody treated him like something special because he had brought Raven back to life—well, almost everyone—but what would they think if they understood that he stole life from the earth and permanently gave it to another being? What if he kept using the power this way? How long would it be until the balance of life was irreversibly altered? Maybe that line of thought was a bit extreme, but it felt wrong to steal life from one living thing and place it in another.

He walked under the portcullis and through the lower courtyard toward the main doors. Genea had already gone inside. Demaris was supposed to go to healing studies with Lore Master Daria, but that would only remind him of his inability to heal the ground. The thought of looking out the windows of the school every day and seeing that dead circle of ground in the middle of such verdant life made him sick to his stomach—he would be reminded of what he did every day. Maybe he'd just skip his classes today and hide in the back of the library.

Demaris read the ancient marble plaque above the massive wooden doors of the castle. The top line contained the title, *Universal Axiom*. Beneath that were the words: *If all do as thou, will life and peace flourish?* He'd read those words numerous times, but now they seemed to judge and condemn him.

He would soon take the test to be raised to the level of Healer, and he'd only been here four months. He didn't need a full year of training from each master, which the school was obligated to provide to each student. Skipping out on one day of lessons wouldn't hurt his chances of reaching the level of Wizard before his complimentary training ended.

Demaris entered the great hall and hurried to the grand marble stairs at the far end, which led to the second level of the castle where the library was located. Balrin, the castle steward, passed him coming down the stairs but was so engaged with reviewing documents he didn't even acknowledge

Demaris, which was fine with him. He didn't want to talk to anybody right now—not even the kindly old steward.

The library consisted of a large hall with a series of adjoining rooms that occupied nearly one half of the second floor, divided into sections based on subject. Demaris made his way past students quietly reading to the back room where the histories were kept. This section was least visited, so it would be the perfect refuge for his current mood. To complete his concealment, he picked up a large leather-bound book from a shelf and buried his face behind it while sitting at a table in the far corner.

Before long, someone else entered the room, and Demaris lowered himself in the chair so as not to be seen. His staff leaned against the wall. He should've put it in his dorm before coming here. It would give him away as sure as if they saw his face. But whoever entered didn't approach him. Demaris peeked around the corner of his book and saw Harlow looking over his shoulder, apparently watching to see if he was being followed. What was he doing here? Harlow struggled with the most basic spells and would be an Apprentice for several more months; *he* certainly shouldn't be skipping classes. Demaris wasn't about to call him over, however, because the last thing he wanted was to listen to Harlow's nonstop talking.

Harlow tiptoed to the corner opposite Demaris, looking over his shoulder several more times. The boy pulled a handful of books from the shelf, set them on the ground and reached into the opening where the books had been. He fumbled around and then reached in farther until his shoulder was pressed against the shelf. It looked like he was reaching through the wall, because the shelves were only a foot deep. Demaris heard a soft click, and Harlow pulled the heavy shelf away from the wall, revealing a dark opening.

Harlow replaced the books to their previous location on the shelf, and Demaris stood. He grabbed his staff and was almost to Harlow when the boy realized he wasn't alone. A book dropped out of his hands, and he shoved the large shelf back against the wall, before recognizing Demaris.

"Renn! You just about killed me sneaking up like that! Why did you follow me here? Is anybody with you? You didn't see anything—"

"Stop, Harlow." Demaris held up a hand. "I didn't follow you. I was hiding in the corner over there. What is this?"

"Oh, nothing. It's . . ."

Demaris cocked his head to one side and raised his eyebrows. "Out with it, Harlow."

"Okay, but don't tell anybody about this," Harlow whispered conspiratorially. He ran a hand through his dark curly hair and looked around the room. "You know how I'm not good at understanding the lore, Renn—"

"Demaris," Renn corrected him.

"Sorry—Demaris—well, I can't do magic good, nothing works like it's supposed to, and I hate it, and I hate going to my lessons. I just don't think I'm cut out to be a magic user like you and everybody else here at the castle—"

"Harlow, what does that have to do with this secret door?"

"I'm getting to that part. So you know how I hate studying magic and it never works right—"

"I got all that." Demaris nodded.

"But I love the *history* of magic and the castle and the history of the great lore masters over the centuries. So, I've been coming here a lot to read. At first, I came between classes and during my free time, but then I started skipping my classes because it's so exciting learning about different Wizards and events—"

Demaris smacked his forehead. "Harlow, *what* is this secret door for?"

"I'm getting to that. Geez, be patient." Harlow glanced around the room and lowered his voice even further, which forced Demaris to lean in. "I was here really late one night, sitting behind that desk in the corner reading when I heard someone come into the library. I was afraid I'd get in trouble for being up so late, so I hid underneath the table. It was Lore Master Gendul, and I saw him open this door and go inside. After a few minutes, I peeked inside. I didn't see Gendul, and I couldn't hear him, so I looked at the latch to figure out how it works."

"Where does it lead?" Demaris wondered aloud as he peered into the dark opening.

"C'mon, I'll show you." Harlow finished returning the books to the shelf, and then slipped into the darkness with Demaris close behind. Harlow pulled the shelf back into place, leaving them in total darkness. Demaris heard Harlow fumbling in his pockets, the sound of stone scratching against flint and then saw sparks as the gangly teen tried to light a candle.

"There's no need for that." Demaris drew a small amount of energy into his staff—Greyfel's staff, he reminded himself—and created soft blue light.

"Thanks. I . . . I can't do that—yet."

Creating light was a pretty basic spell, and Harlow was obviously embarrassed. But his embarrassment gave way to excitement.

"Wow!" he said. "I've never noticed the markings on the walls before." Harlow went to the smooth stone wall and ran his hands along the runes carved into them. Demaris didn't recognize them, but the staff pulsated with distant memory—it had been here before. "My candle just cast enough light to keep me from falling down the steps," Harlow said as he felt the rock engravings. "I'll have to see if I can find a book that talks about what these are."

"What is this place, Harlow?" Demaris touched the engravings, too. The rock was cold but smooth.

"This, my friend, is the *real* library," Harlow said with an expansive smile. "Well, actually it's more like a museum. Come with me, and you'll see what I mean.

Harlow led Demaris down a long, spiraling stairwell. The steps were stone slabs cut and placed by hand—presumably during the construction of the castle. But, after a while, the even slabs changed to rough steps cut into the earth and the walls changed from smooth, hand set stones, to rough cut. They were clearly underground now and the air grew noticeably cooler.

At the bottom of the winding steps, they entered a large room hewn into the rock beneath the castle. The smell reminded Demaris of taking out a book that had rested on a shelf for years and blowing the dust off the spine—he had done that one time in Artio's little cave back home. This room reminded him of the Mage's rock walled study chamber, only much larger.

"Can you increase the light?" Harlow asked.

Demaris channeled more aeon myriad into the staff with a mere thought to increase the light.

"Wow," Harlow said. "This is so much better than using a candle. I've been here lots of times and never realized how big this first room is."

"First room?"

"Yeah. There's a lot of rooms and levels down here."

Sturdy wooden bookshelves, stacked with tomes and rolled parchment, lined the walls. Smaller bookshelves, arranged in rows down either side of the room held more books and papers. The right side of the room had larger shelves, and rather than books, they held various objects. Ancient porcelain and metal jars, bowls and goblets, rolled tapestries, glass containers with strange-colored stones, metal devices with gears—a person could spend years in this room and still not explore or read everything it held.

"How many rooms are there?"

"I don't know," Harlow said. "I haven't found all of them yet, but I've seen a few dozen so far."

"It doesn't look like anybody uses this room," Demaris said. "Everything is covered in dust and cobwebs."

"Yeah, the only master I've seen down here is Gendul, and he always goes deep in the catacombs. He never stops to study or get anything out of the rooms."

"What does he do down here?"

"I don't know." Harlow shrugged his shoulders and scratched his head. "I tried to follow him a few times, but I got lost at the sixth level."

"Sixth level? These catacombs go down six levels?" Demaris asked. "And do all the levels have rooms like this?"

"Oh, some are even bigger, with amazing things!" Harlow's eyes widened and he gestured expansively. "One room is filled with nothing but old Wizard staffs. And there's a room of armor and swords—I think some of the weapons might be enchanted somehow—and some of the rooms are locked so I haven't been able to look in those yet, but I figure if I keep trying, I can—"

"Okay, okay, I get the idea," Demaris said to stop Harlow's rambling. He thought he knew his friend pretty well, but he was gaining a new respect for him. "I can't believe you followed one of the masters. What if he caught you?"

"Well, he was pretty drunk both times," Harlow said with a shrug.

"Yeah, but it's dark and dusty and . . . a bit creepy down here. I can't believe you've kept it a secret and been exploring all by yourself."

"Well, now we can explore it together."

Demaris clapped Harlow on the shoulder and smiled broadly. He felt excited for the first time in weeks.

"Yes. Yes, we can!"

High Lore Master Salas's lungs rattled as he released his breath. Hopefully, a draft of Daria's special berry tea would take care of it. He smiled at the thought of the youngest lore master. She reminded him of Girshla. His smile faded at the memory of his daughter. Girshla had died giving birth six decades ago. Perhaps Daria was Girshla reborn. Their mannerisms and personalities were so much alike, it was uncanny.

"How old is Daria?" Salas asked Gendul. His old friend was sober— mostly sober anyway—which was a nice change.

"I don't know. I think she came to the school thirty or forty years ago." Gendul rubbed at his long white sideburns with one of his hands and sniffed. "It's not polite to ask a woman about her age, but I'd guess she's about fifty now."

Salas's smiled returned. Perhaps his daughter had rested in Valhasgar for a decade and then chose to be reborn as Daria. Then again, that was probably just the wishful thinking of a sentimental old fool.

"You've been staring down at that dead circle of ground for the past fifteen minutes, Salas," Gendul said. He walked to the window and followed Salas's gaze to the meadow six stories below. "I don't think staring will change anything."

"Perhaps we should build a fountain there."

"Oh, that would be great," Gendul said. He walked to the cabinet and helped himself to a goblet of Salas's personal Blaylok wine. "And what shall we carve into the fountain? 'Here marks the spot where Demaris killed Kahn Devin and raised a man from the dead'? Forever reminding the world that a Grand Warlock broke through our defenses as though they didn't even exist?"

Salas turned from the window, leaned on his staff, and let out an exasperated sigh. His body still ached in places from the battle with Kahn four months ago.

"Is that why you've turned to drink so often these past months, my old friend?" Salas walked to the small table where his ancient set of stones was set up and ready for their match. He sat at his usual chair—dark stained wood with a comfortable green velvet cushion—and motioned for Gendul to take the chair opposite him.

"The Grand Warlock waltzed through our defenses and attacked a child on our very doorstep!" Gendul emphasized each word, then took his seat and drained his goblet, which he promptly refilled with the bottle he'd taken from the cabinet. "I don't like the implications of that. It makes me nervous."

"You think we have a traitor in our midst?"

"How could it be otherwise?"

Salas stroked his long beard. He'd asked himself the same question every day since Demaris had killed the Grand Warlock. But who would betray them? Only the lore masters knew all of the defenses in place.

"I don't like the implications, either, my Concordian friend." Salas tossed three sticks and placed his stone on the game board. "But drinking yourself into oblivion isn't going to help matters—not to mention, that's expensive wine, and you're consuming it as though it were goat's milk."

Gendul looked at the half-empty bottle and harrumphed, picked up the three sticks, tossed them, and placed one of his stones.

"In all seriousness, Gendul," Salas continued, "I could use your help figuring this out. Another set of eyes and ears, so to speak. But I need you to stay sober."

"Isn't Phaedra your eyes and ears?" Gendul poured more wine into his goblet. "She'll be madder than Varanu if she learns I'm to become part of your spy network." He winked and took a long draft from the goblet.

Salas chuckled and shook his head at Gendul's subtle comedic irony.

Gendul knew Salas didn't approve of his references to the pagan gods of Concordia, but the practice made Phaedra livid. She was also proud of her spy network and extremely defensive of the fact that she couldn't uncover who had passed secret information to Kahn.

"She has an extensive network throughout the continent, but it never occurred to us we might need eyes and ears in our own home." Salas frowned. "You have an uncanny way of learning secrets."

"Don't patronize me, Salas; we're too good of friends for that."

"I wouldn't dream of it. We both know you have a talent for uncovering hidden knowledge."

"Speaking of which," Gendul said, setting down the goblet and leaning forward, "have you been in the catacombs lately?"

Salas looked over his spectacles and raised his brows. "No, why do you ask?"

"It might be nothing, but over the past two months I've noticed a few items out of place. Perhaps one of the others—"

"I don't think so," Salas interrupted. "I don't believe the others even *know* about the secret catacombs." He rubbed his beard. "Perhaps it is nothing, but it's a start. So what do you say, Gendul? Can you stay sober and help me solve this problem?"

Gendul rubbed at his bulbous red nose and sniffed. Salas watched his friend with steady piercing eyes—he didn't want the man to assume this was just a ploy to help him stop drinking.

"All right," Gendul said. "I'll *cut back* on drinking until we solve this riddle. But before I do, I need a last hurrah."

"A last hurrah?" Salas scrunched his forehead.

"Just the usual," Gendul winked. "I'll only be gone a few days."

"*By Azur's love*, Gendul, I don't understand why you visit that seedy tavern." Salas picked up the three sticks and tossed them.

"The Fish 'n' Hook reminds me of home," Gendul said. "The music, dancing barmaids, the smell of meat roasting over flame, and real Concordian whiskey. Besides, Pitané is much closer than Concordia." He smiled and took another drink as if that settled the matter.

AVEN BLADE

"She set fire to Kahn's grimoire," Shamael told him.

Torin Dak'Thralin raised his eyebrows. He sat in the Grand Warlock's study, listening to Shamael Daro who sat on the opposite side of a black, oak desk. Shamael had completed the ritual of dominance and already acted as if he were Grand Warlock. For all intents and purposes, he was. However, Torin and the two other high priests still needed to accept Shamael at the well of sacrifice and perform the preeminence blessing for his position to be official. Torin didn't tell Shamael that his acceptance by the high priest was a forgone conclusion at this point, because it was the only leverage he had. Hopefully, Shamael would prove to be more farsighted than his predecessor.

Shamael rested his chin on peaked fingers. His piercing black eyes stared into the distance as he relayed that particular aspect of the battle that led him to his current status. He wore a high collared red shirt, but his black hooded cloak had been discarded on the settee near the wall. A small fire burning in a large fireplace cut into the rock kept the study warm. Torin idly wondered about the engineering and time it took to cut a vent through the stone, and where might lead. It certainly wasn't drafting the smoke all the way to the surface. He vaguely remembered reading about a series of vents cut into the stone above the major corridors that allowed for fresh air exchange and transferring heat from the eternal fire in the well of sacrifice to many parts of the caves. He made a mental note to find one of the engineers and discuss it in more detail, but that could wait for another day.

"I understand you came to the Aven-Lore later in life than most. Why is that?" Torin asked.

Shamael's brow drew downward. "I lost my parents young in life and wasn't aware I'd been marked by the gods. Ancilia Biment, the Shapeshifter, found and convinced me to leave Valdivar to study in the caves."

"Your rise in the Aven society has been uncommonly fast." Torin knew Shamael had only been in the lore for about thirty years. It took some that long just to attain the level of Warlock, let alone become leader of the entire Aven society.

"If I remember correctly," Torin continued, "Ancilia was sent by Kahn to infiltrate the thieves' guild in Valdivar . . ." Torin let his words trail off. He'd heard the rumors of Shamael's past, but he wanted to see how the man would react when confronted with it.

Shamael's jaw tightened, causing the scar running from his right ear to the corner of his mouth to become more prominent. "Your memory serves you well, High Priest Torin." Shamael rose and walked to a sturdy wooden cabinet, took two pewter goblets from a shelf, unstopped a bottle of brandy, and poured a glass. He held the bottle up and cast a questioning look at Torin. Devlyn Brandy—Torin's favorite. He nodded his approval, and Shamael poured some for him as well. Torin didn't think it a coincidence that Shamael would have Torin's favorite spirits. Shamael had clearly prepared for Torin's visit.

"Not only did Ancilia find me in the thieves' guild," Shamael said, "but I was also the youngest thieves' guild master in the history of Valdivar." Shamael handed a goblet to Torin, then returned to his seat behind the ancient wooden desk. "I'm an ambitious man, Torin. I hope you won't hold that against me."

"On the contrary, I despise those with no ambition." Torin took a sip, let the liquid rest in his mouth, enjoying the flavor, before swallowing with a contented sigh. "I simply want to understand you a little better, before I give you my blessing."

"Then it doesn't bother you that I was a thief?" Shamael asked, and Torin barked a quick laugh.

"We're all thieves, Shamael. The Nortian Kings and priests have taken the proclamation that Ba Aven hates thievery above all else out of context." Torin took another drink—this was some of the finest brandy he'd had in years. "Ba Aven hates all life and considers all of us thieves simply because we exist. He doesn't care what we do to one another. By the way, what vintage is this?"

"1179," Shamael said. "It was aged for more than fifty years before being bottled. I found this tucked away in Kahn's spirits cellar. Apparently, he knew you favored Devlyn Brandy, so he kept a bottle in case you paid a visit."

"Speaking of Kahn." Torin took advantage of the change of subject to pursue other questions he wanted answers to. "How do you think he died?"

"I'm sure you've heard the same rumors as I," Shamael said. "He was killed by a Child of the Blessing."

"And you believe the rumors?"

"The keepers of the wayfires reported that Lord Monguinir instructed Kahn to either bring the boy to our side or kill him. Kahn left alone, was gone for several days, and then the well went dark."

Torin studied the remaining brandy in his glass while he considered how best to reply. He knew Shamael had been Kahn's second-in-command, but Torin wasn't sure how deep Shamael's loyalties ran—probably not deep at all. Torin set down his goblet, pulled his cloak back and drew the sword on his hip from the scabbard. It made a metallic ring as it slid free and a soft thud when he set it on the desk.

"If Kahn had had this sword when he fought the boy, he would be alive today."

"It appears to be a fine weapon," Shamael said, "but how would a sword help a Warlock in battle."

"This isn't an ordinary sword, Shamael. It's an Aven blade, forged by one of my predecessors more than a thousand years ago—before the binding."

Shamael lifted the sword from the desk and held it in the light cast by a Magician's globe in the ceiling. "I've never heard of an Aven blade. What does it do?"

"The blade has been infused with power." Torin said. "When a person wields this, he is able to draw on and absorb the strength and life force of his enemy. When used against magic, it absorbs the energy of the magic."

"Do you have more?"

"This is the only one in existence," Torin admitted. "The knowledge to forge a weapon like this was lost with the death of its maker. But, I believe there is a tome in the archives that contains the knowledge."

"And Kahn didn't trust you enough to grant you free access to the archives," Shamael said matter-of-factly. Obviously, the new Grand Warlock had had his own experiences with Kahn's lack of trust.

"Well, not until recently. But, then he died—"

"You will learn I am different than my predecessor." Shamael set the sword back onto the desk. "People assume trust is a luxury Warlocks can't enjoy. But I learned in Valdivar that even thieves must learn to trust one another. My plans are bold, Torin, and they require others to be a part of them if I am to succeed. You will have free access to the archives. I want you to learn how to forge more of these weapons—weapons like this could move my plans along more quickly."

Torin smiled and raised his goblet in salute. "Here's to your plans, Grand Warlock Shamael."

Their drink was interrupted by a timid knock on the door, and a flash of irritation crossed Shamael's face.

"Come."

An initiate in black robes shuffled inside and cleared her throat.

"The Warlock, Jenot Lexton, has come to see you, Lord Daro." She kept her eyes to the floor—as protocol required. "I know you didn't want to be interrupted, but Warlock Lexton insists his message is urgent."

Shamael pursed his lips and his brows furrowed. "Send him in."

Torin didn't know Jenot Lexton well, but he'd never cared for the man. He remembered why when the Warlock slinked into the room. Jenot's tight leather breeches and jerkin were dirty and stained with blood, and his greasy hair was matted against his cheeks as it fell to his shoulders. Jenot reminded Torin of an unwashed mummer in a low-rate performing troupe. The kind who would try to trick you out of your coins, steal the virtue of the town girls, and then disappear the following day before he could be brought to justice. He smelled like an unwashed mummer, too.

"Well?" Shamael asked, and Jenot rubbed his hands together and licked his lips.

"It wasn't my fault, Grand Warlock," Jenot pleaded. "I was on the verge of killing the boy when Kintara came at us from behind!"

"Where is the boy now, Jenot?" Shamael's voice was dangerously void of inflection.

Jenot's green eyes darted between Torin and Shamael. The serpentlike Warlock continued to wring his hands.

"Jenot?" Shamael repeated.

"All of my team was killed, Lord Daro. I . . . I had no choice but to flee."

Silence filled the study. Torin had no idea what Jenot was talking about, but he'd obviously failed an assignment Shamael had given him. It would be interesting to see how this would play out.

"You had a dozen magic users and Demon Dogs to help you kill a single boy and capture a couple of slaves and a girl," Shamael said. "Kintara killed all of them but you?"

"Actually, the boy is powerful in the lore, Lord Daro," Jenot said. "He killed several of my team, but we almost had him when Kintara arrived and intervened on his behalf."

"*Azur be damned!*" Shamael slammed his fist into the desk, and Jenot flinched. "Not only did you fail, miserably, but now that traitor Kintara has Avaris!"

"Perhaps if you personally lead a team—"

"There's no time for that!" Shamael stood. "The high priests are here, and I must be presented and receive the preeminence blessings at the well tomorrow night. By now, Kintara's probably shielded them from scrying and who knows where she'll go." Shamael rubbed his head, grimaced and then held his hands behind his back. He paced from one side of the study to the other and stopped abruptly when his eyes fell upon the Aven blade that still lay on his desk. The corners of his mouth turned up as he reached for the blade and held it up—studying the edge and the runes decorating the steel. Torin's raised his eyebrows. It would be entertaining to see how the blade would respond to a Grand Warlock wielding it against another Warlock.

"In Nortia they cut off the right hand of thieves," Shamael said. "I think it's a waste of good men, a waste of valuable tools." His back was to Jenot as he spoke, and he still considered the weapon in his hands. "Don't move, Jenot."

Shamael wheeled around and brought the sword down with deadly force, but stopped just above Jenot's left shoulder. The weapon pulsed with crimson energy. Torin's brows drew downward. Fresh blood beaded in droplets on the blade—at least until the weapon absorbed it—but Shamael had stopped before striking. Then Jenot cried out, fell to his knees, and grabbed at the side of his head. His ear lay on the floor next to him.

"Interesting," Torin observed clinically. "Jenot's aura has faded while yours has brightened."

"It's intoxicating," Shamael said, staring at the sword like it was a dangerous animal. "My senses are enhanced. I can smell the iron in Jenot's blood!" He turned his eyes to Jenot, who toppled to the floor, whimpering, blood dripping between his fingers from the wound on the side of his head where his ear once was.

"Jenot, stop blubbering like an initiate and attack me with bone and fire—here, use this." Shamael reached into a drawer, withdrew a skull and thighbone, and handed them to Jenot.

"I . . . I don't think I have the strength."

"Just a little blast will do. Think of it as an experiment."

Jenot nodded, sweat and blood dripped down his face as he fumbled for the bone implements and rose to his knees. A look of panic overtook the injured Warlock when the magic didn't immediately come, but he continued to focus, and at last the skull and thighbone glowed with red power.

"Now, release it at me," Shamael said.

"Are you certain, my lord?" Holding the Aven magic gave Jenot a replenishment of some lost energy. Torin took mental notes of every detail—he should've brought a notebook with him.

"Release it." Shamael raised the sword between himself and Jenot. A blast of red energy shot from the tip of the thighbone, but instead of engulfing Shamael, the sword sucked in the power like lightning changing direction to strike at a lone tree in a field. Jenot cried out, and the bones made a clacking sound as they dropped to the floor. The greasy-haired Warlock fell next to the skull, his skin ashen and his breathing coming in quick, shallow puffs.

"This is wonderful!" Shamael said. His skin virtually glowed with power. "I wonder if it works the same against the Azur-Lore. Think of the magic a person could wield if they used this weapon against multiple lore users at once."

Torin frowned. This experiment was turning dangerous. Perhaps making weapons like this wasn't such a great idea after all. Followers of the Aven-Lore had one thing in common—a lust for power. With weapons like this, they would kill incessantly. Chaos would ensue. Torin smiled. A man could make a healthy profit and amass great power in times of chaos.

"Set the sword down, please," Torin said. "It's part of the experiment."

Shamael longed to use the weapon again; Torin could see it in the man's dark eyes. Shamael nodded and placed the sword on the desk. His eyes widened and his mouth dropped open. His aura returned to its usual hue, and he snatched the sword back up, but it was too late. The stolen power was gone.

"Very interesting," Torin observed. "Once the sword is released, the power it stole is released as well. I wonder how long the additional power would last if one never released the sword." That last he said thoughtfully more to himself than to Shamael.

"Perhaps I should try out that theory on you." Shamael's veins on his neck and forehead bulged as he glared at Torin.

"Your sense of loss should pass soon," Torin said. He stood and held his hand out to Shamael, suggesting he return the sword. The new Grand Warlock stared at Torin's hand for a long moment.

"I want this sword, Torin."

"I know you do, Shamael," the high priest of Danisyr said, "but it will destroy you. Trust me in this."

"How?"

"The folklore surrounding Aven blades suggests that magic users didn't wield them. They were mostly used by elite soldiers guarding the most powerful lore users. Now we know why. The increased power is obviously addicting."

"Then why did you let me use it?" Shamael demanded.

"I didn't know what you intended to do. And I've never actually seen it used, so I didn't quite know what to expect."

A large Kiroc knocked on the door and entered before Shamael gave him leave.

"General Nishkral," Shamael said. "You may be one of my advisors, but you can't just barge in without permission."

"Sorry, Shamael." The general didn't look sorry, but Torin couldn't tell with his red skin stretched so tightly over his skeletal face. "I asked the initiates if you were busy, but they didn't reply. They just stared at me."

No wonder, Torin thought. They'd probably never seen a massive red-skinned Kiroc with bat-like wings and a row of short spiky horns lining its forehead. "They probably soiled themselves, too," Torin said.

The general nodded respectfully to Torin. "Welcome, high priest of Danisyr." Nishkral frowned as he noticed the sword in Shamael's hand and then saw Jenot on the floor.

"What happened to him?"

Shamael looked at the injured Warlock panting on the floor. "He failed in his mission to capture the slaves and kill the boy." General Nishkral nodded as if that explained everything.

"I have news, Lord Daro," the general said. Then he saw the bottle of brandy on the desk and the pewter goblets. "Perhaps I could have a drink." He walked toward the cabinet. "I traveled quickly, and my throat is dry."

Shamael's lips drew to a tight line, and he looked thoughtfully at the sword in his hand. Torin thought Shamael might decide to strike the general, but instead the young Grand Warlock shook his head in resignation and said, "Why not? Have two or three while you're at it."

"That's kind of you, but one will be fine." Although the general was one of the more intelligent Kirocs, the sarcasm in Shamael's response was clearly lost on him. The general poured a drink and drained it as though it were a shot of whiskey. He had no appreciation of fine spirits.

"That's better." General Nishkral pulled a map from underneath his coat and unrolled it on Shamael's desk. He pointed to a spot and said, "We have an army of ten thousand training here."

"What?" Shamael's eyes shot open, and he leaned over the map. "That's only a few miles from our north entrance. How is it possible an army could be here and our scouts wouldn't know?"

The general tilted his head, and the row of horns on his forehead furrowed like eyebrows. "Ah." Nishkral's eyes widened, and he tapped the map. "It's *our* army, Grand Warlock," he said. "A secret army Kahn has been training for the past several years."

"And why are you just telling me about this now?"

"I just learned about it myself. Like you, Kahn only shared with me what he thought I needed to know. I recently expanded the routes of our scouts to include a larger area north of the caves and discovered them. Kahn had his own scouts patrol the northern Cragg Mountains. Once you put me in charge, I reassigned all scouts and they now report to me."

"Who oversees this . . . secret army?"

"A man named Deegan. Claims he was made a general and put in charge by Kahn nearly ten years ago."

"W-Will I r-recover?" Jenot asked. Blood still streamed down his cheek from his missing ear.

"I'm not sure," Torin said. "I will be curious to learn if you do and to what extent."

"Yes, it would be good to understand how the sword works," Shamael agreed as he handed the weapon back to Torin. "You're right, High

Priest. The pull of the sword is lessening the longer I refrain from using it."

"Initiates!" Shamael called, and the girl who had announced Jenot moments ago hurried into the study followed by a taller dark-haired teenage boy also wearing the black, unbelted robe of an initiate.

"Yes, Grand Warlock?" they said in unison, casting their eyes to the rock floor. Both carefully avoided looking at General Nishkral.

"Take Warlock Lexton to his rooms. Let me know if he recovers."

Shamael returned to his seat behind the desk as the initiates dragged the moaning Warlock from the room and closed the door. Shamael opened the center drawer of the desk and removed a worn leather journal that was sealed with a clasp and held it up.

"This belonged to Kahn," he said. "It's a record of his contacts, spies, plans, and even appointments. It mentions an army of ten thousand, but I assumed he was referring to our regular standing army." Shamael set the journal on the map, released a deep breath and rubbed at his temples. "There is much to be done."

He stood, locked his hands behind his back, and paced. "General, reassign ten of your best scouts to search for Kintara. She will be traveling with a boy and was last seen about twenty miles south of the east entrance to the caves.

"Tomorrow night is the new moon, and we must conduct the blessing of preeminence at the well. Once that is over I need to travel east." Shamael rested a hand on the worn journal lying on his desk. "Kahn's journal states that he is to meet his highest placed spy at a tavern in Pitané on the third night after the new moon—I am curious to learn who this spy is."

"High Priest Torin." Shamael changed the subject. "I think you'll find Clenmon Mishlok to be quite accommodating. He's a bit of a hermit and he doesn't care if you die in the archives—but you'd better not damage any of the books or tomes stored there, or he'll skin you alive."

"So I've heard," Torin smiled and sheathed the Aven blade.

"If anybody knows of a book describing swords like that, it will be him," Shamael said. "Now, if you two will excuse me, I need to learn how the search for potential vitiate is going."

HANDLESS SHADOW KING

Triaklon peered over the boulder and surveyed the seldom used road below—just two well-worn ruts in the dirt from the infrequent merchant caravans that occasionally braved the mountain pass. Even from his vantage point on the mountainside, he could barely see fifty paces down the road. Spring had made its entrance in the valleys, but winter still had a good grip this high up. The light snow flurries and gray clouds made it difficult to see specific details, but, if a caravan rounded the bend, he should at least be able to see shapes and movement.

"I don't like it, Triak," Glavin said for at least the tenth time in the past hour. "It's too early in the season for travel on this road."

Triaklon felt the same, but they needed supplies. This setup was too good, too easy, an obvious trap.

"I'm just reporting what I heard and saw," Radlyn said, responding as he had the last ten times Glavin voiced his concerns. Radlyn had joined the handless band a few months ago and was one of Triaklon's better scouts. Like the rest, he had his own story for how he came to be a one-handed outcast from Nortian society. Trying to feed his family, out of work, just took a loaf of bread . . . an all-too-familiar tale. But this common experience caused his people to bond in a way that folks in the cities didn't understand.

"Lord Thaklard has a contract with a general in Aven City," Radlyn said, "and he has an urgent shipment. They're bringing the supplies through the pass because there's no time to take the king's road."

"I heard you the first time, Radlyn," Glavin said, "but it doesn't feel right."

"If the caravan is heavily guarded, we can just stay hidden," Radlyn said, "but it's worth a look-see."

Triaklon peered across the narrow pass. He could only make out a few of his men hidden in the trees—there were twenty-five of his best fighters in all. Plenty to waylay a regular caravan, but Radlyn was right. If this shipment was too well guarded, they would just sit tight and let them pass.

Triaklon heard the scraping of boots on loose, shale rock, and turned as Jack Cobbler hurried from the trees on the slope above and slid next to them behind the boulder.

"They're coming, milord," the skinny man said as he caught his breath.

"I'm not a lord," Triaklon had said this a lot lately. "How many?"

"Four wagons with six mounted guards in the front and six in the rear."

"What's in the wagons?"

"Don't know, milord. They're all covered."

"I'm not a lord."

"What about the guards?" Glavin asked.

Jack ran a hand through his sweaty blond hair and screwed up his face. "What do you mean? There are twelve in all."

"Heavy armor or light armor, swords or spears?" Glavin asked.

"Oh, two knights in full armor at the front with swords and spears. The rest are wearing chain mail and short swords."

"I don't like it," Glavin repeated.

"We outnumber them two to one, and we have the advantage of position." Triaklon wasn't certain if he was trying to convince himself or his friend. They desperately needed supplies, and if he could capture more weapons, it would enable him to equip more men for future sorties.

"Pass the word to the others, Jack," Triaklon said. "Wait for my signal. If I don't give the sign, nobody moves. If we do stop them, we'll try to get them to surrender their supplies without a fight."

"You think a dozen soldiers are going to surrender without a fight?" Glavin raised a brow, and his voice held a note of incredulity.

"It's worth a try." Triaklon still wondered if he was convincing himself or his friend. "Stealing supplies upsets the plains lords. Killing their men takes matters to a whole new level."

"You heard him, Jack. Get moving," Glavin said, and Jack scurried away.

The caravan rolled into view, and Triaklon checked the sword in the scabbard on his back. He had a blade at his hip, too. He couldn't use two at a time, but he liked to have an extra, in case he lost one in battle. Necrosys willing, nobody would have to die today.

"Hold this while I tighten the strap." Glavin steadied the round, hard leather shield while Triaklon pulled the straps tight on his right forearm. He could do this himself, but having somebody hold the shield made it easier. With the shield secured, he pulled the sword from the scabbard on his hip, and gave Glavin a single nod.

"Wait for my signal." Triaklon half slid, half walked to the narrow section of road below. He'd picked this location because once inside the pass the travelers couldn't turn the wagons, and his men had the high ground; they could come out of the trees and surround them on either side.

Triaklon positioned himself behind a large bush to the side of the rutted road and waited. He surveyed the steep rocky hills on both sides and the line of trees that began about twenty paces up the rocks. He couldn't see any of his men from this location, which meant the soldiers guarding the wagons wouldn't be able to see them, either.

He didn't have to wait long before the vanguard rounded the corner, followed closely by the first wagons. Once they were well into the pass, Triaklon stepped into the middle of the road about a stone's throw in front of them, causing the lead horseman to curse and signal for a halt.

"It's a little early in the season to be using my roads, Captain," Triaklon called to the man. The soldiers guarding the caravan looked up the hills on either side and over their shoulders. They obviously realized this was a perfect spot for an ambush and drew their swords.

"It's lieutenant, not captain, and last time I looked at a map, the road through these mountains belonged to the king—the true king, not the *handless king*."

So the man recognized Triaklon—probably from the wanted posters. The lieutenant acted confident, even trapped in the pass as he and his men were.

"No need to argue over technicalities," Triaklon said. "I'll let you pass unmolested, once you've paid my toll."

"*By the dark of K'Thrak*, you are brazen. But let's not play games, *thief.*" The lieutenant spat the word like it left a disgusting taste on his tongue. "I have heavily armed, well-trained soldiers with me, and you are alone. Surrender yourself without a fight, and I might let you live to plead your case to Lord Thaklard. It really makes no difference to me—you're worth the same, dead or alive."

"That's where you're wrong." Triaklon raised his sword, and his men stepped out from the trees. Glavin slid down the hillside to join him on his left, and Radlyn materialized from behind a boulder to join Triaklon on the right. That was odd. He had told Radlyn to join Skunk in the rear.

The lieutenant threw back his head and laughed at the sight of the men, and Triaklon clenched his jaw.

"And I'm supposed to be afraid of a bunch of one-handed thieves with no training and nothing but mismatched weapons?"

Triaklon pointed his sword toward the man and an arrow whistled through the air and made a loud *thunk* in the wood of the wagon directly behind him.

"I'm not playing games, either, Lieutenant." He pointed his sword toward the still vibrating arrow. "I could've had my man send that arrow through your neck. I don't want to hurt anybody today, but I have a dozen more bowmen hidden in the trees, and we won't hesitate to cut you down if necessary." Triaklon let his words sink in. "Now, give me one fourth of your cargo, and I'll let you pass."

"I happen to know, *Triaklon*," the man emphasized his name and Triaklon tried to act as though he wasn't surprised. How could he possibly know his name? "That you have a single cross-bow and few bolts. However, I will relent and give you what you ask for. But instead of a fourth of my cargo, you can have it all!"

The sides and backs of the wagons dropped open, and soldiers shouted a battle cry as they poured out. They charged up both sides of the pass toward his hidden men. Archers kneeling in a row in the center of each wagon drew their bows and sent a wave of deadly arrows ahead of the advancing footman, taking the advantage of the high ground away from Triaklon's men.

A sharp pain flared in Triaklon's right side. He looked down and saw a dagger shoved into his waist. Glavin dove at Radlyn and knocked him to the ground before he could shove the knife all the way to the hilt. Triaklon watched, momentarily stunned, as the two men wrestled on the ground. He knocked the dagger from his waist but was then hit hard in the shoulder. He staggered backward, nearly falling to the ground by the impact of the arrow embedded in his right shoulder.

He barely dove to the side in time, as the lieutenant and three other mounted knights bore down on him with their war mounts. As the men turned their steeds, Triaklon grimaced and pulled out the arrow. Fortunately, it hadn't hit bone, but he bled now from both wounds. He rose and turned as one of the knights charged him. Triaklon silently cursed for allowing himself and his men to fall into such a blatant trap. He didn't have time to see how the others were doing, but he hoped they were running away. The armored soldier swung his sword as his horse ran past Triaklon, but he parried the blow and continued the motion of the blade into the tendon of the horse's hind leg as it ran by.

He heard the crashing of armor hitting the ground and the whinny of pain from the horse, but had no time to watch the result of his counterattack, because the other two mounted soldiers were charging back toward him now. They positioned themselves so one would pass on his left and the other on his right. The two men raised their swords, poised to strike at the same time. The shield fixed to Triaklon's right arm was still attached, so at the last moment he dropped to a knee and raised both arms above his head. His shield took the brunt of one blow, and the other slid off his sword. Again, he continued the motion of his sword as the war horses charged past him and sliced open a thigh muscle of one of the horses. However, the impact of sword against bone caused the weapon to fly out of his grip. He rolled to the side as the lieutenant charged past again, and Triaklon felt the rush of air brush by his neck and heard the *swoosh* of the blade as it narrowly missed taking off his head.

"Let him go, Glavin," Triaklon shouted. Glavin was chasing a limping Radlyn toward the wagons. Glavin skidded to a halt as the lieutenant waved a group of footman with short swords forward. Apparently, the lieutenant decided mounted attacks against Triaklon weren't a good idea.

"Fall back, Glavin!" Triaklon yelled as he drew the sword from the scabbard on his back. Glavin didn't need to be told twice. He ran to Triaklon's side and drew his own sword. A half dozen men rushed their position. If the footmen surrounded them, it would be over for sure.

"Up the mountain!" Triaklon shouted at Glavin, who followed him as he tried to scramble up the slope. If they could just make it to the tree line, they'd have a chance. But the loose rock made a fast ascent impossible, especially with one hand holding a sword and the other hand missing. Glavin screamed in pain, and Triaklon turned to see his friend go down to his knees and roll over, clutching at a wound on his lower leg.

Triaklon slid down the shale toward the attackers, cursing and shouting as he plunged into them. His sword removed one man's head as he spun, and his shield blocked a strike coming down toward Glavin's chest. Triaklon jumped as two soldiers thrust long swords at his thighs, rolled and came up in the middle of his surprised assailants. His shield smashed the face of the man on his right, and he drove his sword to the hilt into the neck of the one on his left.

As the three remaining soldiers backed up to regroup, Triaklon retrieved a long sword from one of the fallen soldiers and helped Glavin stand. From the corner of his eye, he saw a streak of light and heard a shout of alarm coming from the wagon train. Something was happening near the back wagon, but he couldn't spare a glance to see what had occurred, because five more soldiers rushed to join the three who were regrouping on the road in front of him. Glavin's leg was bleeding badly, and he couldn't put any weight on it. Triaklon could carry the man, but they'd never make the trees before they were cut down from behind.

Rather than wait for the other five, Triaklon yelled and rushed toward the three soldiers who were waiting for the reinforcements. He cut down the first before the man had a chance to raise his sword, and Triaklon slammed the edge of his shield into the throat of the second man at the same time, but the third swung unchecked and left a deep cut in Triaklon's left shoulder. Blood dripped down his arm, making the hilt slippery and difficult to hold; he couldn't swing his weapon with the same force he had moments ago.

Glavin hobbled next to him and raised his sword just in time to parry a strike from a newcomer. The five additional soldiers joined the battle. Behind the soldiers, Triaklon saw flames and realized one of the wagons was burning.

"You've lost the battle!" Triaklon shouted, trying to confuse the attackers. "Look! Your wagons are burning!"

The men looked back long enough for him and Glavin to regain their footing and brace for the next round of fighting, but then the men turned and charged him. Triaklon was tired and growing weak. He bled from his side and both arms now and was winded from the extended battle. Glavin fell to the ground and raised his sword to block a vicious attack from a bearded man.

The others all focused on Triaklon. His sword arm was sluggish, and he was barely able to move his weapon fast enough to block the attacks. If the soldiers were smarter, they would've just attacked two at a time instead of all four. They got in each other's way more often than not. Apparently, they came to the same realization, because two of them backed off and worked their way behind him as the other two continued their attack.

Triaklon stepped back to defend the blows, but he'd forgotten Glavin was on the ground and tripped over his friend. He landed on his back, and his head hit the hard ground. Still, he was able to bring his sword up in time to block the two swords swinging down toward him. The soldiers standing above him raised their swords again, and now four blades raced down to end his life.

Triaklon positioned his blade to block the blows and braced himself for the inevitable. As the blades arced down, a loud booming shout interrupted the strange silence of his impending death, and a large object bowled into the soldiers, sending them flying and crashing to the ground.

Triaklon winced with pain as he pushed himself off the ground. He wasn't sure what had happened, but he had to regain his feet if he hoped to defend himself when the next attack came. He scanned the battle scene to ascertain his best course of action. Bull lay on top of one of the soldiers and struggled to get back to his feet. The remaining three, seeing Triaklon on his feet holding his sword, Bull's massive size rising up preparing to fight, and the burning wagon behind them, turned and ran for reinforcements.

"Bull, help me with Glavin." Triaklon winced when he placed the sword into the scabbard on his hip and wiped a long strand of brown hair, wet with sweat, from his face. Bull pushed him aside, reached down, and threw Glavin over his shoulder like a sack of grain.

"Let's get out of here." Triaklon pointed to the tree line and pulled himself up the rocky mountainside.

"I know I'm not your mother, but you should rest, Triaklon." Skunk hadn't been injured in the battle; he was one of the few who had made it out alive. Triaklon's side burned, and his arms throbbed and hung weakly at his side. Skunk was right. He needed sleep, but his men needed to see him more. When did he start thinking of them as *his* men? They were just a bunch of expelled, one-handed thieves like him. Maybe that was the reason. They were like him—homeless, cast off from society. And now that they were organizing and trying to make some kind of life for themselves in the mountains, society was coming after them again. The plains lords didn't care if a bunch of indigent, starving, and freezing handless people roamed the mountains. But now that they had turned themselves into something more than roaming scavengers, the *decent* folks in society wanted to hasten their death. Maybe he shouldn't have started organizing raids. But it was either that or die during the winter—which was exactly what the good people of Nortia expected them to do.

"They call me the Handless Shadow King," Triaklon said as he walked through their makeshift village. The high mountain meadow and surrounding trees were dotted with hundreds of twinkling camp fires. More than a thousand had gathered during the winter months because word had spread that Triaklon was able to keep them safe, fed, and warm.

"Who cares what they call you, Triaklon?" Skunk spat on the ground for emphasis. "Those plains lords are the biggest thieves of all—who are they to judge us?"

"Do you know why they call me that?"

"Does it matter? They're not worth a brass denar—although I'd gladly pay a gold denar to watch them burn in the well of Monguinir." He spat again.

"Did you know Jack was a cobbler?"

"What?"

Triaklon knew his random conversation confused Skunk, but he kept walking through the cooking fires, smelling the aroma of rabbit stew, smiling at the people, and talking. It helped him sort things out to walk and talk.

"And Thanojen was a blacksmith. Skantin was a fletcher. Krytner was a tanner. I wonder how many other valuable skills exist among this sorry lot of handless refugees."

"Triaklon, you've lost a lot of blood. You really need to—"

"All those skills, right in front of us, and we've been letting them go to waste."

"They've lost their *hands*, Triaklon. Thanojen can't hold the tongs while he strikes with a hammer, Skantin can't hold the shaft while he carves, and Krytner can't stretch leather while he scrapes it—they *all* have only one hand!"

Triaklon turned and looked Skunk in the eye. "We have children among us, Skunk. They need to learn a trade if they ever hope to make something of their lives."

Skunk's mouth dropped open, and for once he was speechless. Triaklon almost laughed at his friend's expression.

"Make something of their life? Are you crazy? Look around you, Triaklon!"

"I am, my friend. For the first time, I *am* looking around me. They call me the Handless Shadow King because they want to encourage their soldiers and citizens to hate me. They want to create fear. They want a king in these mountains? Well, I will give them a king. And I will turn this group of thieves into a mighty people."

As he turned to walk to his tent, he could feel Skunk's incredulous eyes bore into his back. Triaklon smiled. He felt something grow inside that he hadn't felt in many years—hope.

BASILEA

Drake Basil, the grand duke of Boranica, slammed his fist down, and one of the stacks of gold Borans on his desk fell over—at least his goblet of Boranica red didn't spill on the papers and maps spread across the dark oak surface. He held a crumpled letter in his other hand from his son, Danu.

"It's unraveling, Ishtar."

Drake's advisor, who was a Wizard of the Azur-Lore, sat cross-legged on a red pillow on the other side of the study. The room smelled sweet, like a mix of tobacco and cloves due to the exotic weed Ishtar smoked through an elaborate pipe—the kind they used in Divarlyn. A small bowl held the leaf on top of a large gourd-shaped, colored glass container filled with liquid—probably wine—where the smoke was filtered and given additional flavor, then passed through a series of circular tubes before it entered the mouth of the Wizard.

"Decades of work falling apart!" Drake said. "*By K'Thrak's dark heart,* Ishtar, Kahn Devin is *dead*! What do we do now?"

Ishtar blew a smoke ring into the air. His eyes were circled with dark makeup, and he wore deep blue velvet robes with a matching velvet hat embroidered with gold symbols around the band.

"How can you sit calmly and smoke, Ishtar?"

Drake felt like ripping the pipe out of the man's hands and throwing him through the stained-glass window. The late evening sun streamed through the colored sections of the old window, lighting up a depiction of King Lanistin Basil mounted on his war horse, raising his sword and preparing to charge into battle. More than seven hundred years had gone by since a Basil sat on the high throne. On second thought, this particular window was Drake's favorite piece of art in the ancient Basil castle. It would be a shame to ruin it, even if it would be a gratifying way to satiate his temper.

Drake paced behind his desk. "Rumor of Kahn's death is spreading, and our contacts are growing afraid! My agents in Tauret and Mylitta have vanished, and our spy in Boria City, the one who was trained in the temple of K'Thrak, is demanding proof that the Grand Warlock is still calling the shots. And this letter from my son confirms it. *Kahn is dead!*" Drake grabbed a date from the dish on his desk and threw it at Ishtar. "And you're as useless as a Nortian beggar. Are you going to do anything or just sit there and smoke that fancy pipe of yours?"

The Wizard raised his eyebrows and glared at Drake. "I'll let your little outburst pass . . . this time," Ishtar said.

Drake glared back, but he broke eye contact first and took a deep drink from his goblet.

"Perhaps, when Danu returns, you can send him out to reestablish our network," Ishtar said. "After all, he is much more effective than any of us gave him credit for, including the late Kahn Devin."

"I should've paid more attention to how Danu was raised." Drake rubbed his temples and stared at his reflection on the side of his brass goblet. His white hair and the wrinkles around his eyes made him look older than his fifty-five years. "His mother ruined him with her undying devotion to El Azur and her . . . unnatural affection for commoners."

Drake knew that Danu's sense of honor would get in the way of being involved in the scheme to overthrow King Kimael of Boranica. It shouldn't have mattered. If Kahn wouldn't have been so blasted meticulous and slow, Drake would already be king of Boranica. Danu wouldn't ever have had to know the details. He would've been made high prince and eventually the next king.

"We proceed according to plan," Ishtar said.

"How?" Drake ran his fingers through his hair and tossed the crumpled letter onto his desk. "We need the armies of Nortia to attack the northern dukes to put our plan into play. Without Kahn controlling King Thrakus, I don't think we'll get any cooperation from him. And even if he agreed to continue with the plan, I don't trust the man."

"There will be another Grand Warlock." Ishtar took another drag on his pipe, blew a smoke ring into the air, and smiled. "Whoever that is will want an alliance with Boranica just as badly as Kahn did. You and I, my friend, are the only means to accomplish that."

Shamael wiped a bead of sweat from his forehead. The great cavern that housed the well of sacrifice was filled with the din of a thousand conversations that hummed and reverberated off the rock walls and ceiling. The glowing well and the dozens of Magician's globes affixed to the cavern walls cast a crimson hue over the assembled crowd. The three eternal wayfires were burning, adding to the light, and causing shadows to dance on the cave walls like giant black curtains blowing in the wind. The fires, combined with the mass of people, made the immense chamber hot.

Shamael had never seen the cavern so crowded. Probably the last time this many people filled the room was when Kahn Devin had become Grand Warlock—over a hundred years ago. Clenmon Mishlok, the old archivist, was likely the only one here who was present for Kahn's preeminence blessing. Perhaps Siersha, the high priestess of Necrosys, had been there as well. She was rumored to be nearly one hundred and thirty.

Shamael pursed his lips and looked at the high priestess standing across the well near her wayfire. She only looked to be in her forties. Her long red hair and pale skin cast a stark contrast to the deep black velvet dress she wore. The full-length dress was tight in all the right places so that her figure effectively drew the eyes of the men standing near her. The only loose part of the garment was where the sleeves drooped from her elbows to her wrists. In her right hand, she held a long wooden staff—its length coiled with a live serpent. The staff was topped with a skull. Warlocks didn't normally use a staff. Perhaps the practice was more common a hundred years ago when Siersha had advanced to that rank.

She caught him looking at her and gave him a sultry smile. Great. Now she'd think he was attracted to her. The last thing he needed was Siersha believing she could manipulate him with sex. He blushed thinking of the prospect and silently cursed himself. Now she'd definitely think he was just another man she could control with her body. Well, he'd have to make it clear that that wasn't the case. Women brought about the ruin of many great men, and he had no intention of becoming another casualty on that long list.

"I see you invited a non-magic user, Shamael," Hodran said. "And a Kiroc at that."

The high priest of K'Thrak had worked his way through the crowd and now stood next to Shamael at the well of sacrifice. Shamael's irritation with the man for insinuating that he'd done something wrong was washed away in his relief to have a good excuse to look away from Siersha. He didn't want to break eye contact first and appear intimidated.

Hodran's long dark hair and ghostly skin was fitting for a man who represented the god of darkness, K'Thrak. Hodran nodded toward the dais on the opposite side of the well to where General Nishkral sat at the place of honor with Shamael's other advisors.

High Priest Hodran wore a deep purple velvet doublet over a silk shirt and a long purple cloak embroidered with black designs over his shoulders. The man covered his mouth and coughed—Shamael couldn't remember a time when Hodran was in good health. During the past thirty years, the high priest of K'Thrak never seemed to improve. He didn't get any worse, either.

"His name is General Nishkral," Shamael said. "He's one of my advisors, and I choose to give them the respect they deserve—all of them." Shamael knew he was taking out his irritation with himself on Hodran, and that wouldn't accomplish what he ultimately wanted. He took a deep breath and softened his tone. "Just as I intend to give you and your temple the respect and prominence you deserve."

Hodran raised his eyebrows and nodded.

Shamael spotted Torin walking toward him and Hodran. It was almost time to begin. But first, Shamael needed to be certain all three high priests would not only bless him, but also willingly give him their support.

"You there," Shamael called to a Demonologist who was trying to squeeze through the crowd. The black-robed girl had dirty brown hair and an up-turned nose. The color drained from her face, and she looked around to be certain the Grand Warlock was, indeed, calling to her.

"M-Me . . . Are you t-talking to me, Your Highness?"

Shamael nearly laughed, but, on second thought, a young Demonologist should fear him. Although, calling him Your Highness was humorous.

"Yes, I am speaking to you. Go tell High Priestess Siersha I would like to speak with her."

The girl's face turned sickly pale as she looked across the crowd to where a group of men surrounded Siersha. The girl looked back at Shamael, swallowed hard, curtsied, and hurried off to do as she was bidden. Hodran chuckled but his laugh was cut short by another bout of coughing.

"Siersha isn't going to appreciate being summoned like a servant," Torin said as he joined them. "This should be interesting."

Shamael counted on that. He didn't want to humiliate the high priest-ess, but he *did* need to reaffirm his position of ultimate authority in the Aven-Lore with her. This would hopefully be enough of a reminder without pushing her too far.

"It's better than me shouting and waving at her across the cavern," Sha-mael said. To which Torin raised his eyebrows and nodded with a frown.

The mass of magic users fell back like servants making room for a queen when Siersha approached. If the high priestess was upset at being summoned, she didn't show any sign of it as she crossed from her wayfire to where Shamael and the others were standing. Instead, she walked as though she chose to grace them with her presence, and they should be thankful for it.

"Hello, boys," she said with a coy smile. "Your combined auras are just oozing with authority and power. It's quite tantalizing to a girl of the Aven persuasion."

"Likewise," Shamael said. "I'm sure you've succeeded in tantalizing the men of the Aven persuasion."

Siersha continued to smile but hesitated at his words, apparently not sure if she should consider them a compliment or something else. Instead, she changed the subject. "I see you've invited General Nishkral to sit in a seat of honor. That's quite liberal of you, Shamael."

He didn't correct her for not referring to him as Grand Warlock. Her respect would come in time. Aven-Lore users tended to demand respect by virtue of their strength and not anything they'd done to earn it. There were men like that in the thieves' guild, too—they usually didn't live long.

"Nishkral is one of my key advisors, *High Priestess*." Shamael emphasized her title as he nodded to the Kiroc general who sat on a high back chair on the raised dais on the opposite side of the well. He looked proud of himself as he surveyed the mass of Aven magic users milling about the great cavern. "I reward those who support me."

Siersha cocked an eyebrow and tilted her head to one side. "That doesn't sound very Grand Warlocky of you."

"With all due respect to my predecessors, High Priestess, I do not fear those with power. On the contrary, I place trust in them."

"That could be . . . dangerous," Hodran said.

"Perhaps, but it's a philosophy that has produced great results for me in the past."

"And what do you intend to do with that trust?" Siersha replaced her smile with narrowed eyes and pursed lips.

"Reward those who deserve it." He nodded toward his five advisors, who were clearly being publically rewarded with seats of honor. Even the Warlock Jenot was seated among them, although he still looked rather pallid and weak. "The irony of this"—Shamael looked at each of them in turn—"is that the unity that comes from *our* trust will breed chaos across Lemuria."

The three Warlocks looked at each other as if confirming they all heard the same thing. Distrust was taken for granted among their ranks. It had been that way since before the binding. Shamael hoped they had come to the same conclusion as him. Namely, that this distrust was the very thing that had kept the Aven community perpetually floundering in these caves. Working together might just be what was needed to break the back of the Azur-Lore once and for all and bring all nations of Lemuria to heel.

"Then what are we waiting for?" Siersha asked. "Let's get on with your preeminence ceremony."

THE FISH 'N' HOOK

Four miles off the coast of Pitané, in the frigid blue waters of the Northern Lemurian Sea, a dolphin cut effortlessly through the waves. The dolphin had been swimming for nearly a day and realized that his splitting headache was due to the fact that he'd consumed no alcohol for even longer. But the freedom and pristine beauty of the ocean was almost enough to make him forget about his troubles and desire for drink—almost.

The dolphin dove beneath the water and scattered a school of fish swimming in a complex formation. One day, he would take time to study how the fish communicated with one another to swim that way. It was ingenious because they appeared to be a single large animal instead of a thousand small, tasty fish. Watching them reminded the dolphin that he was famished, so he scooped up a dozen as he swam.

The dolphin looked up through thirty feet of water. The shimmering light from the sun was low in the western horizon; it would set soon. He turned upward and used his powerful tail to propel his sleek body toward the surface. He gained speed and pushed even harder as he approached the watery ceiling. He burst out of the water with enough force to climb more than ten feet into the air. At the apex of his jump, rather than rotate and dive back into the water, the dolphin's body shimmered and transformed into a bald eagle.

The great bird screeched, spread his powerful wings, and took to the sky. He was grateful for the thick down feathers covering him, because the air was colder than the water, yet he stayed warm even though he was wet. The air rushing by dried his feathers, and he climbed ever higher as he flew toward the shore.

The small fishing village of Pitané boasted a general store, a cobbler, a blacksmith, an inn, and three taverns lining a solitary dirt road. The eagle guessed no more than a thousand people lived and worked in the area surrounding the village. However, the little harbor always teemed with fishing boats and merchant vessels—the waters here produced the best crab, lobster, and tuna in all of Lemuria.

The eagle flew south of the village and perched on a tree overlooking the seldom-used road that led from Pitané to Port Andrus, a town some hundred leagues to the south. The eagle's keen eyes told him he was alone—at least as far as humans were concerned—so he glided to the road and shimmered into his true form.

Lore Master Gendul Rocknest looked up and down the road, just to be sure he hadn't been spotted—word would spread fast if a lore master was seen here, and that was the last thing he wanted. He held his staff in one hand, rubbed at the white ring of hair that circled his bald head, and then traced his thick sideburns with his other hand. He would stand out like a Kiroc in Alfheina if he walked into the village looking like this. At least he remembered to change his favorite high-collared white sweater for a tattered, plaid buttoned shirt before leaving Elder Island. He also wore a thick brown coat, rugged trousers, and deck boots. In these clothes, the villagers would assume he was just another boat hand. He needed to cast an illusion to change how his face appeared, and he'd need to hide his staff in the woods, where he could call it if an emergency arose.

Gendul drew on the aeon myriad and gave himself full head of black hair and a thick beard. It was a bit of a stereotypical sailor look, but it would be an easy image to hold if he accidentally drank too much. The more complex the illusion, the more focus he'd need to maintain it. He looked thirty years younger as he left the road and headed to the seashore. He walked along the muddy beach until he reached the wooden docks of the wharf. Approaching the village from this direction would reinforce his disguise.

Dusk had fallen by the time Gendul walked into the center of the village, looking much like every other thirsty, hungry sailor with a single purpose. Which was partly true—his head pounded, and a drink was his first single purpose. The few shops lining the road were closing or already locked up for the night. He approached the first two taverns—both already noisy and filled with men anxious to spend their coin on wenches and whiskey. But Gendul walked past both of them without breaking stride. His destination was on the northernmost edge of the village—the Fish 'n' Hook.

The Fish 'n' Hook was marked by a weather-beaten, wooden sign hanging from the front of a single-level log structure with a large main room and a few rooms out back for let. The paint on the sign was faded and dull, but he could still read the words and make out the image of a large fish dangling from a barbed hook. The few windows along the front were grimy with years of grease and soot buildup, but a steady stream of smoke puffed out of the center of the roof with the promise of a good fire to warm the patrons.

Gendul ran his fingers through his illusionary hair and stole a quick look down the road before opening the heavy wooden door. Although the sun had set just minutes ago, the din of the room spoke of men already well on their way to a good drunk. The smell of burning wood blended with grease drippings from a boar turning on a spit over the fire in the center of the great room.

Three serving wenches in low cut, tight-busted dresses whirled from table to table, serving tall steins of ale, goblets of wine, and glasses of whiskey. The innkeeper was a barrel-chested man with short cropped gray hair and a week's growth of salt-and-pepper stubble on his face. His apron, once white, was stained with grease and blood—presumably from butchering the boar he now turned over the fire.

Gendul found a small table in the rear of the room and took a seat with his back against the wall, giving him a view of the entire place. A quick look around told him his appointment hadn't arrived yet—at least, he didn't think they had; he really wasn't sure who to look for. There were a couple of toughs leaning against the far wall, but they worked for the innkeeper and were mostly keeping an eye on the serving girls to make sure none of the guests tried to get too familiar with them. He passed over them and looked around the room again; perhaps nobody would come tonight—after all, Kahn was dead. That might be for the best. Then again, Gendul *had* to keep their agreement in place.

He gripped his knees to make himself stop wringing his hands beneath the table. He was a lore master, *for Azur's sake*—not some Apprentice preparing for their first exam. He would control the meeting. Whoever he met tonight, assuming someone appeared to meet with him, would be new in their role as Grand Warlock. Gendul could set the tone. This time, he wouldn't be bullied. This time, he would strike a better bargain.

His pounding head reminded him that his first order of business was a glass of good Concordian whiskey—after all, that's what he'd told Salas he was coming here for. He didn't want to let his old friend down.

A pretty, well-endowed redhead took his order and gave him a wink as she walked away. No wonder the owner hired security ruffians. The girls used all their assets to sell as much drink and food as they could. She returned with his whiskey and gave him her best smile when he tossed her a silver rukaht.

"Bring me some ribs off that boar when it's ready," he said as she tucked the coin from Kahaal in her brazier. Since Dekla had no king and was mostly peopled by the Dekla Devi, they didn't mint their own coin. So a person could use tender from any other country of Lemuria here. Coins from Kahaal were most common and preferred.

As the girl retreated into the growing crowd, Gendul took a swallow of whiskey, savoring the burning sensation as it warmed his throat. He sucked breath through his teeth and settled in to wait.

A dark hawk circled above the northern fishing village of Pitané. Night had fallen more than an hour ago, but the bird's golden eyes had no difficulty discerning the sign above the door of the Fish 'n' Hook. The sign creaked as it swayed in the breeze, affixed to the inn on a twisted iron rod. The door flew open and two men practically fell out, each with a bottle in one hand and his arm around the other's shoulder, laughing as though they'd just been told the funniest story ever. The hawk felt a little envious. The men hadn't a care in the world as they staggered down the road toward the next tavern.

The bird dropped toward the shadowed dirt road, and with a burst of red energy Shamael Daro transitioned from flight to walking without missing a step. The two men stopped laughing, their eyes opened wide and jaws dropped. One of them looked at the bottle in his hand and then back to Shamael as he walked past them. Shamael smiled. Rumors would run like a grass fire once these two got to the other taverns and started wagging their tongues about a bird that changed into a man.

Shamael had been flying hard for two days and nights to get to this meeting on the date listed in Kahn's appointment book. No doubt Kahn hadn't planned on attending a preeminence blessing and the celebrations that accompanied such an event when he'd set the date. But, there was nothing to do for it other than press on. Shamael had looked forward to this meeting—he just wished he wasn't so tired.

He reached up to rub his head, but paused and forced his hands to remain calmly at his side. He'd done his research, and he was prepared. There was no need for him to be nervous about this meeting. He cursed his sweating palms, rubbed them on his cloak and then walked confidently into the crowded room.

It took his eyes a moment to adjust to the light and smoke. The fire in the center of the room sizzled with grease dripping from a boar on a spit. Shamael's stomach grumbled. A middle-aged man missing a few teeth was playing a lively jig on a lute and smiling affectionately at the portly woman singing on the stage beside him. She held up the front of her dirty red dress and danced as she sang. A group of sweaty men surrounding her clapped their hands to the rhythm of the tune and tossed coins.

The noisy room was crowded, but it didn't take Shamael long to locate his man—sitting alone at a table near the back wall. The man looked like a common sailor, perhaps thirty-five years old, minding his own business and having a drink. But the dull green glow of an Azur illusion was visible to Shamael's Warlock enhanced senses. The man looked up and they locked eyes. Since Shamael made no pretenses at a disguise, he would be easy to spot. He didn't care if people recognized what he was, it would simply help to spread rumor and fear—both good things as far as he was concerned.

Shamael made his way through the tables and serving girls, stopping one of them to ask for a bottle of Boranica red. He was pleasantly surprised when she smiled and replied, "Right away, sir." He didn't think a tavern in a small fishing village would carry something so refined—especially this far from Boranica. He indicated to the table where he would be sitting, and then continued through the bustle.

Shamael pulled out a chair but remained standing. "Hello, Gendul, you look younger than the descriptions I've read."

Only a Wizard could cast such a convincing illusion and the bottle of Concordian whiskey was enough of a clue for Shamael to guess who this was.

"Shh! Careful what you say," Gendul whispered, confirming that Shamael's guess was correct. The man's eyes darted around the hazy room, presumably to make sure nobody was listening. "I'm wearing this illusion for a reason."

"I'm sure you are."

Shamael removed his cloak and hung it neatly over his chair. He would need to have his clothing laundered after leaving this pungent tavern. The young redheaded serving girl swept to the table with his wine and leaned over as she poured in such a way as to make sure the men noticed her ample bosom, practically bursting out of her dress. Shamael appreciated the gesture, so he handed her a Gold Denar, told her to leave the bottle and keep the change. Boranica red was expensive wine, but the Denar was easily worth five bottles.

The girl looked suspiciously at the Nortian coin—but apparently forgot about whatever prejudice she held toward Nortia as she calculated the value.

"Thank you, good sir." She blushed and curtsied. "You are too kind. Let me know if you need anything else . . . and I do mean *anything*." She smiled and gave a sultry laugh as she walked away.

"Really, sir!" Gendul's face turned red, and he spoke in a forced whisper. "Can you please try to be less conspicuous?"

"No, I don't think I can, actually." Shamael sat, swirled his glass of wine and smelled the aroma. The liquid clung to the glass, running down the sides of the goblet like multiple little rivulets, and the aroma was rich and slightly woody. Perfect.

"I think I'd like people to know there is a new Grand Warlock, and he may show up anywhere, anytime, for any purpose." Shamael lifted his eyes from studying the wine and stared into Gendul's eyes—there was a warning implied in his words, and he wanted to be sure it wasn't lost on the lore master.

"For the love of Magaia, I don't even know what your name is or if you *really* are the new Grand Warlock, but respect my wishes in this, otherwise I might rethink working with you."

Shamael smiled and sipped his wine. Once Gendul learned that Shamael knew his darkest secrets, the man would work with him. Of that Shamael had no doubt.

"My name is Shamael Daro. I am the new Grand Warlock." He leaned forward and broadened his smile. "If you'd like, I'd be happy to demonstrate my power for you."

"No, no." Gendul sniffed and rubbed at his nose. "The fact you're here for this meeting is enough evidence to me that you replaced Kahn," he said with a wink, as though he were trying to lighten the tone of their discussion.

"Yes, speaking of Kahn," Shamael said, "I'm not certain his alliance with you was helpful." He locked his gaze with Gendul and took another drink. "After all, your *help* got him killed in the end." He still didn't know exactly how his predecessor was killed, but he didn't want Gendul to know that he lacked that particular piece of information.

"I didn't get him killed!" Gendul said, probably louder than he intended. A skinny, young sailor at the next table glanced at them, and the lore master lowered his voice. "All I did was tell him how to get past our defenses. I had no idea he would attack the Demaris boy right on our doorstep. It was foolhardy of him to do such a thing."

"And you expect me to believe a fourteen-year-old boy killed him?"

"I wouldn't have believed it myself if I wasn't there to witness it." Gendul sniffed and rubbed his nose. "By the time the rest of us arrived, they were locked in battle. Salas told us not to intervene. I've never seen anybody draw the amount of power that boy did on that night." The man eyes looked haunted as he remembered the scene, and Shamael knew Gendul was telling the truth.

"And what of Kahn's body?" Shamael said. "Did it occur to you we might want the remains of our Grand Warlock?"

Gendul stared at him and slowly shook his head. "There were no remains, Shamael. The boy completely obliterated him. There wasn't even a pile of ash left on the ground." Gendul's eyes stared off in the distance like he was reliving the scene. He barked out a short laugh and said, "And then Demaris brought a man back to life that Kahn had killed moments before! I've never even heard of such a thing." The lore master threw back his whiskey and then looked mournfully at his empty glass.

This was a lot worse than Shamael thought possible. It was unbelievable, and yet, he knew Gendul was speaking the truth.

"Your first task, my Azur friend, is to kill this Demaris boy."

"Are you crazy?" Gendul glanced around the room, leaned forward, and whispered, "Didn't you hear what I just said? He killed a Grand Warlock in a fair battle and then turned around and raised a man from the dead like he was some kind of a god! I'm powerful in the lore, but nobody's that powerful." He took Shamael's bottle of Boranica red, poured some in his own glass, and drank it like it was water. Shamael didn't object—he just stared at Gendul, who fidgeted with his empty glass.

"There are other ways to kill, Gendul," Shamael said. "Don't use magic. In fact, make it look like an accident. It's your choice, but I want him dead."

"I'm not a murderer, Shamael." Gendul reached for the bottle of wine, and Shamael put his hand on it. The lore master looked up.

"You're a hypocrite, Gendul," Shamael hissed. "How many lives have been lost because of the information you gave Kahn over the years? It makes no difference that somebody else's hand dealt the killing blow."

Gendul let go of the wine bottle and looked genuinely troubled by the accusation. Apparently, the man had some semblance of a conscience remaining.

"You *will* kill the boy, old man."

Gendul's mouth dropped open while he stared at Shamael. He apparently gathered a little courage because he straightened and took a deep breath. "I owe you nothing, Shamael. Kahn is dead, and my agreement with your kind is dead with him."

Shamael gave a half smile and leaned back in his chair. He knew it would come to this. He let out a loud breath, slapped his knees, stood, and picked up his cloak as though he were leaving.

"As you wish." He turned to walk away, then looked over his shoulder. "By the way, one of my Warlocks will be leading a team into Concordia tomorrow morning to begin harvesting. Did you know it's been a decade since we've looked for marked children there? I think we'll begin in North Port. I hear there is a particularly gifted young lady who lives there— Katerina is her name, I believe."

Gendul's illusion shimmered as the old man nearly dropped his disguise. He maintained it, but his face turned ghostly white.

"You . . . You . . ." Shamael thought Gendul was about to curse and shout, but he stopped himself short and looked around to be certain no one was listening in on their conversation. "Wait, don't go." He stood and indicated for Shamael to sit back down. "There must be something else I can offer you? Some other way I can be of service?"

Shamael placed his cloak back onto the chair and sat down. "This isn't a negotiation, Gendul Rocknest." Shamael poured himself another glass of wine and then poured the balance of the bottle into Gendul's glass.

"If you want to protect your secret daughter and her Witch mother, you will do as I tell you."

Gendul's jaw clenched, and sweat dripped down his cheek. He sniffed and rubbed at his nose. "I need time to consider this," he said.

"Fair enough," Shamael said. "You have until I finish this glass of wine to give me your answer."

"That's ridiculous!" Gendul slammed the table with his fist. "What you ask of me is too weighty a matter to rush me this way!"

Shamael simply smiled, picked up his glass, and sipped his drink.

What have I gotten myself into? Gendul thought as he watched the young Grand Warlock set down his empty wine glass. Those black eyes studied him the way a mountain cat peered at its prey. The scar running down the man's face, and his bald head made him look like a street fighter in fine clothing. Gendul was tempted to strike him unexpectedly and kill the man right here and now, but that would likely end in his own death. Then Katerina would certainly be forced into the Aven-Lore and his wife, Maloreen, would be taken back to the caves and probably sacrificed at the well. If she wasn't a Witch of the Aven-Lore, he could bring them both to the school with him, and they'd be safe there. What a mess.

He'd hid the existence of his small family from everybody. Even the other lore masters knew nothing of his wife and daughter. This was actually the second time he'd started a family. He'd had no intention of beginning again after the tragic loss of his first wife and children. He hadn't even wanted to fall in love with Maloreen—after all, she was fifty years younger than him and a Witch in the Aven-Lore—it just happened. He foolishly believed he could keep it secret and protect them if he only visited occasionally. He cared for them financially, and Maloreen grew to hate the ways of the Aven-Lore so he hoped they could eventually just live a simple life. It worked for the first seven years, but then Kahn somehow discovered his secret and used it to extort him.

Shamael raised a single eyebrow, stood, took his cloak from the chair, and walked away.

"I'll do it," Gendul said.

"What was that?" Shamael asked, turning back.

"I said I'll do it. Just make sure you hold up your end of the bargain."

The Grand Warlock left, and Gendul signaled to the redheaded serving girl. He slid three silver rukahts across the table to her.

"Concordian whiskey—the bottle."

KURULAN

"Watch for rocks!" Raven shouted above the storm.

Aleah looked from side to side as she rowed. Her husband's black hair and clothing clung to his body as he worked the rudder and battled the sleet and waves. His soaked coat and shirt had been ripped open by the swinging mast as he lowered the sail when the storm first rose.

"It's too dark. I can't see a thi—" The small craft made a loud crunching sound and stopped, causing her to pitch forward. Raven also fell forward, cursing as he lost his grip on the rudder and slammed into the deck.

The next wave lifted them off the rock and thrust the small craft sideways. Water seeped into the bottom of the single mast sloop at an alarming rate. Aleah's arms ached, but she forced herself to row faster toward the shore.

"Raven, we're taking on water!" She didn't need to tell him because his hands were already immersed in water as he pushed himself to his feet.

Yesterday morning, Cael had escorted Aleah and Raven to a calm lake tucked into the coast of southwestern Bremenon where the Avuman kept their ragged fleet of washed up boats. The lake was fed by waterfalls from tall cliffs on one side and surrounded by fragrant pine trees. A river left the lake and twisted through a stretch of forest before heading into the Lemurian Inlet—the finger-shaped part of the Northern Lemurian Sea that separated the west shore of Bremenon from main part of the Lemurian continent.

Aleah had emptied her stomach more than once over the side of the boat as it pitched and tossed on the water during the past two days. Now, she ignored the blisters on her hands and her aching muscles as she shivered and rowed with all her strength toward the land and lights of Kurulan.

"How well can you swim?" Raven shouted and stumbled toward her.

"Are you crazy? In this storm?"

"It's not far, and we should be able to touch bottom soon."

When they had left the Avuman and their "haunted" forest, it had been a bright, crisp spring morning. They had expected to reach their destination by nightfall because this far south, the Lemurian Inlet was only a few leagues wide. But by noon of that same day, storm clouds rolled in, turning the sky lead gray and bringing with it a stiff wind that whipped the waves into a white-capped frenzy.

"I don't think we have a choice!" Raven pointed at the six inches of water in the bottom of their boat. "Take off your boots and cloak and leave them here."

Aleah was already wet and cold, but jumping into the frigid inlet sent a shock through her entire body. The dark water disoriented her, but, mercifully, her feet felt solid ground almost as soon as she went under. She pushed upward and swam toward the shore. A wave washed over her and filled her mouth with cold salt water. She sputtered and coughed. She pushed through another wave and then her muscles cramped. As her head was about to go under, a strong hand gripped her shirt and kept her from sinking. Raven was tall enough he could walk with his head above water, bobbing between the wave crests. Her sisters would laugh and call her a man-sick dry lander for letting him rescue her this way, but she was long past caring about any of that.

"You'll miss midsummer's Azur-Aven, Aerik!" Katryline complained for at least the tenth time today. Aerik's wife sat on a cushioned leather chair braiding Adrilla's long golden hair. Their daughter knelt on the floor in front of her mother and played with a rag doll while her hair was prepared for bed.

Aerik grunted, took a drink of ale, and stared at the Kurulan banner hanging on the wall above the mantel. A strong fire burned in the massive fireplace that kept the great hall of their castle warm during cold nights. The banner brandished a golden lightning bolt underneath a crossed hammer and axe on a field of dark blue—the hammer and axe had been his family crest for generations. The worst thing about missing midsummer's Azur-Aven was that he'd not be here to defend his axe-throwing title. That meant his youngest brother, Radlik, would likely win the tournament this year.

Although the snows had mostly thawed, winter still clung on in Kurulan, and his trip south would be difficult through the Kuru-Kulla forest with snow covering much of the way. Winter might even still be hanging on here during the midsummer's events—it sometimes did. It felt like a spring festival most years because the summer solstice was about the time the runoff was at its peak. The air was crisp, flowers were beginning to bloom and, well, it felt like spring.

"You were just there a few months ago," Katryline continued. "*Lunaryn love me*, but I don't understand why you must rush back down to Kah-Tarku just because Melista called another meeting."

"Ouch, that hurt," Adrilla complained.

"Sorry, dear," Katryline said. "But you really need to take better care of your hair. It's a mess of snarls. After all, you'll be a young woman soon and—Jim and Jam, stop chasing that cat!" A spotted cat leaped over the chair where Katryline sat, then ran under the table next to Aerik, across the great room and into the long hallway that led to the children's wing of the castle. A barking dog and the twin boys, Jimosyn and Jamisyn, followed shortly after, laughing and shouting.

"Lunathail!" Katryline shouted. "Where is that woman? Lunathail!"

"Yes, Your Highness?" Aerik grimaced and took another sip of ale as their skinny nanny hurried into the room, curtsied, and then tucked an errant strand of mousy brown hair behind her ear. He tried to get people to just call him Aerik or sir, but his wife insisted they use honorific titles. In some ways, she was similar to Melista Tarku, although he'd never point that out to Katryline.

"Will you *please* gather the twins and get them ready for bed?"

"Yes, of course, Your Highness." She rushed out of the room after the boys, stopping long enough to make a quick curtsy to Aerik as she ran by him.

"Melista didn't even bother to say what the urgent matter was?" Katryline asked.

Aerik had let her read the letter so she already knew the answer to that question. Melista simply wrote that an urgent matter required an immediate gathering of the rulers of Kahaal. She insisted they be at her palace one week prior to summer solstice. Even if the meetings only lasted a day, Aerik didn't think he'd make it back for midsummer's Azur-Aven, because that took place the first new moon after the solstice. This year that was only a week later.

"The problem with Melista is that she has nothing better to do with her time," Katryline said. "If she had six children, a husband, and a mother-in-law living in her castle, she wouldn't be so quick to call these grand councils, *by Lunaryn's love.*"

Aerik grunted and stared at his empty stein. Maybe he should refill it with whiskey this time. It looked to be a long night. The Bremenon winds were blowing, and Katryline was on a rant.

"Off to bed, Adrilla." His wife smiled at their youngest daughter and sent her off with a swat on her bottom. "Tell your older sister and brothers to prepare for bed, too." Katryline walked to the fire, tossed two more logs in, picked up the long iron poker, and positioned the logs just right. She insisted on being called Your Highness but didn't think twice about doing menial tasks like brushing hair and stoking a fire. Aerik smiled. In this, she was *nothing* like Melista and the soft, noble women of the southland. He'd take the solid stock of Kurulan woman over the sophisticated ladies of a southern court any day.

"I don't think it's right for Melista to order you about—don't you agree, Mother?"

Aerik's mother sat near the fire, knitting a wool sweater and humming. "Did you say something, dearie?" She was nearly seventy and could barely hear these days.

"I said, I don't think it's right for Melista Tarku to give orders to your son. Don't you agree?"

"Oh, that's lovely, dearie. Be a sweetie and pour me a glass of wine." Katryline let out an exasperated breath and walked to the cabinet where they stocked wine, whiskey, and ale.

"Perhaps you should purchase one of those hearing horns for your mother when you're in Kah-Tarku." She poured the wine and handed it to her mother-in-law.

"So you're giving in to the fact that I have to make this trip?"

Before Katryline could respond, there was a loud knock at the massive double doors that led outside to the courtyard.

"Who in the name of Thail would be out in this storm?" Aerik wondered out loud. His wife gave him an exasperated look—she wasn't through complaining—but she brushed at her dress and fussed with her hair as she hurried to open the small speakeasy that was cut into the door.

"Gregor, what brings you out of the gatehouse on a night like this?"

"Visitors washed up from the inlet." The castle guard captain's voice was muffled by the wind, but Aerik could hear him well enough. "Insisted on seeing the prince tonight. Claims to be an old family friend."

Katryline closed the small wooden window and opened one of the iron studded doors.

"*By Lunaryn's love*," Aerik said. "Thail himself wouldn't travel the inlet in a storm like this—especially at night!" He stood and walked over to see who the unexpected visitors might be.

"Raven, is that you?" Katryline said. "*By Thail's beard*, the two of you look like half-drowned rats. You'd best get inside and sit by the fire. We can figure out what this is about after we get some hot stew and a bit of whiskey in you."

"Raven?" He was the last person Aerik expected to see at his doorstep. He hadn't seen or heard from the man in a decade. "Raven, you son of a Warlock, it *is* you!" Aerik pulled the man into an awkward, wet bear hug. "I haven't seen you in years, and you show up on a night like this, with a woman at your side, no less." He held Raven at arm's length and looked him over. He was a little older but still had hair as black as K'Thrak's heart and without a spot of gray in it.

"Come inside, and let's get you two warmed up." Aerik slapped Raven on the back. "We'll have a night of stories from you, and I've got a bottle of whiskey to share while we hear them."

"Gregor," Katryline said to the captain of the guard.

"Yes, Your Highness."

"Fetch Blimron."

The captain's eyes widened. "In the middle of a storm . . . at night?"

Aerik smiled at the thought of the captain trying to rouse the ornery Meskhoni at this hour and convince him to cross the courtyard in the midst of a storm. The old man only willingly left his tower to go fishing.

"Tell him to bring his medicines," Katryline said. As the captain turned to carry out her orders, she added, "And tell the old Mage to be quick about it!"

Aerik rubbed the length of his long, blond beard and grunted. "So, Kahn is dead?" He raised his brows and caught his wife's eyes. "I'd wager my finest axe and a hundred sheep that Melista knows about this. That's why she's called this emergency meeting."

"And it changes things," Katryline said. She sat in the chair closest to Aerik and sipped wine as she listened to Raven. Raven and Aleah looked a lot better now. Blimron had dressed their wounds and given them a nasty tasting tincture.

"Unless there is some other pressing, late night emergency," Blimron said with a scowl, "I'll be returning to my tower to get some sleep."

Raven and Aleah were dressed in furs now, had eaten a bowl of stew, and they both held mugs of spiced ale. Aerik still couldn't believe Raven had gone and gotten married. He claimed this girl was a warrior, but Aerik wondered how strong she could be. She didn't have much meat on her bones, but she did have a warrior's look in her eyes. She didn't say much, but she noticed everything. She was pretty enough, Aerik supposed, but he preferred a woman with a little more meat and curves on her.

"Aye," Aerik agreed with his wife. "This changes things a lot. I'd wager a year's worth of fine whiskey Melista and Narkash are both scheming to become the next king."

Aleah set her stein down and leaned forward. "I know Kahn was considered the true king of Kahaal, sir." At least she remembered to call him sir instead of Your Highness. "But you've had a regent act in his place for decades. Why does his death change things so much?"

"His regents were able to keep power by using Kahn's name as a threat."

Katryline nodded in agreement and then jumped into the conversation, cutting Aerik off. "That weaselly little rat Lamon of Devlyn has been funneling tax dollars into his pet projects for years. Every time my husband or one of the other princes says anything about it, Lamon claims he's doing what Kahn would want and they can complain to him if they'd like."

"With Kahn dead"—Aerik rubbed at his beard and stared at the fire—"it won't take Narkash or Melista long to make a move."

Aleah's stomach growled at breakfast the next morning, but she let the food sit untouched in front of her while she stared. She had been raised in the royal palace in Domeria, served in the guard at the castle in Achtan, and visited a dozen other castles and great manors over the years, but she never saw a castle or a royal household function like Aerik and Katryline's.

The stoic castle was beautifully rustic and, like others she'd been in, expensively furnished with lavish rugs, tapestries, hand-carved chairs and tables—all the luxuries simple folk would never enjoy in this life. A warm fire burned in the large fireplace on one end of the long room, and the dark polished walnut table was set with highly polished silver dishes. But breakfast with Aerik's family was pure chaos.

First, a cat and two dogs charged into the room, and the twins jumped from their chairs, shouted, and chased after the animals. The oldest two boys—Rodrik and Aerik the younger—sat on opposite sides of the table tossing pieces of pork sausage at each other to see who could catch the most in their mouth at one time. The girls, Clynthia and Adrilla, were arguing about who was taking whose clothing without permission, and their father, Aerik, sat at the head of the table, already drinking his second stein of ale.

Princess Katryline insisted the staff refer to her with the honorific title Your Highness, but she had just got up and left with a servant to visit the kitchens because the egg soufflé wasn't cooked quite how she liked, and she was going to help them whip up another batch to show them her secret process for getting it just right.

Aleah didn't realize she was gawking until she glanced at Raven and saw him grinning at her. Truth be told, she preferred a relaxed and noisy atmosphere to the stuffy airs put on by most families of the nobility. But now she understood why the other regions of Kahaal consider Kurulan to be a bunch of barbarians.

"I've got it!" Aerik slapped the table, and Aleah flinched in her seat at his sudden outburst. The twins—Jim and Jam—continued chasing the dogs and cat, but the other children stopped what they were doing and looked to their father.

"Since I can't be here for midsummer's Azur-Aven, we'll just have our festival before I leave!" He smiled broadly as though he'd just solved a major dilemma. "Better yet, we'll hold it before Raven and Aleah leave—that will give me a chance to redeem myself against you in the axe-throwing event." That last comment he directed at Raven.

"I hope you've spent more time practicing than drinking ale, otherwise you'll likely lose to me *and* my wife. Women are allowed to participate in the games, are they not?"

Aerik rubbed his hands together and let out a hearty laugh. "Of course women participate in the games—although usually in archery and wrestling."

"Wrestling?" Aleah asked. Woman participating in games of strength and athleticism was nothing new to her. After all, *men* were not allowed to participate in her home country of Domeria—the games there were reserved for female champions. But she found it odd that dry lander women would compete against men in this way.

"In the mud, of course," Aerik said happily. "There's nothing so entertaining as watching your wife get covered in mud as she slips around on the ground wrestling another woman."

"Your wife . . . the princess? She wrestles other women in the mud?"

"Of course," Adrilla, the youngest sister chimed in. "Mother has won the event seven years in a row!"

"Wow, that's truly . . . impressive." Aleah forced a smile.

After breakfast, Raven and Aleah went for a walk around the castle grounds. Now that the sun was out and the sky was blue, the estate looked much more inviting. A thin blanket of snow covered the ground, but it glistened under the warmth of the early spring sun and was beginning to melt. They crossed a courtyard, a practice arena, and a garden area before reaching the outer wall of the castle grounds, then climbed a set of rock steps cut into the stone so they could see the view from atop the parapets.

Aleah caught her breath as she got her first glimpse of Kurulan in the daylight. The water of the inlet was bright blue and as calm as glass. Like a mirror, it reflected the Bremenon Mountains on the opposite side of the inlet. To the southwest, beyond the farms, a taller, distant mountain range rose up—the Kuru-Kulla range. Directly south rose a forest.

She'd studied the forest and both mountain ranges on maps many times but never realized how majestic they were. The forest was thick and endless from her vantage point, and the mountain peaks cut into the sky like snow-covered rocky spires reaching toward the realm of gods—like green-and-white giants.

Directly across the narrowest part of the inlet, a stretch of land appeared to be cultivated with farms and what looked to be another small town, but from this distance she couldn't make out any structures. Just north of that town was where the Bremenon Mountains began their impressive stretch to the sky.

"Is that a town across the inlet?" Aleah asked.

"Yes, it's called Kanor," Raven said.

"Why didn't we just go there, rather than nearly drown and freeze crossing this stupid inlet?"

"Two reasons. First, we had no horses, and it would take much longer to walk. Second, the townsfolk would be suspicious of two strangers wandering out of Bremenon."

That made sense, she decided. And the fact that Raven was friends of the Kurulan prince was a plus, too.

"We should return to this place someday," she said. "When it's warmer and we can explore the mountains."

Raven nodded, put his arm around her waist, and pulled her close to him.

Aleah looked down at the city below. A single cobblestone road wound its way from the castle southward, like a rocky brown snake cutting a line in the snow, wrapping in and out of buildings and homes. The city stretched generally southward along the road. Homes, businesses, and small farms hugged both sides. On the left—the east side of the road—the buildings stretched from the road to the water of the inlet. On the west side of the road, beyond the buildings, there were farms stretching toward the foothills of the Kuru-Kulla Mountains.

"So are you going to challenge the princess?"

"Challenge her?" Aleah scrunched her forehead and looked at Raven.

"To a wrestling match, of course." Raven grinned, and Aleah punched him in the arm.

"I just barely got warm and dry. The last thing I'm going to do is wrestle in mud with other women for the enjoyment of a bunch of barbarian dry landers."

Raven laughed and looked back out over the expansive view.

"How about you?" Aleah asked. "You plan to join the axe-throwing contest?"

"Yes I do," he answered with a smirk. "But I don't think it will be much of a contest."

"Really?" Aleah said. "That confident of your skill, huh?"

He shrugged his shoulders and continued to grin.

"Perhaps I should join the axe throwing and make it challenging for you. Who knows—maybe women will win both the wrestling *and* the axe-throwing events this year."

THE TIARAK LOCK

"You did well," Shamael told Ancilia and Shadin as he inspected the fifty prospective vitiate. The recruits stood in a line in the center of the Demonologist cavern. Their faces various shades of red due to the crimson light cast from the dozens of Magician's globes spread throughout the large chamber. Some trembled as he walked by and all kept their eyes on the floor rather than straight ahead the way a soldier would.

"Ancilia," Shamael said and lifted the chin of a young female recruit. Her eyes were wide and haunted. "Did these recruits . . . volunteer?"

"Yes, milord."

"And they understand what they will become?"

"Yes, milord."

"Good." Shamael finished walking the line, turned, and faced the recruits.

"If any of you wish to reconsider," Shamael said to the assembly of black-robed students—a dozen or more also wore the red belt marking them as Witches—"now is your chance to back out. I assure you, it will not affect your standing in the Aven-Lore."

There were furtive glances from one student to another. Nine stepped forward and shyly asked to be dismissed—all young Demonologists. Ancilia and Shadin drew their lips to a thin line. They had obviously used coercion to reach fifty "volunteers." Despite his assurances that students who backed out wouldn't be affected, he almost pitied the nine. Ancilia and Shadin had only coerced them because they knew these students wouldn't go far in the lore. Now, the nine would be left with little talent *and* instructors who resented them. *Oh well*, Ancilia thought, *it couldn't be avoided.*

"Ancilia," Shamael said to the old woman who had been his first mentor in the Aven-Lore, "select twenty-four of these and send the remainder back to their studies."

"Forgive me, Lord Daro, but did you not request fifty?"

"So I did," Shamael said. "However, Monguinir only gave me leave to create twenty-four."

"The demon lord agreed to your request?" Ancilia's eyebrows raised. Shamael didn't blame her for appearing surprised. Monguinir hadn't allowed a Grand Warlock to create vitiate in nearly two thousand years—not since he was betrayed by Nefarion Drakkas.

"Not entirely. I requested fifty."

"But, still, how did you convince him?" Ancilia asked. Shadin stepped closer to presumably hear Shamael's answer. "After all," she continued, "Nefarion only had twelve vitiate."

"I reminded him that Nefarion betrayed him *before* the binding. Now he is bound in the well and any action I take and any power I lay claim on will only increase chaos, which, in turn, will increase his own strength and help him escape."

Ancilia nodded. "Very bold approach, Shamael, but Monguinir isn't known for his generosity. What else did he require?"

Even now, thirty years after Shamael and Ancilia left Valdivar for the caves, she had the ability to read him like no other. It annoyed him at times, but was one of the reasons she was a good advisor.

"He laughed when I asked for fifty," Shamael pulled her aside so Shadin couldn't hear them. "He said I would thank him later for not allowing me to pay the price for so many."

"What is the price?"

"He said I would discover that once I reach the West Asgar Island with the twenty-four. He said I must find someone called the Guardian, and he would teach me how to turn them into vitiate and tell me what the payment is."

"Are you sure this is wise?"

Shamael pursed his lips. "No." He clasped his hands behind his back and turned back to the line of Demonologists, wondering what he was getting himself into. "Select the twenty-four strongest and have them ready to leave at dawn."

When Shamael looked back at Ancilia, she gave him a look of motherly concern, and then nodded. Shamael gave her a single nod in return.

"Shadin," Shamael said loud enough for all to hear. "Follow Ancilia's orders as if they were my own. The chosen twenty-four need to meet me at the north gate at first light." Shadin's eyes widened and his mouth dropped open. Most people believed the caverns and corridors of the northern section to be haunted. Additionally, these recruits would have to march all night to arrive on time. Demonologists and Witches couldn't Shapeshift, so they would have to walk the several miles of tunnels to the north gate.

Shadin must have realized his expression made him look like a novice, because he smiled as though the task were simple and bowed. "As you wish, Grand Warlock."

The recruits, however, continued to gape and tremble, presumably at the prospect of marching to the north gate. Simple minded fools. But, their fear would make it easier for him to manipulate and mold them, so he didn't bother to tell them there was nothing to fear in the north section. Perhaps, with the help of these vitiate, there would be enough followers of the Aven-Lore in the near future to rebuild and reopen the northern caves.

Shamael didn't touch his amulet as he took the form of a black hawk and flew down the corridor. He wanted the recruits to see that he needed no help to use his magic, that he was far more powerful than any of them would ever be.

Thirty minutes later, he transformed from bird to man in midflight and landed gracefully at the threshold of the solid door to his study. The two Demonologists serving at the door jumped to attention and straightened their robes.

"G-General Narkash is waiting inside for you, Master."

What in the dark of K'Thrak *does that Kiroc want now?* Shamael wondered. He needed to prepare for his journey with the vitiate. He didn't have time to deal with the general.

"General," Shamael said as he marched into his study. "In the future, you are to wait outside."

The Kiroc bowed, nearly spilling the goblet of wine he was holding. So not only did he enter Shamael's study uninvited, but Narkash also helped himself to wine. No wonder Kahn kept this room warded and locked all the time. Shamael wanted to be different than Kahn, but this was one habit his previous master had that he decided he would embrace.

"What is so urgent you must see me now?"

"My scouts have located Kintara and the boy."

Shamael stopped removing his cloak and turned to face the massive Kiroc.

"Where?"

"They are just entering the Mord Mountains, milord. There is another boy and girl with them, so they travel slowly."

Shamael clutched his hands behind his back and pursed his lips. Then he pulled parchment from his desk, dipped a quill in the inkwell, and scratched out a letter.

"Give this to Jenot," he said as he dripped hot, red wax onto the folded paper and pressed his seal into it. "Tell him I've decided to give him a final chance to redeem himself. This time, he is to take two hundred Kiroc soldiers, Demon Dogs with their handlers, and as many magic users as he deems necessary to kill them. I want them all dead. I would personally go, but I have a greater task."

Tellio twisted his waxed mustache with his thumb and index finger and watched the merchant vessel rise with the water in the lock's chamber. The lock canal was cut to the side of the waterfall in the Tiarak River. The waterfall only dropped three feet, but was five hundred paces wide. He took a deep breath and rubbed at his bald head. The stubble was longer than he liked. It'd be easier to let his hair grow, but a completely bald man looked stronger than a man with a ring of hair circling his head.

"Can we cripple those locks and make it look like an accident, Gustov?" He asked the skinny engineer crouched beside him. The old man lowered the spy scope and rubbed at the gray whiskers on his chin.

"Mayhap we can." He put the scope back to his eye, extended the tube-like cylinder, and studied the boat and the men operating the valves. He shut the scope, put it in his belt, and pulled a rolled parchment out of his bag.

"It wearies my heart to damage such a work of ancient beauty," he said as he rolled out a drawing of the lock system on a boulder and pointed to the upper gate. "Look at this."

Tellio grunted, slid behind the man, and looked over his shoulder.

"This gate is made of oak and only four inches thick. The balance is weighted perfectly so a single man can turn the screw and open or close the gates. But that's not the impressive part. The gates close at an eighteen-degree angle with the wedge facing the current—it's beautifully simple yet brilliant engineering."

"I don't get it."

"It's all about water pressure. That wedge uses the river current to create a watertight seal and ensure the gate can't accidentally break open when the chamber is at the lower level. It's a thing of beauty."

"If you say so, Gustov. How do we destroy it and make it look like an accident?" Tellio asked. "I want that thing out of commission long enough to force the Valdivarian boats to drop anchor and wait. But I don't want them suspecting a trap until we're ready to spring it."

"Light it," Gustov said.

"What?"

"We're going to light the trap with naphtha. We aren't going to 'spring' it," the old man said with a wry smile.

Were all engineers this annoying or just Gustov? Tellio was fully aware they planned to use naphtha when the trap was ready—it was a figure of speech, and the old man knew it. But, Gustov was the top engineer in the

Anytos guild, so Tellio figured he could put up with his annoying humor.

"We've been studying this thing for three days," Tellio said. "It's time for us to get to work. I want to do it tonight."

"Then we'd better get started." Gustov rolled the parchment and returned it to his worn, leather bag. "We've only a few hours until nightfall, and then we can implement phase one of our plan." His grin showed his stained and crooked teeth.

"Phase one?"

"You want that out of commission for two weeks, right?"

Tellio nodded. It would take that long for a good line of merchant vessels to back up along the river.

"That crew down there manning the locks is small, but you can bet they know how to repair it. We'll need to do a series of things to keep it down," Gustov said as they walked toward their hidden camp and the rest of Tellio's small force. "First, we'll strip the teeth on the axle of the pinion gear in the upper gate—that will take a few days to fix, and they'll keep the water level in the chamber low while they make the repairs. While they repair the gear, we'll sabotage the hinges, so the gates will break off when they reopen the lock. Then we'll get to work on the paddle of the lower gate so the chamber won't fill properly once they repair the doors."

"And that will shut them down for two weeks?"

"Give or take a few days," Gustov said. "If not, we'll think of more games to play with them."

LYNMARIA

L ord Danu stood at the ramparts of Tiaron's city walls and stared at the dancing lights of a thousand gleaming campfires. He longed to get back to Basilea and his band of misfits, but bypassing the blockade of the Valdivarian army was proving to be more challenging than he'd thought.

Danu, Kivas, and Durham had made good time after they left Anytos. They'd arrived in Menet after a week and stayed for two days—just long enough to meet with Danu's agent in the city and pay a quick visit to the temple of Azur. But they'd been stuck here in Tiaron for more than two weeks now.

"Even if we get Valdivarian uniforms," Danu mused, "I don't think we'd be able to get through that army—we'd be questioned by every officer along the way. And if we made it to the back of the army, we'd be caught trying to leave and treated as deserters."

Durham, who stood next to Danu, chuckled a deep rumbling sound from his chest.

"Why is that funny?" Danu asked with a little more irritation in his voice than he intended.

"Sorry, my Lord," Durham answered, his wispy blond hair blew fitfully in the light breeze. "But I think if we put on Valdivarian uniforms, we wouldn't even make it out of the gates of Tiaron. They'd be a bit curious as to how three Valdivarian soldiers got into the city and why they were trying to leave."

Danu took a deep breath and let it go in frustration. Durham was right. He'd thought through this ploy a few times already, and there were just too many holes in it to safely carry it out. He wished for at least the hundredth time that Raven were there to help. Kivas tried, but subterfuge wasn't his strength.

That was another problem. Kivas spent every night in the common room of the Broken Crown, drinking and playing dice. Each night, a growing crowd showed up to join in the game, which meant people might figure out who they really were. If Danu and his men were discovered by the queen regent, it would complicate matters and delay them even further.

"Excuse me, Lord Danu Basil of Basilea, I presume?" a voice said from Danu's left side. The outer walls were a popular place for people from the city to come at night and watch the army, so Danu hadn't paid a lot of attention to the short man wearing brown hose, a loose white shirt, and a green traveling cloak—but he had his attention now. Danu's eyes widened, but he recovered from his surprise and looked around, as though wondering if the man were addressing him.

"I think you're mistaken, my good man. My friend and I—"

"I'm Yorbin, spy master to Queen Regent Jenica Wolcott," the man said with a wry smile that barely touched the corners of his mouth. His brown hair looked like it needed a wash and a comb, and his beard had maybe a week's worth of growth with a sparse amount of gray peppered on his cheeks. "We've been watching you since you arrived. In fact, Her Highness is a little upset you didn't pay her a proper visit when you passed this way a few months ago with the Child of the Blessing."

Danu opened his mouth to repeat that the man was mistaken about his identity, but changed his mind; continuing the ruse would only make him look silly at this point.

"I assume she sent you to fetch me, Yorbin?"

"Something like that, Lord Danu." His mild-mannered grin was irritating. How was Danu going to explain trying to pass through Jenica's city—twice—without paying her an official state visit? After all, Boranica and Tiaron had been trading partners for centuries. He'd even trained with the knights of Tiaron for six months when he was a younger man. She would certainly view this as a slight against her.

"I suppose I don't have a choice in the matter?"

"She could send the city guard to escort you, if you'd prefer that over me."

"That won't be necessary, spy master," Danu replied dryly. "When has she asked I attend her?"

"Now would be good."

Of course. He hadn't been courteous to her, so why should she extend courtesy to him? "Durham," he said, turning to his soldier—was he actually grinning? "Tell Kivas what happened. I should be back by morning."

Danu nodded to the spy master and followed him down the wooden stairs. On top of the ramparts, the wind blew in from the plains and smelled like campfires. Once Danu neared the street, the pungent odors of urine and rotting trash assaulted his nose. He and his unassuming escort passed crowds of refugees and headed to a black carriage waiting near a group of other carriages across the dirt-packed road that circled the perimeter wall of the city. The carriage could have belonged to any one of a hundred merchants, and the driver wore the clothing of a lowly coachman. This was not a coach fit for state business; it was perfectly inconspicuous.

The coach lurched, and Danu watched the crowds as he and the spy master rolled down the road. Refugees from the surrounding farms, displaced when the military first appeared on the horizon, milled about—most looking to pick up odd jobs, but some had already resorted to begging. The stone wall that surrounded the city was lined with makeshift shelters. Dozens of gray-clad Azur priests passed out foodstuffs from baskets, attracting large groups of people. Danu frowned as he watched a small child get pushed aside by a group of older children who were trying to secure morsels of food.

Their coach climbed the gentle slope that led to the center of the city, the dirt road changed to cobbled, and the tenements and food markets turned to clothiers and other fine stores. When they entered through the gates of the inner city the road turned to smooth stone and the aroma in the air was more pleasant. Danu smelled roasting meat as they passed one large manor and fresh bread wafting from another.

Once within the inner walls, the castle fortress of Tiaron was visible—exactly in the center of the city, surrounded by a moat filled with water pumped up from the Wanderove Divide. The drawbridge lowered, and the portcullis opened, allowing them to pass underneath the gatehouse and into the outer courtyard where a line of soldiers stood at attention with spears resting on their right shoulders.

Checkered red-and-white flags—with a knight's helm in the white squares and a castle tower in the red squares—hung from either side of the gatehouse and from both sides of the archway that led to the inner courtyard. Conspicuously missing were the yellow flags of Valdivar with its black dragon sigil.

Yorbin escorted Danu through the large brass doors of the palace and into the grand foyer.

"I assume you've met Cowen, lord steward to our lady," the spy master nodded toward a stately old man who was waiting for them. "He'll take over from here. Now, if you'll please excuse me, I have other business to attend to."

"Yes, of course." Danu was as pleased to see the old steward as he was to be rid of Yorbin. "Master Cowen, you look as hale and fit as the last time I saw you," Danu said happily, taking the man in a warm embrace. "How long has it been—ten or eleven years?"

"Ten years, three months, and five days to be precise, Marquis Danu." Cowen served as lord steward to the Wolcott royal family for the past two kings and now the queen regent. His hair was white and meticulously combed to the side, and his robe was scarlet with gold cording.

Danu groaned. "Nobody has called me the marquis in years, Cowen. I hate the formality in titles. Please just call me Danu."

The old man chuckled. "You are the marquis, like it or not. Your father is cousin to your king and that makes him grand duke. You are the duke's oldest son, and that makes you a marquis. Besides, I enjoy making you uncomfortable."

"Then you should really enjoy the next few hours, Cowen," a matronly voice said from the balcony overhead. Danu looked up and suppressed a sigh. Jenica Wolcott, formerly the regent duchess of Tiaron, now the queen regent of Tiaron, stood above them looking down from a gallery that surrounded the grand foyer. Her furrowed brow and tightly drawn lips confirmed the irritation in her voice. Her thick, dark hair fell from underneath a sturdy silver crown and over her shoulders. She wore a stately, lavender gown and large silver earrings with the same intricate scroll work as the crown on her head.

"I'm beginning to think you don't like me, Lord Danu," she said as she descended the grand staircase. "This is twice, in as many months, you've visited my city without so much as a 'hello.'"

"I sincerely apologize, Queen Regent Jenica," Danu bowed his head. "I assure you, I meant no disrespect to you and your esteemed house."

"I'm sure. Nevertheless, I don't appreciate the lack of faith you place in our alliance." She walked past him and indicated he and the lord steward should follow. "I understand your reticence the first time you passed through—after all, you were trying to avoid notice from Kahn Devin and his spies. A visit to my castle with Renn in tow would've certainly drawn attention, but really, Danu, you can't even take a little time for a visit now?"

"Umm, would it be an inappropriate time to mention you haven't aged a bit since I last saw you?" Danu said, trying to lighten the mood. "Still regal and as graceful as a swan."

Jenica stopped and gave him a withering look. "It's inappropriate *and* impertinent. I'm old enough to be your mother, Danu."

He regretted his attempt at levity. They had been on good terms while he was in Tiaron for his training with her knights several years ago, but perhaps the stress of the war—

"Now, if you add *beautiful* to your list of compliments," she continued, "it would help . . . a little." A small smile touched the corner of her mouth. "Honestly, Danu, I understand your desire to be discreet in your movements, but you could have visited if only to say hello to Taythor. He idolizes you. After you left, he asked about you every day for a year. It made us all crazy."

"He is a special boy," Danu said. "He studied and worked so hard to be like me and the other knights—and he has a quick mind."

"He's practically a man now," she said. "He'll be nineteen soon, and I'm sure the people will vote for him to ask King Nalbron's daughter, Isabella, to become his betrothed."

Danu laughed, earning him another scowl from Jenica. "I'm sorry, Your Majesty, but the thought of commoners voting for who the future king should marry is such a strange concept to me."

"It's been our custom since General Riverford reunified the Twin Cities more than three centuries ago," the lord steward said defensively. "It's a custom that has brought loyalty from the peasants and peace between the cities. Pardon my interruption, Your Majesty."

"No need for pardon, Cowen," Jenica said.

They walked past a pair of guards and through a set of arched doors that led to a large garden, lit by beautiful iron rod lamps posted along the several paths at strategic locations—near fountains, reflection pools, or next to benches where one could sit and admire the topiaries. There were others enjoying the gardens as well. Two men in fine clothing chatted quietly as they walked along a path—stopping frequently to admire the manicured shrubs and flowers that Danu could smell from the moment they'd stepped outside. A group of young ladies and children sat on a grassy area, surrounding a woman with long brown hair and full lips, who had an inviting smile and an easy laugh

"Come sit with me." The queen regent walked to a bench under a lamp near the central fountain that bore a knight on a rearing steed holding a drawn sword. Streams of water shot up from the edge of the fountain and over the statue. "We have matters to discuss, and then there is someone I'd like you to meet."

Danu was curious but also worried. It sounded like she had favors to ask of him—things that would take extra time, which was exactly why he'd hoped to avoid a visit to the castle and Jenica. The queen regent indicated for Danu to sit next to her, then sent Cowen to find the Lord Marshal Tarcott.

"You haven't been able to devise a way to return to Boranica, Danu," Jenica said matter-of-factly. "You are trapped in the Broken Crown." She twisted her face with obvious disdain at the mention of the seedy inn.

"Yes," Danu said. "Perhaps you've noticed: there's an army of fifty thousand camped on your doorstep."

"Don't be insolent, Danu," she snapped, "I've had little rest and thought of nothing else during these past weeks." She took a deep breath and squared her shoulders while she straightened her gown. A servant in livery approached holding a tray, and she indicated the man could advance. He gave her a cup of hot tea and asked if Danu required anything. Danu smiled and shook his head.

"On my way through Anytos, my men and I stayed with Mytton," Danu said. "He tried to get me involved in this . . . conflict. I know it sounds like a hollow excuse, but that is the reason I tried to keep a low profile here, my lady. I simply cannot appear to take sides in this war until I know the will of my king."

"I wouldn't mind a few additional swords," she said, "but don't flatter yourself—even *your* sword wouldn't make much difference against the host outside my gates." She took a sip of tea then set it on the bench. "We are going to do each other a favor, Danu." she turned to him and peered in his eyes. "I'm going to clear a path for you to leave. In return, you and your men are going to take Lynmaria with you and see her safely to Leedsdale." She indicated to the woman surrounded by the small group of ladies and children on the grassy area opposite the fountain.

"Your Majesty." Danu held up his hands. "I mean no offense, but I can't guarantee my own safety out on those plains. Having a woman along would make safe travel more difficult."

"Lynmaria isn't just a woman, Danu. She is a Mage of the Azur-Lore and Artio's replacement."

"What is she doing here? I assumed Artio's replacement would be to Leedsdale by now."

"She arrived precisely one day after the army and has been my guest since that time," Jenica answered. "As you can see, my entire household absolutely adores her." The queen picked the teacup off the bench and blew on the hot drink. "I'm tempted to offer her the position of Court Meskhoni and send Leland in her place, but that would be selfish of me."

"Leland?" Danu asked.

"My Court Meskhoni," Jenica said. "He's capable enough, but gets frustrated with me because I counsel with Mastedelia—the high priestess of Lunaryn—more frequently than with him."

Danu watched Lynmaria interact with those around her. He couldn't hear what she said over the pitter-patter of the fountain, but she was clearly the center of attention.

"It would be helpful having a Mage accompany us," he said, "but how do you intend to get us past that army?"

Jenica frowned. "We've sent emissaries to Valdivar, we've petitioned for peace . . . we've tried to let diplomacy and cooler heads prevail." She got a far-off look in her eyes, and her jaw grew rigid. "But King Reollyn won't even give us an audience. Instead, he cuts off my city with his army and threatens my people."

Danu pursed his lips and nodded.

"You've seen the refugees in the streets," the queen regent said. "I'm running out of food, and the priests can only do so much. If the farmers don't return to their fields and plant crops soon, my city won't survive next winter."

"What about imports from the East? I saw many caravans from Kahaal on my way here—"

"It's not enough," Jenica interrupted him. "By the time the Kahaal traders reach my city, they've already passed through Anytos and Menet and most their goods are already sold. The blockade is hurting everybody, but it's crippling me."

"I can't stay trapped behind our walls while King Reollyn's soldiers plunder the farmsteads and ranches in the plains surrounding my city." Jenica narrowed her eyes. "I may not have as large of an army as Reollyn, but I have the best knights in all of Lemuria, and he is about to experience the havoc they can create among his ranks."

"What is your plan?"

"Two hours past midnight, I'm sending one thousand mounted knights out of the front gates to cut a large swath through that army as their men sleep. I'm sending another five hundred through the north gate and five hundred through the south gate. While the larger force cuts through the middle of the army, the smaller detachments will charge west toward the main gate, killing and driving out the Valdivarian troops camped near the walls along the way. The smaller detachments will meet with the first thousand knights as they are returning to the main gates to clear the way for them to retreat back into the city."

"Does General Wheelhouse of Anytos know about this plan?"

"Of course." Jenica let out an exasperated sigh. She probably considered the answer to his question to be obvious. "The generals from Menet and Anytos counsel with Lord Marshal Tarcott daily to coordinate our efforts." She closed her eyes and took a deep breath. "They've already secured the river and the southern gate. They will leave a force of four thousand to hold those positions. Their heavy and light cavalries, along with eight thousand infantry troops will follow my knights—half along the south wall and the other half along the north wall to hold those positions. Once my knights clear those areas, I don't want the Valdivarian army to take them back."

Danu frowned as he considered the amount of damage these knights would inflict upon a sleeping army. "So the bloodshed begins."

"And what would you have me do, Danu? Hide behind these walls and ignore this affront?"

Danu shook his head and took her hand. "I would do the same as you, Jenica. I was just hoping—"

"You were hoping for the same as all of us," she said. "A peaceful resolution. The time for that has passed. When my knights charge out of the north gates, you will wait ten minutes and then follow with Lynmaria and your men. You'll be given fresh horses and supplies. Head north until you are far enough into the plains to avoid the Valdivarian army scouts and then go west until you've circumvented the blockade."

"What about the Tiaro Devi?" Danu asked. "Mytton said they have splintered into small bands of raiders looking for easy targets."

"*King* Mytton," she said with emphasis on the new title. "There is that risk, but I trust with your skills you can avoid them. Ah, here comes Lady Lynmaria," Jenica said with a broad smile as the Mage approached.

"I hope I'm not interrupting you," the brown-haired woman said as she joined them. "And please, just Lynmaria is fine." She had deep brown eyes that lit up with her easy smile, and beautiful olive skin that was sun browned just enough to give her a golden radiance.

"Not at all," the queen regent said. "This is Lord Danu. He and I were just discussing the arrangements for your journey."

"I'm pleased to make your acquaintance, Lynmaria," Danu said, rising and lightly kissing her on the hand. "I understand you will be replacing Artio as Leedsdale's Meskhoni."

"The pleasure is mine," the woman said, "and yes, I am his replacement."

"Well, you're certainly more pleasant on the eyes than Artio, but you have some big shoes to fill. Artio was a wonderful man and good friend."

Lynmaria sat on the bench and now Danu was between the two women. The Mage leaned back and looked up to the stars. "Artio was a great man, indeed," she said. "I first met him when I was a young girl entering the school on Elder Island. Artio had just completed his Mage tests." She laughed lightly, and her eyes glimmered when she looked back to Danu. "I actually had a bit of a crush on him. I wanted so badly to be like him and the other Mages and Wizards. I wasted a lot of time and energy trying to be something I wasn't. It took me many years to realize I just needed to be myself."

Danu nodded thoughtfully, wondering how old Lynmaria was. She looked to be no more than thirty, but Artio had left the school more than fifty years ago.

"But what of you, Danu?" Lynmaria asked. "I've heard stories about acts of gallantry and valor."

"I'm flattered, but you know how stories are," he said. "They get more fantastic with each telling."

"Is it true you call your regiment a band of strangers?"

Danu laughed. "That story is true, but I'm afraid it isn't gallant or filled with valor."

"They say many of your men lost everything in life, some even have questionable backgrounds, and yet you train them and accept them—you give them a second chance."

"They have their quirks, I'll admit, but they are good men deep down," Danu said, not sure he liked where this was heading.

"I'm told the people in the provinces you govern for your father are quite fond of you, and you treat even the lowest members of society with fairness and respect."

Danu blushed. "I don't see any reason to be unkind—"

"Did you learn these traits from your father?"

Again, Danu laughed out loud, "*By Azur*, no. My father is a strict and hard disciplinarian—everybody knows that." Danu narrowed his eyes and tapped at his chin. "I'd have to say I picked up those traits from my mother. She spent a lot of time with me as a child—more than most noble ladies spend with their children."

Lynmaria smiled and her brown eyes were bright with apparent interest. "These are powerful traits, Danu, and they will serve you well if you are true to them throughout your life." She took a deep breath, clasped her hands together and rested them on her lap. "So tell me, Lord Danu, when the time comes for you to replace your father, will you try to fill his shoes?"

"I . . . uh, well . . ."

Danu wanted to defend his father, but he also knew he would do things much differently than his father. Lynmaria locked eyes with him. Her smile was comforting and warm—not the smile of someone who'd just got the best of a discussion.

"Well, I'd better go to my quarters and prepare if we are to leave tonight," she said to Jenica, who stood and gave her a warm embrace.

"I won't be at the gate," the queen regent said, "and I don't know when I'll see you again." Danu knew Jenica well enough to realize she was working hard to hold back tears and maintain a modicum of dignity. "Visit us often, Lynmaria. You are always welcome in my home."

"Thank you, Majesty." The Mage smiled with genuine affection. "I will visit when I can."

Danu and Jenica watched her cross the courtyard. Before the Mage reached the door, she was besought upon by more young women of the house staff, and they were joined by others wanting to talk with her.

"How did she do that?" Danu asked.

"Do what, dear?"

"Turn a pleasant conversation into a powerful lesson, without making me feel like I'd been lectured."

"Well, she's a Mage. Magic, I suppose." Jenica winked at him, then said, "I've already sent a carriage to fetch your men and belongings. Here comes the lord marshal. He will fill you in on the rest of the details. Good luck."

TO TRADE A STORY

Danu sat on the back of a roan whose multicolored coat was nearly black at its head and points. Kivas hunched in the saddle of a large brown gelding. The courtyard in front of the northern gate was filled with row after row of mounted knights wearing heavy armor covered with red tabards brandishing a single Tiaron-style knight helm embroidered over the breast plate. Each knight was mounted on an armored warhorse—lethal weapons in their own right.

"I pity the Valdivarian army," Kivas whispered loud enough for Danu to hear. The lieutenant's eyes were glossed over from being forced to leave the Broken Crown in the middle of his nightly ritual of emptying the innkeeper's ale keg, and he rubbed at his matted black hair. "Five hundred men in full armor, mounted on war horses. They haven't broken formation or even flinched."

Danu looked the knights over—again. He'd trained with these men years ago, but he, too, was in awe of their discipline as they awaited the order to charge. A contingent of knights this large should make more noise, yet it was eerily quiet. A gentle breeze tugged at the red-and-white flags hoisted on either side of the gates and atop the crenellated walls. Danu could hear them snapping in the wind. The smell of horse sweat was the only indication of the knights' presence.

Judging by the position of the small and large ladle constellations in the sky, it was approaching two hours past midnight, which explained why the surrounding streets and alleys were nearly empty of common citizenry. A few stray cats and curious street beggars hid in shadows and watched the knights—sensing something big was about to happen.

Lynmaria wore a dark traveling cloak with the hood pulled over her head and sat on a sturdy white mare behind Danu and Kivas. In her left hand, she held a staff. A crystal at the top glowed with faint green light. The folds of her cowl hid her eyes, but the shadows cast by her staff lighted her nose, cheeks, and full lips. If she was nervous, it didn't show in her smooth features.

Durham sat stoically in his saddle next to her. He also wore a heavy riding cloak, but his hood was pulled back, and his square chin was set with determination as he waited for the captain in charge of this detachment of five hundred knights to lead the charge. They each gave Danu a slight nod of the head when he sent them a look that asked the question: "are you ready"?

A regular rotation of city guard walked the ramparts of the wall, and the knights watched them. Tonight, the city guard had an additional task: watch the high tower of the castle and give a sign to the knights in the courtyard below, letting them know when Lord Marshal Tarcott lit the signal fire. The castle was built on a hill in the exact center of the city, so the fire would be seen by this knight regiment as well as the regiments waiting at the south and east gates—ensuring a simultaneous assault.

Danu watched the people manning the gates. They had quietly opened the inner portcullis a few moments ago and now awaited the signal to raise the outer portcullis. Danu's heart pounded with anticipation—both excited and sad for what was about to happen.

His horse snorted and fidgeted, and Danu patted the animal's neck. "Steady, boy. Calm down." The words were as much for him as the horse.

Two of the city guards stopped pacing, turned toward the knights and gave them a smart salute. The knights spurred their mounts and charged through the gatehouse as the outer portcullis was raised. The torrent of knights pouring from the gates and onto the plains was like a flash flood of man, beast, and metal. There were no trumpets. None of the knights shouted or yelled as they attacked—they wanted to maintain the element of surprise for as long as possible. However, within moments, the screams of dying men and shouts of alarm from the soldiers of the Valdivarian army filled the night.

The standoff was over. The war had begun.

The thundering of the knights' charge faded, and in minutes Danu and his small group were alone. The city guard had stopped pacing and watched over the wall at the fighting below. Danu knew it would be a route. Hundreds of men would be killed; the rest would flee with whatever they could carry to escape the knights and reach the safety of the main force, which was camped in front of the east gate.

Danu looked at each face in his group and gave them a reassuring smile. "Time for us to leave, friends." He spurred his mount into a fast gallop. No one would notice them riding out to the plains—there was nothing to flee from. He could've led his group away from the city at a comfortable walk because the knights had very efficiently cleared the area of enemies. But, Danu wanted to get as far away from the screams and shouts of the dying as he could. So he rode fast, straight north into the grassy plains until he could no longer smell, see, or hear any sign of civilization before he slowed his horse to a gentle walk.

"What are your plans, Lord Danu?" Lynmaria asked as the others brought their mounts beside his. "Travel by day or by night?"

"We ride until the moon sets," he pointed with his chin at the moon as he bobbed in the saddle. "It'll be too dark to travel safely after that, so we'll rest until dawn. If we get an early start in the morning, we should be able to be get to the far side of the army and join back with the main road before evening tomorrow."

Kivas, riding on the other side of the Mage, pulled out his leather canteen and drank deeply before coughing and spitting the liquid onto the ground. Danu smiled and pretended not to notice as Kivas wiped his mouth.

"All right, very funny," Kivas boomed. "Who put water in this?"

Durham laughed—a deep rumbling sound from his chest. "That's what's supposed to be in there, Lieutenant," the big man said. "After all, it *is* called a *water*skin."

"*You* did this?" Kivas sounded incredulous. Durham never played practical jokes.

"I did not," he replied, "but I do think it's funny."

"Quiet, you two," Danu said. "Voices carry a long way out here. We don't want any visitors." Kivas gave him a withering look. Danu raised a single eyebrow and smiled. The last thing he needed was for Kivas to be inebriated if they came across a roaming band of Devi warriors.

The group whispered when communication was necessary as they traveled westward during the night. The moon sank below the horizon, and Danu guessed dawn was only a couple of hours away. The predawn air was cold, and the grasses were already moist with dew. At least it was spring, so the grass wasn't waist high yet. Still, he didn't relish the prospect of sleeping on cold, wet plants. He looked toward Lynmaria to see how she was faring. If she was tired or cold, her body language and facial expression didn't give her away.

"I don't suppose you could do something about the dew?" Danu asked. "I'd like to sleep dry if possible."

"I could," she answered. "However, the light from my staff would be visible for some distance. It might draw unwanted attention."

Danu decided it would be better to be uncomfortable for a few hours than deal with Devi raiders, so he rolled out a canvas tarpaulin, and they laid their bedrolls on that. It would be wet by the time they woke, but he could take time to dry it out once they were past the army and out of danger from the Tiaro Devi.

In the morning, they ate a breakfast of salted pork, bread, and cheese and washed it down—much to Kivas's chagrin—with water. By the time the sun was fully over the eastern horizon, casting long shadows in front of them as they rode, they had already put another mile behind them.

The sun climbed to the center of the sky and Danu felt sweat bead down his chest, so he put his riding cloak away. A warm breeze blew from the south, causing the green spring prairie grasses to lean gently northward.

In a couple of months, the plains would be a sea of gold as the grasses grew longer and changed color. As he watched the swaying of the plants, he noticed that the grass, in some places, wasn't moving in unison with the breeze.

"We've got company," Danu said. "Straight ahead about fifty paces and a little to the right." Kivas and Durham shifted in their saddles and placed a hand on their swords. Lynmaria pulled back her cowl and looked to where Danu indicated, but she appeared more curious than concerned.

"Let's veer southward and see if we can avoid them." Danu pulled left on his reins and said, "Keep pace with me." He continued scanning the ground, looking for unusual movement. Whoever was in the spot he first noticed reacted to their change of direction—the grass moved in the wrong direction of the wind as it closed toward Danu and his little company. He looked behind, left, and directly ahead, and realized they were being surrounded.

"Now!" Danu shouted. "Run!" He spurred his horse and shifted course again, back to the right—just enough to hopefully squeeze between the gap he could see in the shifting grasses.

They didn't get far before a group of ten Devi tribesman, wearing clumps of grass like hats over their long dark hair, stood in front of them. Each warrior held a bow and arrow, drawn and ready to fire.

Danu veered hard left, heading back the direction they'd come, hoping to find an open lane out of this trap. If they could break through to the open plains, there was no way the band of Tiaro Devi warriors could catch them on foot.

He heard a whistling sound and flattened himself to the back of his horse as an arrow whizzed by his head. A line of Devi warriors stood up in the grass in front of him. Five held drawn bows and released another volley directly at their small group. A green barrier materialized in the air just before the arrows struck, and they fell harmlessly to the ground. Another group of warriors stood, and behind them, three warriors who had—until now—been secreted behind the knoll crested a hill on horseback.

"Stop!" Lynmaria shouted.

Danu pulled back on his reins. There was no chance they would escape if they kept running in circles, only to be met by Devi warriors with bows at every turn. He drew his sword and hurried to the Mage's side. Kivas and Durham followed suit and soon the three soldiers circled her, each facing outward to fend off an assault from any direction.

"We're not going to fight our way out of this," Lynmaria said, just loud enough that her would-be protectors could hear. "Let me talk with them."

"Can't you do something with your magic?" Kivas asked. "If you protect us from their arrows, we can cut a path straight through and be out of here before they know what hit 'em."

"I could," she said, "but I'm not about to help you massacre these men when there are other options."

"Other options?" Kivas cocked his head and raised his eyebrows. "We're surrounded and they're shooting at us!"

"There are almost always other options." She looked earnestly into Kivas's eyes, and Danu saw the lieutenant's features relax before he nodded.

Lynmaria maintained a soft, green, pulsing shield around the small group as she walked her horse in front to address the leader of the Devi fighters.

Danu had studied the language of the barbarians when he was younger, but he wasn't fluent in Devinese, so he struggled to understand the terse replies to Lynmaria's questions. The leader was on horseback and had thick, long dark hair braided with colorful cords that framed his face and hung below his shoulders. Like the other warriors, he wore leather that had been dyed green to match the spring vegetation, except—unlike those on foot—he didn't go to the extent of tying clumps of grass to his head and back to further camouflage himself.

"I hope she knows what she's doing," Danu whispered out of the corner of his mouth to Durham and Kivas.

The warriors on foot eased closer as Lynmaria spoke with their leader—holding arrows nocked in their bowstrings and tightening the circle in which Danu and his group were trapped. The grass on their head looked like messy green wigs and dirt from the grass clumps stuck to their faces. Danu thought it would have made for a comical picture in any other setting.

"They want our horses and weapons," Lynmaria said over her shoulder.

"We'd never get out of the plains alive," Danu said.

"I know. I'll barter with something else."

"We don't have anything else of value," Kivas said. "Now, if we had some whiskey to give them . . ." He left the thought hanging but gave Danu a pointed look, which Danu answered by rolling his eyes.

"We have stories and knowledge." Lynmaria smiled. She spoke to the leader again, leaving Danu, Kivas, and Durham to stare at her back as though she'd lost her mind. Danu looked at the other men and shrugged his shoulders.

Although he couldn't understand all that was being said, the body language and facial expressions were clear—guarded hostility shifted to curiosity. Bows were lowered, crouching tribesman stood at ease, and the leader's face grew thoughtful.

"They're going to take us to their camp," Lynmaria said. "Their small tribe doesn't have a Meskhoni, but S'kata—that's the leader's name—says they have an old woman who treats their wounds and illnesses. I'm going to teach her some things about healing, and we'll share stories with them tonight around their fire."

"And they'll let us go if you do this?"

Lynmaria nodded in response to Danu's question.

"Are you sure we can trust them?" Kivas's voice was quiet but filled with concern. "King Mytton warned us—"

"If our lady Mage trusts them, that's good enough for me," Durham cut Kivas off with his rumbling voice. Durham didn't say much, but Danu had learned over the years to trust the man's judgment.

Danu didn't like the idea of losing another day or two. He'd been away from Basilea for six months already and still had to stop in Achtland. At this rate, he wouldn't be home until midsummer's Azur-Aven. However, he didn't see any choice.

"Like Durham said"—Danu smiled at Lynmaria—"if our lady Mage trusts them, so do I."

She rolled her eyes at the honorific title, but smiled in return. She faced the leader of the Tiaronea Devi and said a few words. The man shouted a command, turned his horse to the north, and led the way.

Danu and his small band followed behind the leader and the other two Devi riders. The warriors on foot brought up the rear—no doubt making sure their "guests" didn't change their minds and decide to flee.

They rode through unchanging landscape for nearly three hours—rolling hills of new spring grasses, sage brush, wild flowering plants, and rocks. If this place had a reliable source of water, it would be amazing farmland. Danu wondered how deep a man would need to dig before hitting the water table. Maybe he could teach these people to farm—that would solve the never-ending skirmishes between the plains cities and the Devi nation. Rather than raid the outlying farms and ranches, they could grow their own food and build permanent dwellings.

They crested a knoll that was larger than most, and saw a small copse of trees in a little valley below. Several conical tents—made of thin logs with leather stretched tightly around them—encircled the thicket of trees. As they drew near the camp, Danu noticed a larger tent, set on a platform of solid wood, in the middle of the trees. He was surprised to see a structure this complex out here among savages. They apparently returned to this place every year as it had a sort of transient permanence to it.

Curious children ran out of tents to greet the warriors. Women stopped doing chores—grinding meal, scraping animal skins, chopping edible roots—to watch their men ride into the settlement. The women talked and pointed at the white-skinned strangers, but unlike the children, they stayed well back.

S'kata raised a fist and the company came to a halt. He dismounted and handed his reins to a boy with long dark hair who Danu guessed was no more than ten. An old woman stepped out of the large tent on the platform. She shuffled toward the group with the help of a gnarled wooden walking stick until she stood in front of S'kata. Her bent frame and silvered head barely came to the man's chest, but he bowed and dropped to a knee until she touched his chin, giving him leave to rise.

S'kata spoke to her and pointed toward Danu's group and she turned her gaze thoughtfully in their direction. She pointed her walking stick at Lynmaria and said something in an angry voice. S'kata shook his head and replied confidently. Danu understood the words Aven and Azur, and he recognized the name Sambuta, who he knew was the leader of the entire Tiaronea Devi nation who had been controlled by a Kiroc Warlock. He could guess the old Devi woman was worried about getting involved with magic users after what happened last fall to Sambuta. That was the event that caused the Tiaronea Devi nation to splinter into multiple smaller tribes.

The old lady listened to S'kata defend his decision to bring the small group to their camp, then she walked past him and approached Lynmaria.

"What do you want with us, Witch woman?" She had an accent, but Danu was surprised by how well she spoke the common tongue. Durham tensed visibly at the words *Witch woman*. The tone in the old woman's voice sounded like she was describing the vilest creature imaginable. If a man had spoken that way to Lynmaria, Danu had no doubt Durham would've already drawn his sword and demanded an apology.

"My name is Lynmaria." If the Mage was offended, no one would have been able to tell by her mild mannered reply. "My friends and I are merely travelers wishing to cross your land. In exchange for this boon, I have offered to give you a gift that will be of great worth to your family."

"What *gift*?" the old woman's eyes narrowed and her lips tightened. Lynmaria climbed down from her horse, bent over, and plucked a tall weed that had feathered leaves and clumps of tiny white flowers. "This is my gift," she held out the plant and smiled. "It grows wild in your land and contains powerful healing properties."

"Chuck tail weed?" the woman said, clearly unimpressed. "Your gift to us is chuck tail weed? Do you take me for a fool? My grandmothers', grandmothers', grandmother had this knowledge, as did many grandmothers before her."

"You use this as a remedy for fevers, correct?"

"Of course."

"Sanguinary," Lynmaria said, "or chuck tail weed as you call it, can do much more. It can cure infections, stop bleeding, help digestion and relieve pain. The preparations are different. I will show you how to make and use Sanguinary for each of these ailments."

The woman leaned on her walking stick and stood on her tip toes as she looked into the Mage's eyes, then at the chuck tail weed and back to the Mage. The old lady settled back to her bent position and harrumphed. "I believe you are telling the truth." Her eyes narrowed, "you're not bewitching me with your magic like Sambuta, are you?"

Lynmaria smiled and placed the plant in the woman's free hand. "Trust your instincts," she said. "What does your heart tell you?"

The old woman stared again into Lynmaria's eyes and sighed loudly. "My name is Magdka. If what you say is true, I will grant you a boon of safe passage for you and your man servants."

Danu frowned at being referred to as a man servant. He looked at Kivas and Durham. Both men twisted their lips and shrugged their shoulders.

"Is there anything we can do to assist you, my lady?" Danu asked Lynmaria when she locked arms with Magdka and headed toward the large round tent on the platform.

"Perhaps you could teach the men of the tribe something useful," she said.

"I could teach them how to play cards," Kivas murmured once the Mage was out of ear shot.

"Not that," Lynmaria called over her shoulder. Apparently, her hearing was better than Kivas realized. Durham chuckled and smiled as he watched her disappear into the tent. Danu couldn't recall seeing the former sailor smile so openly before. It wasn't that Durham was unpleasant; he was just solid and consistent.

The men couldn't communicate well with the warriors of the Devi tribe, but after caring for the horses, they discovered they did have something in common—knives. Soon, they were engaged in a game of knife throwing. After that got tiresome, Durham showed them tricks for whittling different animal calls. He became popular with the children when he made wooden whistles and showed them how to play them.

The women of the tribe built a roaring fire, cooked roots on the coals, and set a side of bison roasting on a spit above it. When the sun sank below the horizon, Lynmaria and Magdka emerged from the tent arm in arm, laughing, and joined the rest of the tribe for the meal.

After they ate, the men produced drums made from skins stretched across small, hollowed logs and played rhythmic beats and sang while the girls of the tribe danced. Danu looked at Kivas. He was smiling and laughing at a broken comment an older warrior said. Kivas was laughing, and he hadn't had a drop of ale!

"Story!" S'kata said in broken common. He stood and held up his hands to get everybody's attention. "Friends promised story." He began to chant. "Story, story, story . . ." Soon, the entire tribe clapped and shouted for a story.

"The Mage tells me you fought in the battle six moons ago when the Warlock who bewitched Sambuta was defeated," Magdka said. "We would hear that tale."

Danu's stomach tightened, and his heart dropped. That had been nearly six months ago, yet the pain of Artio's death still weighed heavy on him. He didn't relish the thought of telling that tale.

"I don't speak your language, Magdka," he said politely, bowing slightly in deference to the medicine women. "Perhaps the lady, Lynmaria, could give them a story from her adventures."

"That's not a problem, Danu," the Mage said, "If you'll let me gently touch your thoughts, I can show them the story through your memory." Danu bit his lip and tried to think of a kind way to avert her suggestion.

"I would be happy to volunteer my memories of the battle." Durham gave Danu a knowing smile. Danu nodded to him, silently thanking the man for coming to his rescue.

"As you wish, good man Durham." Lynmaria noticed the subtle, non-verbal exchange between the two men—Danu could see the understanding sympathy in the quick look she shared with him. She stood and led Durham into the center of the gathering. She placed the fingertips of her left hand on his right temple and closed her eyes.

"You will feel a gentle touch in your mind, Durham," she said. "Just relax and think of what happened that day."

He nodded. Lynmaria held her staff in the air and moved it in a circular motion. Green mist formed and swirled in the air and images took shape. The members of the Devi tribe gasped and let out choruses of *oohs* and *ahs* as the scene unfolded.

Danu found it strange to witness the battle from somebody else's vantage point. Durham had been on the opposite side of the field from Danu during the battle and it was peculiar to watch himself ride Thorn out of the circle of wagons to meet the oncoming Devi charge. The scene changed then to focus on the battle Durham and Aleah led on their side of the wagon circle. Lynmaria told the story in Devinese as she showed the events. Danu could hear the awe in her voice as she realized the overwhelming odds they had faced and the courage in which Danu's men carried out their duty to protect Renn and the other children.

The view changed again when a sudden blaze of red and green light lit up the battlefield accompanied by a booming crack. The attack from the Warlock met the shield Artio had put in place around Thorn and Danu. He winced as he watched himself fly off Thorn's back from the impact of the energies converging as witnessed by Durham from across the battlefield. He saw himself get buried by attacking warriors, and then Aleah charged in swinging a sword in each hand, trying to cut a path to him and Raven— who also fought to save Danu. His eyes welled up with tears, watching his friends recklessly put themselves in danger to rescue him.

The green mists shifted, and the scene changed, with Durham's thoughts, to the wagons now burning from a volley of fire arrows. Chaos ensued after that—horses running to escape the flames caused a breach in the line of defense, and Devi warriors rushed toward Artio. Durham must have been running to meet them because the memory showed him engaging with one warrior and then another.

A Devi warrior raised a sword to cut Artio down, but Thorn rushed into view, reared up, and came down on the warrior. Thorn continued to kick and buck, but then he was hit by several arrows and went down. Danu had to turn and look away as two arrows struck Artio.

Danu wiped a tear that streamed down his cheek. He composed himself and looked back to the memory just as Renn stopped the fighting with the thunderous sound of his shouts. He saw the Kiroc Warlock shoot red fire at Renn who, somehow, caught the fire in his left hand and then sent it back, much stronger and faster, through his right.

White power shot from Renn's fingertips, consuming the warriors who had killed Artio, and then Danu watched as Renn pounded his fists into the ground, causing the earth to shake. When Renn shouted to the Kiroc, "Die, you pawn of filth!" and white power blazed from his eyes and fingers to consume the massive Warlock, the entire group, including Lynmaria, gasped in awe.

The green mists faded away and were replaced by silence. Tears streamed down Lynmaria's face. She leaned against Durham for support. Danu remembered Artio had been a close friend of hers, too. Watching his death must have been hard on the Mage.

Magdka stood and joined Lynmaria and Durham in the center of the gathering. She spoke in Devinese to her tribe, and they all nodded agreement with her. S'kata stood and signaled for Danu and Kivas to join them in the middle of the circle. He placed his hand on Danu's shoulder as he addressed the tribe. He then placed his hand on Kivas and the other on Durham and spoke again. The tribe members jumped off the ground and cheered. Before Danu realized what was happening, he was swept from his feet and raised in the air, along with Kivas and Durham, while the people sang and clapped.

"What's going on?" he shouted down to Lynmaria.

"They've made you official warriors of their tribe," she shouted back with a smile. "Rather than leave a trail of dead enemies through the plains, we will leave a trail of devoted friends."

CLOAK AND KNIFE

Gendul scraped his long knife against the wood in his hand. A small pile of shavings lay on the ground at his feet, but the wood hadn't taken on any particular form—it just got smaller as he absentmindedly whittled.

He wore a dark cloak with the cowl pulled over his head and sat on a barrel at the base of the wall of the school-castle. The stables were directly across the courtyard from where he sat and he could hear the occasional whinny of the horses and smell manure. The boy he waited for had returned from his early morning ride several minutes ago, so he should be coming out soon.

Gendul sat next to a small, iron studded door that opened into a storage room. It was a good place to hide a body. It would be days before anyone found it.

Nobody else was in the yard due to the early hour. There was enough light to see by, but the sun hadn't risen above the horizon yet. The lore masters and most students would still be sleeping. And if by odd chance anybody looked out of a window and saw him, they would just see a person in a dark cloak. Nobody would suspect Gendul was up at this hour. His reputation of being a drunk would be useful in completing his task this morning.

At last, the boy walked out of the stable and made his way across the courtyard.

"Who goes there?" Gendul said, loud enough for the boy to hear, but soft enough his voice wouldn't carry to the rooms above.

"It's Demaris." The boy paused—he clearly hadn't noticed Gendul sitting in the shadows of the castle wall.

"It's awful early to be out riding, don't you think?"

"I ride Thorn every morning." Demaris walked closer. "Usually, I'm finished before anyone else is up. Who are you?" He kept a little distance between them.

"Sorry, my boy." Gendul looked up so Demaris could see his face but kept his hood on so nobody looking down from above would recognize him. "It's just me. I didn't mean to startle you." It was early spring but still cold enough for a cloak; Demaris wouldn't suspect anything.

"Master Gendul?" Demaris cocked his head. "What are you doing out so early?"

He walked up to Gendul. That was good. All he'd have to do now is drive the knife into the boy's heart and drag him through the door. Just a little closer.

"I couldn't sleep. Whittling helps calm the nerves."

It wasn't a lie. Ever since his meeting with Shamael last week, Gendul hadn't been able to sleep. Now, he just needed to finish the task Shamael gave him, and his daughter would be safe. Not only his daughter, but all the children of Concordia would be safe from the harvesting of recruits for the Aven-Lore. Certainly, killing one boy to save thousands was justified.

"What are you carving?" Demaris stepped closer and peered at the wood.

He is close enough now, Gendul thought. *Just stand and thrust the knife in a single motion.* The boy would never know what happened. Gendul looked around the courtyard and rubbed his nose—they were still alone. *What am I waiting for?* he thought. *It will be simple. Just stand and drive the knife into his heart. He's right there!*

"Are you okay?" Demaris asked. "Your hands are shaking."

"What? Oh . . . so they are—"

"What's that going to be?" The boy pointed at the shapeless piece of wood.

"Umm . . . It's . . . Well, I'm not really sure. I just whittle to calm the nerves."

"I don't think it's working," Demaris replied. "Your hands are trembling like you've got the shakes or something."

Why was he shaking? Just stand, thrust the knife into Demaris's heart, and drag him through the door. It would never be easier than this.

"Who's over there?" an old tired voice called out. Gendul nearly dropped the knife but quickly composed himself. He looked to the sound of the voice and saw a plump old man with beady blue eyes, shoulder-length white hair, and a goatee walking toward them. He'd just rounded the corner of the castle, presumably on his way to the stables.

"Master Flynton," Demaris said enthusiastically. "You're just the man I wanted to see."

"Oh, it's you. I might have known," Flynton said, recognizing Demaris. "You're always about in the morning." His eyes widened, however, when he recognized the lore master. "Master Gendul, what a pleasant surprise. I'd never expect to see you . . . Uh, what I mean is, it's a nice surprise to see you out and about on such a beautiful morn as this."

Gendul knew the man caught himself before saying something like, *I can't believe you're sober and out of bed at this early hour.*

"I haven't been able to sleep in lately, Flynton," Gendul answered. "Magaia knows I try, but sleep eludes me."

"Who's Magaia?" Flynton asked as he scratched at the whiskers on his chin.

"She's the Concordian goddess of the earth," Gendul said, grateful for the diversion. "Her tri-swirl rune is one of the symbols on the school flag. Phaedra hates it when I invoke the old gods," he said with a chuckle.

"You shouldn't go about upsetting Master Phaedra." Flynton was defensive when it came to her. It was no secret he fancied her. "She is a great woman."

Gendul smiled and nodded in deference to the man's praise of her.

"Master Flynton," Demaris asked. "Could you please leave Thorn's stall open so he can come and go as he pleases? You don't need to leave hay or water for him—he'll just graze in the meadows and drink from the stream."

Flynton's jaw went slack, and he gave the boy a blank stare at this request. Gendul nearly laughed, despite his dour mood.

"Leave open . . . come and go . . . Are you crazy, Demaris?" The stable master stammered. But then he must have remembered he was talking to the boy who'd single-handedly killed the Grand Warlock last winter, and his face paled. "I don't mean you no offense, young master," he apologized, "but if you don't put the horse in at night, he may never return. It's easy to get lost in the Oraima Mountains and . . . and there're bears out there, to boot."

"Don't worry. Thorn won't get lost, and he's much too big for a bear. They prefer smaller prey. But if you could leave a few apples in his stall each day, he would appreciate it. He'll come by from time to time and eat those."

Flynton put his hands on his hips. "How about a little wine and cheese? I could set it on a table with a linen cloth in the center of his stall?"

"Fine." Demaris obviously didn't appreciate the man's sarcasm. "I'll bring apples myself. Just don't lock the door to his stall."

"No, no." Flynton held up his hands. "If you say he needs apples every day, then apples he gets." The horse master turned and stomped off toward the stables, muttering irritably. Demaris and Gendul stared after him.

"Was my request really *that* difficult?" Demaris asked as Flynton disappeared into the stable.

"I wouldn't worry about Flynton," Gendul said, amused by the entire exchange. "He's been stable master here for four decades and he's set in his ways."

Do it now! he thought. He scanned the courtyard—they were alone again. Of course, Flynton had seen them together, but nobody would suspect a lore master, and it would be days before Demaris's body was found. They wouldn't connect his death to Gendul.

"Are you certain everything is all right, Master Gendul?" Demaris asked again. "You're shaking like a rabbit staring down a mountain lion."

He looked at his hands and tightened his grip on the knife to steady his hands. He would do it for Katerina. He'd do it for all the children of Concordia. It would be over in a heartbeat . . .

"Demaris," a high musical voice said. "There you are!"

Gendul jerked and almost fell off the barrel.

"Harlow told me you'd probably be at the stables with your horse, so I came here to find you."

"Estilla!" Demaris's face turned bright red. "You're looking for me? I mean, good morning. Umm, what can I do for you?"

For the love of Magaia, Gendul thought as the girl joined them. He had hesitated too long. *Why were so many people up this early in the morning anyway?*

Estilla wore exercise attire and held two long, thin swords in her hands. She had a bright smile on her face, and to her credit, she barely flinched when she realized the man in the cloak was Gendul.

"Good morning, Master Gendul." She curtsied to him. "You don't mind my borrowing Demaris, do you?"

Gendul gave her a half-hearted smile, which she must have interpreted as him granting her leave.

She turned to the boy and held out one of the swords. "Derisela isn't feeling well this morning. I thought you might like to join me for some fencing practice before breakfast."

"Umm, y-you want me to . . ." Demaris stammered, and his face turned a brighter shade of red than it already was. "I mean, sure . . . yeah, I'd love to."

"Great!" She took him by the arm, and dragged him away, but she looked back and smiled. "Thanks, Master Gendul! Have a nice day."

Gendul watched them go and then looked down at the knife in his hand. What a coward he was. He had the perfect opportunity and he couldn't bring himself to do it. He wasn't a killer, despite what Shamael said. But, somehow, Demaris had to die. It was the right thing to do. It would save thousands from the horrors of the Cragg Caves and the Aven-Lore.

Tristan sat at the vanity and intertwined the thin flower wreath she'd made yesterday with a circular braid in her hair.

"I wonder who Renn is talking to down there," Genea said thoughtfully.

"Really, Genea?" Tristan turned the mirror enough to see Genea's reflection looking out the window and down at the courtyard. "You're going to drive yourself crazy watching Renn every morning like this."

"I don't watch him *every* morning," she protested. "I just happened to see him talking to someone in a dark cloak, and it's unusual, that's all." She twisted a strand of hair in her finger and pursed her lips. "It isn't horse master Flynton, because he just walked into the stables, and—" She breathed in sharply and stopped talking, then stormed away from the window and gathered her books.

"What's wrong?"

"It's nothing! I'm going down to breakfast. Are you going to join me?" It was a bit early for that; the dining hall wouldn't have food for another thirty minutes.

Tristan went to the window to see what caused Genea to become so upset. She watched Estilla take Renn by the arm and lead him away from the person in the dark cloak. "Oh, I see. It looks like they're just going to practice swords, Genea. I'm sure it's nothing more than that."

"I don't care what they're doing," she said, clearly trying to control the rising pitch of her voice. "I've got more important things to do than . . . than worry about what he's doing with that girl."

Tristan tried not to laugh, which would upset Genea further. Instead, she said, "It's still a bit early for breakfast. Why don't you let me help you brush out your hair?"

Shamael Daro tapped his upper lip with his forefinger and reread the entries in Kahn's diary regarding the blue scythe. The only possible person this could represent was the Grand Duke Drake Basil. But these notes claimed the blue scythe spent two years at the caves studying the Aven-Lore. How could a man of high station like Drake be trained at the caves and nobody know about it?

The constant pelting of icy rain beating against the large canvas tent was distracting, but at least General Deegan was civilized enough to keep it comfortable and well stocked. Shamael raised a pewter goblet and sipped the Boranica red he'd poured from the general's private collection and then stared at the dark liquid. The grapes for this wine could have been grown on Duke Basil's lands. What would motivate a man with his position and power to join Kahn? It didn't take long to deduce the answer to that question. The only thing men with power lusted for was more power—ultimate power.

A sudden gust of cold air rushed into the tent, followed by a soaked General Deegan. Frozen rain clung to the man's brown beard, and his cloak and mail were drenched.

"The horses, mules and supplies are being sequestered, Grand Warlock." He stood at attention as he made his report. "I also have a cook, two scouts, and my best captain joining you. A team of engineers is leaving in the morning, so they can build a boat once they reach the shore. All will be ready for you and your . . . recruits to depart for the West Asgar Island within the week. Although, I'd suggest you stay in camp for a few weeks more. There's no use getting to the beach just to sit around while the engineers finish building the boat."

"Thanks, Deegan. At ease."

The general hurried to the wood-burning stove that radiated enough heat to keep the tent warm, despite the cold rains. The burning wood combined with the wet canvas tent created an aroma that reminded Shamael of a winter hunting shack.

That was the problem with having the Aven-Lore's center of power this far north. Winter held on to the upper Cragg Mountains like a starving urchin clung to its last piece of bread. In Valdivar, it would already be spring. Flowers would be blooming, and thieves would have easy work on the streets, cutting purses without the bother of moving aside the winter rain cloaks of their victims.

Shamael rubbed the scar on his cheek and thought about the cold trek ahead for his twenty-four vitiate recruits. Hopefully, they'd all survive. Maybe he should have brought a few extra, just in case some died along the way. The horses and pack mules would make a big difference, but it would still be a hard, cold three or four weeks—especially once they began the ascent up the high peaks on the West Asgar Island.

"I'm glad you have your best captain going on the journey north," Shamael said. "They'll need a good man to lead them—remind your captain they are students, *not* soldiers."

"Understood, milord, but I thought you would be with them as well."

"I'm going south first to meet with some . . . allies. I'll be leaving in the morning, so have your men build a large fire for me after breakfast."

"As you command, Master Shamael."

"Deegan, what do you know of King Boran?"

"Not much." The general turned from the wood-burning stove and looked at Shamael. If he wondered why the Grand Warlock asked such a random question, he did a good job of hiding it. "He's the king of Boranica. He's old. His heir is his young nephew."

"But what about Boran the man?" Shamael pressed. "You were a captain in the Devlyn army, and then you fought with mercenaries all over Kahaal before Kahn brought you here to train this secret army. What did you hear about Boran, the *man*, in your travels?"

Deegan poured himself a goblet of wine from the bottle Shamael had already opened and sat across from him.

"Mercenaries don't like to talk about their past. It's too painful," the general said. "Most of them are running from something and don't want anybody knowing too much about where they've been. But when they get to drinking, they like to complain about the men who did them wrong— they often complain about lords and dukes and kings." He took a drink of his wine and shook his head. "When I was a captain in the Devlyn army, our intelligence on King Boran was that he is a kind old man . . . and trustworthy. Unusual, if you ask me. Most stories I heard about kings make me think they're a bunch of greedy ingrates."

Shamael nodded thoughtfully. Kahn had probably selected Drake Basil as an ally because King Boran of Boranica was incorruptible.

"And what were Kahn's plans for you and your men, General?" Shamael set down his wine and picked up a map of northwest Lemuria. "Where and when did he intend to deploy your ten thousand troops?"

"Kahn was a . . . guarded man, milord," Deegan answered cautiously. "He never shared his plans with me." The general swirled his wine and watched it roll in the glass. "He only told me to have my men ready at all times."

"That doesn't surprise me, General," Shamael said. "My predecessor didn't place a lot of trust in others. I was his second-in-command, and even I knew little of his overall designs. You'll find I am different in that regard." Shamael took a sheet of parchment, dipped a feather quill in ink and wrote a letter.

"Have your runner take this to General Narkash." Shamael dipped his ring in hot wax and placed the Grand Warlock seal at the bottom of the note. "It informs him you are on my council of advisors and are to have access to the treasury and stores to equip you and your men as you deem necessary." After seeing the discipline in Deegan's army of ten thousand, and the fact that the general had already been loyal for a decade, Shamael was convinced this man was somebody he wanted in his inner circle.

General Deegan's eyebrows rose as he read, then he set the letter on the table and looked at Shamael.

"I am honored you judge me worthy to sit on your council, Grand Warlock," he said slowly, "and unrestrained access to the treasury will certainly help me maintain a top notch army. But I grow weary of hiding in these mountains." He leaned forward and looked earnestly at Shamael. "As you said, I've been doing this now for ten years, and I ask myself: for what? I'll be honest with you, Shamael, I'm not a man of religious conviction, and I don't care about the Aven-Lore or the Azur-Lore. To me, they're just different sides of the same silver rukaht. I only took this post because Kahn offered me a lot of gold, but what good is gold? I have nothing to spend it on as long as I am stuck here in the upper Cragg Mountains."

"What is it you want, then?" Shamael asked. Every man had a price. You just needed to understand his motivations.

"I want to feel *alive*." Deegan hit his fist into the palm of his hand and raised his eyebrows. "I miss the thrill of battle, the glory of victory. I've built this army, and I want to *use* it."

"That, my friend, is something we both agree on." Shamael leaned forward and turned the map so the general could see it better. "Chaos is about to grip the nations of Lemuria, General. Your army is going increase the chaos . . . and enjoy the spoils of war."

THE TOURNAMENTS

A leah shaded her eyes from the bright morning sun with her hand as Aerik climbed to the hastily built log stage to address the crowd. Midsummer's Azur-Aven was still five weeks away, but Prince Aerik of Kurulan decreed that the festivities associated with the biggest celebration of the year would be held early on account of his need to travel to Kah-Tarku.

Fortunately, there had been no storms since the night Aleah and Raven had arrived, so the spring sun had melted most of the snow in the valley and, more importantly, melted the snow in the large field located southwest of the castle where the events would be held.

For the past two days, merchants of all kinds set up canvas tents in rows in and around the field, so they could display their wares for the attendees. Aleah was amazed by how quickly the festival grounds changed from a muddy field to a temporary village of tents, stages, and rowdy taverns, complete with the smells of ale and roasting pigs.

Minstrels and actors were scheduled to perform at different stages throughout the next three days; mystics told fortunes in small, colorful tents; jesters juggled balls while walking on stilts; and, of course, men sat at the makeshift taverns having drinking contests while playing games of chance. Earlier that morning, Raven had pulled her out of the way as two men tumbled out of one such establishment, grappling with one another in the mud, cursing and throwing fists as they rolled on the ground.

"My friends and brothers," shouted Prince Aerik as he raised a stein that was likely filled with ale . . . or perhaps something stronger. "Raise your mugs with me as we drink our thanks to Thail for yet another prosperous year!"

Aerik took a deep pull from his mug, as did everybody in the crowd who had a drink in their hand, and then he wiped the excess froth from his blond beard. There were at least ten thousand people at the massive celebration, but everyone could hear the prince because Blimron, Aerik's court Meskhoni, stood next to the prince using the Azur-Lore to amplify his voice. The squat Mage grimaced at Aerik's supplication to the pagan sky god.

Blimron didn't look like a typical magic user to Aleah. He wore high boots with brown breeches tucked inside, a thick wool shirt, and a warm vest. His white hair was unkempt, like he hadn't washed it in weeks. Maybe the Mage's grimace wasn't due to the king's reference to Thail, but because Blimron wanted to be done with his duties so he could go fishing. Whenever anybody in the prince's staff wanted to find the Meskhoni, they would send out runners to each of his favorite fishing spots—without fail, he would be at one of them.

"The Meskhoni Blimron here"—Aerik gestured with his thumb toward the Mage—"will bless the babes on the night of Azur-Aven, so we won't be doing any of that during this celebration."

"I'm sure Aerik is pleased he won't have to sit through all those blessings," Raven whispered. "That's why he's got such a big grin on his face."

"Either that, or the fact that he started drinking at the crow of the rooster," Aleah whispered back.

"This year," Aerik shouted even though he didn't need to—the Meskhoni's magic would've carried his voice either way—"we have two special friends joining us." He looked down at Aleah and Raven and waved for them to join him on the stage. That was the last thing Aleah expected. Had she known he would call them up, she'd have made sure they were far enough back in the crowd so he couldn't see them. Raven gave her half a smile, shrugged his shoulders, and pulled her up to the wooden platform.

"Some of you may remember my good friend Raven." Aerik put his arm round Raven's shoulder, pulling him away from Aleah. "Ten years ago, he joined our celebration and left with the first place prize in axe throwing!" The prince shook his head and looked over the crowd. "How about that? An outsider came into Kurulan and bested us all at axe throwing!"

The crowd erupted in a friendly chorus of boos.

"So men of Kurulan, are we going to let him beat us again?"

"No!" Their shouts echoed across the field.

"And this time around he's brought his pretty little wife, Aleah." Aerik released Raven and pulled Aleah to his side. "Raven claims she's going to beat us in the archery event! What do you say to that?"

"No!" the crowd's shout was even louder this time. He released Aleah, and she looked at Raven who had a broad smile on his face. He was actually *enjoying* this. Really? She would rather just watch and fade into the shadows than be held up as the local nemesis.

"Then do your best to make Thail proud," the prince said, "and let's show our friends what Kurulan is made of!" Aerik raised his mug and the crowd cheered.

At least the people love their prince, Aleah thought.

"Axe throwing today, archery tomorrow, and ladies wrestling the final day," the prince continued. "First place winner in each event gets a barrel of fine ale, and the person with the highest overall standing from the combined events wins this!" He signaled to a spindly man with a narrow face to join them.

Aleah caught her breath when she saw what the man carried. He bowed before the prince and held out a perfectly carved, longbow. Aerik looked annoyed with the man's genuflecting. "Thanks, Elzmeas," he said under his breath, although his voice still carried through the Mage's spell to the crowd. "You can stand now."

"This bow," Aerik shouted to the crowd again, "was expertly handmade by our own master bowyer, Elzmeas Coldwater, using a single stave of yew from my secret grove high in the Kuru-Kulla Mountains. I believe it is the most balanced bow I've ever held." He gave the man a hard pat on the back, which nearly caused him to fall off the stage. But, the bowyer caught himself, smiled and waved to the crowd—obviously pleased to be publicly recognized as a master of his craft by the prince.

Aleah's mouth fell open and her eyes widened. Everything faded from her vision except the beautiful weapon. She stepped forward and ran a finger along the smooth wood. The longbow's maker truly was a master craftsman. The grain was true and straight, and the pale, creamy sap wood perfectly offset the honey-colored heartwood. Obviously, Elzmeas had spent weeks, if not months, reading and getting to know this single piece of sacred yew before he ever put a knife to it.

"I take it you like the bow," Raven said, pulling her back to him. Aleah flushed, realizing the prince and the crowd were all staring at her.

"Obviously, the bow has the approval of our guest," Aerik said, holding up the bow for the crowd to see. The prince handed the bow back to Elzmeas, then took a parchment from the Meskhoni and read aloud the list of rules for the events.

"I'm going to win that bow, Raven," Aleah whispered. Her eyes never left the beautiful weapon.

"Or I could win it for you," he said playfully.

That comment broke the spell. Aleah looked at Raven and placed a hand on her hip. "Just because we're married, don't think I'm going to start acting like other dry lander women, Raven. I am *not* letting a man win for me—even if you are my husband." She wanted to punch him in the stomach when he chuckled, but she decided against it, since they were standing in front of thousands of people and next to the prince of Kurulan.

By the time the axe-throwing contest began, over three hundred people—men, older boys, and a handful of women—had signed up for the event. It took the greater part of the day to narrow the field, until only ten entrants remained. Aleah was the only woman still in the event—the other nine were Raven, the king, and seven of what she assumed were the best warriors of

Kurulan. Her arms were tired, as she had already competed in four other elimination matches prior to this final round.

The axes were provided from the prince's armory to ensure everybody threw similar sized and weighted weapons. But these axes were designed to be wielded by burly Kurulan soldiers who averaged more than six feet in height and over two hundred pounds. At five foot nine and a bit under one hundred fifty pounds, she felt she was at a distinct disadvantage. Still, years of practice throwing smaller blades helped her adjust to the extra weight and size. Accuracy was more important than strength in this event, as long as you had enough of the latter to throw the weapon fifty paces and make it stick in the targets. The targetswere large cut sections of tree logs, about two feet in diameter, set on stands five feet above the ground with red painted targets on them.

By the time the sun was only a finger's width from setting, the contest was narrowed to the final three challengers—Prince Aerik, Raven, and Aleah. They each drew a small twig to determine the throwing order. Raven would throw first, followed by Aerik, and Aleah last. That was a bit of luck. Being last to throw meant she would see the others' throws first and know what she would need to do to win. Each of them would get two throws, and the person with the two closest to the center eye would win.

Raven stepped up, took the long axe with both hands, raised it above his head, and threw it end over end. The crowd alternated between cheers and playful boos as the axe struck the target with a thump, nearly at the exact center of the eye. Two young soldiers ran to the target, now tilted from the impact of the axe, removed the weapon, straightened the stand, and marked the spot where Raven's axe stuck with a black dot—Raven's color.

The prince made his first throw next and received wild cheers and shouts of congratulations when his throw landed next to Raven's mark, but slightly farther from the center. The soldiers marked his spot with a red dot.

Aleah stepped up and a group of young girls cheered and shouted words of encouragement. She'd already become something of a hero to the teenage girls of the town, who all dreamed of being great warriors like her one day. Somehow, word had spread that she had been trained by the mythic female warriors at the jungle city of Tanis in Domeria. She would certainly have a word with Raven later tonight about how that particular story got started.

She gripped the heavy axe in two hands and raised it over her head. She stepped back so she could get a running start to increase the momentum of her throw. She smiled to herself as she released the weapon and watched it sail end over end toward the target—she hit the eye, exactly in the center. The girls and women in the crowd went wild. She gave Raven and the prince a curtsy and a smug grin as she stepped aside for their final throws. Raven grinned back, but didn't appear worried. The king, on the other hand, licked his lips and wiped a bead of sweat from his brow.

Raven's last throw whistled through the cold evening air, thudded solidly against the target, and again the crowd cheered and booed as they saw the axe sticking firmly into exact center of the eye—splitting the blue spot that marked where Aleah's first throw landed. Raven turned to her and bowed deeply with a flourishing wave of his hand—like some dandy at a royal ball.

Aerik was muttering under his breath as he walked up to the mark. He wiped his brow again, then spit in his hands and rubbed them together while he studied the target. The crowd grew silent as their prince took the axe, raised it above his head, and let the weapon fly. There was a stunned gasp from the crowd before they remembered that proper etiquette required them to cheer for their prince. It wasn't a particularly bad throw, but it landed a full hand away from the center mark, and not enough to beat Raven's throws. And worse, based on the throws Aleah had been making all day, it likely wouldn't be enough to beat her final throw, either.

Aerik's face was red as he walked, tight lipped, past Aleah and stood next to Raven to watch her final throw. This time, as she stepped up to the waiting axe, the cheers from the girls in the gathering weren't so boisterous. The crowd seemed to realize the embarrassment and emasculation their prince was about to endure as he watched a woman beat him at his best event. Aleah thought about how Aerik had won the event nine years in a row—his last defeat coming at the hands of Raven.

She rubbed her hands together. The temperature had dropped, and she could see her breath. The crowd was silent as she picked up the axe, raised it above her head, and stepped backward. She breathed deeply and ran forward, making her decision as she let the weapon fly.

The axe sunk deep with a loud *thunk*. The target swayed. When the wood stopped shaking the crowd let out a roaring cheer. The prince squinted at the target, then jumped in the air and gave a shout of joy, pumping his fist. Aleah's final throw was three finger widths farther from the center than the prince's final throw. Aerik didn't beat Raven, but his combined throws were just good enough to beat Aleah. She took third place in the first event. A group of burly, blond men slapped the prince on the back and handed him a stein of ale.

"That was . . . generous of you," Raven whispered, stepping next to her.

"I don't know what you're talking about," she said with a self-satisfied smile. Before he could argue, the prince turned, grabbed Raven by the shoulder, and pulled him into the revelry. A big mug of ale was forced into his hands, and Raven was lifted up on the shoulders of a group of men who sang as they carried the champion off to the nearest makeshift tavern. Aleah felt a stab of jealousy—after all, she had taken third place, and nobody rushed to congratulate her. But tomorrow was archery. She wouldn't lose that event.

"Excuse me, Lady Aleah?"

She turned and found a gaggle of teenage girls gathered behind her. A tall, pretty girl with blond hair and brown eyes—unusual, considering blue was most common in Kurulan—stood in front of the others. This was the group who had been loudly cheering for her all day.

"I'm Frija," the girl in front said, "and these are my friends."

"It's nice to meet you, and please just call me Aleah," she said.

"Umm, well, Aleah, we were wondering—my friends and I, that is—did you let the prince beat you? I mean, we totally understand if you did because

Thail only knows how embarrassed he'd be if a woman beat him at axes."
That last part rushed out of her in an avalanche of words.

Aleah smiled at her young fans. "I wish I were that good," she said. "But
the truth is the prince beat me in a fair match."

"Oh, I see." Frija was clearly disappointed as were her friends.

"Will you girls be cheering for me tomorrow?" Aleah asked, wanting to
change the subject to something less awkward. Frija's face turned bright
red, and the other girls giggled and whispered to one another.

"Well, the thing is, I'm actually in the archery tournament, too, so . . ."

"That's wonderful," Aleah interjected to save the girl from more embarrassment. "Prince Aerik and these Kurulan men need some decent
competition to keep them humble."

All of the girls laughed. "I couldn't agree more," Frija said with a bit
more confidence than Aleah expected from a young girl.

"How old are you, Frija?"

"I just turned sixteen this month past."

"Are you good with a bow?" Frija's face turned red again, but she raised
her chin and straightened her shoulders.

Before she could answer, her friend chimed in, "She's the best archer
in all of Kurulan!"

"She would've won last year," a strawberry blond with light freckles said
angrily, "but somebody swiped her arrows and Frija had to borrow some
at the last minute!"

"Then I look forward to our competition, Frija. Good luck tomorrow."

ARCHERY

"It appears that Aerik drank too much of your winnings last night," Aleah said, referring to the barrel of ale Raven won in the axe-throwing event the day before. The high prince stood on the wooden platform, addressing the crowd to begin the archery tournament. His hair was tangled in his beard, and his cloak hung crooked off one shoulder.

"Probably," Raven agreed, "but more than ale is ailing him. Once he finished celebrating not being bested by a woman, it occurred to him that he didn't actually win." Raven smiled and shrugged his shoulders. "I think the fact that I gave him my winnings was even more irksome, once he had time to think things through."

"Maybe so, but he obviously drank a healthy portion of your winnings nonetheless," Aleah said. "I can see the dark circles under his eyes from here."

Blimron sat on the platform near Aerik, ensuring the high prince's voice carried over the masses. The Meskhoni looked to be as bored as the high prince was disheartened. The Mage wore tall black boots with his pants tucked inside, a lightweight shirt, and a wide-brimmed straw hat. There wasn't a cloud in the sky, and the morning sun warmed the air.

Once again, Aerik shouted unnecessarily. "The archery event will be held on the west field, and all targets will face away from the festivities, so we shouldn't have trouble with errant shots this year."

Some in the crowd chuckled. Aleah wondered what had happened last year to cause Aerik to make this clarification.

"We have some five hundred entrants this year, so the event will take most of the day," the prince continued. "Of course, the music and theater stages will be going all day, and the merchant tents will be manned at all hours, so feel free to enjoy whatever . . ." He turned to Blimron and lowered his voice—although the entire crowd heard him because the Mage was still amplifying his words. "Have I missed anything, Blimron? My head feels like Thail cracked it with the blunt side of his axe."

"*For the love of Azur*, Aerik," the Mage said. He dropped the voice amplification spell, but Aleah was standing close to the platform, so she still heard him. "You've already droned on too long. If I give you something to cure your hangover, will you just start the event so I can go fishing?"

"That's just great," the prince said. "I have to watch the tournament all day while you fish!" Aerik rubbed at his head and signaled for the Mage to amplify his voice. "May the gods bless our festival," Aerik shouted, forcing a smile on his face, "and let the events begin!"

The crowd cheered, and the high prince winced and rubbed at his head. He held his hand out to Blimron who rifled through a leather pouch hanging from his hip, handed the prince a small stoppered brown bottle, and bolted from the platform.

Aleah and Raven followed the crowd to the archery range in the west field. The high prince and his family sat on tall chairs with soft cushions under a canopied grandstand. Captain Gregor Thailson—whom Aleah and Raven had met the night they washed up on shore—sat in the seat left of the king, opposite Princess Katryline. Men in uniform, whom Aleah assumed were generals of the king's army, also sat on the grandstand. The prince didn't appear to be in a better mood, but he was working on it. He held a stein in one hand as he raised and dropped a ceremonial axe in the other to officially start the competition.

The tournament was far enough away from the merchant tents so that the aroma of roasting meat gave way to the smell of fresh spring grasses, carried through the air by a light breeze that rolled down the Andrikan foothills and across the fields.

Twenty-five archers lined up to shoot at targets placed one hundred paces away. Each contestant was allowed two shots—the first was a practice shot, and the second was judged against their competitors. The ten best would advance to round two. Aleah wasn't up to shoot until the sixth group, so she and Raven stood back and watched.

"See the girl with the long blond braids." Aleah pointed to an archer near the far end of the line during the second group. "Her name is Frija. Her friends tell me she's the best archer in Kurulan."

"Oh, and when did you become so familiar with the locals?"

"When you left me alone to celebrate with the prince," she said, arching one brow.

"That's not fair." Raven held up his hands. "You can't expect me to say no to a high prince in his own kingdom."

Aleah harrumphed and turned her attention back to the event. Frija's practice shot was only a hand from the target's eye, and her competition shot was within three fingers of the center. She easily advanced to the next round. But unlike the other archers, she jogged forward to retrieve her arrows before leaving the field to wait for her next match.

Aleah had selected a bow from the king's armory—a well-balanced weapon, also made from yew, but not nearly as fine as the longbow she intended to win. She'd had a few hours to practice with it, and so both of her shots hit dead center of the target, drawing oohs and ahs from the onlookers. She turned and bowed, as all the contestants did after their round, toward the grandstand where the royal family sat presiding over the event. Prince Aerik appeared to be in better spirits now. He raised his mug and gave her a congratulatory smile.

Raven didn't shoot until the fifteenth group of twenty-five contestants. He also used a borrowed weapon but easily made it to the next round. His first shot only missed by half a hand, and his second was within two fingers of the eye.

Aleah watched Frija again during the second round. The total field of contestants had been narrowed from five hundred to two hundred. Frija's shots were both closer but still off-center, and the frustration on her face was evident. Still, her second shot was easily good enough to advance to the next round of eighty. Once again, both of Aleah's shots were exactly on target.

When they took an hour break for lunch, Aleah saw Frija and her friends sharing their meal on the grass. Aleah picked up a leg of lamb, told Raven she'd be back shortly, and approached the girls.

As she advanced, several of the girls—including Frija—stood, wiped their greasy hands on their aprons, and greeted Aleah with giggles and praise for her amazing marksmanship.

"Frija, could I have a word with you?" she asked. The girl looked nervously at her friends, who encouraged her to go. "Bring your leg of lamb," Aleah said. "We'll eat while we walk."

The girl grabbed her food and followed Aleah, who walked in the direction of the Kuru-Kulla Mountains. Frija was as tall as Aleah and walked with confidence even though Aleah could sense the younger woman was nervous.

"I noticed that you retrieve your arrows after each round rather than let the attendants gather them," Aleah said.

"They're *my* arrows," Frija snapped.

Aleah raised an eyebrow and looked at her askance as they walked.

"I'm sorry," the girl said more softly, cheeks turning red. "I make my own arrows. The reason I didn't win first place last year is because someone stole my quiver of arrows in the last round. I'm more cautious now."

Aleah nodded and took a bite of the greasy leg of meat. She wiped her mouth on her sleeve—it was brown wool, so the grease didn't leave an obvious mark.

"You're a natural archer," Aleah said. "I've trained with a lot of people and I can honestly say you have the makings of a great archer."

"You really think so?" Frija's voice rose in pitch, and she turned to face Aleah, her eyes glistening with excitement.

"I'm certain of it."

"I heard that you trained with the fabled women warriors of Domeria and the archers of Achtan! Is that really true?"

Great, Aleah thought. She would have to punch Raven in the gut when she got him alone for letting that much of her past out. At least he didn't tell anyone who she *really* was. He'd probably been bragging about her to the prince who, in turn, got drunk and bragged about her to an entire tavern.

"Yes, it's true," she confirmed but didn't elaborate. "That's why I recognize talent when I see it."

"Could you give me some pointers?" Frija asked. "After the tournament, of course," she quickly added. "I wouldn't expect you to help me in the middle of a competition."

"I'll give you some pointers right now," Aleah said. "After all, a victory is only truly satisfying if your enemy is at their best when you defeat them."

"Oh."

By Frija's frown and downcast eyes, Aleah could tell she'd hurt the girl's feelings, so she said, "That's a Domerian concept, Frija; I'm not saying you're my enemy. I'll give you a pointer right now that will help you. Your technique is great. You just need to learn to trust yourself."

"What do you mean?"

"You hesitate after you draw the string to your ear, like you're second-guessing your aim," she said. "You have great instincts. Trust them. Make your decision and go with it."

As they walked back to the waiting group of girls, who were obviously anxious to ask Frija about their conversation, Frija thanked Aleah and gave her a quick hug.

Raven had a curious look on his face when Aleah rejoined him. His black hair was neatly combed but fell partially over his right eye, and he picked at his teeth with a small stick.

"What was that about?" he asked.

Aleah sat next to him and took up his mug of ale. "Just giving her a couple pointers."

"What if she beats you?" Raven smiled and flipped his hair out of his eye.

"I'm not worried about me," she teased. "You, on the other hand . . ."

"Oh, I see." Raven narrowed his dark eyes. "You're hoping to put some distance between us in the final standings, so you'll have the best overall score and win the bow."

Aleah smiled, raised the mug to salute him, and took another drink.

"Well"—Raven took the mug back—"the girl is good, I'll give you that, but it's going to take more than a few *pointers* for her to beat me."

The contest finished as the last light of day faded to twilight. Aleah could smell the burning pitch of the torches that lit the stage and the crowd as she stood next to the high prince and his wife to accept their praise for her victory.

"As high prince of Kurulan, I'm honored, and I must admit, a little embarrassed to congratulate Raven's wife as victor of today's event." Aleah had to force herself to keep smiling. Did Aerik *really* just refer to her as "Raven's wife"?

The high prince was shouting as he spoke to the crowd, but this time it *was* necessary, because Blimron hadn't returned from fishing. Or, more likely, he finished fishing a long time ago and was hiding in one of the makeshift taverns with a tall stein of mead or ale.

"Raven told me his woman would win this event," the high prince continued. "I guess he'd seen her shoot a time or two in the past."

Raven's woman? Now Aleah wanted to slug the prince in the mouth—and Raven, too, for that matter. And that grin on Raven's face made it impossible for her not to scowl at both of them.

"But how is it," the prince slurred a little as he continued to address the spectators, "that my best archers where all defeated, not by just one woman . . . but *two*?!" Now it was Aleah's turn to grin. Frija stood on the other side of the prince, her smile reaching ear to ear, and her cheeks flushed with either pride or embarrassment—perhaps a little of both. Raven stood on the other side of Frija in the spot for the third-place champion. Why was he still grinning at her like that? When they got back to their room, she was going to hit him and then kiss him—maybe not in that order.

"At least we have the consolation that young Frija here is a citizen of Kurulan, and I, like her father, am proud of that fact. She represented her high prince and nation with honor." Everyone cheered and shouted for Frija, especially the group of girls standing together near the front of the platform.

"This would all be well and good," Aerik said, "except the third-place honors go to, yet again, my friend Raven." The prince reached behind Frija and slapped Raven on the back. The crowd erupted in a chorus of mixed boos and cheers. Raven smiled indulgently and bowed with a flourish. This only caused the boos to grow louder.

"Aleah, you won the barrel of ale for taking first place," the prince said. "Shall we send it to your rooms?"

"Actually," Aleah said, "following the example of *my man*, I'd like to give the barrel to someone else."

The high prince smiled broadly and patted his stomach. "Well, my friends and I will be sure to put it to good use." Men on the platform and in the crowd raised their steins and cheered.

"Actually, Your Highness," Aleah interrupted, and the high prince winced—apparently at her use of the honorific. "I think your cellar is filled with enough spirits." Now the king's face showed outright disappointment, but the crowd laughed as Aleah gave him a playful kiss on the cheek. This earned her a scowl from Raven, which was even better. It also made the prince blush and his wife, Katryline, roll her eyes.

"I will give the ale to the second-place winner," Aleah said. "But since Frija is too young for ale, I thought perhaps her father would like it delivered to his home." Aleah smiled at the tall, heavyset man who stood at the center of the first row of onlookers. He beamed with pride, and the flush on his cheeks reached all the way to his balding scalp.

"That's my girl!" he shouted and raised his empty mug. "That's my Frija!"

His wife and a little boy and girl stood next to Frija's father, smiling and cheering.

Aleah raised her hand to silence the crowd. "And I'd like to ask a small boon."

The high prince raised an eyebrow but motioned for her to continue.

"I ask that Frija be given an opportunity to train with the royal archers." The high prince stared at her, and a hush fell over the crowd. Aleah kept her eyes fixed on Aerik. He looked around the grandstand until he found Gregor Thailson—captain of his guard—and waved him over. The two men discussed something under their breath and then Aerik boomed with laughter.

"Aleah," he said with a broad smile and put an arm around her shoulder, pulling her to his side. "I'll do better than that!" He put his other arm around Frija, spilling ale on her shoulder from the mug in his hand as he pulled her to his other side. "After what we witnessed today, Gregor and I have decided to offer Frija a position in my court as master archer. She will be *training* archers."

The crowd went wild. Her parents and friends ran up to the stands and carried Frija away on their shoulders. Aleah shook her head as the high prince and his family followed the crowd away from the field, singing and carousing as they made their way back to the fairgrounds, likely to find a purveyor of spirits to continue the celebration.

It wasn't long before she and Raven stood alone on the covered grandstand. He still had that half grin on his face. She punched him in the stomach and smiled as the air exploded from his lungs. He doubled over melodramatically.

"That's for the prince calling me your *woman*," she said, then pulled him into an embrace and gave him a long, hard kiss. "And that's for being so handsome."

He pulled back and smiled so broadly she thought he was about to break out in laughter.

"What is so funny?"

"You and Frija may have beaten me," Raven answered, "but we are tied in the overall standings. I have a first- and third-place finish and so do you." Raven smiled that half smile of his and said, "I guess we'll have to share that bow."

Aleah narrowed her eyes and considered punching him again.

"However," Raven said, "if you behave yourself and treat me well, I might decide to let you have it for yourself." Raven moved to the side as Aleah tried to punch him again, grabbed her arm, and used her forward momentum to pull her into him and wrapped her in a tight hug. "Hitting me is definitely *not* behaving," he said with a chuckle. "You're going to have to do much better if you want that bow all to yourself."

"We'll see about that, *Camden*." She emphasized his real name because she only used it when she was irritated with him. He only laughed harder and led her back to their room at the castle.

TO WIN A BOW

The noon sun burned away the morning dew, making it warm enough for Raven to remove his black vest. An attendant, who stood at the back of the royal grandstand, hurried forward to take it and offer him a glass of wine. He smiled and shook his head—it was too early for wine. The prince, on the other hand, had no objections to starting this early in the day, especially during celebrations, and so he held out his empty stein. "Ale for me. I'll save the wine for later."

The crowd was by far the largest of the three-day festival. A square area, directly in front of the grandstand where the high prince, his family, and honored guests sat, had been cleared of grass, rocks, and plants. Wagons carrying barrels of water were used to turn the cleared ground into a square, muddy, wrestling pit. They drove four corner posts into the ground and ran thick ropes from post to post to create a genuine fighting ring.

Raven shook his head as the last wagon pulled away, having emptied its water on the saturated ground. He remembered the last time he'd attended these events ten years ago. He was shocked to see women wrestling each other, but the added element of mud was even more disturbing. It *was* funny to watch them slip and slide and struggle to stand as they battled, but it also seemed a bit . . . barbaric. And to think, the princess herself was something of a celebrity with the citizenry of Kurulan because she was the perennial champion. He chuckled at the thought of one of the southern noble women, like Melista of Kah-Tarku, competing in such a public display.

The way the wrestling area was roped off reminded him of the fighting pits in Nortia, minus the mud. Except in Nortia, women weren't even allowed to attend the fights—unless, of course, they were serving wine or selling themselves to the highest bidder for the night. But if King Thrakus of Nortia ever saw this event, Raven was sure the man would add it to his regular activities.

The crowd chanted for the first match to begin. Men, women, and children surrounded the other three sides of the wrestling arena and additional stands with seats were set up behind them so more people could watch.

"Blimron," Prince Aerik said. "Let's get this started so you can go fishing."

"What? And miss the best event of the year?" the short old Mage said. "Not on your life. This is the one thing better than a day of fishing."

The prince walked to the front of the wooden platform to address the crowd. Raven looked around, wondering where Aleah was. She had been sitting next to him earlier and excused herself to use the privy, but that was half an hour ago.

". . . just under fifty contestants this year," Raven heard the high prince say. "The ladies drew random numbers for the first bout, and the winner of each match will move on to the next round and so on, until we have a champion." Aerik still shouted, even though Blimron was making his voice carry. "Gregor will read off the names of the contestants before each match." The captain of the guard got up and walked to the front to stand by the prince. He held a long piece of parchment.

"Our first match today"—Gregor also shouted. Raven smiled at Blimron, who rolled his eyes, shook his head, and smiled in return—"will be Gianna Tannerson against Aleah, wife of Raven."

The crowd went wild, and Raven jumped out of his seat. Maybe he misheard . . .

Aerik turned, a wide grin splitting his face. "Hah!" he boomed. "That little wife of yours has a lot of spirit, Raven. Why didn't you tell me she was joining in the mud-wrestling event?"

"Why, indeed?" Raven frowned.

He wasn't sure if he was dreading the match or looking forward to it. It would've been nice if Aleah had at least warned him. Then again, she did say she wouldn't let a man win the bow for her. He should have known she'd do whatever it took to get that weapon on her own.

His eyebrows rose when Aleah stepped out of the crowd. She wore a sleeveless red shirt covered by a tight leather vest, leather pants, and her hair was pulled back off her face. Her thin, athletic frame, with her hair pulled back like that made her look like a pretty, eighteen-year-old maiden. Men in the crowd hooped and hollered and whistled. Surrounded by Frija and her friends, Aleah ducked under the rope and walked into the muddy ring.

Raven's brows rose higher when Gianna, her opponent, waddled into the ring. She was easily six feet tall and probably weighed three times what Aleah did. Her long blond hair was done up in braids on either side and then brought together in a ponytail. She also wore tight clothing—although the affect was starkly different. If that woman got on top of Aleah, it would be over—Raven wasn't even sure *he* could lift the big Kurulan woman.

Gregor raised a curved animal horn to his lips and blew, signaling the start of the fight. The hefty woman charged Aleah, who stood calmly until Gianna was nearly on top of her. At the last moment, Aleah turned to the side, grabbed the woman's outstretched arm, and used her momentum to throw her into the rope. Gianna flipped out of the ring, landing on her back on the hard dirt with an explosion of breath.

The woman writhed on the ground, and Raven thought she might stay down. But she rolled over, pushed herself to her feet, and staggered back into the ring, clearly dazed by the hard fall. Aleah faced her from the middle of the ring, and Gianna approached more cautiously this time. She circled Aleah, feinting at charging her. Aleah didn't react; instead, she calmly watched her opponent's eyes. When the woman got close enough, Aleah dropped to a crouch and with a sweep kick cut Gianna's legs out from underneath her, causing the woman to, once again land on her back—this time in the soft mud.

Gianna struggled to push her weight out of the mud, her face red with apparent anger at Aleah's unorthodox wrestling technique. She growled and ran at Aleah. The woman reached out to take hold of Aleah, who grabbed Gianna's hand, leaned backward, and then turned in an arc—causing Gianna to swing around her like children playing a spinning game. Once Gianna was off-balance and twisting, Aleah let go, causing the woman to, once again, fly into the ropes, flip outside of the muddy pit, and land on her back on the hard dirt.

Gianna was limping now and breathing hard as she struggled to get back into the ring. But rather than change her tactics, she charged again with similar results. It looked like Gianna was going to tackle Aleah, but she dropped low and, as the bigger woman fell over her, Aleah stood and pushed up as hard as she could. Gianna flipped one and a half times, landing face-first in the mud. She tried to push herself up again but was too exhausted. Aleah serenely walked to the woman, placed a knee on her back, and looked to the royal grandstand for a ruling.

Gregor blew three quick notes on the horn and shouted, "Aleah, wife of Raven, is the winner."

The crowd cheered as Aleah wiped the mud from her hands on Gianna's back and then left the ring, scowling at Gregor—no doubt for referring to her as if she were Raven's possession. A few men—probably Gianna's husband and brothers—hurried into the arena to help the muddy and exhausted woman stumble from the ring.

The wrestling matches continued throughout the day, and Raven wasn't able to get a moment alone with Aleah until the dinner break. By that time, the field of wrestlers was narrowed down to the final four women; of course, Aleah was one of the four.

"So," Raven said as they sat at the only vacant table in one of the large tavern tents, "are you enjoying rolling in the mud with women for the amusement of dry lander men?" It irritated him that she hadn't even bothered to ask his opinion of her joining the wrestling event. He stood up to signal the barmaid, knocking his wooden stool over as he did.

"I haven't been rolling in the mud," she said with her nose in the air. "In case you haven't noticed, I've stayed relatively clean."

"Very funny. I just wish you would've warned me, instead of lying so you could leave me stranded on the grandstand."

"I didn't lie," she said. "I did go to the privy. I just didn't return to my seat."

The barmaid worked her way to the corner where Raven and Aleah sat and took their order. There wasn't a lot of variety on the menu—lamb and ale or lamb and mead. A few places had been serving fish, but three days into the festival, those tent-taverns were beginning to stink.

"You know what, Camden?" Raven cocked an eyebrow at her use of his real name. "I think you're jealous."

"Jealous?" Raven shouted. He looked around the tent and lowered his voice. "If you want to debase yourself for a bunch of men and a yew bow, that's your choice."

"You're jealous," she repeated and folded her arms. "You don't like all those *barbarians* seeing your wife in tight clothing wrestling with women."

Up until now, their marriage of a few weeks had been blissful. This was the first time Raven truly felt irritated with her. He felt betrayed. He narrowed his eyes and glared at her. In the silence, she smiled as though she'd guessed correctly.

"I'm not jealous." He let out an exasperated breath. "I just feel like you went behind my back."

"So now that we're married I have to ask permission to do the things I want? Is that the way it is?"

"That's not—"

"Who's being treated like property now?" she said. "You were so concerned my Domerian upbringing would make me want to control you, but you're the one acting like the slave owner. Typical dry lander male pig ego. And the worst part is you don't even recognize you're doing it! I'll spit on the crown of Darlynria before I let somebody own me—that includes you."

She stood and stormed away, nearly knocking over the young barmaid as she brought their drinks and food. Aleah steadied the girl, grabbed a leg of lamb, a mug of ale, and glared once more at Raven before she marched out of the canvas tavern. Who was Darlynria? He'd have to remember to ask Aleah about that . . . after she calmed down.

The serving girl watched Aleah go and then looked back to Raven, apparently unsure of what to do.

"Umm, are you staying to eat your meal, sir?" Raven shifted his eyes from where Aleah left the tent, to the girl, and nodded.

"Okay, that will be eighteen copper rukahts." She set the other leg of lamb and ale on the table, and Raven flipped a silver rukaht to her.

"Keep the change."

She smiled, curtsied and retreated back to help other customers.

Raven took a bite of lamb, then dropped it onto the plate—he'd lost his appetite. Why did he allow himself to fall in love? It was a lot more work than he'd realized. He took a long pull on his ale, leaned on his elbows, and stared at his food. Was he really a dry lander pig? All he wanted was the courtesy of her telling him what she planned to do. That wasn't asking too much, was it? Then again, she was raised in a country where men are property and women control everything. She probably had a hard time adjusting to a world where everybody assumed male dominance over women.

The sun was sinking behind the Kuru-Kulla Mountains when Aleah faced off against the princess for the final match. Raven cringed when Gregor, once again, introduced Aleah as "wife of Raven." Now he understood why she had been so cross. All day long she'd been introduced this way. She easily bested every opponent—except for the match that just ended a few moments ago—and yet Gregor still announced her according to her relationship with Raven.

He hadn't been certain Aleah would be victorious in the quarter-final match that just ended. Her opponent had been head taller, extremely athletic, and a good fighter. Aleah was no longer clean. Mud streaked her face, and her hair was matted against her head. She'd rolled around in the mud for more than five minutes before slipping through her opponent's grip. She won by locking her hands together with one arm behind the woman's head and the other wrapped around one of her legs.

Now she stood opposite Princess Katryline waiting for the championship battle to begin. She could have stopped long ago, Raven realized. She held a high enough standing after the third bout that her combined event scores had already assured her sole victory of the bow. But it wasn't in Aleah's nature to quit. She had joined the event and would give it her all until she either won or was beaten. But Aleah was exhausted now. Raven could see it in the deep breaths she took and in the way her shoulders drooped. But the princess also moved slower than she had earlier in the day. She'd wrestled just as many times as Aleah had.

"Ha, ha!" Aerik boomed to his right. "It doesn't get any better than this, my friend! A day of drinking ale and wrestling, and now our women fight for the victor's spoils!"

Raven gave the prince a half-hearted smile and raised his still full mug of ale in salute. The high prince was happy now, but if Aleah won this match, it wouldn't be good. The princess's pride was at stake. And while Aerik was able to overlook being bested at throwing axes by Raven, he didn't think Katryline would take losing well.

Soldiers placed a dozen stands with torches around the outside of the muddy arena and lit them. The flames caused light and shadows to dance across the contestant's dirty faces as they sized one another up from opposite sides of the ring.

Gregor did his best to build up anticipation with the crowd: ". . . seven championships in a row, our own Princess Katryline, will battle against the female warrior Aleah, wife of Raven." Raven groaned at the flash of fiery anger in Aleah's eyes.

Aerik shouted, "Show that little southern girl what a real woman can do, Katryline!" Then the high prince laughed and signaled at a server to refill his mug.

Gregor blew the horn, and the crowd quieted as the two women circled each other. Raven sensed a tense emotion in the air and realized the people were likely concerned that their princess might finally lose. What would the ramifications of that be? Raven looked past the mud pit to the group of girls on the other side—Aleah's teenage fans—even they weren't shouting and cheering like they had during previous bouts.

Aleah feinted toward the princess's leg. The princess bent forward to take Aleah to the ground. Aleah spun to the side and jumped onto Katryline's now exposed back and used the princess's momentum to shove her, face-first, into the mud. Raven cringed, and the crowd groaned. Prince Aerik gave a half-hearted laugh and ran a hand through his long blond hair.

The princess slid out of the neck hold and then rolled and jumped back to her feet. Raven shook his head at the agility Katryline had for a mother of four who was tall and a little rotund—especially since she'd already wrestled several times that day. These Kurulan women were impressively strong and had a lot of stamina.

Once again, the muddy ladies circled each other, looking for vulner-abilities. The princess dropped to a knee and tried to grab both of Aleah's legs—a move the princess had used in earlier matches to take down her opponents. But Aleah, anticipating it, dove over top of Katryline and rolled back to her feet. The princess adjusted and this time she ap-proached Aleah in a more upright position—probably thinking to use her height and weight as an advantage. However, Aleah cartwheeled toward the princess, wrapping her legs around the larger woman's neck, and then continued her rotating momentum to cause them both to spin onto the ground. They landed with the princess on her stomach and Aleah on the woman's back. Aleah shot her hand under the princess and grabbed her wrists, rolled them under, and then pulled one arm out to the side just enough to get her forearm underneath the princess's elbow. She leaned to the center of the princess's back, keeping the el-bow locked and driving her knuckles into the woman's spine. Then she grabbed the woman's other wrist and pulled it out so the princess lay flat on her face with one arm locked like a wing and the other extended. Aleah used her body weight to push Katryline's shoulder toward her ear, forcing the bigger woman to roll over onto her back. Keeping hold of the woman's arm and wrist, she pressed her hip into her shoulder. The princess arched her back and pushed with her feet, but all that did was drive her shoulders deeper into the mud.

Raven had seen this move before—it was called the arm bar, and there was no way to get out of it once your opponent had you in the correct position. Gregor stood and slowly raised the horn to his lips. Aleah glanced to the stage where the high prince and guests earnestly watched. She then, for the briefest of moments, locked eyes with Raven and gave him an almost imperceptible smile.

Just as Gregor pressed the horn to his lips, Aleah's hold on the princess's wrist was broken, and Aleah rolled off to the side as the princess thrust her hips upward once more. Aleah was a too slow at getting back to her feet. The princess grabbed hold of her leg, pulled her backward and over at the same time and then dropped heavily onto her chest. Aleah struggled and pushed but couldn't lift the heavier woman off of her.

Raven saw a smile of relief on the captain of the castle guard just before he blew the horn to end the match. Prince Aerik jumped to his feet, shouting and cheering as loud as he could, drenching Raven with ale from his stein. Raven didn't mind. He also stood and gave Aerik a smile and a congratulatory handshake.

"I gotta hand it to you, Raven!" he shouted over the cheers of the celebrating crowd. "That little woman of yours has a lot of spirit." The high prince slapped him on the back and, noticing his mug was empty again, signaled for the servant to bring wine. "You'd better watch yourself around that one," Aerik said as a servant filled goblets for both of them, "or you might wake up one morning missing your man parts!" He laughed at his own joke and then jumped off the stage into the mud pit to officially congratulate his wife.

Aleah was breathing hard when she approached the grandstand, and she smiled up at Raven.

"So," Raven said, "you lost the match but won the yew bow—without the help of your dry lander pig husband." She gave him an exhausted nod, but her smile widened. "Have you forgiven me for acting like you're my property?" Raven asked.

"Help me out of here, and we'll discuss it," she said breathlessly. Raven reached down from the stage to help her up. But when Aleah grasped his hand, she pulled backward as hard as she could and threw him face-first into the mud.

"We can discuss your apology over a hot bath," she said with a laugh.

WARBREAKER

On the third morning after the celebration ended, Raven stood next to a tall, sturdy brown gelding. He inspected the saddle and knots that attached his pack and bedroll. Aleah did the same with a blond mare that Aerik's stable master had prepared for her. She fidgeted with the beautiful yew longbow that she won for taking first place in the combined events. She wrapped it in a blanket and secured it beneath her bedroll. Raven smiled because he knew she was debating between having it more accessible or hidden and tucked away for protection.

"Sooner or later, you'll need to break that thing in, you know." He walked behind her, held her shoulders, and kissed her on the neck.

"It's Warbreaker," she said, pulling it back out from under the bedroll.

"What?"

"My bow isn't that *thing*; her name is Warbreaker." She unwrapped the bow, turned, and smiled at him.

"You named your bow?"

"She's too beautiful to be without a name."

"So why Warbreaker?"

"That was the name of my favorite panther my mother had when I was a little girl—that panther saved me from an angry boar once."

"And your bow is 'smooth like a panther'?" Raven said with a grin.

"Where did you learn that phrase?" Aleah put her arms around him, still holding her bow in one hand. "You're starting to sound like a Domerian."

"That's enough, you two love doves." Aerik walked into the courtyard, and he appeared to be in a foul mood. He wore traveling clothes and his long blond hair was neatly braided and pulled back. "Come with me." In one hand, he held an axe and in the other he held a white rabbit by the ears. They followed the prince across the inner courtyard to a plain wooden door with iron studs.

"Here, hold this." The prince handed the rabbit to Raven, reached into his pocket with his free hand, produced a rusty skeleton key and unlocked the door. He led them into a room with no exit, closed the door and locked it behind them. Torches on either side of the door and on stands in the center of the room burned brightly, but the cloying warmth and flickering shadows on the walls were mostly caused by a fire on the far side of the room beneath a massive granite mantel. Two giant sized axes made of gold hung on the wall above the mantel, crossed and reflecting the irregular light of the torches on their shiny surfaces.

"What is this place?" Aleah walked toward a large granite grind-stone set in the center of the room between two torches. A stylistic axe carved from the gray rock was balanced against the circular stone as though it were being sharpened by an invisible giant. She noticed that the side of one wall was painted with a great battle scene. The warriors wore leather and fur and battled strange beasts and monsters. A massive lightning bolt shot from a cloud and struck the center of the army of beasts giving the human's the victory.

"Raven," Aerik looked at him with feigned surprise. "I can't believe you would bring your wife to our lands without teaching her about Thail." Turning to Aleah, he said, "This is my shrine to Thail, god of the sky."

"And the rabbit," she asked, "what's that about?"

The prince's sour expression returned. "An offering to Thail to give us good weather and a safe return from our travels." He harrumphed, plopped the rabbit onto the grindstone, and exposed its neck. "The gods know I'll need protection to get through another week of meetings with the other rulers of Kahaal—especially that woman." Raven assumed Aerik was referring to Melista Tarku.

"And some good weather would be welcome for all of us," Raven added. Aleah looked at him with a crooked smile—as if asking him if he really believed this would help.

"Judging by the way the two of you washed up on my shores like a couple of drowned rats," Aerik said, "I assume Raven didn't give Thail a peace offering before your last journey." He brought the axe down on the rabbit's neck, severing its head. It kicked a few times and then went still. Aleah gave Raven a look of mock accusation. Raven smiled apologetically and shrugged. Aerik grabbed a lock of his hair and, using the bloody axe, cut it from his head.

"Here," the prince said, handing the axe to Raven. "Both of you need to cut a lock of your hair with the same axe that took the life of the sacrifice."

Raven cut off a small bit of hair from the back of his head with the axe, then handed the blade to his dubious wife, who did the same. High Prince Aerik Kurulan took the lockets of hair in one hand and the rabbit in the other. He held the offerings above his head, closed his eyes for a few moments, and then tossed it all into the roaring fire. The smell of singed hair and burning meat poured into the small chamber. Fortunately, the flue was well ventilated so the smoke from the sacrifice didn't overwhelm them.

"All right then," Aerik said. "We'd better be on our way."

"Is that all?" Aleah asked. "Aren't you going to, I don't know, say something?" Raven realized Aleah had probably witnessed a lot of different religious ceremonies and was expecting more formality than this.

"Not me. I'm a warrior—not a priest."

In most royal households, the Meskhoni would officiate at religious ceremonies. Raven had watched Ishmael and Artio perform various rites on numerous occasions in their service to the Basil family. But Thail was a pagan god and not recognized by magic users of the Azur-Lore, so Blimron wasn't likely to participate in something like this. When Raven was in Kurulan ten years ago, the old Mage would mix in a bit of preaching of El Azur and true religion when he wasn't fishing. Come to think of it, he hadn't heard Blimron mention El Azur at all these past few weeks. He'd probably given up preaching to the folk of Kurulan as a lost cause.

As they walked back to their horses, a group of archers filed into the large interior courtyard and lined up across from a dozen targets. Raven saw Frija inspecting them from the side as she stood next to Gregor, fidgeting with her vest and shifting her weight. Raven looked at Aleah and smiled. She beamed with pride, watching her young student take on this new role.

"Aleah! Raven!" They turned at the sound of the princess's voice. She was hurrying across the courtyard with the dog barking excitedly at her skirt. Jim and Jam bumped her as they ran past, causing her to nearly drop the basket she carried. She glared at the boys, kicked at the dog, and then hurried forward.

"I thought you and the children said your goodbyes last night," Aerik said as the princess handed her husband the basket.

"We did, but I thought it would be nice if Raven and Aleah had some fresh bread and my famous mountain berry jam to take with them—after all, once they're past the farmlands to the west they won't come across any villages until they reach the trading post on the Ava River."

She opened the basket and gave them each a loaf of hot bread and a sealed earthenware jar. Aleah opened the jar, stuck in her finger, and tasted the sweet, purple preserves.

"That's wonderful." She gave the princess a quick hug. "You have been an amazing host to Raven and me. We've enjoyed our time here."

"Well, there's no need to rush off," she said. "You're welcome to stay as long as you'd like."

"You two need to come back next year so we can win back the axe-throwing and archery championships." Aerik smiled and punched Raven on the shoulder, but Aleah knew the prince was more than half serious. He really didn't like his countrymen being bested at their own games by outsiders—even if they were friends.

"Yes," the princess agreed. "Aleah will have a better chance at becoming the wrestling champion." She cleared her throat, stood a little taller, and said, "I've decided to retire as the undisputed wrestling champion, so next year you won't have to face me."

Aerik raised his eyebrows and cast a furtive glance at Raven. They both knew Aleah let the princess win, but no one was willing to say it out loud. It was best to let the princess have her pride.

"Well, we'd best get started or I'll miss the tide, and you two will be here all day long," the high prince said.

"The tide?" Raven asked. "You're sailing around Bremenon to Kah-Tarku?"

"Don't be daft, Raven," the high prince laughed. "I'm being ferried across the finger to Kanor. I'll take a horse from there to the Bremen River and catch a riverboat down into the capital city." Raven nodded as he listened. It made sense. It would be faster and easier to make the journey that way than riding a horse across the forest and the Blaylok plains.

The prince unrolled a large map on tattered parchment and laid it across the rump of Raven's gelding.

"Memorize this," he pointed at a spot on the map. Aleah and Raven looked over the prince's shoulder. "Head northwest when you leave the castle until you circle around the Kuru-Kulla Mountains. Once you are on the west side of the mountain range, head south along the Ava river until you reach a trading post."

"Northwest around the mountains and then south to the trading post," Raven said. "Sounds easy enough."

"Don't try to cut across the Kuru-Kulla Mountains—there's still snow in the passes and roaming bands of thieves who torment travelers going to and from the mining and trapping villages. The thieves usually stay in the mountains, but they have been known to attack travelers on the north trail on rare occasion, so keep an eye out for them."

"Aleah and I can deal with thieves," Raven said with a grin.

"I'm sure you can." Aerik laughed and slapped Raven on the back. "If we're lucky, the two of you *will* be attacked, and you can rid me of some of the vermin! When you get to the trading post, they prefer dealing in valdins rather than rukahts. This should be enough to buy passage for the riverboat and the lift at Anytos." He handed Raven a heavy black purse that clinked. Raven tossed it back.

"That's generous, Your Highness," Raven said, "but we have enough valdins for our needs."

"Just Aerik is fine," he growled, reminding Raven he hated the honorific. "And take it anyway. Consider it an advance for ridding me of any thieves you happen to cross swords with on your way." Aerik handed the bag to Aleah.

"What shall we do with the horses?" Aleah asked.

"Send them home."

"Just like that?" Raven said. "Send them home? Is there a special command or something we have to do?"

The prince looked at him like he was speaking to a simpleton. "Of course there's a special command," he answered. "Slap them on the rump and say, 'Go home!'"

As Raven and Aleah mounted their horses and rode out the castle gates, Aerik, his wife, and all six children stood in the courtyard and waved goodbye.

"You know what?" Aleah asked. Raven looked at her and raised a brow. "I think we should come back here. After we're done doing . . . whatever it is the Seeress saw in our future, this would be a good place to make a home."

"Really? They're a bit rough around the edges, don't you think?" Raven asked. "And the winters here are long and brutal."

Aleah looked back at the castle and took a deep breath of the mountain breeze. "Okay, we'll make a summer home here and a winter home in Divarlyn."

"Why Divarlyn?" Raven asked. "Why not Tanith?"

"Divarlyn's beaches are fantastic, and I don't stand out there. In Tanith, I'm a princess and, let's face it, you'd be my property." She smiled at him and gave him a sultry wink.

Raven laughed. "Divarlyn it is."

LIGHT A TRAP

A light rainfall made it difficult for Tellio to see through the spy glass. He guessed it was nearly sunset, but the clouds were so dark he didn't know for certain.

"A bad storm is rolling in, Captain," Donelvan whispered. Tellio had grown to respect Donelvan over the past several weeks. He was one of the twenty elite soldiers Tellio had brought with him from Anytos. Donelvan's red hair and freckled skin were unusual for a man of Anytos, but he wore his mustache in the traditional waxed fashion and had a single tower tattooed on his right forearm—the sigil of their city.

Tellio wiped the water from the lens of the spy glass and gave the contraption back to Gustov, the old engineer.

"Your tricks have worked well, Gustov," Tellio said. The engineer took the spy glass and studied the scene from behind the ridge where they were hiding.

Tellio rubbed his hands together. "There're seven boats anchored in that river waiting for the lock workers to fix the paddle. We're going to light 'em up tonight, men."

"I've a few more ideas to keep those locks down for another week," Gustov said. "What's the hurry?"

"They're beginning to suspect foul play," Tellio answered. "They're posting guards at the upper and lower lock gates." He rubbed at his stubbled head. Stubble again. It felt like he'd shaved only yesterday. He crouched lower and turned to face his men. All of them were covered with mud to camouflage themselves from the men milling around on the decks of boats and at the locks. Tellio and his men had avoided being seen—so far. But hiding a force of twenty on the plains was difficult—twenty-two counting himself and Gustov.

"With that storm, it will be dark and blustery," Tellio said. "Perfect for us to strike." He could see the excitement on the faces of the soldiers. They were men of action. Hiding and waiting wasn't why they had joined the army.

"We work in teams of three." Tellio counted with his fingers. "A painter, a holder, and an archer. My team will take out the front vessel. When it lights up, that's the signal to shoot at your boats. Any questions?" He scanned his men, and the old engineer shifted and raised his hand. "Gustov, you'll stay back with the horses and supplies."

The quick nod and smile that broke out on the old man's face confirmed to Tellio that he had correctly guessed Gustov was worried about getting too close to the action.

Two hours later, Tellio lay in the mud on the riverbank with rain pelting his back and a strong south wind making it difficult to hear the men lying in the mud next to him.

"Why am I the painter?" Joakin asked, clearly unhappy at the idea of swimming in the cold river to paint the boat anchored in the middle with naphtha. "I'm the best archer of the three of us."

"You're also the stealthiest," Tellio said, just loud enough for the mousy, hatchet-faced soldier to hear, but not loud enough for his voice to carry in the wind. "Donelvan is good enough with a bow to hit your mark on the boat." The younger man wouldn't argue—he was too well trained for that. But the blank look on his thin, boyish face made it clear he still didn't like his assignment.

Without another word, Joakin slipped the loop of a long rope around his waist and walked into the lazy river. He pulled a small raft that carried a brass spittoon filled with dark, sticky naphtha—that smelled of paint—and a long staff wrapped tightly with cloth around one end. Tellio held the other end of the rope that was attached to Joakin and watched the small soldier disappear into the dark storm.

The plan was simple enough—so long as Gustov was right about the properties of the tar-like naphtha he'd prepared for them. Once Joakin reached the boat, he would dip the end of the long-handled staff into the jar of naphtha. Then he would smear it liberally in a large circle near the aft and the bow of the side of the boat. Last, he would light the cloth on the end of the staff and slap it against the center of the boat. As soon as Tellio saw the fire in the center of the boat, he would pull hard and fast on the rope to bring Joakin back to shore while Donelvan lit arrows dipped in naphtha and shot them at the aft and then at the bow of the vessel, setting the entire side of the boat on fire.

"Are you sure this stuff will burn?" Donelvan asked while they waited. "It's raining pretty hard."

Tellio sniffed and rubbed his chin. "Gustov says it will. Claims it will make the surface of the water burn as it drips off the side of the boats, too. He's the most brilliant engineer in Anytos so . . ." Tellio let his words trail off into the storm.

Donelvan ran his fingers through his wet red hair. "It's a small step between brilliant and crazy," he said. He dipped four arrows into the naphtha and laid them against a small branch so the tips didn't touch the ground. Donelvan placed them far enough apart so that when he struck one with a spark from his flint, it wouldn't light the arrow next to it.

"Be careful not to let any of that liquid fire drip onto your skin or clothing," Tellio said. "Gustov said it will burn right through you with no way to put out the flame."

A burst of flame lit up the dark about fifty paces away, straight in front of them. "Finally," Tellio said. "Joakin's done his job. Time for you to do yours, Donelvan." Tellio pulled the rope, hand over hand, as fast as he could.

"*Ba Aven's Breath!*" Donelvan said. "Gustov wasn't exaggerating about this stuff. It lit with my first strike." He raised the bow and shot the flaming arrow toward where he guessed the front of the vessel would be—but the arrow continued to sail past the boat and fall harmlessly into the river.

"Too far!" Tellio said. "Only aim a finger's width to the right of Joakin's mark!"

In a few seconds, Donelvan had another fiery arrow streaking across the dark stormy sky toward the boat. This time it struck, and within moments, the entire front of the boat was burning. A shout of alarm from the boat, followed by men yelling commands at each other, cut through the wind. As Tellio pulled Joakin out of the river, Donelvan's third flaming arrow arced toward the boat. This one hit near the top of the aft end, but fire dripped down the side until it made contact with the spot Joakin had painted moments ago with an explosion of light.

The three men stood on the shore and watched in awe as the boat was engulfed by flames that wouldn't be satiated. Burning wood fell into the water but rather than hiss as the water doused the flames, it continued to burn. Soon, it looked like the burning boat was floating on a black river with tongues of flame leaping out of water, hungry to consume it.

Down river, a volley of flaming arrows streaked through the sky toward the other waiting boats. Merchant vessels carrying supplies, some boats bringing reinforcements and weapons—all were like goats tied to a post just waiting for the butcher's axe to fall.

"That fiery line would make a dragon proud," Tellio said as he watched all seven boats go up in flames. He and his men were jerked out of admiring their handiwork when the second to last boat downstream shot a volley of flaming arrows toward the shore—dozens of arrows at a time. By the light of the arrows, Tellio saw three of his men running from the shore for the safety of the ridge. Another volley arced across the sky, and this time Tellio only counted two runners.

"Get back to the horses," he shouted. "Those ships may burn, but there will soon be hundreds of soldiers on shore looking for us, and they'll be madder than a jilted Roamali lass."

Donelvan and Joakin grabbed their remaining supplies and ran to where Gustov waited with the horses.

Tellio wondered what they should do next. He hadn't really thought beyond this first attack. *It sure would be nice to have Danu or Raven here right now,* he thought. He missed playing cards and drinking ale with Kivas and the boys, but he never realized how much he depended on Danu and his dark-haired captain for strategy. It amazed him that Danu was able to stay lighthearted under the weight of leadership. *What would Danu do now?* he wondered as he approached the picketed horses and the old engineer. Some of the men were already back and climbing onto their horses. They would all look to him for direction.

Danu was the one who had suggested slowing the supply line. If Danu was here, that's probably what he'd keep doing. Soon, all of the teams returned, and Tellio did a quick count.

"Where's Tynoveo?"

The two men who had been partnered with the young soldier clenched their jaws and shook their heads.

Tynoveo was barely twenty. His mother and fiancé had come to see him off the day he left Anytos with Tellio and his small band of soldiers. Tellio turned and looked in the direction of the burning river. Not because he wanted to see the destruction; he didn't want the men to see his tears. Stupid, really—with all the rain, they wouldn't be able to tell any different.

They didn't have time to recover the boy's body or give him a proper burial. At least his soldiers weren't wearing the colors of Anytos. Tynoveo didn't even have a waxed mustache or any tattoos. The Valdivarian soldiers wouldn't be able to identify him or where he was from. Tellio coughed and took a deep breath.

By Lunaryn's light, *I wish Danu were here,* he thought again. He steeled his resolve and turned back to his soldiers.

"We head south, men, toward Valdivar." He hoped the storm would cover their tracks. "There's more work to do."

SHACK BONES

Avaris shielded his eyes from the burst of red light when Kintara landed in front of him and transformed back into human form.

"Quickly, get what you need," she said. "Shamael isn't taking chances this time. There's a small army of Kirocs, Demon Dogs, and lore users on our trail."

"An *army?*" Avaris rushed into the shack he had lived in with Myrrah, Lekiah on his heels. "Is the new Grand Warlock with them?" Avaris called out loud enough for the black-haired Warlock to hear.

"I didn't fly close enough to be certain," Kintara answered, "I can't take the chance of letting them recognize me, but I don't think so." Avaris glanced out the door and saw Kintara look up in the sky as though making sure she hadn't been followed.

"They have scouts with Demon Dogs and they're moving fast. They'll catch up to us in two or three days." she walked into the musty shack. "Once we're finished here, it's time to separate. We're moving too slow." Avaris saw her glance toward Kalisha who was sitting outside on a three-legged stool—Myrrah used to sit on that stool.

"Don't worry about us," Lekiah said to Avaris, who was about to protest Kintara's plan. "I'll gather a few things from the hold, take Kalisha south down the river and then disappear into the plains."

As Avaris filled a leather pack with the necessities—clothing, boots, blanket, knife—Kintara wandered around the room, looking at the objects Myrrah had left behind.

"I'm surprised Kahn didn't send anyone to investigate her cabin," she mused, picking up Myrrah's grimoire. "Then again, he had never told anyone where she was hiding. He didn't trust us with the knowledge of your exact location."

Avaris thought about the implications of that. It had probably saved him from being abducted years ago by some ambitious Warlock. In a roundabout way, Kahn had probably saved him more times than just sending Myrrah to raise him.

"You should take Myrrah's grimoire—" Kintara stopped midsentence as she approached Avaris with the thick tome and looked at the floorboards in the corner of the room. "What's under there?" she asked.

"I don't know. I've never liked the feeling of that side of the cabin." He realized that saying this out loud seemed odd. "I stayed away from there."

"That's because it's warded," Kintara said. "A simple spell designed to hide something you don't want others to find. Usually, a warding will collapse when the one who makes it dies. It looks like she anchored it to . . . whatever it's hiding. Clever."

Kintara walked toward the corner but stopped three steps in front of it. She studied something Avaris couldn't see, took a thighbone from underneath her cloak, and drew power into it. She inched the bone forward, causing red sparks to crackle in the air. The musty smell of the cabin was replaced by the acrid smell of the Aven power. Then a shimmering wave parted the air as though a curtain had been pulled back. Kintara set the bone on the ground and said, "Avaris, Lekiah, pull these floorboards up, right here."

The boys shared a look and then did as she asked. They pulled away the first board and fell back in disgust.

"Where did she get all those bones?" Kintara wondered aloud—voicing one of the many questions that had just entered Avaris's mind. "Are those . . . children?" She crouched down for a closer inspection. Then understanding dawned on Avaris.

"Not children," he said. "Mordvins." No wonder they were so afraid of her. And that explained where she got her human skulls and thighbones.

"Get another bag and pack as many bones as you can carry."

As many as *he* could carry? He wondered what *she* was going to carry. Probably nothing—she spent most of her time flying. Then a thought occurred to him.

"Kintara, why don't you teach me to transform into a bird?" he asked. "We'd be able to travel much faster." *Especially now that Lekiah and Kalisha won't be with us.* That last thought he left unspoken.

Kintara rolled her eyes and harrumphed.

"Necromancers take years to become Shapeshifters and some never do." She pushed an errant strand of black hair away from her eye. "You will probably learn to transform faster, but that army will be here long before you do. It may look easy, but one mistake, and you'll kill yourself."

Avaris bit his lip against the retort that shot to his tongue. He was a Child of the Blessing. He had a lot more power than those Shapeshifters. He'd killed six of them using simple animal bones before Kintara had bothered to step in and help during the battle on the mountain. He was pretty sure he could learn to transform a lot faster than Kintara believed. He glared at her before turning to carry out her instructions.

He couldn't find another pack, so he laid out a blanket, set bones on the middle, and tied it together at the corners. By the time they walked out of the shack, they were in shadows because the sun was setting behind the mountains. Kintara looked at the sky and then at their immediate surroundings.

"It's probably best we don't travel these mountains in the dark, so I suppose we'll have to camp here tonight," she said. "Lekiah, you make dinner while Avaris and I study common tongue."

Avaris nearly laughed out loud at the sour look his friend leveled at the dangerously pretty Warlock. Avaris was really going to miss him. Lekiah was truly his brother—his oath brother and soon his brother in marriage. Avaris was past thinking it strange that his best friend loved his sister. He was happy for it. He couldn't think of anyone better to protect her than

Lekiah. Avaris hated to leave them, but he knew they would be safer away from him.

The following morning, Kintara took to the skies as the three Devi youth hiked down the mountain and across the cold, swift river. They stopped at the hole blasted into the fortress gates nearly six months ago by Kahn Devin, and none of them spoke. Avaris took a sharp breath and rubbed his thighs. He wasn't prepared for the memories and emotions that flooded his heart and mind. He thought he'd buried those feelings along with his mother and younger brother that cold morning after the last Kiroc flew away from the massacre. A warrior didn't cry, but he wasn't ashamed of the tears rolling down his cheeks.

Kalisha shook and sobbed—she couldn't enter the hold. Lekiah took her into his arms. "It will be all right," he whispered. "I will protect you."

"I can stay with my sister," Avaris said. "Get what you need, and we'll wait at the river." Lekiah wiped a tear from Kalisha's cheek and raised his brows.

"Go on," she whispered. "I'll be . . ." She didn't finish the thought, but Avaris nodded for Lekiah to go ahead.

Lekiah crept into the abandoned hold. It reminded Avaris of the night he'd escaped and then quietly returned, afraid there would be a trap waiting for him. He chewed on his lip when Lekiah disappeared behind the tents and held his breath. Once he was certain Lekiah wasn't going to barge back out with enemies on his heels, he let out a sigh of relief and smiled at his sister. She was shaking and silently crying.

"Come on, Kalisha." He took her hand. "Let's go to the river and see if the canoes are still there." He thought they would be. It appeared the hold, like Myrrah's cabin, had remained abandoned after Kahn Devin killed and captured their tribe. Aven-Lore users hadn't returned—they were preoccupied by the succession battle—and the other Devi clans wouldn't return to a place of such great evil. They would fear that the spirits of the dead would bring similar troubles to their families. Avaris and Lekiah didn't need to fear that, because the spirits roaming this place *were* their family. Avaris wondered what had happened to the spirits of his clan. Would they wander among these ruins forever? Or did spirits go to Valhasgar like his father's Meskhoni taught? That would be a good question to ask Kintara, he decided.

Avaris directed Kalisha to the path that led to a small inlet that the tribe had dug on the side of the river to launch their canoes from.

"I can't believe how this much this path is already grown over," Avaris said to draw Kalisha into conversation. She made a noncommittal noise that sounded like agreement. "I guess in another year it won't even look like a path anymore." That was a dumb thing to say. She began to cry again. The path was overgrown because their clan no longer used it—and never again would.

"At least the boats are still here," he said, hoping to cheer her up, "stacked neatly right where they belong." He pointed to eight canoes, stacked in four rows of two, in a clearing protected from the elements by a thick canopy of tree branches. "There's a bit of leaves and dirt on them, but that's not a problem. Here." He walked to the far side of the first stack of canoes. "Help me flip this over and put it into the water."

She woodenly followed his lead. Her eyes remained vacant, but at least she was moving and somewhat responsive. The last thing Avaris wanted was for Kalisha to revert to the state she was in when they had found her in the Grand Warlock's study.

As they placed the second canoe into the shallow water of the little inlet, Lekiah came down the path, carrying bows, arrows, swords, and a pack filled with clothing, bedding, and other necessary implements.

"Put another canoe into the water," Lekiah said as he loaded his supplies into one of the waiting boats.

"A third canoe?" Avaris asked.

"I don't plan on ever coming back here," Lekiah said. "So I'm going back for more gear. I'll fill this canoe with supplies and tie it to the one Kalisha and I will be riding in." He started back to the hold, and Avaris and Kalisha overturned a third boat.

By the time they finished their preparations, the sun was straight overhead, but Kintara hadn't returned from scouting. They ate dried meat, nuts, and bread that Lekiah had taken from the hold.

"Do you think we should wait for Kintara?" Avaris asked.

Lekiah swallowed his food and shook his head. "We're traveling down a big river." He bent down to drink from the river then tossed the food pack into his canoe. "If she can't find us from the air, she's not a good scout." He helped Kalisha into the canoe, shoved it into the river, and hopped in.

Avaris shrugged his shoulders, pushed his own canoe into the river, and let the current take him away from the hold. As he watched it disappear around the bend, he wondered if he'd ever see it again.

SECURING ALLIANCES

The wayfire sputtered and flared. Raul Lucian looked up from scrubbing the stone floor to see who was coming to the temple. Only Warlocks, Shapeshifters, and sometimes Necromancers arrived this way. He hoped it was Siersha, the high priestess of Necrosys. The only pleasure he ever got in this miserable place was watching her supple form glide past him during her infrequent visits. She, of course, would probably kill him if she knew the kind of thoughts that played in his mind as he stared at her. He didn't care; death would be preferable to his current life.

His knees ached, and his hands were red from hours of scrubbing floors with hot water—red like his mottled beard and hair. Siersha had red hair, too—beautiful, long, silky red hair that framed her face and cascaded over her shoulders. He stood and faced the fire. Whoever was coming would expect a proper welcome from the servants of the Night Temple, the temple of Ba Aven's son K'Thrak.

Raul's lips curled downward in disappointment as a bald man with a scar that angled from his right ear to his mouth, wearing a dark traveling cloak, stepped out of the flames. He looked vaguely familiar—perhaps Raul had seen this man once before . . . years ago. The two magic users in dark robes who had the job of tending the wayfire dropped to their knees in genuflection when he appeared. He glanced at them and then glared at Raul for daring to stand in his presence. Raul dropped to his knees and touched his head to the floor. He didn't know who this was, but he clearly wasn't a man to be trifled with.

"Take me to your master," the man said to the magic users. His accent was subtle. Raul couldn't quite place it, but the man wasn't from Nortia. Raul turned his head just enough to see the exchange.

"I'm sorry, M-Master Grand Warlock," the lore user closest to the fire stammered.

Did he say Grand *Warlock?* Raul squinted to better see the man in the black cloak. *This certainly wasn't Kahn Devin.*

"High Priest Hodran is at the castle, c-counseling the k-k-king. If we'd known you were—"

"Compose yourself," the bald man snapped. "What is your name?"

"Chandel, m-milord."

"Aven-Lore users don't stammer like whimpering slaves, Chandel, regardless of whom they're addressing."

"Yes, of course, Grand Warlock Shamael." The man made an obvious effort to stand more erect and speak more confidently. "I can, umm . . . show you to the castle if you wish."

Raul raised his body from the stone floor as the two men left the inner sanctum of the temple. If this man was the Grand Warlock . . . what had happened to Kahn Devin?

King Thrakus Druger VI grimaced when Hodran coughed into his sleeve and wheezed. The man took a sip of wine from a crystal goblet the serving girl had set before him and coughed again. Was he never healthy? Maybe it had something to do with his position as high priest to the god of night, K'Thrak. Then again, maybe he was just a sickly person.

"I don't envy those of you who dedicate your life to the lore," Thrakus said, hiding his contempt, "but it would be nice to have the ability to shape shift and fly to Balek, or better yet, use a wayfire and instantly arrive."

"Magic does have its advantages," the Warlock said.

"Maybe I should've insisted Dromak and Arikka have the wedding here. After all, it is a state wedding." Thrakus didn't look forward to the two weeks' journey through the western Cragg Mountains to Baron Dromak Wytrane's castle in Balek, even if the view overlooking Beartooth Bay *was* amazing. Thrakus's young wife, on the other hand, was beside herself with excitement. She'd never been to Balek and was also anxious to see her mother—Kronan's wife, Princess Deliana.

"I should've insisted the wedding be at Avengate." The king chuckled. "Let my brother host a week-long celebration and laugh at him while everybody consumed his food and wine."

Then again, that would be a longer journey, and even in early summer the high northern plains of Nortia were sometimes hit with snowstorms. At least his journey to Balek should have decent weather.

A knock at the solid wooden door of his war room brought him out of his thoughts. He hadn't called for anyone and didn't feel like being bothered. In fact, it was high time Hodran left as well. But what *really* bothered him was that the person knocking didn't wait for permission to enter—the door opened, and one of Hodran's temple workers rushed in and bowed to the night Warlock; he didn't even acknowledge Thrakus. The king was about to angrily protest, but the words of the black-robed servant made him catch his breath.

"Master Hodran, the Grand Warlock requires an audience with you."

Hodran stood, and a man in a dark traveling cloak entered the room. He wasn't tall or particularly large, but the confidence in which he held himself commanded respect. His head was shaved, and the scar running from his right eye down to his mouth caused the piercing scrutiny of his nearly black eyes to be even more imposing. Thrakus followed Hodran's lead and bowed to the new comer.

"Hodran, I trust all is well?" the man asked.

The night Warlock nodded. "Master Daro, allow me to introduce King Thrakus Druger." Thrakus bowed lower.

"I am honored by your visit, Grand Warlock Daro," he said as he straightened from his bow. "My staff and I are at your service."

"Thank you, King Druger," the Grand Warlock said. "I am Shamael

Daro. You and your forefathers have been loyal subjects for many years—I assure you that loyalty will soon be rewarded."

Thrakus didn't like being referred to as a loyal subject, but the promise of reward piqued his interest. This certainly wasn't the way Kahn Devin would have begun a conversation.

"Can I offer you a drink, Master Daro?"

"Boranica red, if you have it."

Thrakus forced a smile and bowed. Kahn, Hodran, and now the new Grand Warlock all drank Boranica red wine; maybe drinking like a woman was a requirement if one aspired to be a Warlock.

"I don't have much time, High Priest Hodran." Shamael removed his dark cloak and took a seat at the table. "I have several other visits to make during the next two weeks, so I must be brief and to the point."

"No offense, milord," Hodran said and then coughed sickly into his sleeve, "but quick visits are the best in my experience—unless you're visiting a beautiful, young wench."

"Actually, I will take issue with that," Shamael said and stared hard at Hodran, who paused in the middle of raising his goblet of wine. "Brief and to the point is *especially* best when visiting a beautiful wench." He chuckled, and the other men in the room laughed, more in relief than at the joke. Shamael took the glass of wine from the dark-haired serving girl and smiled as he raised it in salute to the others.

"It's convenient to find the two of you together," Shamael continued. "Hodran, I want you to send some of your best spies to Siersha's temple in Cragmur—maybe five or six."

"It will take time to place that many spies in the temple of Necrosys. Might I ask what they should be looking to discover?"

Shamael genuinely laughed at this comment, set down his wine and held up his hands. "You misunderstand me, Hodran," he said. "I don't want them to spy on her; I want her to train them. In return, you will train some of her best assassins in the art of spying."

Hodran nodded thoughtfully, but Thrakus could tell the night Warlock was uncomfortable with the idea.

"I'm surprised you didn't think of this before, Hodran," Shamael continued. "Spies who are trained assassins are twice as useful."

Thrakus had to admit it would open a lot of possibilities as he considered the idea. And Hodran could charge a small fortune for such a man.

"Is there a particular assignment or skill you want us to emphasize in their training?"

"Spying and killing, of course," Shamael said as though Hodran were an idiot.

"King Druger, I am tripling the amount of gold you are receiving from our mines—I want you to double the size of your army and have them ready for battle within six months."

Thrakus smiled—the Grand Warlock might drink wine, but at least he was a man of action. "Gladly, Master Daro." The king bowed again. "My men have been training long and hard for the battles to come. Might I be so bold as to ask where you intend to attack?"

"Actually, Thrakus, you can." Shamael's eyes glimmered with apparent mischief as he took a sip of wine. "You see, unlike my predecessor, I believe in sharing my strategies with my allies." That certainly was a departure from what Thrakus was accustomed to.

"I will be creating a great deal of chaos throughout Boranica during the next several months, and when the moment is right, your armies will invade from the north and press as far south as Mylitta and Tauret."

"Master Daro"—Thrakus raised his stein of ale—"the armies of Nortia will be ready."

"Excellent." The Grand Warlock joined Thrakus by raising his own glass and finishing its contents.

"Now, I require food and lodging before I begin the next leg of my journey," Shamael said. "I trust you have guest quarters in your castle."

"Of course, milord." Thrakus didn't care for magic users as a matter of principle—use them for what they can do for you but don't associate more than absolutely necessary was his standard practice—but somebody as powerful and influential as the Grand Warlock required his best. "We will have a feast in your honor tonight, complete with pit fighting and dancing wenches."

"I trust you will be joining us, Hodran?" Shamael said, turning to the pale-skinned high priest. The night Warlock dipped his head in respect, causing his long black hair to fall over one eye, and said, "Of course, Master Daro."

The following morning, as the sun rose over the city, the three men walked across the courtyard to the gatehouse of the castle complex, discussing the details of the assignments Shamael had given them the evening before. Thrakus's head pounded from the late night festivities. How the Grand Warlock was so alert at such an early hour after a night like that was beyond impressive. All in all, Thrakus was surprised to find he was pleased with the Grand Warlock's visit. His treasury would soon receive an influx of gold from the Cragg mines, and all it cost him was one night of feasting and revelry.

"High Priest Hodran," Shamael said as he turned to leave. "It may be a few weeks before I am able to visit Siersha to outline my plans with her. In the meantime, select your men and have them begin their journey to her temple."

Hodran inclined his head toward Shamael.

As the Grand Warlock walked away, his body shimmered red and smoothly transformed into a large, black dog. The animal bounded through the portcullis and disappeared down the hard-packed dirt road of Nabal, causing people and animals to scurry and jump out of the way to escape his path.

"That's curious," Hodran said in a wheezy voice. "I didn't know Shamael could transform into a Demon Dog. Come to think of it, I don't know of any Warlock who uses that form."

"Why is that curious? He is the Grand Warlock, after all."

Hodran looked down his nose at the king. Thrakus thought the man wasn't going to condescend to offer an explanation. He wondered if a quick, solid punch to the throat would kill a Warlock the same as any other man. Thrakus was tempted, especially at times like this, to try this theory on Hodran.

"It's curious," the night Warlock explained as though speaking to a child, "because transformation is difficult and dangerous. Only the most gifted lore users can do it safely, and only a select few can shift to more than one type of animal. When you transform, you take on the animal's characteristics. Their instincts have to be controlled because they constantly threaten to take over the person who has assumed the form. Demon Dogs have insanely powerful instincts. Most lore users would lose their identity if they transformed into such a beast."

An incredible lust for blood tore at Shamael's mind as he ran through the city. He felt immense satisfaction at the terror the sight of him inspired in the eyes of people and animals as his powerful body ran effortlessly past them through the streets. He wanted to kill and feed. He *needed* to kill and feed. It took intense focus to control the demands of this form, but the exhilaration of this shape was worth the danger.

Once he was outside of the city and into the forest, he would give into the desires. He would need the energy of a good meal for the next leg of his journey, and he didn't fancy eating mice, which was what he would kill and eat in his bird form. He would eat venison for breakfast before changing form and flying south to his next appointment.

He displayed his sharp fanged teeth as he tried to smile at the thought of leaving Hodran and Thrakus the way he did. He didn't even care if the antic was pretentious. Hodran would be surprised and impressed by the power it took to control this form. Thrakus might not appreciate the subtle nuances, but seeing a man transform into a massive Demon Dog before your eyes would send a strong message to anyone. A more powerful message would be the ability to travel instantly to any major city on the continent. Once his vitiate were in place, he wouldn't have to travel long distances as a bird *or* a Dog—he would simply order his vitiate to build a wayfire and he could arrive in the space of a few heartbeats.

Finding a herd of deer was easy with the enhanced senses of this form—the crisp scent of pine was distinctly different than the earthy smell of dirt and, likewise, every animal and plant had a strong, distinct smell. Making the kill was even easier—he didn't even bother to single out the weakest or slowest member of the herd.

The fresh meat and warm blood was intoxicating and filled him with a bloodlust to kill just for the thrill of the hunt and the feel of warm blood dripping through his fangs. He resisted these urges and instead ran as fast as he could to the south. Trees and plants whipped past in a blur as he charged through the forested foothills south of Nabal. The wind blowing through his thick black fur was cool and invigorating. In the distance he could see the rise of a hill with a sudden drop at the top. He sped up the hill forcing his powerful legs to leap boulders, bushes, and streams. The strength of this form was overwhelming and exhilarating. As he crested the rise, he leaped out into the sky, unconcerned with the several hundred foot drop below him. The massive black Dog shimmered in the air, and with a piercing cry it flew into the sky in the shape of a large, black hawk.

The view from this vantage was nearly as thrilling as his race through the foothills. The energy from the stag he'd eaten while in the form of the Demon Dog would fuel this form for several days.

He followed the western Cragg foothills southward all day. As the sun was melting into the water to the west, he saw the silver ribbon of the T'Karn River meandering through the plains on its journey from Lake Tanisyr to the Drbal Divide. Once he crossed the river, he would be in northern Boranica. The kings of Nortia had disputed that fact for centuries, but since there was no major city within one hundred leagues of the river on either side, the debate was pointless.

There was no moon when the sun sank into the Drbal Divide. The waning half-moon wouldn't crest the eastern horizon for several hours yet. It would soon be difficult to see specific ground features, even with his hawk eyes.

A waning half-moon meant summer solstice was still three weeks away.

That meant that midsummer's Azur-Aven, which was celebrated during the first new moon after the solstice, would be in five weeks. He wouldn't be able to officiate at the ceremony in Aven City located just inside the west gate of the caves. He and his vitiate recruits would likely just be arriving at the dark pool where the Guardian would show him how to work the magic necessary to transform them.

He didn't particularly care for large celebrations anyway, but it would've been good to be at Aven City for the first midsummer ceremony following his ascension to Grand Warlock. Perhaps Torin, the high priest to the storm goddess, Danisyr, could cover for him. After all, he'd been in the archives nearly every day searching for a lost tome that would give him the knowledge he lacked to make Aven blades, so he'd likely be there anyway. However, that might upset Prince Kronan, seeing as how Torin should be at Avengate officiating the prince's ceremony. There was nothing he could do about it. Completing the vitiate ritual and getting them placed around Lemuria was the most urgent matter of business.

It took longer to reach Mylitta than Shamael had hoped. When the moon rose, there was dense cloud cover, so he had to fly slower and change altitude several times in order to make certain he was on the correct course.

Although the sun hadn't yet crested the eastern horizon when he circled the crenelated walls and parapets of the northernmost city of Boranica, the sky was growing lighter and the clouds had dissipated. The night watch languidly made their rounds on the battlements—one soldier had even tucked himself into a dark corner, asleep behind a pile of boxes.

It's been too long since they've had to fight, Shamael thought. *This is what happens when there's no danger—men grow careless.* His hawk's beak wasn't capable of contorting into an expression that showed the contempt Shamael felt. *Well, they'll have danger soon enough. And if they aren't prepared to face it, all the better.*

Merchants, bakers, and other shop owners entered the cobbled streets below as they began their various morning routines. Shamael found a tall, sturdy tree with thick foliage and settled on a branch high above the ground.

It would be easier to rest this way than to transform back to a human and rouse an innkeeper, just to sleep in a bed for a couple of hours.

Shamael didn't get much sleep, however. The constant din of the street rose in earnest soon after he'd settled in the tree. As the sun approached its apex, he flew from the tree, over the market and a park, and landed in a dark, abandoned alley. The hawk looked around before transforming back into a man. Instead of taking the image of an imposing Warlock, Shamael wore the face of a haggard old beggar, complete with wispy gray hair, a wrinkled, sun-beaten face with several days' growth of silver stubble, and a worn and torn homespun shirt and breeches. He reached into the inner pocket of his cloak—to anybody watching, it would've appeared he was reaching into his ratty shirt—and pulled out a thighbone, which he transformed into a knotted, bent walking stick.

MYLITTA THIEVES' GUILD

The old man limped through the park, into the market, and settled himself on a busy corner—opposite another beggar—and held out a trembling hand to passersby.

"Oy, old man." It didn't take the thin beggar across the road long to get upset with the new competition. "This is my beat. You can't work here, so bug off before I turn you in."

Shamael ignored the man and continued holding out his hand, accepting a silver coin from a merchant. Not bad. He'd only just started begging, and he already had a silver Boran to show for his efforts.

"Hey! Gimme that money!" The younger beggar supposedly had a bad leg, but he made his way across the road to where Shamael sat fast enough. "That's *my* money! This is *my* corner."

"I don't know what yer yappin' 'bout," Shamael said in a shaky, old man voice.

"That's my money!" The thin man got right in his face as he shouted. He was missing most of his teeth and had bits of tobacco stuck between those that remained.

The red-faced beggar reached down to take the money from Shamael. "Give me that and get out—"

Shamael swung his walking stick around much faster than an old man should have been able to and swept the beggar's feet out from underneath him in midsentence. People paused to watch the beggars' argument. Shamael gave the other panhandler a toothy grin, and the man jumped up, his bad leg completely forgotten. The beggar noticed the gathering crowd, and his eyes darted nervously back and forth.

"This isn't the end of it, old man," he hissed as he brushed himself off. "I'll be back."

Shamael just smiled, held out his hands to people in the crowd, and was rewarded with a dozen or more coppers tossed to him from bystanders who had enjoyed his antics with the other beggar. The skinny beggar with bad teeth spit at him, turned on his heels, and pushed his way through the crowd. Hopefully, he would be back sooner than later. Amusing as it was to sit here pretending to be an old beggar, the ground was uncomfortable, and he didn't care for debasing himself this way.

Less than a quarter hour later, the beggar pushed his way through the crowd, followed by a couple of toughs who struggled to keep up with him. The beggar pointed at Shamael, turned to shout something to the men following him, then gave a glare to Shamael that said, *you're in for it, now.*

That took less time than Shamael feared it would. A sign that the thieves' guild was well organized here in Mylitta.

"Oy! Old man." A tough man who looked to be in his early twenties with blond hair and built like an ox stopped in front of Shamael. Next to him stood a man who was massive, but not from muscle. He was a few years older, had a full beard with bits of food clinging to it and a rotund stomach that spilled over his belt. The skinny beggar stood to the side with a self-satisfied look of anticipation on his face.

"Git yer things and move along," the first thug continued. "This 'ere is Jindy's spot."

"I don't see no name anywhere," Shamael said, looking on the ground and walls behind him.

"I don't *need* no name written anywhere—"

"Shut yer pie-hole, Jindy," the blond thug said. "Listen up, old man, 'cuz I'm only tellin' ya once. These streets belong to Vardan, and *he* makes the rules." He pointed to the leather cap on the ground next to Shamael that held the fruits of his begging and said, "Give us them coins. They belong to Vardan now. Beat it!"

"Why don't you take me to this *Vardan* guy, and I'll give them to him m'self," Shamael said with a taunting grin.

"You'll give 'em to me now, or we'll thump you on the head and toss you in the river," the fat man said.

"No, you *will* take me to Vardan." The small amount of red energy that flowed from his walking stick wasn't visible in the bright sun, but it caused the ruffians to believe the idea was their own.

"Get up, old man," the oxlike thug said. "You're going to see Vardan."

The skinny beggar looked at the big tough like he'd lost his mind.

"What you lookin' at?" the blond man said. "Git back to yer post before I toss *you* into the river."

Shamael made a show of trying to raise his old frame off the hard ground and allowed the men to escort him roughly down the street. They left the main thoroughfare and wound through shaded back alleys, always heading in a general direction toward the river front.

After taking three side streets and two more alleys, they ducked into a nondescript doorway that led into a dark store room with old wooden chairs and furniture covered with cobwebs and dust. They walked to the opposite side of the room to a doorway that opened onto another road—but this one had more traffic, and from the smell of things the river was nearby.

"Keep him 'ere till I give the signal," the blond man said.

"Whatever you say, Veril."

"You daft o' what?!" The oxlike thug cuffed the dark-haired man with the big gut upside the head. "Don't be using my real name around the likes o' him!"

"What's the problem?" The other man rubbed at his head. "It's not like he's gonna live to repeat it."

"Just wait for the signal." With that, he stepped out of the door and walked across the street to a large warehouse. He walked in an open door, then reappeared moments later, and made a few quick movements with the fingers on one of his hands.

"That's our cue, old man." He shoved Shamael through the door and across the street. They followed the other man around the corner of the building, down an alley that smelled of fish and sewage and stopped at a small door with a speakeasy cut into it. The blond ruffian, Veril, tapped on the door in a series of short and long knocks and the small cutout slid open.

"What's the cargo on the afternoon shipment?" a mousy voice on the other side of the door asked.

"Smooth furs and fish."

The speakeasy slid shut, and Shamael heard someone fumbling with locks on the other side of the door, which opened just enough for them to slip inside.

"Whatcha got 'ere?" a short balding man holding a clipboard asked.

"Takin' him to see Vardan."

"What would Vardan the smooth want with an old beggar?" The bald man lowered his clipboard and peered more closely at Shamael—seeing nothing but a dirty old beggar.

"That's none of your concern," the blond thug said. "Just release the lever and make sure nobody followed us."

The bald man sucked in a breath, apparently to argue, but looked at Veril's massive arms and instead nodded and said, "It's yer hide, not mine."

Veril tilted his head, narrowed his eyes, and stared at Shamael, obviously second-guessing himself and wondering why he was taking this unimportant beggar to personally meet with the guild's master thief. Shamael pushed more power through the walking stick into his escorts' minds, persuading them to continue moving onward.

The men led him inside another door into a small storage closet. They moved a barrel to the side, revealing a trap door. Shamael heard a clicking sound—apparently, the bald man released the lever Veril had referred to earlier—and the big-bellied man grunted as he bent over and pulled open the door, revealing a stairway.

They walked down the steps into cool, damp air. Once his eyes adjusted, Shamael saw a wooden walkway built on top of the muddy floor of the tunnel. He was surprised it wasn't flooded, being so close to the river. They walked, Shamael assumed, away from the river because they soon left the mud and continued a few hundred more paces on dry dirt. They entered a door into an underground storage room, and after going around several bolts of cloth, some furniture, wine casks, and other goods, they came to a massive wall painting. Veril pulled on the frame, and the picture opened to reveal a short-carpeted hallway.

Shamael heard voices and giggling women in the distance, and shafts of light sliced in from the far end of the hall. Two guards stood at the end of the short hallway facing the voices. One guard, a woman in tight, sleeveless leather armor, turned to face them. Her brown wavy hair was held off her face by a braided strip of leather tied around her forehead.

"Who goes there?" She drew two throwing knives.

A Kiel-Don, Shamael realized. He could tell by the weapons and the way she carried herself. He was impressed that a thieves' guild could afford the service of one of Siersha's acolytes.

"The smooth otter cuts through the rapid river," Veril said. The woman put her knives away and motioned them forward.

They entered a circular chamber as large as a king's throne room, complete with red-carpeted floors and a massive fire pit feature in the center. A large fire burned in the pit, providing both heat and light to the immense space. Hard-looking men lounged about the room—some seated at tables, playing games of chance with dice or cards, and others on overstuffed sofas, flirting with prostitutes. Paintings with impressive gilded frames and finely woven tapestries covered nearly every inch of the wood paneled walls, and a gallery ran the length of both sides of the room above the wall hangings.

At the far side of the room, a pair of ornate, golden candle holders—each bearing five lit candles—stood on either side of a large round sofa with colorful pillows and throw blankets. Animal furs lay on the carpet in front of the sofa—a large white bear hide as well as jaguar and panther skins from Domeria.

Resting comfortably on the sofa, surrounded by three barely clothed women—one feeding him grapes, one massaging his shoulders, and the last sitting next to him playing a small harp—was a man who looked to be in his late thirties or possibly early forties. He had dark hair with a tightly manicured goatee, and wore a flat-topped, black hat sporting a long blue feather on one side. His black silk shirt was covered by a silver jerkin with gold threaded designs. Around his neck hung a chain with blue, black, and silver gemstones held in place by gold settings. He also wore a black dress cloak with a large ruby brooch clasped at his throat and high riding boots.

Shamael's escorts walked confidently into the room, forcing him forward as they advanced toward the man he assumed could only be Vardan the smooth.

The two ruffians didn't notice the sudden silence in the room or the curious stares from the other thieves. The spell Shamael had used kept them from being observant of such things, but the master of the guild noticed the sudden change in the room. He pushed the girl feeding him grapes aside and leaned forward.

"What is the meaning of this?" he demanded. "Sonshil, why did you admit these men into my lair?"

"They gave the password." The Kiel-Don didn't offer any other explanation, so the thief master stood and took a step forward.

"Drogir!" Vardan called and a large man with a thick beard stepped out from behind a screen that stood between the round sofa and the back wall. The man's dark hair was pulled back into a pony tail and he wore a black shirt and an animal tooth necklace.

"Yes, Master Vardan."

"Are these your men?"

"Yes," he answered and then addressed the men standing on either side of Shamael.

"Veril, Thad, what is this about?"

"Umm, well, this old man . . . He . . ." Veril's brow furrowed in apparent confusion, and his eyes darted from Shamael and back at the men at the front of the room. Shamael dropped the coercion spell and the man couldn't remember the reason for bringing a stranger to the center of their secret guild.

"Spit it out, Veril!" the man called Drogir shouted. He stepped forward and balled his fists.

"We brought him. He . . . was . . ."

"Wait," Vardan the smooth pushed Drogir aside and approached Shamael. "Where did you get that ring, old man?"

Shamael grinned. This Vardan was more observant than he'd given him credit for. But that wasn't surprising. A man didn't become master of a thieves' guild without paying close attention to details and, of course, without being a ruthless killer. Vardan wore a nearly identical ring on his hand—gold with a large black stone encircled by smaller rubies. The master of each thieves' guild owned and wore such a ring.

"I'll not ask you again," he said with venom dripping from his words. "Where did you get that ring?"

Shamael heard a shuffling sound on the gallery and looked up to see at least twenty men with bows and arrows trained at him. He moved forward, straightening his bent body as he did, and let his disguise vanish. Vardan stepped backward but held up a hand to stay the arrows.

"I am Shamael Daro, former guild master of Valdivar." The walking stick transformed back to a thighbone, and it glowed with barely restrained red power crackling over its surface.

"I've never met a thief who was accomplished in the Aven-Lore," Vardan said in an imperious tone, apparently recovered from his surprise. "Did Kahn Devin send you?"

"Kahn is dead," Shamael replied coolly. "I am the Grand Warlock now."

"Dead, you say? So the rumors are true." He glanced toward the Kiel-Don he called Sonshil. She had probably heard about the events and passed them on to him. "Kahn was still in his prime," the man continued. "I'm surprised to learn he was killed." Obviously, Vardan knew more than he was letting on. Shamael kept his gaze leveled on the man.

"I didn't think it possible to kill a Warlock, especially the Grand Warlock. I guess all men must eventually die." He gave Shamael a pleasant smile. He was *actually* threatening him. Well, that may be a good sign, depending . . .

"Kahn is dead," Shamael said. "Your contract with him is now held by me."

"I see." Vardan pursed his lips and he fingered his brooch, probably a signal for his men to be prepared to attack. "And what would you require of us, now that you hold my contract?"

"If you follow my instructions, you will gain power and riches beyond what you now possess," Shamael answered. "I won't bother to illustrate the consequences of not following my instructions."

"And what, pray tell, are the *instructions* we are to follow, Master Daro?"

"Shortly after midsummer's Azur-Aven, your guild will create chaos in Mylitta. Soon, all of Boranica will be at war."

Vardan looked at Drogir, raised his eyebrows, and looked back at Shamael. "I'm sure, as a former guild master, you understand the difficulty of what you ask. After all, much of my income comes from extorting the other guilds and nobles—they pay me, handsomely I might add, to maintain order and keep a workable balance. Chaos is not good for business." Shamael didn't respond. He continued to stare at the man and wait.

"I also own many legitimate business enterprises in the city and . . . well, I simply can't do what you are asking." He made another small movement with his hand as he spoke.

The bone in Shamael's hand flared to life, encircling him in a shield of crimson energy. The whirring of flying arrows filled the throne-like room, but they fell harmlessly to the ground around him—although Veril and Thad dropped to the ground, each looking like a pin cushion with multiple arrows protruding from their bodies. Shamael's free hand flicked toward the master thief and Vardan dropped to a knee, grasping his stomach. His eyes grew wide and his mouth dropped open when he saw the knife imbedded in his gut and a pool of blood soaking his rich jerkin.

Shamael maintained his shield and sauntered toward Vardan. Drogir drew two swords and advanced toward Shamael. Drogir's loyalty was admirable after witnessing how the Grand Warlock had just negated the attack of the entire thieves' guild. With a gesture and another surge of red energy, Drogir flew out of the way and landed on his back some thirty paces away.

"You are right about one thing, Vardan," Shamael said loud enough for all in the room to hear. "A Warlock can be killed, but not by the likes of you."

"I can . . . can still be of service . . ."

"Yes, you can," Shamael smiled as he interrupted the man's pleas for mercy. Vardan got a look of hope in his eyes.

"My predecessor would send others to kill for him. If he did personally kill, he used magic to do so." Shamael looked around the room, including the gallery, so there would be no mistake he was addressing them all. "Vardan, you can be of service by showing your guild that I have no qualms about killing with my bare hands." He turned and punched the guild master in the throat.

Vardan grabbed at his neck, struggling for air. He squirmed on the ground at Shamael's feet, and the Grand Warlock turned to Drogir, who was just now lifting himself off the floor.

"Drogir, come here."

The large man obeyed. He didn't grovel or show fear. He walked with purpose—like a man resigned to his fate, whatever it may be.

"What do they call you?" Shamael asked.

"Drogir the Dagger," he said.

"How fitting. You may well become my dagger, indeed. Vardan was shortsighted." Shamael pointed to the dead master thief. "War and chaos present the perfect opportunity for men of action to become powerful and wealthy beyond measure. My contract is now with you, as Vardan's second-in-command. That is, if you are willing to accept the terms."

"I am and I will." The man bowed his head in acquiescence. "What would you have me do, Grand Warlock Daro?"

Shamael raised his voice. "Drogir is now master of the Mylitta thieves' guild." Men and women standing on the main floor and watching from the gallery lowered their weapons and stared. "You will obey his every command."

Turning back to Drogir, he lowered his voice. "You will obey my every command." Shamael looked hard into his eyes. The man didn't flinch, but the look he returned confirmed to Shamael he would follow orders. "My first instruction to you is this: starting on the night of midsummer's Azur-Aven, you will maintain this fire at full strength for a period of two hours—from an hour prior to midnight to an hour after. You will do this every night until I return."

Drogir brought his fist to his chest in salute and bowed his head.

"It will be done, milord."

KING'S CANDY

"All right, King's Candy, break time is over."

Cremin cringed at the nickname the staff used for him and the other pages when no one with any real authority was around.

"You have ten minutes to get down to the beach veranda where the king will be taking his supper."

Cremin and the four other pages hurried out of Page Hall and rushed through the back corridors, down several sets of stairs, and out the west doors of the palace to one of the many verandas that overlooked the Drbal Divide. Now that the rainy season was over, the king was prone to eat his evening meals overlooking the gardens and beach as the sun melted into the ocean.

A cool breeze was blowing in from the water, and the sound of surf and sea birds was a welcome change of scenery to Cremin's way of thinking. And there was nothing more respectful to Solra, may his name be blessed, than to reverently watch the sun rise in the morning or set in the evening. Although, Cremin knew the king didn't view this as a religious duty. He simply was a man who appreciated beauty . . . maybe a little too much.

A plush red carpet led from the palace door to the king's table, which was set on the edge of the veranda. The pages stood in a line on one side of the carpet, and the cooking staff, wearing livery, stood opposite them on the other side. Giggling and chatter preceded the king as he walked onto the balcony with his entourage, which consisted of the court Meskhoni—the Wizard Desmantor—Lord Steward Halbert, the captain of the house guard, and two of his soldiers who wore white pants tucked into shiny black boots, a black coat with yellow cording and a yellow armband with the black dragon insignia.

The soldiers carried ceremonial spears, wore a sword on their hip, and took a position on either side of the door. Their captain was distinguished by his rich green doublet and black hat with a yellow feathered plume coming from the top. He was younger than Cremin would've expected for a person of such high position, but he was handsome and had perfectly combed blond hair, which probably had something to do with his fast rise in the king's court.

King Reollyn had obviously just come from his appointment with the royal hairdresser—his wig was immaculately combed, and his face was powdered and pale, which drew attention to the black, heart-shaped mole drawn onto his right cheekbone. He wore tight, cream-colored hose and a richly embroidered purple, gold, and black jerkin covered by a thick purple cape. Halbert, the lord steward, undid a golden clasp from around the king's neck, removed the cape, and helped the king into his seat at the table.

The Wizard took his place to the right of the king. Desmantor's makeup was even more outlandish than the king's. His face and lips were painted white, and his eyes were lined with black and purple. He had a black stripe coloring the middle of his lips, leaving the outer edges of his mouth white. He wore a high collared white robe with a jeweled breastplate of red leather, and a red and white striped head dress that reached a hand's length above his head.

Halbert sat at the table to the king's left, and one of the liveried servants removed the shiny metal lids from the several dishes of food that had been laid out for their meal.

"Ooh, lamb chops with mint sauce." Reollyn clapped his hands. "One of my favorites." The cook beamed with pride.

"Now, Halbert," the king said between bites of food, "while we are at the theater tonight, I want you to instruct the conductor to play the third movement from Idavadi's *Nightsongs of the Goddess* prior to starting the opera. I haven't heard that piece in ages, and I simply love the melody. The king was always in high spirits when he was going to the theater. Cremin was also pleased to hear the king talk of his night out, because it meant a night off for him as well.

The sound of boots rushing down the hallway caused everyone on the balcony to look expectantly toward the door. The captain of the city guard, wearing tan pants tucked into black boots and a black hat with a yellow plume, entered the balcony and bowed deeply, removing his hat as he did so, revealing a balding and sweaty scalp.

"I'm terribly sorry to disturb your meal, Your Majesty," the man blurted, out of breath and red faced. "But I have urgent news for the captain of the house guard."

"Well, out with it, Captain Ganderal," the king said, clearly unhappy about having his meal interrupted by business.

"Perhaps, my liege," Halbert intervened, "it would be best if Captain Ganderal consulted with Captain Taneral elsewhere. I'm sure they can resolve the issue without bothering us."

"Nonsense," the king snapped. "Taneral is taking his supper with us, and then we are all going to the theater—I don't want to be delayed."

"That might be a problem, Your Majesty," Captain Ganderal of the city guard said. "There's been a riot."

Everybody on the veranda stopped what they were doing and stared at Ganderal. He licked his lips and rubbed at his tight dark mustache.

"What? Where?" King Reollyn asked.

"It began in the poor quarter but spread to the art district. Most of the rioters have been contained and jailed," the captain hastily added when he saw the concerned looks on the faces of his leaders. "But others barricaded themselves in the theater—I expect we will have them out shortly, but there will be no show tonight as the performers and the conductor are quiet unsettled by the entire affair."

"This is outrageous!" King Reollyn pounded his fist on the table and stood. "How dare they ruin my night out!" He paced and touched his wig as though he wanted to run his hand through his hair as he considered the news. "I should send the city guard to tear down the shanties from the outer wall in the poor district and drive them all out of the city!" he shouted.

Cremin arched his eyebrows. He'd never seen the king so angry. After the king looked from face to shocked face, he released a breath and plopped back into his seat.

"Number three." He waved in resignation to the page holding his favorite white cat. The page's name was Brekia, but Cremin knew the king would never bother to remember any of their names. Reollyn sighed and began petting the cat. "Captain," he asked, "why have I not heard my subjects are unhappy before today?"

"Umm, Your Majesty, I have reported it to . . . to my superior many times. I'm not sure—"

"Perhaps I can shed some light on this, Your Majesty," the lord steward interrupted Captain Taneral and cleared his throat. "I have received some reports from the captain, but the concerns were of a trivial nature—"

"Trivial?" The king's eyebrows rose, and he sat taller in his seat. "You call a riot that spoils my plans trivial?"

Cremin had to make an effort not to smile. Finally, the king was showing some backbone toward his manipulative lord steward. Halbert was good though, and he adjusted his tactic.

"You are absolutely correct, Your Majesty," Halbert continued. "Clearly we underestimated the discontent of the poor in our city—"

"Why are they discontented?" The king's forehead creased. "We have the most beautiful and sophisticated city in all of Lemuria. I love my people. I throw parties and encourage art and learning. What more could they want?"

In the uncomfortable silence that followed, the two captain's lips were drawn in tight lines, and Halbert scratched at the shadow of whiskers that always darkened his face by the end of the day.

"Well," the king prodded, "what did the reports say they wanted? Why are they rioting?"

"They are poor and hungry, my liege." Halbert used his most placating voice, obviously trying to calm the king. "They are simple minded and don't understand the stresses you face as a king. Some of them accuse us of wasting money on feasts that could be used instead to feed and clothe the poor. But the poor in every city across the continent complain of the same thing. I'm sure you can see why we didn't think the matter important enough to bother Your Majesty."

"How dare they—" The king's voice rose, but he broke off his rant in midsentence as another servant burst onto the balcony followed by a dirty and travel-worn soldier. The servant's face turned white when she realized that the king was on the veranda where she had led the messenger.

"B-Beggin' your pardon, Your Majesty." She bowed several times and backed away as she spoke. "I was told the captain was out here . . . I didn't know you . . . I mean, I'm sorry—"

"Jefson?" Captain Taneral's eyes opened wide. "What's happened? Your regiment should be at the front lines by now."

"Sorry to disturb your meal, Your Majesty—"

"Oh, my meal was *disturbed* long before you arrived," the king said to the disheveled messenger. "Might as well give your report quickly and get it over with."

The man genuflected awkwardly and rolled his hat in his fingers as his eyes darted between the king and Captain Taneral.

"Continue your report, soldier," Taneral said sternly.

"The northern locks on the Tiarak River were impassable for several weeks—sabotaged." The man looked at the captain as he spoke but shot furtive glances toward the king and lord steward. "Seven boats were moored in the river, waiting to pass, and we were ambushed in the night." He licked his lips and twisted his hat. "I regret to report that every boat was destroyed."

"How did an army large enough to destroy seven boats travel unnoticed to the locks and ambush us?" Captain Taneral asked.

"It weren't no army, Captain," he said. "The tracks we found the next morning couldn't have been made by more than twenty men."

"Twenty men?" Halbert shot to his feet. "How did twenty men destroyed seven boats—some carrying complete battalions of soldiers?"

"They attacked at night in a storm using Ba Aven's own fire," he sounded like he was pleading for his life as he tried to explain. "We couldn't put out the flames. Even the water was on fire."

"What was salvaged?" the bald captain of the city guard asked. "How many men and supplies did we lose?"

"Most of the men were able to swim to shore, but we lost nearly all the supplies."

"This will make things difficult on General Prothus and his armies," Captain Taneral of the house guard said. "At least, until we can secure additional boats and supplies, and then pick up the soldiers who are stranded at the docks and send them north."

"Yes, well . . ." the messenger licked his lips and continued rolling his hat in his hands. "I also have word from the general," he said. "A messenger arrived from the front lines the morning I left." The man's eyes darted from face to face.

"Well, out with it," Halbert said.

"The knights of Menet launched a surprise attack while most of the army was sleeping. It was . . . very bad for our troops. By the time they could organize a counteroffensive, the knights had pulled back into the city and secured the gates."

"How many?" Captain Ganderal asked, his voice quiet and his eyes hard. Cremin realized the man probably had friends and family serving in the army up north.

"Nearly five thousand dead and several thousand wounded."

"How could this happen?" The king's face turned red, and he pounded the table again as he stood. "How dare Duchess Wolcott send her knights against us! We haven't attacked her city yet!"

No one said anything about the absurdity of his comment, but the king must've read it in the looks on their faces that he should've expected the ruler of Tiaron to respond when her city was under siege.

"And *what* in the name of Azur is Prothus doing up there?" Reollyn didn't wait for an answer. "He is supposed to be our greatest general, and he wasn't prepared for something like this?"

No one spoke as the king looked from face to face. Captain Ganderal of the city guard looked to the messenger and asked, "How many casualties did the enemy suffer?"

The messenger looked down and said something, too soft for anybody to hear.

"Speak up, man!" the king shouted.

"Twenty-three, my liege," he genuflected to avoid the wrath of his superiors.

Cremin was shocked. He couldn't imagine how a smaller force of knights could inflict so much damage on the Valdivarian army without taking greater losses. Solra, may his name be blessed, was not protecting the armies of Valdivar in this siege.

The king's mouth opened and closed several times before he finally said, "Twenty-three?" He looked imploringly from face to face. "We lost five thousand men, boats, and supplies. How much did we spend on those supplies, Halbert?"

The lord steward pursed his lips. "Nearly four hundred thousand gold valdins."

"How could General Prothus be so careless with my army?"

Again, nobody answered—the king obviously didn't expect an answer.

"Halbert, I want General Prothus back here immediately to answer for his incompetency! Number three," the king dropped into his chair and waved for the page to bring his cat back to him. He visibly relaxed as he stroked the white fur.

"What am I to do?" he asked, and Cremin could tell by his posture and tone that this time he really did want his advisors to answer.

"We still have superior numbers, my liege," Captain Ganderal said tersely. His balding head and face were flush with anger. "I say we order General Prothus to attack. This outrage must not go unpunished!"

"General Prothus?" The king stopped petting the cat and sat up straight. "General Prothus just lost five thousand troops and only killed twenty-three in return."

"If I may, Your Majesty." The blond captain of the house guard bowed, and the king signaled for him to speak. "A direct assault against the city would not be advised. The walls and gates give our enemy the advantage." He held up a hand to forestall Captain Ganderal who looked ready to explode. "But I agree with the captain—Prothus should counter this affront. The general is, after all, the best military mind our country has had in a generation, and I'm sure he can mount a surprise attack of his own. Your father trusted—"

"I don't care what my father did!" The king jumped off the chair sending page number three with the cat reeling backward. Cremin caught Brekia with one hand and the cat in the other before they both hit the ground.

"Oh, *for the love of Azur*, look what you made me do, Taneral." The king's tone instantly changed, and he rushed to take his cat from Cremin. "Thank you number five, for saving my little kitty." He petted the animal, but as he placed it back onto the red pillow, the cat meowed loudly, jumped down, and ran off.

"Oh bother, I've upset her." The king looked to the door where the cat disappeared. "Number three, go and find her." As the page left, the king sat down and said, "I've lost my appetite, and my show is cancelled. What a miserable evening. At least I have my ball next week to look forward to."

"Your Majesty." Halbert cleared his throat. Cremin noticed the man always paid close attention to what was said by others before he revealed his thoughts. He was like one of Cremin's father's glass makers—carefully manipulating the heat and sands until just the right moment to insert his influence and create the bauble he desired. "I believe there is a way to resolve all of these setbacks and still satisfy your well-deserved entertainment needs—it will require a little sacrifice, but nothing we can't afford."

"Go on, Halbert." The king's face lit up for the first time since the captain of the city guard brought news of the riot.

"First, we publically announce that you have magnanimously decided to forgo your state ball next week so the funds can instead be used to feed the poor." Halbert held up a hand to check Reollyn's objection. "Just a moment, allow me to continue, please." The king sighed and waved for him to continue.

"You will still have your celebration," Halbert said conspiratorially. "We'll just keep it to a smaller group—only invite those guests you actually *like*, and bring them here by boat so they aren't parading through the streets."

"Oh, that's much better. Perhaps I won't invite my older sister, Stellarys, and her husband, the Baron Renton. Lately, she's been getting on me to marry. I can just let her think I actually cancelled the affair." He chuckled and clapped his hands together as he thought about this new idea. "The evenings are so lovely now. Perhaps we will have a floating party right on my beach!"

"That would be wonderful, Your Majesty," Halbert agreed. "Now, for the rest of the plan: I will give money to a few of the priests in the poor quarters and inform them of your generosity. That way word will spread to everyone so they will no longer wish to riot."

"I don't see how this plan of yours is going to help with the war effort, Lord Steward," Captain Taneral said, and Captain Ganderal grunted in agreement.

"I'm getting to that." Halbert raised a hand and cleared his throat once more. "We need more recruits to replace those we've lost. What better way to help the poor than by giving them employment?" He smiled and let the idea sink in with the others.

"Are you suggesting we round up poor people off the streets and put them in the army?" Ganderal sounded incredulous.

"Only every male age twelve or over who isn't currently gainfully employed. Think of it," he said with a mischievous smile. "We feed them, we train them for—I don't know—three or four weeks, and then ship them to the front lines."

"That's not long enough to train competent soldiers," Captain Taneral objected.

"We don't need them to be competent, Captain," the lord steward said. "We just need them to get in the way of the first assault from the Tiaron knights—slow them down long enough for our real soldiers to do their job."

"You'll be sending them to their death!" Captain Ganderal protested.

"Oh, isn't that a shame. I guess there will be no one left to riot in our streets or complain about being hungry." He raised an eyebrow and gave them all a self-satisfied smile. The captains looked appalled, but King Reollyn clapped his hands together and said, "I love it! Oh, Halbert, what would I do without you?"

Cremin noticed both captains had to regain their composure at the king's acceptance of this strategy. Cremin was also sure that Solra, may his name be blessed, would not approve of using one's poor subjects in this manner.

"I've suddenly regained my appetite," the king declared. "After supper, I want you to proceed with making the announcement about next week's ball and distribute the money this very night to the priests. Number one and number four, I am in the mood to celebrate. Come to my rooms tonight, and we'll . . . have some entertainment."

APPEASE AND INFLAME

Cremin examined brightly decorated sun runes that hung from a display rack next to the open door of a merchant shop. The glass and ceramic runes outside the shop were small enough to hang unobtrusively from a doorjamb. Just inside the shop, Cremin could see larger sun runes displayed on the wall; some were paintings, some elaborate stained glass windows that could be installed in the homes of the wealthy.

The doorjambs of every home and building that Cremin saw displayed a sun rune for protection. He knew that even the poor, living in makeshift shanties near the outer walls of the city, had painted runes on their doors.

In the palace, paintings, tapestries and stained glass windows with the sun rune were strategically placed, but the king and others of the noble class only appreciated the runes for the sake of art—it was beneath them to actually believe the rune would truly offer some form of protection. But the common citizens nodded their heads in reverence to the runes as they walked inside buildings and homes, and some kissed their fingertips and pressed them against the symbol. It reminded Cremin of Divarlyn, except the citizens of his home city were strict in their observance to the sun runes—even the noble class kissed their fingers and touched the runes in Divarlyn.

"If you're not going to purchase anything, old lady, move along. You're getting in the way of real customers."

Cremin startled when he realized the shop keeper was speaking to him. The man wore a velvet doublet and a stylish hat with a thin, purple feather banded on the side above the brim. After leaving the palace, Cremin had changed into a disguise: a dirty homespun dress and a veil—the attire some women wore to hide their face in deference to the goddess Lunaryn. He didn't think Solra, may his name be blessed, would take offense at him pretending to be a worshipper of the goddess—after all, he was doing the bidding of his father, the Raji Matla, to learn as much as he could of these people to help him secure a treaty that would give *the people* an advantage in the glass trade throughout all of Tiaronea.

He hobbled away from the store, mimicking the gate of an old woman, and looked up the main avenue to the palace at the top of Turoth Hill. Halbert should be coming any moment now. At least, Cremin hoped the lord steward would take this route; it was the most direct course to where he suspected Halbert was going.

The streets here in the merchant district of Valdivar bustled with activity, even though the sun was setting behind the palace. Shouts from across the cobbled road drew his attention. Young men—probably sons of minor nobles judging from their bright, long-tailed suits and powdered wigs—boisterously greeted one another. They bumped their right then left shoulders together and gripped each other's right hand in the air as though they were about to arm wrestle while they laughed.

Some of the shopkeepers were locking their doors as dusk fell, and lamplighters walked up and down the avenue, lighting the tall lamps lining the busy thoroughfare. There weren't beggars or urchins in this part of the city because it was too close to the noble district and the city guard kept them away.

The sound of horse hoofs clacking against stone drew Cremin's attention back toward the direction of the palace, and he breathed a sigh of relief—Halbert was, indeed, coming this way to carry out the task assigned to him by the king. When the lord steward's carriage passed by, Cremin followed it up the crowded street. Fortunately, the press of the evening crowd kept Halbert and his guard from traveling too quickly.

Cremin had walked these streets many times since coming to act as a page to King Reollyn. The other pages spent their free time being pampered in the palace, but Cremin wanted to learn all he could about the people of Valdivar and their customs. So far he hadn't been restricted in his movements as long as he was back to the palace in time to carry out his duties.

The lord steward's entourage headed eastward and gently upward through the city toward the poorer districts. The change was gradual at first. Cobbled streets bordered by shops and beautiful estates made of stone gave way to shops built of wood where the regular people of the city purchased clothing, medicines, food, and other necessities.

A dirt-covered old man in rags with his leg bandaged and a crutch lying on the ground next to him lifted a wooden cup as Cremin shuffled by.

"Spare a copper palin for a fellow worshipper of Lunaryn?" he asked in a shaky voice.

Cremin raised his empty hands and shook his head, wishing he had something to give the man.

"Stop those thieves!" a voice shouted over the general noise of the street. Cremin looked to the source and saw two urchins running between people as they tried to evade an overweight city guardsman.

On the opposite corner, an old man with wispy white hair and a sparse beard stood on a wooden box, crying out to the people to repent and return to the worship of El Azur, lest the city be destroyed. When the lord steward's retinue rode by, the old man shouted at Halbert that the king was leading the people to destruction, but Halbert ignored him.

The shift from the common streets to the slums was rather sudden and drastic. Grimy men and women in ragged clothing lounged about in alleys and on street corners. Shops were closed once the sun set because the lamplighters wouldn't work these streets. The only businesses open now were seedy taverns and inns. This was why Cremin chose to disguise himself as a poor old woman who worshipped Lunaryn—he could pass through most parts of the city without raising much interest. Even here in the slums, people knew he wouldn't have anything of value or interest. Still, he carried a dagger under his dress, just in case.

Now that the streets weren't so crowded, he had to hurry and even take calculated short cuts through small alleyways to keep up with Halbert. But he had a good idea where the lord steward was going—the small Azur temple where the gray-clad priests preached and administered to the poor. There was a larger temple closer to the palace, where the upper class citizenry went for healing and to occasionally worship, but that wasn't the priest Halbert was referring to when he told the king about his plans.

Fortunately, there was a small grotto in a weedy garden area near the temple built by the Sisters of Lunaryn—a cultlike group who worshipped the goddess. As far as Cremin could tell, the worship of Lunaryn wasn't strictly forbidden by the priests of Azur, because she was, after-all, one of El Azur's daughters. Solra, may his name be blessed, wouldn't tolerate such heresy. Sure, he had children—one was even the essence of the moon, like Lunaryn—but true worship was reserved strictly for him.

Cremin walked through the crowd of hungry and sick milling around waiting for the priests to feed or otherwise help them, and walked toward Lunaryn's Grotto. He entered the small garden surrounding it, slipped behind a row of bushes, pulled off his dress and veil, rolled them into a ball and hid them. The clothing he wore underneath was dark and tight. The sun was fully set now, so if he stayed in the shadows, he was pretty certain he could move without being seen.

He crept to the back of the temple and through a service door that opened into a hall leading to the kitchens. He pressed his body against the wall of the hallway before entering the kitchen. He heard voices and the constant clanking of pots and pans, but judging from the dancing shadows that reached the corridor, the only light came from a large fireplace in the far wall.

He peeked around the corner. Three gray-clad, fully shaved priests worked preparing food. One stirred a large kettle that hung above the fire while the other two chopped vegetables and chatted. Cremin moved silently to a large bureau in the kitchen, pressed himself into the shadowed corner, and waited to be sure the men hadn't seen him. From there, he crawled a short distance along the floor to the opposite door and into another corridor.

Once out of the kitchen, he heard voices moving toward him so he slipped into a supply closet, leaving the door slightly ajar until the speakers walked past.

". . . once you take supper to High Priest Chalmer, you are to help me feed the children in the . . ." Their voices faded as they entered the kitchen. That name was familiar, and it only took Cremin a moment to remember— Chalmer was the priest Halbert had met with in a secret room under the palace a few months ago.

A priest left the kitchen, carrying a tray of food, and Cremin slipped out of the closet behind the man. Cremin followed him to the end of the service hall and up a twisting, narrow stone stairway. Cremin desperately hoped no one else would come from the opposite direction, because there was nowhere to hide if they did. He wished he had taken a robe from the supply closet so he could blend in with the priests.

They passed a small landing in the twisting stairway with a closed wooden door. Through a cutaway window with iron rungs, Cremin could see dozens of beggars and homeless women and children milling about a large central room on the other side—this must be the main level, he decided. He checked the door, and it wasn't locked. If he needed to make a quick exit, he could probably get out this way without drawing too much attention. Then again, his skin color and hair would stand out—he seldom saw others of *the people* here in Valdivar, and everybody knew King Reollyn kept one as a page.

He continued up the spiraling staircase, listening to the footsteps of the priest ahead of him, careful not to make noise as he climbed. The footsteps stopped, and the sound of an iron knocker hitting against a metal plate on a door reverberated throughout the stairwell.

"Your dinner, Priest Chalmer," the man said loudly enough to be heard through a closed door. Cremin heard the clicking of a latch and wood scraping across stone.

"Ah, my favorite time of the day!" a cheerful voice said. "Come in, come in." The door closed, and Cremin hurried up the remaining steps, which ended at another small landing with an iron-studded door, behind which he presumed Chalmer, the priest, was taking his meal. There was also a small table underneath an open window that allowed for a cool evening breeze to enter, but there was nowhere to hide, and the serving priest would likely come back out at any moment.

Cremin looked out the open window and took a deep breath to steady his nerves. He'd trained for this, but he still didn't enjoy the thought of climbing out an upper-story window—especially when the ledge was only a hand wide. The ledge continued around the side of the building, being interrupted occasionally by statuary recesses. The street below was dark, but he knew he was at the front of the temple by the din coming from people below. He could barely make out the dark shapes of people walking in, out, and around the temple on the street far below. But there was also a window only ten paces farther along the ledge on the other side of an alcove that held a statue of what he assumed was the image of El Azur looking down at the people.

Cremin climbed onto the ledge and pressed himself against the cold stone wall. You never look down when you're doing this sort of thing. He remembered walking across a rope stretched tightly between two trees for hours during his training when he was younger. You lose your balance when you look down. He shuffled toward the niche with the statue. Fortunately, there was enough space for him to climb inside and around the back of the giant work of stone art. It appeared much larger now that he was standing next to it, than when he looked at it from the street.

Climbing back onto the ledge, he inched his way to the window. He couldn't crouch down to peek inside, because doing so would certainly cause him to lose his balance, but there was no need. The window was open, and the men didn't bother to lower their voices.

"A regiment from the city guard was at the temple until only an hour ago." Cremin recognized the voice; it belonged to a priest. "They took away young men they suspected were involved in the riots and looting. I'd be lying if I told you this was over, Halbert. Azur knows I wish it was, but the people are fed up with the king."

The lord steward cleared his throat. "I share your concern, Chalmer. These are difficult times for our city. The king was furious when he heard about the riots and insisted we send the city guard to clear the streets and drive the poor away. 'Throw the trash out and let them become feed for the vultures,' the king said."

"No!" The priest sounded horror-struck. "You can't let them do it, Lord Steward!"

"Settle down, Chalmer," Halbert said. Cremin imagined the man making soothing gestures with his hands as he tried to calm the upset priest. "I managed to convince the king to try a different approach."

"Go on." The priest said when Halbert didn't say how he had calmed the king.

"I tried to get the king to cancel his scheduled balls and festivities at the palace and instead give the money to the poor. I argued if we used our resources to feed and clothe them, and perhaps work with the city guilds to pay for their men and young boys to be taught a trade . . ." Halbert trailed off and sighed.

Cremin shook his head as he listened. He had heard the conversation at the palace between Halbert and the king, and this wasn't what they agreed to at all.

After a moment, Halbert continued, "But the king came up with a different plan. He said to announce that the balls have been cancelled, and he has a plan to put the poor to work."

"That doesn't sound too bad," the priest said. "Why do you have that look in your eyes, Halbert? I can tell when a man's heart is troubled, and yours is troubled something fierce."

"I'm sorry, Priest Chalmer. I should know I could never hide something from a servant of El Azur such as you."

Cremin thought he would puke if he had to listen to much more of Halbert's disingenuous sentiments. The man was as good a liar as Cremin had ever met.

"The king is still going to have his balls and parties. But he'll keep it secret and be cleverer about how his guests arrive in the city so the commoners don't catch on. And the work he has in mind for the poor is to conscript them into the army and send them to the front lines to . . . to die."

The sound of a fist pounding the table and silverware bouncing against dishes was followed by the priest's angry voice. "That man's heart is darker than Turoth's soul!"

Cremin thought it ironic that the people of Valdivar cursed in the name of the dragon emblazoned on their state flag. If they hated Turoth the dragon so much, why put his image on their flag?

"The riots of today will pale in comparison to what will come if the king enacts this plan," the priest vowed. "I'm sorry, Halbert, but how can we stand idly by and let such things happen?"

"Be at peace, my old friend," Halbert said in a calming tone. "Here's a little money from the treasury. The king doesn't know I took it—he still trusts me—so please keep quiet about where it came from. Once the king has his parties and entertainment to distract him, he will forget all about his plan to ship the poor off to war."

"How can you be certain?"

"I can only promise that I will do all in my power to stop it from happening."

Cremin had heard enough. The citizens of Valdivar had cause to dislike their king, but for some reason, Halbert was doing everything he could to turn their dislike into hatred—hatred that would lead to revolution.

YOU CAN FLY?

Danu placed his hand on S'kata's chest and the Tiaronea Devi Warrior placed his on Danu's in return.

"You always welcome my land," S'kata said in broken common. "You visit Devi family again."

"Thank you. We are honored by your friendship."

They stood next to the tree line of the Tiarak Mountains that marked the border of Tiaronea and Achtland as they said their goodbyes. S'kata and a dozen Devi warriors had accompanied them to ensure their safety. Because most of the warriors had to walk, it took much longer than Danu had hoped.

"I have one more gift for your tribe, S'kata," Lynmaria said as she untied her bags from her white horse. "I think you could make better use of this horse than I."

Danu held up his hand to forestall Kivas's objections, inwardly wondering what the Mage was up to. They still had a long way to travel, and giving up one of the horses would slow them down.

"Mage Lynmaria, you have high honor above all friends." S'kata bowed to her, something Danu only saw him do for Magdka when they had left the camp. "This is great gift. The gods will remember well."

Durham and Kivas said their goodbyes also, not just to S'kata but to all the warriors who had joined them. Danu was surprised to realize he was going to miss these men. Their way of life was simple, but they had accepted the four of them as tribe members and treated them like family.

Once the Devi warriors left, Danu asked, "Why did you give them your horse, my lady?"

"They brought us safely out of the plains and they will make better use of it than I."

"But now we have one less—" Kivas started to complain, but Durham cut him off.

"The Lady Mage can ride my horse," he announced. "I will gladly walk."

Danu had to suppress a smile at the chivalrous manner in which Durham made his offer.

Lynmaria smiled openly and said, "Thank you, good man Durham. However, there is no need for you to walk. I'm certain your horse is strong enough to carry us both."

His face turned red, and Danu saw a flash of excitement in the man's blue eyes, which Durham tried to subdue. He cleared his throat, took the bedroll and bag from her, and helped her into the saddle.

"You honor me, my lady."

Lynmaria nodded graciously and accepted his hand as though it were common behavior between them. Danu coughed to cover up a laugh caused by the dumbfounded look on the face of Kivas. The lieutenant watched the exchange with open mouth and wide eyes and then rubbed thoughtfully at his black beard.

Once Durham had secured the Mage's belongings, he climbed up in front of her, and she held on to his waist lightly.

"Shall we go, gentlemen?" she asked. "If we hurry, we should make the king's road by nightfall."

They made good time and were actually able to travel several miles on the road before dark. Although they were still a good three days' journey from Achtan, they had already come across a detachments of soldiers from the city patrolling for bandits. Danu felt like he could finally relax.

The waning crescent moon wouldn't rise for several more hours and when it did, it wouldn't add much light. Not a good time for traveling, so the men found a small clearing to make camp.

Danu walked to where Lynmaria stood, looking up at the stars.

"You were right, Lynmaria," he said. "I'm glad you stopped us from fighting S'kata and his men. I have the feeling that alliance will prove to be a good thing in the future."

"There is a time for everything, is there not?" she said, still looking at the stars. "A time for fighting and a time for talking; a time for finding new friends . . . and a time for finding new love." That last she said softer and with a wistful smile. Kivas and Durham walked up as she finished speaking, so Danu turned his attention to them.

"Durham, get a fire started. Kivas, set up a tent for Lynmaria."

"That won't be necessary, Lord Danu," she said. "In two days, it will be a new moon, and the people of Leedsdale will have babies to bless during Azur-Aven. Next new moon is midsummer's Azur-Aven, and I'd like to have at least one blessing day to get to know the citizens before the biggest festival of the year." She looked at them and smiled. "I think I'll fly to Leedsdale from here."

"Fly?" Danu said at the same time as the others. "You can fly?"

"Of course," she said and laughed lightheartedly. "I am a Mage after all."

"Well, then why did we need to escort you through the plains?" Kivas asked.

"We didn't escort her," Danu said, understanding dawning on him. "She escorted us."

"I had a feeling you might need assistance," she said with a coy smile.

"So can you see the future?" Durham asked.

"Not exactly, good man Durham," she said fondly. "Perhaps it was the whisperings of the aeon myriad or perhaps just a woman's intuition. Either way, I enjoyed getting to meet each of you. Do be careful during the remainder of your journey."

She smiled and the air around her staff glowed a bright green. With a shimmer, she turned into a white hawk with brown-tipped wings and flew west into the clear night sky toward Leedsdale.

⋈⋈⋈

Raven could see his breath in the cool evening air as he ran through the trees. He climbed every large boulder he saw. He jumped up to every branch sturdy enough to hold him and then did ten pull-ups before dropping to the ground to start running again. He had been doing this for the better part of an hour. His heart was beating fast, and he was breathing deeply and sweating, but he should've been exhausted thirty minutes ago at this pace. He felt like he could easily run for another hour. He loved the extra energy, but it made him a little concerned. He had always had greater stamina than other humans, but this wasn't normal—even for him.

Maybe it was the location. After all, they *were* in the northernmost tip of the Avalian Forest. But that didn't explain the other times he'd done this in the past few weeks. When he had exercised in Bremenon, he credited the spirit of Bremen, the essence of the Bremenon forest, for his additional stamina. But what about the days he spent training in the yard at High Prince Kurulan's castle? To what could he attribute the additional stamina there—Thail's ghost?

He stopped running when he reached the small campsite he and Aleah had set up earlier that evening. She'd been practicing with her new bow—something she did every chance she could—while he trained. She wasn't back yet, so he built a fire and turned his thoughts to something less disconcerting—like supper. He heard a snapping of twigs and rustling of leaves. Aleah wasn't trying to mask her approach.

"Ooh, you are smooth like a panther," she purred as she walked into camp. "I could get used to watching you walk around with no shirt on." She favored him with a seductive smile. Raven felt a little self-conscious because of the big white scar on the center of his chest. The pendant Lumornel had given him, and his rune necklace rested against his exposed skin.

"You look quite alluring yourself," he said with a mischievous grin, pushing his own discomfort aside, "in that tight leather vest over your low-cut shirt. Your long brown hair flowing over your shoulders—it really complements the rabbit blood smeared on your left cheek."

She held her prized bow in one hand and a dead rabbit by the ears in the other.

"Well, someone has to keep us fed." She set the rabbit down and pulled Raven down to kiss her soft, smiling lips.

"There," she said with a laugh. "Now we match."

He realized she'd held his cheek with the same bloody hand that had just held the rabbit.

"Very funny," he said. "I guess we're going to have to take a bath in the stream to clean up."

The idea of making a fire and cleaning the rabbit for dinner was abandoned for an hour while they "bathed" in the river. The late spring runoff was so cold, they spent most of their time on the bank. When Raven finally did get around to making a fire, it was already dark. Aleah skinned the rabbit and prepared it for the fire.

"It looks like we'll need to take another plunge in the river after we eat." Raven was excited at the prospect of bathing with her again. Maybe having extra stamina wasn't so bad after all.

"Very funny." She sounded irritated. "I should've let you clean the rabbit while I made the fire—after all, I am the one who shot it. I shouldn't also have to do the dirty work."

"And judging by where the arrow entered, I'd say it was a pretty good shot. I guess you like that bow?"

"Shot it on the run at over eighty paces." She flashed him a proud smile.

"Wow. Was it a lucky shot?" Raven regretted his attempt at humor when a handful of entrails hit him in the face.

"Looks like you need to bathe again, too."

Later that evening, they relaxed by the fire, and Raven licked the grease from his fingers and took a long drink of water.

"I'd wager that river runs all the way through the Avalian plain to the Ava River," Raven said. "I'd also wager the trading post is near there as well."

"Probably," Aleah answered half-heartedly and sighed.

"What's wrong?"

"Every day we travel is one day closer to the time we'll have to separate."

Raven pulled her close and kissed her on the head.

"I wish we could just forget about duty and all those things Lumornel told us in Forvendale," he said. "I wish we could just stay here and live in this forest."

"There *is* something about these forests," she agreed. "It feels . . . like home. I know that doesn't make sense, but I feel a connection here. I felt it last winter when I came through with Renn."

"Speaking of home." Raven latched on to her comment and decided to dig a little deeper. "Why did you leave your home in Domeria? You were a princess living in one of the most beautiful palaces in all of Lemuria."

"I don't know. I guess I wanted . . . adventure."

"I'm your husband now, Aleah." Raven could tell she was holding back. "You can let down your wall and talk to me."

She stared at him, searching his eyes, and then let out a deep breath.

"My earliest memory as a little girl was watching my older sister, Leandaria, practice with her bow." She smiled wistfully as she recalled the memory. "I wanted to be like her in every way. She was tall and beautiful, smart and strong. But I was always shorter than my sisters and looked different, too. I didn't really fit in. When I was fifteen, a spy who had trained at the temple of K'Thrak fell in love with one of our captains. He turned double agent for us, and I spent a year under his tutelage, in addition to my regular warrior training." She picked up a long stick and stirred idly at the embers in the fire that was nearly burned out.

Raven waited without speaking. He knew she would say more when she was ready.

"I was eighteen when I discovered that Kinled wasn't my real father. I guess I should've been excited to learn my true father was the king of Achtan, but I felt betrayed. I wanted Kinled to be my father, just like he was for my sisters."

Raven didn't wipe the tear that trickled down her cheek. She'd probably be embarrassed by her show of emotion and stop talking.

"Shortly after that, I convinced my mother I would be best utilized as a spy in the court of my father. King Torleif wanted to meet his daughter, even if he wouldn't acknowledge me. Once he realized how useful I was as a spy, scout, tracker—pretty much anything he needed—he asked me to stay as a permanent part of his court. I don't think he even cared that I was passing on state secrets to my mother."

She fell silent, and Raven just held her. He wanted to say something, but he had never been good at giving comfort. He was the silent one who just listened and only gave his opinion when necessary.

"What about you?" Aleah asked. "Is revenge truly the only reason you left Forvendale?"

"Ever since I learned the truth of what happened to my mother, I've wanted to kill Drake Basil," he answered woodenly. He clenched his jaw and stared at the trees.

She looked up, studying his face. "Are you ever going to kill him?"

"I still fantasize about it . . . but probably not."

"I don't believe you."

"What? You think I *will* kill him?"

"Not that," Aleah said. "I think there are other reasons you left the land of the Avuman."

Raven didn't reply.

"You loved Annel. You had your friends, your mother."

Raven took a deep breath and watched the flames of their campfire dance. "Like you, I felt out of place. The revenge I felt for Drake was intense and a convenient excuse to help me avoid facing the other reasons."

"If you loved her, why did you leave her?" Aleah had a strange note of concern in her tone of voice. "Will you leave me one day, too?"

"Never!" Raven said without hesitation. "I will never leave you."

"How can you be sure?"

"Annel is Avuman, Aleah," he said. "She's going to live seven hundred years or more. When I'm an old man, she will still be a young woman. I thought if I left, she would be able to forget me and move on."

"But that didn't happen."

Raven looked up at the stars, then shook his head.

"No . . . no, it didn't." He sighed and looked at her. She still studied his face. "Once Avuman give their heart. . . it's difficult, almost impossible, for them to move on. I had hoped . . ." He left the thought unspoken.

"You hoped that since you were human and both of you were young, it would be different."

Raven hesitated and then nodded.

"I suppose that was it."

They listened to the crack of the fire until Aleah pulled out an instrument of small hollow reeds tied together with twine. She played a slow, pretty melody. She'd taken to doing this occasionally after they left Elder Island.

"Why didn't you ever play that on our journey to Elder Island last year?" Raven asked. He enjoyed listening to the music, and it showed a softer side of her.

"Cole was such a good musician. I guess I was embarrassed."

Raven listened for a little while longer before he said, "But you play from the heart. It's so . . . passionately haunting."

She stopped and cocked an eyebrow. "When did you become a poet?"

He smiled. Her melody perfectly fit his mood—beautiful, yet sad. Just like this night and just like the prospect of having to part so soon.

"We'll be to Anytos in another week," he said. "Another week after that, we'll be to Menet, and then—"

"I don't want to think about it," Aleah cut him off. "Let's just enjoy the time we have now."

Aerik thought that Melista looked like an ugly old cat ready to pounce on her prey.

"I think we all know why I convened this special meeting, gentlemen," she said. The woman stood at the end of the table, leaning forward. "Kahn Devin is dead."

"I rescheduled my Azur-Aven festival just so you could tell me something I already know?" Aerik was in a foul mood after all the secrecy Melista had subjected him and the others to. She stiffened and looked down her nose at him. She, no doubt, considered the Azur-Aven festivals to be beneath the educated and sophisticated class. They barely even celebrated it here in Kah-Tarku.

"Is that the reason for all this secrecy?" Narkash also seemed irritated with Melista's subterfuge. The flag of the Dahka family—a silver centaur shooting a bow on a black field—hung behind him on the stone wall, clearly signifying where he was to sit during this gathering. Melista had written to each of them, insisting on a special meeting, and then once they reached the gatehouse of the city walls, they had all been stopped by the guard and taken through tunnels, back alleys and hidden passageways to a secluded, underground network of rooms. Aerik was pretty certain they were somewhere deep below Melista's palace. Each of their armed escorts were also taken through the tunnels, but their accommodations were in a large underground barracks a short distance from the luxurious rooms he and the other rulers of Kahaal had been assigned. Melista obviously wanted to keep this particular visit a secret.

"Don't you think our own spy networks already informed us of that?" Narkash continued. His blue velvet, long-coat with gold cording elaborately weaved into it rested on the arm of his chair. He had loosened the collar of his white silk shirt, but his ruffled cuffs were still held together by diamond cuff-links and his jewel pommeled sword rested against the wall under his sigil. Aerik shook his head. He had always considered Narkash to be a man of action, but here he was practically dressed like a court dandy. It was all that money from his diamond mines—too much money can ruin anybody. Aerik would take the simple life in Kurulan over the wealth and troubles of these city people any day.

"I assume there is a reason Lamon and his advisors haven't joined us, Melista," Karn Blaylok said as he indicated to the empty chair. The flag of house Devlyn—a green sea serpent on a yellow field with red jagged trim—hung on the wall behind the vacant seat. Karn always got to the heart of things. That was one reason Aerik liked the man. His practical and straight-forward nature was likely a result of his country being a rural land of farms and ranches. Open air and honest work made a man see things straight. It also caused Karn's skin to be a bit weathered—something other nobles looked down on because it meant Karn was frequently working rather than sitting in the shade while others did the work for him. But as far as Aerik was concerned, that was a good thing, too.

"You assume correctly, Karn." Melista nodded to him. She wore a dark green dress with silver thread and pearls embroidered in a circular pattern on the bodice. Her hair was held in a bun atop her head, with a single ringlet falling down her right shoulder. Aerik thought that if she was twenty years younger and had a fuller figure, she might actually be attractive. But she wouldn't last more than a week in the mountains. He smiled inwardly at the thought of her being pounded into the mud by his wife at the games. Now *that* would be a battle he would pay to watch.

The flag behind her seat was a purple field with two diagonal yellow stripes—same as the national flag that loomed large on the wall in the front of the room. The difference was the national flag also bore a crown in the center of the field with five points and three jewels. The five points represented the five rulers, and the three jewels represented the king and his two advisors.

"I think we can all agree on one thing, gentlemen," the high princess of Kah-Tarku continued, "Lamon must not be crowned king when next we meet."

"And you want us to place you on the throne in his stead, Melista," Narkash snarled.

"Actually, I don't." Melista gave them a self-satisfied smile as she looked from face to face. Aerik twisted one of the braids in his beard as he eyed her. She was up to something. You can't know much about a woman's mind; that was something he'd learned long ago. But, when a woman says she doesn't want something you know she's had her eye on for a long time, you'd best be prepared for a conniving plan to follow.

"What then?" Narkash asked. "Are you going to vouch for one of us?"

"Not exactly, but I have a proposal I think will be beneficial to all of us, and most importantly, to the people of our nation." She removed the glove from her right hand, sat down, and took a sip of wine from a long-stemmed crystal goblet that a servant had just handed to her. Aerik was given a pewter tankard of ale—at least they remembered what he liked to drink. Of course, with this lot, he'd rather be drinking whiskey. Maybe he could convince Karn to find a tavern with him after the meeting ended.

"Let's face facts, gentlemen," Melista continued. "If we simply attend our regular standing meeting in three months without a plan, Lamon will almost certainly be named king of all Kahaal. We must have an agreement between us before that time."

Aerik glanced at the men around the table—each eyed Melista with wariness. They didn't trust her as far as they could toss a fat Dahka ram. But he also knew none of them wanted Lamon to become king. When no one disagreed with her, she continued her argument.

"Our laws state that a regent must be confirmed king by a plurality vote of the ruling council or a tie. Lamon already has two votes locked up—his own and the combined vote of his councilors." She looked slowly from face to face and said, "If any one of us votes for him, that gives him three votes, and he is automatically king of Kahaal."

"And without a solid plan, even two votes would likely secure him the throne," Karn confirmed.

"How is that?" Aerik asked. "Two votes aren't a majority."

"*Plurality* of votes," Melista said condescendingly. "Plurality just means he needs more votes than anybody else. In our laws, even a tie secures his bid."

"I'll vote for Karn," Aerik announced. He'd pull on Thail's beard and spit in his face before he was going to let this woman manipulate him.

"And by so doing you would give Lamon the throne!" Narkash snapped. Aerik could feel his face turn red. He felt like slamming Narkash's face, along with his new fancy shirt, into the table. Instead, he picked up his ale and slammed back the rest of the liquid, then held out the tankard for the servant to refill.

"They're right, my friend," Karn said kindly. "If we don't have an agreement going into this thing, it will lead to split votes, giving the throne to Lamon, and—if I judge correctly—civil war." That last he said with a hint of accusation as he gave a hard look to Melista and Narkash. The room fell silent while they considered his words.

"Nobody *wants* war," Melista said, "but I refuse to submit my subjects to his rule any longer."

"I won't commit my cavalry to a civil war," Karn said.

Narkash and Melista's lips pursed, and their eyes narrowed. Aerik was proud that Karn glared right back at them until they looked away.

"What's your offer, Melista?" Narkash's long brown hair was still a bit wild, despite his fancy suit, and his eyes held a glint of steel.

"I will abdicate my throne to my heir, Kahman, and we make him the king."

The room broke out in laughter, Narkash laughing loudest.

Aerik shouted, "I say we make Karn the king."

"I don't *want* to be king, Aerik," Karn said with a scowl. The man took out his pipe and packed it with sweet Domerian tobacco. If Lamon were in the room, Aerik knew his friend would have smoked Devlyn tobacco out of deference to the man.

"Must you smoke that foul thing in here?" Melista said.

"Yes, actually, I must." Karn stood, walked to a torch, and lit a thin, slow-burning stick, which he then used to light the contents of his bowl.

Melista glared at him and waited for the men to settle down before continuing, "I am prepared to offer each of you concessions that I think you will find quite appealing."

"You think you can buy our support?" Karn pulled his pipe from his mouth, and his red eyebrows arched.

"That sounds rather unsavory," she said. "Let's call it . . . favors in exchange for your vote."

Karn rolled his eyes and puffed on his pipe.

"Let's hear it, then," Narkash said. "What are you offering?"

"Karn, you will have free access to the Kuru River from the port at Kiran to your city. No taxes on exports or imports and priority shipping lanes." She waited for a reply, but Karn simply smoked his pipe, practically chewing the end off of it.

"Aerik, you will be given a five percent reduction in all taxes paid to the crown—fifteen percent rather than twenty."

"He already pays less than the rest of us because his economy is so much smaller," Narkash protested, "and I am the one making up the difference."

"And that is why I am offering you the best boon of all," Melista gave him a thin-lipped smile. "Marriage between Kahman and your daughter Kishandra."

Narkash rubbed his chin and stared at her. He narrowed his eyes, harrumphed and said, "I have a different proposal. I will grant the same boons you propose, but we name *me* king. You will have your marriage with Kahman and my daughter to strengthen your position."

"Kah-Tarku is the capital city of our kingdom and the center of education and commerce," Melista said, "and Kahaal Tarkulan himself, my ancestor, unified and established our government. It is natural and the correct order of things to bring the seat of the king back where it belongs."

"That's not a good enough reason." Narkash said.

"I thought you would feel this way, Narkash." Melista smiled and smoothed her dress. "The simple truth is you don't trust my ambition. None of you do." She looked around the room.

Aerik folded his arms and leaned back. Melista was right about that. Nobody in the room trusted her.

"By the same token, I don't trust your ambition, Narkash, and I am fairly confident Aerik and Karn don't, either."

She had a point there, too. Aerik didn't trust either of them, and he knew from conversations with Karn that his friend from Blaylok didn't, either.

"I will step down and act as an advisor to Kahman," Melista said. "I will have some influence, but only half of what the rest of you will have. Are you willing to limit your power, Narkash? If we make you king, what assurances do we have you won't remake our entire culture to your liking?"

Narkash glared at her, but Aerik knew he was considering her offer.

"We don't have to agree to my terms right now, gentlemen," Melista said as she pulled out three envelopes and handed one to each of them. Aerik's name was written on the front of his envelope in calligraphy and sealed with purple wax and Melista's imprint. "The complete details of my offer are outlined in these letters. In three months' time, our laws dictate we must officially inaugurate a king. Arrive two days before that meeting so we can finalize our agreement. If you have changes, I will entertain them at that time. Until then, I bid you farewell. In the words of the merchants' guild: may your dealings be profitable."

AN AXE FOR AN EYE

The cool blue light from Renn Demaris's staff cast a soft, steady glow on the hewn, rock walls of the vault he and Harlow were standing in. They'd explored here before, but today his curly, dark-haired friend was excited and secretive. When Demaris had successfully passed his Sorcerer tests earlier today, he told Harlow he wanted to get away from the other students for a while. Harlow's face lit up, and he anxiously led Demaris to the secret catacombs beneath the library. Demaris was told to "wait" or "trust me" when he questioned his friend about it.

"When are you going to tell me what you're so excited about?"

"Okay, Renn," Harlow whispered, looking around to make sure they were alone—as if anybody else would be there.

"Demaris," Renn corrected him. "Call me Demaris."

"Oh yeah, sorry, Renn—I mean, Demaris." Harlow looked over his shoulder again and the excitement returned to his eyes. "You know how I like to study, and I *really* like reading about Greyfel the Wizard and all his adventures. Did you know one time he snuck into the Cragg Caves and stole a powerful sword? Well he did, but I'll tell you that story another time—"

"Harlow," Demaris interrupted. "Get to the point."

"Oh yeah, sorry." He smiled sheepishly. "So I skipped a class the other day and was going through that old chest of leather-bound books." He pointed at the chest made of smooth black wood they had discovered the last time they came here. "I found this." He held up a small leather tome that was sealed with a rune-embossed iron lock.

"What is it?" Demaris narrowed his eyes and ran his fingers over the cover of the ancient book.

"A diary written by the Whitestone Wizard," Harlow said with a huge grin, barely able to contain his glee.

Demaris wrinkled his brow and cocked an eye toward Harlow. "Umm, who is the Whitestone Wizard?"

"What? You've never heard of him?" Harlow looked genuinely shocked. "He was the nephew of Greyfel's closest friend, Shandizar."

"Harlow, how could you expect anybody to know that? People don't even know about Greyfel's friends, let alone his friends' nephews." Demaris was growing irritated. "So do you need me to remove the warding on the lock or something for you?"

"No, I can do that." Harlow drew in power from the aeon myriad and let it flow into the rune on the locking mechanism. Demaris could see the flows with the aid of his staff, and he instinctively understood the way Harlow instructed the intelligences of the aeon myriad to function.

"I'm impressed," he said. "That was a delicate spell. I thought you said you weren't any good at magic."

"I asked Devera to show me that one, and I worked on it for days," Harlow answered. "A lot of books are warded, and this is usually the best way to remove the spell."

"So you can learn to use the lore if you really put your mind to it?"

Harlow's face grew red with apparent embarrassment, and he shrugged his shoulders. "I guess, but that's not what I wanted to show you." Harlow flipped to a page near the middle of the tome. "Listen to this: *My uncle said the great one sealed many important treasures in the belly of the earth at the seat of learning.*" Harlow's eyes practically glowed as he looked expectantly at Demaris.

"Treasure sounds good," Demaris said, "but the rest of it sounds like gibberish."

"Don't you see?" Harlow waved his free hand through the air. "Greyfel founded this school, and we are standing in catacombs under the ground . . . the *belly of the earth*."

Demaris's imagination came to life as it dawned on him what Harlow was saying.

"So Greyfel buried important treasures here." Demaris looked around the room with a new sense of wonder.

"And what is the greatest treasure Greyfel ever possessed?" Harlow prompted.

Demaris thought for a minute while his friend looked at him with eager eyes. "Well, I already have his staff, so . . . I don't know. You're the one who studies so much; you tell me."

Harlow grinned, looked around again, drew closer to Demaris, and whispered, "The Godstone."

Demaris raised his eyebrows. "You think the Godstone is down here somewhere?"

"Shh!" Harlow held a finger to his lips and looked around once more.

"*For the love of Azur*, Harlow, we're three levels below the library," Demaris said. "Nobody can hear us."

"You can never be too careful," he said, still barely speaking above a whisper. "We're talking about the most powerful talisman in the history of the world, Renn, and based on my research, I *really* think it's down here somewhere."

Demaris studied his friend. Harlow had never been more serious—or more excited—in his life.

"It's Demaris."

"What?"

"You called me Renn again."

"Oh, yeah. Sorry, Renn—I mean, Demaris."

"What are we waiting for, then?" Demaris asked with a sly grin. "Let's find the Godstone."

"Now?" Harlow sounded surprised.

"Why not?"

"Don't you need to get back for the celebration feast? You and the others who advanced today are being honored, you know."

"I know, but we have a few hours before that, and I don't want to mill about before the eating starts and listen to people go on about it," Demaris said.

"Well, you *are* the fastest student to reach the level of Sorcerer—ever."

Demaris clutched the staff of Greyfel a little tighter. He'd heard rumors that some of the lore masters wanted to take his staff away until he became a Wizard. They thought it helped him learn faster, and his latest achievement would only add wood to that fire.

"Exactly," Demaris said. "Maybe I should intentionally slow down for a while."

Harlow scrunched his brows, looking at Demaris like he was crazy.

"Come on." Demaris walked toward the door on the far side of the chamber. "We've already searched every corner of this room. Let's go find the Godstone."

The room wasn't a perfect square. The walls sunk inward with alcoves at some places and jutted forward at others. At the far side of the room, the walls narrowed into a foyer with a cabinet on the right wall that displayed spears, swords, and battle-axes. Demaris led the way, holding the light. But as he walked into the foyer and reached for the iron door handle, a rope on the ground at his feet came to life and lashed him to the wall.

"Look out!" Harlow shouted. Demaris looked up just as his friend reached for the handle of a large battle-axe flying directly at his head. A flash of intense pain seared the right side of his face, and his head cracked against the rock wall he was lashed against.

"Renn! Are you okay, Renn?" Harlow was frantic, and his voice sounded to Demaris like he was miles away. The pain was so incredible he couldn't focus on anything else.

Demaris closed his eyes. "Not Renn," he whispered. "Demaris . . ." Then the pain pulled him into unconsciousness.

"What were you thinking, Gendul!"

Gendul had never seen Salas so angry—and he'd known the man for many decades, so that was saying something.

"I was only trying to catch whoever was trespassing in the catacombs," he said with as contrite a look and voice as he could muster. "I don't know how that axe fell onto the boy. I only placed a spell on the ropes to tie up the first person who stepped near it."

That was a partial truth. He did place a spell on the rope to latch a person to the wall, but he also used some of the boy's hair to make sure it would only be set off by Demaris, and he also attached the spell to the axe so it would be pulled toward the rope.

"If it weren't for the quick actions of Harlow," Salas said, "Demaris would most likely be dead right now!"

And *that* was the real problem. Harlow, the boy who was clumsy and awkward, actually grabbed the axe handle as it flew toward his friend and slowed the momentum enough so it didn't do the job properly. What was he going to tell Shamael? He'd never be able to kill the boy now without raising suspicion.

"*Thanks be to Mag* . . . er, *Azur* that the boy had the wherewithal to stop that axe." Gendul nearly thanked the old goddess instead of El Azur, but now wasn't a good time to aggravate Phaedra. She was standing behind Salas with her hands on her hips, looking like a storm cloud ready to burst.

"How could the axe simply fall with that kind of force?" she said over Salas's shoulder.

Gendul felt sweat drip down his back and kept his expression and voice grief-stricken and remorseful as he answered. "Perhaps the vibration of my trap being set-off caused it to fall—"

"IT WOULD HAVE SPLIT HIS HEAD IN TWO IF NOT FOR HARLOW!" Phaedra pushed past Salas. Gendul closed his eyes and shrunk back from her anger. She took a calming breath and said, "It would take a hard strike to do that kind of damage." She took a step forward and looked hard into his eyes. "I don't believe that axe simply fell," she punctuated each word of her accusation, and Gendul felt his face lose all color. He dropped his mouth in feigned shock and disbelief.

"You can't be suggesting that I . . . that I tried to hurt somebody with the trap?" Gendul looked at the two lore masters with imploring eyes. "I may have my faults, but I would never intentionally hurt anybody."

"Gendul, were you intoxicated when you set the trap?" Salas gave him a way out. It wasn't a good one, but it was the only believable excuse and so he ran with it.

"I . . . I . . . Well, I only had a little . . ."

"You set up a trap while you were drunk!?" Phaedra's face turned bright red.

Salas's shoulders slumped, and he shook his head. He plopped into his overstuffed chair. "I thought we agreed you would quit imbibing, my old friend."

Gendul, in fact, hadn't drank since returning from his meeting with Shamael, but better to let them think him a hopeless drunk than a murderer.

"I suppose it's possible for a spell to spill over to nearby objects," Gendul said quietly, "but I was careful, and I wasn't *that* intoxicated—"

"Obviously you were, and a boy has lost his eye because of your loathsome dependence on spirits," Phaedra hissed.

That was good. It appeared they believed him. Still, how was he going to kill the boy now without being the primary suspect? How was he going to forestall Shamael from harvesting the marked children of Concordia? How was he going to protect his daughter?

"Phaedra, will you please ask the boy to come in?" Salas sounded defeated.

Phaedra glared at Gendul as she brushed past him to the door of Salas's personal study where they were gathered. She opened the door and told the boy with dark curly hair to join them. His face was stained with tears, and he shook visibly as he fidgeted with his robe. Gendul wouldn't be surprised if the teen had wet himself while he was waiting outside the door.

"Harlow, I want you to tell me what you and Demaris were doing in the catacombs," Salas said kindly.

"*I* want to know how you found it in the first place," Phaedra interrupted. "It was that staff of his, wasn't it? I'm beginning to think Tova is right. We should take Greyfel's staff from Demaris until he passes his Wizard exams."

"No, i-it wasn't like that," Harlow stammered. "I followed Master Gendul several weeks ago. I mean, I wasn't spying or anything. I was just reading in the corner and I heard noises like somebody fell into some books and I looked up and it was Master Gendul and then he opened the secret door, so I wanted to see—"

"Slow down, son," Salas said.

Both Salas and Phaedra gave Gendul a withering look. Not only had he nearly killed Demaris, but it was his fault the boys found the secret catacombs to begin with. This was not going well.

"Okay, so tell me why you kept returning," Salas said. "What were you looking for?"

The boy's body shook even more than before, and tears streamed down his red cheeks. Gendul actually felt pity for the boy, even though he did ruin everything.

"I didn't mean for anything bad to happen. I'm sorry. I promise we won't go in there anymore, and we won't ever tell anyone about the secret entrance. I just wanted to explore and find interesting things, and it was my fault Demaris learned about it, and I was the one who told him to come with me today, and now he's going to miss the celebration dinner and—"

"Harlow!" Salas's voice was sharp as he cut the boy off, and the teen closed his mouth with an audible click. "Is this why you've missed so many classes with Devera? To explore where no student should go?"

The boy's face lost all color, and his chin shivered. "I just love studying about history and learning about ancient artifacts. I . . . I'm not good with spells, so I'd rather be in the library."

"And what were you boys looking for today?"

Harlow licked his lips and looked nervously at each of the lore masters. "I found the Whitestone Wizard's diary—you know, the nephew of Shandizar, Greyfel's closest friend."

"I know who he is," Salas replied, "but I confess I'm surprised you do."

"Oh, studying about Greyfel's life is my favorite of all. Did you know that one time he—"

"Not now, Harlow," Phaedra interrupted him. "We all know about the adventures of Greyfel. Tell us more about the diary and what you two were up to."

"Oh yeah, sorry. Well, I read the diary a few times, and one passage really got me excited—"

"Was this diary not warded or locked?" Salas interrupted.

"Umm, well, yes."

"And who helped you remove the warding?"

"Oh, I did that all by myself." The boy was obviously proud of that fact.

"I thought you said you are not good with spells," Salas said. "That particular spell isn't taught until you become an Enchanter and you are still an apprentice."

"And not a very good one at that," Phaedra added.

"I really wanted to read the diary, and so I asked Devera about the spell and then found a book in the library that had the spell in it, and I studied and practiced for days until I could do it. It's the only spell I can do well."

"Probably because it's the only spell you put your mind to," Phaedra said.

"Show me this diary and the passage that excited you so," Salas said, holding out his hand. Harlow slowly reached into his robe and removed an ancient leather tome. He opened it to a page near the middle and showed it to the High Wizard. Salas read the passage and handed the diary to Phaedra.

"And just what artifact do you believe Greyfel has hidden in the catacombs?"

Harlow said something so soft none of them could hear.

"Speak up, child," Phaedra said.

"The Godstone," Harlow mumbled and looked at the floor.

Salas and Phaedra exchange a thoughtful look, and Gendul realized they actually believed the boy was right.

Salas cleared his throat. "Harlow, did you know that we used to have a librarian?" The boy looked up, he looked confused, and shook his head.

"It's true. However, he died a few years back, and Gendul has been keeping things tidy in the library until we find a replacement. So it seems we have only two options for your punishment."

Harlow's eyes widened, and Gendul could see him shaking again.

"The first option is to expel you from the school and send you back home."

"No, please! I'll do anything. I'll scrub dishes and wash the bathrooms, but please don't send me away—"

Salas raised his hand for silence. "Or you can train to become our new librarian. Of course, you'll have to reach the level of Sorcerer before you can officially be named the librarian of Elder Island."

This time, it wasn't just Harlow who dropped his mouth and stuttered. Phaedra joined in, and Gendul had to cough to cover up his laughter.

"Salas, you can't be serious. He's . . . he's just a boy and not a good student—"

Salas held his hand up until the room went silent once more. "If you choose to become our librarian, Harlow, you must commit to at least ten years of service. Are these terms agreeable to you?"

"Yes, yes! Of course! This is the best thing that's ever happened to me!"

"Oh, and no more visits to the catacombs unless you are accompanied by Gendul."

That's just what Gendul needed—a job babysitting this kid. Salas was probably doing it as a punishment to him. Well, at least he wasn't being sent away. Maybe he could think of something else to offer Shamael to protect the people of Concordia.

"Can I go see Renn now?" Harlow was obviously excited to share the news of his good fortune with his friend. Salas smiled and waved him to leave.

"And Harlow," the high lore master said as the boy ran for the door. The boy stopped and turned around. "Best you keep quiet about the catacombs below the library." As Harlow reached for the door handle, Salas added, "By the way, you saved your friend's life today. I'd say that makes you a hero."

Genea wrung her hands as she watched Daria apply an ointment to Renn's wounds. Next, the lore master held the tip of her staff close to Renn's injuries and called on the powers of the aeon myriad to help with healing. The massive gash that started at his hairline, went over his right eye, and down his cheek grew closer together. It didn't seal entirely, but the gash was thinner than before and looked less swollen. His eye, however, had to be removed—it had been damaged beyond repair, despite the lore master's best efforts.

"How long before he wakes?" Genea asked.

"It's difficult to say." Daria was beautiful with dark hair, smooth skin the color of milk, and bright red lips. Genea had heard that the woman was in her sixties, but she appeared to be barely past twenty. "The mind is a complex thing, and when I tried to probe his, he subconsciously created a wall to keep me out. It was . . . blue."

"The shield around his mind was blue? What does that mean?"

Daria looked at Genea and shrugged. "Maybe that's his favorite color," she said with a hint of a smile. "He will wake when his body and mind are ready. You also need to get some rest, Genea. Don't worry. I'll send someone for you if I think he's about to wake."

"Well, it's not like that . . . I mean, so what if he wakes up when I'm not here? It makes—"

"Genea, lies are never good. But when we lie to ourselves, we steal from our happiness." She gave her a patronizing smile.

Genea was about to protest when somebody barged into the infirmary.

"Is Renn awake? How is his eye? Did you fix it? I can't wait to tell him—"

"Slow down . . ."

"Harlow," he supplied and gave Daria an awkward bow.

"Demaris is sleeping now," Daria said. "It's what he needs most, so try to be a little less . . . disorderly."

"And why are you so happy anyway?" Genea could feel the blood rising in her cheeks. "Renn just lost an eye, and his face is going to be scarred for life! And it's *all your fault!*"

Renn stirred when she shouted, and the lore master glared at her.

"The least you can do is show a little concern," Genea whispered angrily.

"Hang on," Harlow protested. "I saved his life! Don't I get any credit for that?"

"Saved his life?" Genea sounded incredulous. "Oh, because you ran back to the castle crying that Renn was hurt after you were horseplaying in the mountains and Renn tripped and hit his head on a rock? If you would have brought him to the celebration like a real friend would've done, this wouldn't have happened!"

"What are you talking about? We didn't go to—"

"It's all right, Harlow," Daria broke in before he could finish his rebuttal. "Salas told us how Demaris was hurt in the woods and your quick actions saved him."

Harlow stared at the lore master with his mouth hanging open.

"I still say you should have made him come back to celebrate his advancement with the rest of us." Genea folded her arms and gave him her best glare.

"Well, he wanted to get away from everything for a while. I guess . . . I thought the mountains would be peaceful."

Why was he acting so weird? Harlow gave Daria a strange look, and she just nodded and smiled at him.

"Off to your rooms, both of you," the lore master said. "I'll send a runner to each of you when he wakes."

BURDENS OF RULE

Danu breathed deeply, enjoying the aroma of King Torleif's garden combined with the glass of Boranica red he swirled in his hand. Bees flew busily in the warm air from blossom to blossom gathering nectar. Danu realized this was the first time he'd felt at peace for months. Even telling Torleif and his grandmother the part of the journey where Artio died felt freeing because his audience knew the Mage intimately and loved him.

"That is quite a tale, Lord Danu," the young king said.

"It saddens my old heart to think of Artio dying on the plains," Torleif's grandmother said. She looked as stately as ever, though more frail than when Danu's party passed through Achtan more than six months ago. In one hand, she clutched the letter Danu had given her from her granddaughter Tristan; in the other, she gingerly held a cup of hot tea. Torleif read his letter from Tristan and gave it to a servant to be delivered to his study for safekeeping.

"I find it almost poetic," the old woman said, "that Artio's replacement saved your lives on the same plains where he died. She sounds wise. I should very much like to meet her."

"Aye," Durham rumbled. "She is wise *and* beautiful."

The queen mother arched a slender brow and looked down her nose at Durham. Danu knew she didn't entertain common soldiers and was probably surprised that he would speak, uninvited, in her presence. Danu was surprised as well. Durham was a quiet man. Both he and Kivas would have been more comfortable relaxing in a tavern while Danu paid this official visit to the king without them, but Torleif insisted the entire returning party join him and his grandmother at the castle.

By the look in Durham's eyes, he was likely lost in thought about the new Meskhoni. Kivas, on the other hand, was comfortably lost in his large stein of ale. He had already emptied one, and a servant replaced it with a new stein before the lieutenant could mourn the lack of liquid in the first. At least it was only ale and not something stronger.

"Will you and your men stay with us for the midsummer's Azur-Aven celebrations, Lord Danu?" Torleif asked. "Or must you return to your own lands to officiate in yours?"

"The latter, I'm afraid, King Achal." The young king cringed at the honorific, and Danu smiled as he sipped his wine. He genuinely would like to stay for a time and spend the holiday in Achtan, but he missed his people, and they needed to see him after all these many months of travel. "As much as we enjoy the comforts of your hospitality, we must leave in the morning so we can arrive in time."

"I am sorry to hear that, but I understand."

"It saddens me, too," Kivas said. "It isn't every day a man can drink his fill of the king's own ale without spending a copper scheling."

The king laughed loudly and slapped his leg. "No, I guess not." He shook his head and said, "I hate to turn our conversation to matters of state, but since you are leaving so soon, I may not have another opportunity." He glanced toward Kivas and Durham.

"You may speak freely in front of them, Your Majesty." Danu grinned as the young king gave him a withering look. He knew Danu enjoyed torturing him with formal titles.

"My . . . network reports that King Kimael Boran's nephew has fallen ill and grows frailer every day."

That wasn't good news—the boy was the king's only legitimate heir.

"The king spends little time on state matters," Torleif said, "because he is preoccupied with his nephew's condition."

Danu realized this was Torleif's polite way of saying the king was neglecting the affairs of the kingdom. King Boran had always been a good and strong king, but matters of the heart could make the strongest man vulnerable.

"Your father," the king's grandmother said, "is watching these matters with great interest." Her tone was pleasant, but Danu saw the innuendo in her comment. Torleif's spy network believed Danu's father might have intentions of taking advantage of the king's weakening position.

Danu pursed his lips and nodded. "Then indeed, it is best that my men and I leave in the morning."

The cliff looked impossibly high as Raven studied the lift from the deck of the riverboat. He was amazed each time he watched it carry people, animals, and even wagons a thousand feet up the vertical rock face to the city of Anytos. He looked at his wife to comment about it, but she was staring, with longing in her eyes, toward the forest to the east—Avalian. She was compelled by it daily. Now that he knew her heritage, he understood why. The blood of the Avalian ran strong in her veins—distant, but strong nonetheless.

He nudged Aleah and pointed her to the gangway. It was their turn to disembark, so they picked up their packs and walked down the wooden ramp.

"There are a lot more soldiers at the base," he observed, "probably due to the war." They'd heard the rumors that a war had broken out between Valdivar and the city-states as they traveled down the river.

"Just because I've been watching the forest, doesn't mean I'm blind, Raven," she sounded irritated. "I can see there are a lot of soldiers."

"I wasn't suggesting otherwise," he said, "I just don't want to be recognized. I'd like to pass through Anytos as quickly as possible so we—" He stopped talking as a soldier holding a helmet with a captain's plume rising from the top walked up to them.

"Captain Raven," the man said. "Welcome back to Anytos. King Mytton would like to see you. I have already taken the liberty of sending a messenger pigeon with a note informing His Majesty that you have arrived."

Raven looked at Aleah and rolled his eyes. She shrugged her shoulders and smiled.

Wait a minute, Raven thought, raising an eyebrow and looking back to the messenger. *Did he say* King *Mytton?*

The king was meeting with Captain Andon in his war room when Raven and Aleah were ushered in an hour later. More than a dozen maps were opened on the table. Various objects rested in locations Raven realized represented troop locations.

"Ah, Captain Raven and Aleah," King Bendigo Mytton said as they were escorted into the room. "So nice of you to join us." He wore tight cream-colored hose tucked inside black riding boots, and a gold doublet.

Captain Andon's plumed helm rested on one end of the table, and the hatchet faced man looked up from the maps he was studying. Danu once said the man's pointed nose, wispy brown hair, and thin mustache made him look like a rat—Raven smiled at the memory.

"Thank you for honoring us with a personal invitation, King Mytton."

"So," the king smiled and looked back and forth at the two of them, "are congratulations in order or condolences?" Their faces must have looked confused, because the king and Andon burst out laughing.

"I'm sorry, but I seem to be missing something," Raven said. He wasn't sure if he should be concerned at the private joke or relieved.

"Danu was here several weeks ago, and he told us of the battle you lost," Andon said. "he said you fought with this beautiful female warrior and lost your heart."

"I saw it coming, you know," Mytton said conspiratorially. "I could see it in Aleah's eyes every time she gazed at you."

Raven looked at his wife. She glared at the king with her lips pursed and a hand on her hip.

"And the great Captain Raven," Mytton continued, "who sees every-thing, was completely blindsided. The hunter became the hunted and lost the battle."

This, at least, made Aleah smile.

"So tonight we will celebrate your union." Mytton looked at them and raised a single eyebrow. "Do I need to call for a priest to perform a marriage ceremony?"

"That's already been taken care of, thank you," Aleah said.

"Great, then tonight we celebrate, and tomorrow you can take your new positions as captains in my city guard."

Raven looked at Aleah. He was pretty sure his own expression mirrored hers. They didn't have time for this, and neither was sure quite what to say.

"I know it isn't what you want to do, but you are in my country, and I'm at war. I need you both. Lord Danu refused to help, but I can't very well conscript King Boran's second cousin into service. You two, on the other hand, are soldiers—soldiers who are needed here."

Aleah looked at Raven. Her eyes communicated volumes to him, and then she nodded once.

Raven turned back to the king and said, "Actually, my wife is Princess Aleah of Domeria, fourth daughter to Queen Leandril."

"Nice try," the king said with a mock grin. "I suppose Raven is Danu's secret brother, too."

"Half brother, actually," Raven said. They looked at Mytton and Andon without breaking eye contact for several moments.

"You're telling the truth, aren't you?" The king laughed and shook his head. "*For the love of Azur*, how many more secret nobles are hiding out with Lord Danu?"

"Just us, I think," Raven said.

"I'm sorry, King Mytton." Aleah stepped forward and held out her hands. "We would like to help you, but we both have urgent business to attend to in our home countries. We really must leave as soon as possible."

The king twisted at his waxed mustache and paced. He shook his head, turned to a window and looked out to his courtyard and city beyond. Raven and Aleah caught each other's eyes and waited.

"Perhaps there is a way we can help each other," the king turned to them. "I have a valuable caravan of supply wagons leaving tomorrow for

Menet where they will be transferred to the river and sent to the front at Tiaron. The Devi tribes have been raiding our supply roads, and this is a prime target. I can't afford to send Andon or his squad captains with the caravan. So if the two of you will lead a team of soldiers to make sure it arrives safely, I will consider your service to my country satisfied."

Raven shared a glance with Aleah, then said, "That sounds fair. We'll both accompany the caravan to Menet. I will continue with your wagons until they reach the front, but Aleah will be turning south to Domeria at Menet."

The mountain reverberated with the sharp ping of hammers striking metal. Triaklon could smell the acrid aroma of steel being forged, but the pungent odor of tanning leather was overpowering. Fletchers and bowyers made crossbows and bolts, and weaponsmiths made spears, swords, and shields that could strap to the forearm.

In only a few short months the camp had turned into a village. The various craftsmen and their apprentices had set their shops in a row. It turned into a road with each trade working side by side, trading with each other for goods and services. Bartering was slowing them down, Triaklon realized; he would need to establish some form of currency. When did he start thinking about things like that?

"I thought you were crazy." Skunk ran his fingers through his red hair while he watched a cobbler tap nails into the sole of a boot inside his makeshift shed. They would need to improve these buildings before winter. In the Cragg Mountains, snow could begin falling in another three months—four, if they were lucky. "But boys are learning trades, and we are acting like a real village," Skunk said.

Triaklon tried to walk through this part of the village a few times each week to see how things progressed. Once the men resumed working in their former trades, they'd found purpose to their lives again. The women among them were sewing, teaching children, cooking, and tending gardens and shops. For the most part, they were good people who had fallen on hard times at a point in their life and made a mistake. For that, they had lost their right hand, and society cast them out. What a loss of talent and resources. They had everything they needed to make a thriving village here in the mountains, as long as the Nortian lords left them alone long enough to get established.

"Come on, Skunk," Triaklon said. "Let's see how our prisoner is doing." They walked past the last trade-smith shanty and then another five hundred paces to a one room cabin. It was the most solid building in the entire mountain village. It had to be—it served as a jail. By far the thing he liked least about being a leader was judging and punishing those who caused problems in their small community. It couldn't be helped though. He'd have to write down a code of laws and make sure everyone understood the consequences of breaking those laws.

When they reached the cabin, Triaklon opened a small pass box and placed fruit and bread into the cell for the prisoner.

"Glavin, you awake?" There was no answer. "Glavin!" Triaklon yelled.

"I'm awake, you hypocrite."

"Still upset, I see." Triaklon had no choice. Glavin was one of his closest friends, but he was caught trying to steal one of the lambs.

"How long are you going to keep me locked up in here, Triak?" Glavin said. "I'm your best friend, *for the love of Lunaryn!*"

"You tried to steal a lamb, Glavin," Triaklon said wearily. "If you did that in any other village, your body would be swinging in a tree at the end of a rope, and your soul would be resting in Valhasgar."

"I was drunk!" The prisoner said each word with emphasis, grabbed hold of the iron bars in the lone window, and looked out at them. Glavin hadn't shaved or bathed in two weeks. He looked haggard and smelled worse.

"Skunk, ask Bull to bring a barrel up here with water so Glavin can wash himself."

"Why don't you just let me out of here, and I'll wash in the river?"

"You know I want to let you out, Glavin, but I have to be consistent. If I let you get away with trying to steal sheep, I'll lose the respect of everyone else."

"C'mon, Triaklon. You and I are like brothers. *By Aven*, I fought by your side more than once. I helped you build this place, *for Azur's sake*. Show some mercy."

"You aren't swinging from a tree, and you still have one hand left," Triaklon was growing angry. Glavin should be one of his top officers, not his biggest problem. "That's more mercy than you'd get from any other ruler."

"Oh, I see. The Great Triaklon is my ruler. He can cast me away just like a real king."

"If I don't hold you accountable for your actions Glavin, then I truly would be like the lords you despise." He realized he was shouting, so Triaklon took a calming breath and then continued in an almost pleading tone. "In our society, everyone will receive equal treatment under the law." Glavin stared back at him through the short iron bars. "We need you, Glavin. *I* need you. I won't leave you in here any longer than I must, but your current attitude isn't helping matters."

With that, he turned and walked away. Skunk followed, and Triaklon asked, "Am I doing the right thing? Locking up one of my closest friends?"

"I don't know . . ."

"But?"

"Well, I have heard others talk about it. I think you have the support of the people in this. They believe you will be a fair leader."

They continued walking in silence. This is why he shouldn't have agreed to be their leader, but it was too late to turn back now.

LEKIAH'S STAND

Avaris adjusted the angle of his canoe—just enough to slide past a large boulder protruding from the Andrus river and through a short span of rapids. Constant navigation of the water was instinctive for him, even though this was the first time he'd traveled this part of the river. In fact, for the past several days, everything was new. He had never been south of the Mord Mountains before today.

Here on the plains, rapids were infrequent and mild. And although he'd never been to these grasslands before, the landscape quickly grew familiar. Day in and day out, reeds, cattails and herds of bison slid by either side of the river as he made his way east. The right side of the river—the southern side—was Dekla and to his left was Andrika. They looked identical.

Occasionally, he saw small groups of various Devi tribe members getting water, washing clothes, fishing, or simply bathing in the river. Most just looked at him with curiosity; some called out to him, and he would wave as he cut through the waters. It wasn't uncommon for a young Devi warrior to canoe through the Andrus, so when he came across these groups, he wasn't too concerned.

Had Kintara been in the canoe with him, it would've been an entirely different matter. A pretty, white-skinned woman with dark, black hair riding in a canoe with a Devi boy would be cause for much speculation. But he only saw Kintara a few hours each day. She would return from scouting long enough to give him his daily lessons in common tongue and drink the bitter tea she made twice each day. After that, he would camp for the night, get up with the dawn, and start downriver once more.

Lekiah and Kalisha had parted ways with him six days ago. Once the Andrus River broke out of the mountains and into the open plains, his sister and oath-brother hid their canoes, took what supplies they could carry, and headed southwest—toward the southern end of the Mord Mountains, where the Wanderove Divide follows the foothills south to the border of Tiaronea. When they left, Avaris got out of the river and made enough tracks to ensure their pursuers would be able to tell that the three of them had separated and that Avaris still headed down the river. He hoped they would leave Lekiah and Kalisha alone if they knew he was no longer with them.

He was drawn out of his thoughts by a loud screech. A big raven flew over him, landed near the riverbank, and transformed into Kintara. He looked at the position of the sun and worked his canoe to the bank. She usually didn't return until later in the day.

"You need to move faster," Kintara said.

"Devinese?" Avaris raised his eyebrows. "Lately, you only speak to me in common tongue."

"Now isn't the time for it," Kintara said. "The magic users who *can't* Shapeshift and some of the Kiroc army have broken off to pursue Lekiah and Kalisha."

"But they're are okay, right?" Avaris thought about turning back to help his family—the only family he had left.

"They have a head start, and Lekiah knows how to survive in the wilderness better than his pursuers do," Kintara said.

Avaris wasn't convinced. Lekiah was a great warrior, but his sword couldn't fight magic.

"Maybe we should turn and fight," Avaris bit his lip and ran his fingers through his long matted hair. "Now that they're divided, we could maybe defeat them one group at a time."

Kintara folded her arms and arched one eyebrow. "You're not invincible—not yet anyway." She blew a strand of dark hair off her face. "We only defeated them the first time because I surprised Jenot, and they were fewer in numbers. They have two dozen magic users, a sizeable Kiroc army, and twenty Demon Dogs following you. Now that they've left the non-Shapeshifters behind, the Demon Dogs and Kirocs are setting the pace. They can run for days without getting tired, and they're moving faster than you are."

"We're going to have to face them sooner or later." Avaris felt strangely calm at the prospect. Maybe that was because he hadn't actually seen them with his own eyes. Maybe because he'd won several battles over the past few months. "And I know a lot more now. You've been training me every day for the past several weeks. We can hide and ambush—"

"I appreciate your enthusiasm"—she shook her head and rolled her eyes—"but you are naïve."

"Then teach me how to change into a bird so we can escape!" he shouted at her. Her insults and insistence that he wasn't strong enough pushed his nerves over the edge. She leveled a cold gaze at him with her dark eyes and put a hand on her hip. Avaris glared at her—he was not going to be intimidated.

"As I said before"—her voice was stern and measured—"you are naïve."

Avaris threw his arms outward, palms up. "Then what are we going to do?"

"You are going to paddle faster," she said, "and I am going to attempt to slow them down without getting killed. We need to reach the Andrus Fens before they overtake you. We'll make our stand there."

"The fens?" Avaris asked. "The Devi do not go into the fens—danger lurks there."

"If you're going to be my Apprentice, you must learn to trust me," she said. Avaris was about to explode at her again, but she softened her expression and added, "The danger in the fens will help us."

Lekiah wiped sweat from his forehead, took the water flask from Kalisha, and drank deeply. The flask was nearly empty, but he wasn't worried about that; there was plenty of water now. They had crossed the grasslands and were back at the foothills of the Mord Mountains and, more importantly, the Wanderove Divide. Of course, this far north, the river was more of a strong mountain stream than the massive dividing thing it grew into as it made its way south.

His main concern now was the approaching line of hunters on the horizon behind them. It gave him mixed feelings. On one hand, the fact that some of their enemies had pursued him and Kalisha meant fewer followed Avaris. On the other hand, Avaris and Kintara were more capable of defeating magic users than he was.

Lekiah had two bows, several dozen arrows, a sword, and a couple of knives among their supplies, but what was that against magic? The fact that their enemies followed their trail so quickly meant they had Demon Dogs with them. He might be able to defeat a few Dogs and Kirocs, but not if Aven-Lore users were hitting him with magic attacks at the same time.

He needed a plan and didn't have any good options. Kalisha knew how to use a bow—all Andrikan Devi women and children learned to use weapons—and that might help if he could get her to snap out of the daze she was in.

"We'll cross the river here and find a place to make a stand," he said as he refilled their waterskin from the clear, cool river. Kalisha didn't answer—he didn't expect her to. She followed him and did what he asked, but her eyes were still haunted by the nightmares of the past several months.

Once they crossed to the far side of the river, Lekiah looked back to the horizon and bit his lip. Their pursuers were gaining ground fast. He surveyed the mountains in front of them—they were jagged and filled with pines and undergrowth, but they were not nearly as big here in the south end of the range as they were farther north.

"I know you're exhausted, Kalisha," Lekiah said, adjusting his pack, "but we need to move as fast as possible." He took the smaller pack she was carrying from her back and replaced it with a quiver and a bow, which he strung for her. He then tied a knife to her hip. "Use these if you need to," he said. "I'll carry your pack so we can travel faster." She didn't answer, but she *did* at least look at the bow and knife.

Lekiah set as fast of a pace as he could, but having one pack on his back and another in his hands made blazing a trail through the virgin mountain underbrush difficult at best.

"Wait here," he said after they'd traveled some distance and stripped the pack from his back to climb a tall tree. Their enemies were still a good distance away, but they would overtake them within an hour. He surveyed the land around him and found what he was hoping for: a narrow gulch cut into the mountain by a stream. It had a waterfall about halfway up that dropped a good twenty paces and then continued down the shoot until it leveled off and meandered out to the Wanderove Divide. The steep ravine was rocky, and a narrow row of pine trees grew in the center like spikes on a ridgeback lizard.

Lekiah hurried down the tree and gave Kalisha an encouraging smile.

"Everything is going to be all right," he told her. "I have a plan. We just have to go a little farther."

He picked up the packs and set a faster pace than before—if they could make it up that ravine they might have a chance. Kalisha was breathing hard and sweating, but she didn't fall behind. She was strong. Lekiah smiled inwardly with pride. She would be a good wife.

He was only able to daydream on that thought for a few seconds, because the bay and howl of a Demon Dog sounded in the distance. The creatures must have found the trail at the river and were now entering the forest. He didn't have much time.

The ravine was difficult to climb. Loose rocks and dirt, combined with the steep and narrow pitch caused them both to slip and slide. They had to hold on to large boulders and tree trunks as they worked their way up to keep from falling all the way back to the base. Once they got above the waterfall the ground leveled some, but was still narrow and grew narrower as it climbed to the peak of the mountain.

A large pine with thick branches stood a little farther up the ravine, and at its base was a large boulder; it would have to do. He set both packs on the ground behind the boulder and handed the waterskin to Kalisha. While she drank, Lekiah buried his face in the stream to cool off and quench his own thirst, and then they took time for a quick meal of dried, salted meat.

"Take your bow and climb the tree." He pointed to a thick branch halfway up the tree that had several other sturdy branches nearby. "Stop at that branch and try to stay out of sight. If . . . if something happens, you'll be able to shoot down at your attackers and move around to avoid anything they fire up at you."

She looked up at the branch and then back at Lekiah, and in her eyes, he saw something different—resolve. She attempted a wan smile and then surprised him by giving him a fast kiss on the cheek before turning and climbing into place.

He felt a twinge of sorrow as he watched her go. There was so much he wanted to say to her. He wished he had time to hold and kiss her properly, just in case.

Once again, his thoughts were interrupted by the excited barking of Demon Dogs; they were close now. Lekiah picked up the other bow and quiver and hurried back to the top of the waterfall. He peered over the edge down the steep, narrow gulch, nocked an arrow and drew the bow. Within range of his arrow were three Demon Dogs, four Kirocs, and three magic users—at least, he assumed they were magic users because they were human.

It only took a moment to decide where to aim. He released the arrow, and the magic user in the front flipped onto his back and slid down the treacherous ravine, a bolt protruding from his throat. Lekiah nocked a second arrow and let it fly before the others realized what had happened to their companion. The second robed lore user looked up the ravine just as Lekiah's next arrow pierced his forehead—he, too, rolled backward down the gulch, until his lifeless body came to a twisted stop against the base of a dark pine.

Lekiah ducked behind a boulder as a bolt of angry crimson energy slammed into his position. He felt the heat of the attack and smelled an acrid stench, but the massive rock protected him. He peered around the boulder to take another shot and red energy blasted into the rocks above him, sending a shower of pebbles and dust raining down on him. They were trying to pin him in until the Dogs and Kirocs could reach his position.

Lekiah scrambled on his hands and knees up the ravine and then hurried to the opposite side. He worked his way back down to where a pine grew virtually sideways out of the mountain near the top of the falls. From here, he could see the magic user holding a skull and thighbone, sending a constant stream of red power at the rocks where Lekiah had been hiding moments ago.

He pulled the string of his bow back to his right ear, took aim, and let an arrow fly. The Aven-Lore user dropped his bone implements, clutched at his throat and fell forward. The Kirocs and Demon Dogs howled in rage and frustration, but they were closer now than before. Lekiah drew another arrow and shot the first Dog in the chest. Another arrow pierced the second Dog through the eye, and it cried out and rolled down the ravine. The third Dog, however, bounded over the trees and rocks before Lekiah could nock another arrow, and he was knocked to the ground by its impact. The greasy black fur of the Dog was hot and wet with sweat, and Lekiah felt saliva drip on his neck as the Dog opened its maw to bite him. He twisted, and the animal missed his throat but latched onto his left shoulder.

Lekiah cried out in pain, but the Dog's howl was louder still, because Lekiah drove his knife deep into the animal's chest. The Demon Dog tried to bite again, its eyes filled with rabid anger, but Lekiah twisted the blade, causing the Dog to yowl and writhe. He rolled the dead beast off himself just in time to see a double-bladed axe driving toward his skull. He rolled, and the blade bit into the rocks, showering him with sparks from metal hammering against stone.

Lekiah rolled again and rose into a fighting stance with his sword drawn. The Kiroc lifted the axe above his boar-like head and charged the Devi warrior. Its arms were as thick as Lekiah's leg, and it was easily twice again his height—but brute strength, recklessly charging forward, left an easy opening for Lekiah. He ran forward to meet the charge, slid under the creature's blow and between its legs, and then hamstrung it as he came up from behind. As the beast fell forward, Lekiah's sword came down, and with two hands, he drove it through the massive back until the sword tip bit into the ground.

Before he could pull the blade from the dead Kiroc, another ran forward, swinging broad swords in each hand, and Lekiah had to abandon his weapon and dive out of the way. This Kiroc was a sickly blue color, with a shock of black hair standing on end from its jackal-like head. It had a bull neck, a thick body and long arms, but was shorter than Lekiah. It grinned, showing decaying and rotted teeth as it realized Lekiah had no weapons. His knife was buried deep into the chest of a Demon Dog, his bow was lying on the ground next to another dead Dog, and his sword was lodged into the back of the Kiroc who lay dead on the ground between Lekiah and the advancing creature.

"You're going to die, human," the Kiroc said in a gravelly voice. "Then Graklin will have your woman." Lekiah assumed the beast was referring to himself. The thought of that thing ravaging Kalisha filled him with rage. He pulled two arrows from his quiver, one in each hand, ran forward and leaped off the back of the dead Kiroc on the ground between them. He flipped over the shorter Kiroc, twisting in the air as he passed over a surprised Graklin, and drove one arrow into his throat. He landed behind the beast and slammed the other arrow into its back.

"You couldn't even defeat a *poor* Devi warrior, Kiroc worm," Lekiah said as the creature gurgled and dark blood dripped from his mouth, "and *I* am the best."

Lekiah looked down the gulch, but didn't see any other attackers. He hurried back to the boulder he'd hidden behind when the battle began, and peered over to get a better look. He thought he saw movement in the shadows of the trees far below, but if it was more enemies they were retreating—nothing advanced on him. No Dogs, no Kirocs, and no magic users. He frowned. The battle had been too easy.

Lekiah made a tally in his head: three magic users, two Kirocs, and three Dogs. He'd killed eight. Not bad, but from what he had seen on the horizon there should have been at least that many again. He clutched at his left shoulder. Now that adrenalin wasn't pumping through his body, he noticed the throbbing pain. He looked down and was surprised by how much blood dripped down his arm.

Lekiah gathered his weapons, made his way back to the tree, and fell at the base. He rested his head on the trunk and closed his eyes. He heard movement above, and Kalisha climbed down to join him. She took stock of his injuries, then went to the packs—Lekiah heard her rummaging through them, but was too tired to watch what she was doing. She went to the stream, filled the waterskin, wet a piece of cloth, and then knelt by his side.

"You fought bravely." She spoke so softly Lekiah almost didn't hear her. She put the waterskin into his right hand and proceeded to clean his shoulder. Lekiah raised the water to his mouth and drank deeply. She took out some more cloth, wrapped it around his shoulder, and tied it off.

"Thanks," he said, and he grabbed her hand before she could move away. He gave her a reassuring smile. She returned the smile, went back to the packs, retrieved some dried meat and bread, and they shared a meal as they watched the sun set.

"Let's get up in that tree with our supplies—we need to rest," Lekiah said. "I don't want to be on the ground if more Demon Dogs or Kirocs decide to sneak up on us in the dark."

Finding a comfortable position thirty feet up a pine tree was difficult. Lekiah tied their packs across two sturdy limbs, and they used those to help secure him and Kalisha so they wouldn't fall. Kalisha wrapped herself around Lekiah, and he held her close. Her brown skin was smooth and her black hair smelled nice—even though they had been traveling for weeks. Despite his fatigue, he'd never felt better. She was still wrapped in his arms several hours later when Lekiah awoke to the distant sound of barking Dogs and the unmistakable glow of red energy in the sky above the mountain pass.

THE DEKLA DEVI

Lekiah woke Kalisha but gently rested his hand over her lips so she would know to be quiet.

"Stay here," he whispered. "Keep your weapons close. I'll be back soon."

She squeezed him, and he kissed her forehead. He gathered his own weapons and climbed down the tree.

Several Demon Dogs were howling now, but they were joined by the barking of other dogs. The sky illuminated again with a burst of red energy, and Lekiah realized a battle *was* taking place, but on the backside of the mountain.

He scrambled up the last several hundred paces of the ravine where he and Kalisha had taken refuge, until he crested the ridge. The sounds of fighting grew louder once he reached the top. The black of night was giving way to the gray light that preceded the rise of the sun—still, he couldn't see anybody as he peered into the trees below.

He hurried down the mountain in near silence, staying hidden in the forest. It wasn't long before he came upon the source of the commotion. He crept around a large trunk and crawled under a bush to get a better view.

A Dekla Devi camp was under attack. Several tents were burning and women, some carrying babies and holding the hands of children, frantically ran from the carnage. Men and boys were engaged with Kirocs, Demon Dogs, and Aven-Lore users, but they were losing the battle. The ground was littered with the bodies of Dekla people and their dogs. A few large dogs still valiantly attacked the Demon Dogs, but they obviously couldn't hold out much longer.

This attack was meant for him, he realized as he watched the little tribe battle the unexpected assault. The band from the Cragg Caves following him and Kalisha had probably realized the ravine was a death trap, and decided to attack from behind when they stumbled upon this camp of Dekla Devi.

Lekiah watched the battle, grinding his teeth. These warriors would do fine against a normal group of invaders, but they had no experience battling enemies like this. He couldn't bear to watch them be butchered. Especially when it was his fault this enemy invaded their territory.

He retreated from under the bush and crept around the camp to get to the downhill side of the battle—behind the attackers. The magic users had stayed safely behind the front line of Demon Dogs and Kirocs—letting their minions engage with the Devi warriors while they created havoc with their powers.

Lekiah snuck up to the Aven-Lore user furthest behind the battle—a dark-robed man who had just discarded a thighbone and was drawing another from beneath his clothing. Before he could summon the red power, a line of red blood gushed out of his throat from the slash of Lekiah's sharp knife. The man dropped silently to his knees and fell on his face.

Lekiah wasted no time locating and dispatching another magic user. He didn't care that it was a woman. She had been sending bolts of crimson fire from the eye sockets of a skull when he drove his sword through her back. The power stopped and she cried out in pain, causing the two remaining lore users to look over to see what had happened.

Lekiah dove behind a large tree to avoid being blasted by the converging crimson streams intended to kill him. He nocked an arrow and waited. The red energy pounded against the tree, and he could tell it would be incinerated by the relentless assault at any moment.

He rolled into the open, came up on one knee, and released an arrow before diving behind a large boulder. The magical onslaught stopped. He knew his arrow had found the throat of one of the magic users, but the other was still out there, probably waiting for him to reappear so he could be more accurate with his next magical attack.

But Lekiah couldn't sit trapped behind a rock. He could hear the screams from the battle that still raged on in the village. Even without the help of the lore users, the Demon Dogs and Kirocs would destroy these people and then they would go after Kalisha.

He peered around the boulder to see what had happened to the last magic user, and saw dark robes fleeing from the battle and into the forest. He nocked another arrow and took aim, but lowered his bow because the man disappeared behind the trees. He hated to let him get away, even though this coward would likely not stop running until he was safely back to the caves under the Cragg Mountains.

He turned his arrow instead to the battle in the small camp and let it fly at the largest Kiroc who was engaged with two warriors—one looked to be no more than ten years old. The creature let out a blood curdling howl and reached for its back, opening itself up to the sword of the bigger of the two warriors. By the time this Kiroc was dead and the warriors noticed there was an arrow in its back, Lekiah had fired two more arrows as he ran into the melee, and the final two Demon Dogs cried out in pain as they fell to the blood-soaked earth.

Lekiah tossed his bow aside, drew his sword and picked up the sword that had been dropped by the Kiroc he shot, and then began a dance of death with the remaining four unholy creatures from caverns beneath the Cragg Mountains. As he spun, parried, and sliced with a sword in each hand, Kirocs cried out in surprise and pain. When they dropped to the ground, the Dekla Devi warriors pounced on them and finished them off. Within moments, the battle was over.

Lekiah stood in the center of the little camp, sweat dripping down his face and panting with exhaustion. He dropped the sword in his left hand and rotated his throbbing shoulder. He probably shouldn't have used two swords.

"Who are you?" an older man asked, stepping forward. He wore only a loincloth, and a gash across his forehead dripped blood into his long gray-and-black peppered hair that was plastered to his sweaty face.

"My name is Lekiah." He brought his fist to his chest. "I am a warrior of the Andrikan Devi."

The other tribesmen muttered to one another. Like Lekiah, they had dark skin and long black hair, but most of them wore multiple thin braids where his hair flowed freely. Women and children crept cautiously from the trees and back into camp to see the stranger.

"An Andrikan Devi." The old man raised his eyebrows. "And you risk your life to help the Dekla tribe?"

"These that attacked you were following me," Lekiah said matter-of-factly. A warrior did not take glory for something he didn't actually do. "It is my fault your land was invaded."

The old man turned and huddled in a circle of his tribesmen to confer with them. A young boy tried to work his way into the group but was pulled back by his mother.

The old man turned and asked, "Why does this host of demon spawn want to kill you, Lekiah of the Andrikan Devi?"

"They seek to capture the woman who travels with me. She is the sister of—"

The baying of Demon Dogs and a flash of crimson power in the sky stopped Lekiah's explanation and stopped his heart.

"Kalisha!" he shouted and turned to look up the mountain. He grabbed his bow, and ran toward the ravine where he had left her. He heard men from the Dekla tribe shouting after him, but he didn't care. Nothing mattered except Kalisha.

Another flash of red energy lit up the morning sky above the ravine before he crested the ridge. He no longer worried about moving silently. He charged down the gully with reckless abandonment. He slipped and slid, nearly falling as the loose rocks gave way under his soft leather boots, but kept himself upright by clinging from tree to tree and boulder to boulder.

There were no more blasts of red power, but he could still hear shouting and the barking of Demon Dogs. A Dog yelped in pain, and he heard more shouting. He slid to a stop behind the tree where he and Kalisha had spent the night.

"Die, you slimy, worthless beast of filth!" Kalisha was covered in blood. She held her knife in her hand and slammed it over and over into the chest and face of a massive Kiroc lying motionless on the ground. Two Demon Dogs and a black-robed lore user lay dead on the ground nearby, each pierced with one or more arrows.

"This is for Toci!" she shouted. "And this is for my mother!" Her words were punctuated with emotion as she continued to stab at the dead Kiroc. "And this is for me!" She left the knife, buried to the hilt in the eye of the bloodied creature, fell to her knees, and cried. Her body shook with her sobs, and she covered her face with blood-soaked hands.

Lekiah dropped his sword and hurried to her side. He dropped to his knees, put his arms around her and held her against his chest. He looked up the ravine to the three Dekla Devi tribesmen who followed him. They stood back a respectful distance, but stared slack jawed and wide eyed.

Later that night, Lekiah and Kalisha shared a meal and fire with the Dekla Devi. They had spent the day burying their dead. They had dragged the bodies of their attackers to a cliff and dropped them over the edge—they had no honor in life, so they deserved no honor in death.

Kalisha no longer had a haunted look in her eyes. Instead, they were hard with firm resolve, but they softened whenever she looked at Lekiah.

"So Lekiah of the Andrikan Devi," the old man said after they shared their story with the tribe. "You and your woman have no tribe?"

"Our tribe will always be with us, here." Lekiah touched his heart. "But we roam the plains alone now."

The man looked at each member of the remaining Dekla tribe. They were small in number, but they each nodded earnestly when he caught their eyes. He looked at Lekiah and Kalisha and smiled broadly.

"My name is Dredan, and you are no longer alone." He opened his arms wide. "We would be honored if you would roam the plains with us as members of our tribe."

Lekiah raised a questioning brow at Kalisha, who smiled at him and nodded.

"We accept with gratitude." Lekiah brought a fist to his chest and bowed his head.

The men cheered and the children clapped their hands and hurried over to welcome them to their family. Kalisha smiled at Lekiah, and for the first time since they left the Cragg Caves, he realized she was finally back. She was going to be all right.

THE ANDRUS FENS

"You need to move faster!" Kintara landed in the canoe and transformed back into her human form. "They are less than a league behind and moving fast!"

"I'm paddling as hard as I can," Avaris shot back at her. His shoulders and back were numb with the exertion of nonstop rowing over the past several days. "It would be nice if *you* helped paddle instead of just yelling at me to go faster."

The Warlock blew a strand of dark hair off her face and gave him a level stare. She was quite pretty, especially when she had that exasperated look on her face. She pursed her lips and her eyes narrowed dangerously. It was disturbingly alluring.

"I have to pay a visit to our friend in the fens. I need to make sure he's . . . prepared to help us." She apparently decided to ignore his outburst. "Just make sure you reach the border of the fens before your pursuers overtake you."

"What if he won't help?" This was the first indication Kintara gave that her friend might have to be persuaded to help.

"He will," she said confidently. "He owes me a favor. One last thing: get to the borders of the fen, but do not enter until I return."

With that, the air around her shimmered with a hint of red, and a large raven flew away to the east.

"Wait!" he yelled, but she was too far away to hear. He stopped shouting; it expended energy he didn't have. "I've never seen the fens," he said. Hopefully it would be obvious when he reached them. He supposed they would look different than the rolling, grassy plains.

He turned himself in the small craft so his back was facing downriver. He needed to switch the direction he was pulling to give his muscles a change, and this would also allow him to see his hunters if they came into view. He pulled with the current, wishing for at least the hundredth time the river wasn't so languid on the plains. The swift currents by the Devi-Hold in the mountains were much better for speed—sometimes they moved too fast. A little help from the water now would be welcome.

The sun dropped three finger widths in the sky before the landscape changed. Avaris pulled his canoe onto the shore at the point where the Andrus River forked into a dozen or more small fingers. These rivulets were more like large streams that spread into marshy wetlands. The streams disappeared into tall rushes and cattail groves. Farther in, he could see trees reaching to the sky. This had to be the border of the fens.

A group of large birds with long beaks dropped from the sky and landed some distance into the marshy land, but Avaris couldn't see where they touched down because his view was blocked by the reedlike vegetation.

He wiped sweat from his face and looked out into the plains behind him. He saw no sign of pursuit, so he walked back to the river's edge, knelt down, cupped his hand and scooped water into his mouth and then splashed his face. He was reaching down to get another handful of water when he stopped short, squinted his eyes, and studied the sky to the west. Several small, dark specks had appeared on the horizon.

He stood and watched them increase in size as they flew closer. Perhaps they were simply another flock of birds making their way to the fens. Still, he kept his eyes on them as he made his way back to his canoe and felt through his pile of supplies for a skull and thighbone.

He looked back toward the fens and chewed absently at his lower lip. He could hide in those reeds, but Kintara had specifically told him to wait at the border of the fens for her. Then again, it would take more than reeds and swamplands to hide him from Demon Dogs.

He squeezed the thighbone in his left hand and drew upon the aeon myriad—forcing red energy into the magical implements. The birds were flying in an unorganized line, not in a uniform formation the way ducks and geese did. And the difference in size from one bird to another suggested they were not all the same species.

He turned, stared into the fens and scanned the sky above it. Where was Kintara? Maybe she realized they were facing hopeless odds and decided to save herself. It wouldn't surprise him. She was a Warlock of the Aven-Lore, after all, and they were the most deceptive liars of all people—everyone knew that. Kahn Devin had almost convinced Avaris to join with him, and that was *after* he saw what the man did to his tribe. It wouldn't be hard to believe Kintara's commitment was only as strong as her belief that she would personally benefit from their alliance.

When he turned back to face the coming fowls, his heart stopped, and he drew a slow, steadying breath. A row of black beasts was now visible, bounding across the grassy plain and chewing up massive amounts of ground at an alarming pace. He drew more power into his bone tools and wiped at the sweat on his face with his sleeve as he prepared to face the onslaught. The feeling of the red power flowing through the skull and thighbone and into his body helped push his fear aside and steel his will for what was coming. He was sick of running. He would destroy them now or be destroyed. Either way, it would end today.

"I told you we are going to make our stand in the fens."

Avaris felt a wave of relief at hearing the female Warlock's voice behind him.

"Let's get inside the fens before they arrive," she said.

"I was afraid you changed your mind about helping me," he said as he released the red energy, tossed the bones back into the canoe and shoved it into the water.

"Which rivulet do I follow?" he asked as she climbed in and sat across from him.

"Take one of the north fingers," she said as she scanned the horizon. "It doesn't matter which one, but be quick about it."

He chose the widest stream, and soon they were encircled by a wall of cattails and tall reeds. Clouds of mosquitos surrounded them as he paddled deeper into the fens. Before long, the stream opened into a shallow swamp with thin, short, skeletal trees pushing up through the murky waters. Pond scum floated on top of the water and parted like a curtain as Avaris and Kintara made their way forward.

"What was that?" Avaris nearly tipped the canoe because he pulled back and shifted his weight too rapidly. The thick long creature sliding through the water toward and then around their canoe was too large to be a snake—at least, Avaris had never seen a snake that large before.

Kintara's mouth twisted into half a smile. "*That* is help."

Avaris watched the massive, scaly black body slither through the water toward the edge of the swamp. The creature was longer than ten men and as thick as a large pine tree.

"Don't stop," Kintara said. "We need to be to the trees before they enter the fens and see us."

He rowed toward an opening in the reeds on the far side of the swamp. As they twisted through a maze cattails and thin crooked trees, another massive snake slithered through the water. This one had a purplish hue to it as its wet black scales reflected the evening sunlight. When it approached the canoe, a massive head burst out of the water directly in front of them and hissed, staring at them with yellow eyes and crescent-shaped pupils. Sticky white liquid dripped from long fangs as big as one of Avaris's legs, and a long forked tongue shot in and out of its maw.

Avaris instinctively stood and jumped backward, not realizing his mistake until he felt cold, dark water engulf him. His shock at being submerged and unable to see caused him to breathe in a large amount of water as he attempted to shout. He landed on the soft peat mud and a few hard rocks. He twisted to get his feet underneath him and pushed back to the surface.

He came up coughing and spitting and whipped his head to get his long hair out of his eyes. The water was only waist deep, but his feet sunk several inches into the loamy bottom. Just when he was able to see again, he felt a massive slippery body brush against and around him beneath the water and then saw enormous yellow eyes peering at him from above.

He wasn't holding any bones, but he instinctively pulled in power from the aeon myriad to protect himself.

"Stop!" a man's voice thundered from the edge of the swamp. The giant snake and Avaris both looked to where the man stood among the grasses and reeds. His skin was caked with mud, and he wore a grass skirt around his waist. His long hair stuck out in clumps and was green like pale summer weeds. His headband was made of white beads that held his matted hair off his face and around his neck he wore loops of red and green reeds. In one hand, he held a skull and in the other a thighbone; both were glowing red.

The man said something Avaris couldn't understand, and the snake dropped into the water and slithered away, following the first serpent.

"Sorry about that," the strange man said. "She thought you were the enemy." As if that explained everything.

"Avaris," Kintara said with an odd concern in her voice. "Look at your hands."

He looked down, and his hands were glowing with green power. He released the energy immediately but stared at his fingers.

"I thought you said this boy is learning the Aven-Lore, Kintara," the man on the shore said.

"He hasn't formally chosen his path yet, Esrath," Kintara said. "Has the power ever manifested itself in you as a green color before?" she asked Avaris.

"No. What does it mean?"

The Warlock pursed her lips and stared at him. The muddy, barbaric man standing in the reeds narrowed his gaze and scratched his armpit.

"We don't have time to discuss this right now," Kintara said. "If you're through swimming, get back in the canoe. We have business with our uninvited guests."

As if on cue, Avaris heard the distant baying of Demon Dogs. The man Kintara called Esrath looked over his shoulder in the direction of the sound.

"It would seem they are nearly at my doorstep," he said, and four birds appeared over the fens, flying in circles. Simultaneous bolts of red power streamed from Kintara and Esrath toward the nearest bird—an eagle or perhaps a vulture. The bird's shriek of surprise and fear lasted only a moment before it fell from the sky. The other birds careened away and dropped to the ground behind the reeds and outside of the fens.

"Ha! Run like the cowards you are!" Esrath shouted and jumped with glee.

"They aren't fleeing, Esrath," Kintara said, "but they won't attempt to fly over the fens again to look for us, and that will help."

"I know that," he answered. "It just felt good to kill one of them after all they've done to me. Now, let's get into position before they get too far into my home."

"Follow that outlet through the reeds to the larger trees," Kintara instructed Avaris. "The Demon Dogs will follow our scent into the fens, but they will be met by Esrath's pets. We'll draw those who survive that attack into the trees, and that's where we'll make our stand."

"Those *things* are his pets?!"

Kintara shrugged at his question, sat down, and waited for him to follow her instructions.

"Oh, great," Avaris groaned. "I lost the oar when I fell in."

"No matter," Kintara said with a twisted smile. "You're already wet and muddy. The water isn't deep. You can push the canoe."

He gave her a level gaze that said, *very funny.*

"I'm serious," she said, "and be quick about it. We need to be in position soon." She returned his level gaze, and he grumbled as he lowered himself back into the murky cold water.

The howling and barking increased in volume as Avaris pushed the canoe through the water toward narrow channels that led from the larger pond back into a maze of reeds and cattails. When they entered the channel, it opened wider, and then the reeds drifted closed behind them. He looked closer and saw a large turtle head peeking above the water, watching them pass.

"What's going on?" His eyes darted back and forth, and he pushed faster. "The land is moving and . . . and I think I saw a giant turtle head."

"Esrath likes to play with creatures and plants," she said, scanning the skies. "Some of the stands of grasses and reeds are actually turtles that grow vegetation on the backs of their shells."

As Avaris pushed forward, he saw smaller water snakes, beavers, musk-rats, and all sorts of flying bugs. "Are you sure it's a good idea for me to be in the water?"

Whatever Kintara was about to say was interrupted by the cry and wail of Dogs. Avaris heard the water splashing in the distance and the hissing of snakes. Then the wailing of the Demon Dogs faded into an eerie silence.

THE SERPENTS

Jenot Lexton ran as fast as he could, but had difficulty keeping pace with the gait of the Demon Dogs—fortunately, the Kiroc soldiers couldn't keep up with the Dogs, either, so the animals weren't running at full speed. Jenot's fox form was fast and agile, but his legs were shorter than the large black Dogs, and a week of nonstop running had taken a toll on him. Fortunately, there were rodents in the Andrikan Plains, so he'd had plenty of food to eat.

Jenot and his small army were finally closing in on their prey—he could tell by the excitement of the Dogs. The Andrus Fens were in sight, and Avaris and Kintara were trapped inside. They would try to hide, and the swampy bog would help a little, but the Dogs could still track inside the fens.

Once Kintara's situation was hopeless, she'd no doubt try to flee and leave the boy to his own devices. Jenot had given the others strict instructions to prepare for that eventuality—that traitorous whore was *not* going to escape him again. He couldn't wait to get his hands on her. The thought of how he would degrade and humiliate her added to his own excitement as the chase was nearing its end. Torturing her slowly and watching her suffer would be supremely satisfying.

Four lore users who could transform into birds were circling above the fens. The others who could fly had landed at the edge of the reeds and transformed into their human bodies. Jenot looked at the birds in the air with a twinge of jealousy. This was one time he wished he'd learned how to transform into a bird. Normally, he preferred his alternate forms: fox or snake. But at times like this, flying would certainly be preferable.

As he watched his companions in the sky over the fens, two crooked streams of red energy shot up from within the dense marsh and converged on one of the birds—it was destroyed before the Shapeshifter could mount a defense. The others careened away and dropped to the grassy plains outside of the fens. Maybe it was a good thing he couldn't take the form of a bird. He wasn't certain which of his companions was just annihilated, but better them than him.

Jenot transformed back into his human body at the edge of the fens and heard the shrill cry of a woman.

"No! They killed my brother!" It was Suro. She and her twin brother Suno could transform into vultures.

"You will pay for this, Kintara!" Suro turned and shouted toward the reeds that marked the border of the fens. "You and that boy will both die!"

All the magic users had transformed into their human forms now, and more than one hundred and fifty Kiroc warriors and a pack of thirty Demon Dogs gathered to await Jenot's orders.

"Suro," he said. "You will get your revenge, but standing here shouting is only going to make you a target."

She glared at him with dark eyes, ringed with shadowy circles from days of exertion and lack of sleep. Her long, brown hair was parted in the middle but otherwise uncombed and her fur coat—which would be useful if she were on the peaks of the Cragg Mountains—hung open. She took a menacing step toward him but, although she was a Shapeshifter, he knew she wouldn't dare challenge him. Instead, she removed her coat and let it drop to the grassy earth.

"Then let's get in there and finish this job," she hissed and pushed up her shirtsleeves. Jenot raised a brow and grinned.

"Don't worry, Suro." He rubbed his hands together. "You'll have your revenge. Kintara has a lot to pay for, and I plan to make her suffering last a long time."

"Captain Ryglunk," Jenot called to the massive, gray-skinned Kiroc who was in charge of the Kiroc warriors. The captain had scars on his square face, and purple veins spider-webbed across his muscled frame. A bony ridge shaded his bright red eyes that shone with anticipation of the hunt.

"Send the Dogs after the trail and follow with your . . . soldiers. Kill the boy but try to take the Warlock harlot alive. Suro and I have a score to settle with Kintara."

The Kiroc turned, raised an immense axe above his head, and shouted a war cry to his motley army of Demon Dogs and Kirocs. Hraldur, a tall, spindly legged Kiroc with red skin and golden eyes, raised a barbed whip and snapped it over the backs of the Demon Dogs, and they raced into the wet bogs, baying and barking in pursuit of what was clearly a fresh trail.

An unorganized mass of Kiroc warriors, some tall, some short, but all fast and strong, charged in on the heels of the Dogs. Some of the Kirocs looked almost human, while others resembled a perverse cross of human and beast. They all had one thing in common—a thirst to kill. This had been a long, hard march, and all of them were anxious to make Kintara and the boy suffer for it.

"Listen up." Two dozen magic users—men, women, and even a few Kirocs, moved closer to Jenot. "Be prepared to draw on the power at a moment's notice. You all saw what just happened to Suno. Kintara has no doubt been training the boy, and believe me when I say he is stronger than any of us."

That comment brought snorts of derision and laughter. Jenot wanted to lash out at the fools, but he held his tongue. They'd all heard of his failure the first time he'd confronted Kintara and Avaris, and they no doubt felt they would've succeeded where he had failed. Well, they would soon learn for themselves how strong the boy was, and Kintara would pay for the shame she'd brought to Jenot with her surprise attack.

"When we find them, we attack together, and as I told Ryglunk, I want Kintara alive. She will be humiliated and die a slow and painful death." The others shouted agreement at this, fell in with Jenot, behind the Dogs and Kirocs, and charged into the swamp.

The ground was muddy and wet when they crossed into the tall reeds. Rivulets broke off from the Andrus River to create smaller streams and murky ponds with scum on the water and banks thick with vegetation.

The howling of the Demon Dogs ahead, changed to frantic yelping. Before Jenot could shout out a question as to what was happening, enormous serpents shot out of the murky pond, each with Demon Dogs squirming in their gargantuan maws. He fell backward in awe of the beautiful creatures. Water cascaded off the snake's shiny black and purple scales, and a Kiroc dangled, impaled, from the razor-sharp fangs of one of the serpents.

Multiple streams of red power shot toward the creatures, but a crimson shield precipitously materialized in front of the giant water snakes and held off the attacks long enough for the serpents to drop into the swamp and disappear beneath the dark water.

The surviving Demon Dogs and Kirocs fled the pond and climbed up the muddy, reed-covered shore.

Jenot stared at the location where the creatures disappeared. He'd never beheld such beauty and majesty before—he'd never dreamed such creatures even existed. Sure, he'd heard stories about dragons that lived more than a thousand ago, and other massive creatures that lived during the god wars, but—

"Jenot!" Yanavah shouted, red-faced. "You didn't even attempt to attack those things! No wonder you were bested by Kintara and that boy."

Only Yanavah, the only other Warlock among Jenot's army, would dare speak to him this way. The man's normally well-kept blond hair was now wet and disheveled, and a piece of green moss hung from his light brown beard. Had Yanavah known of Kahn's death in time to return to the caves, he might be the Grand Warlock instead of Shamael. As it was, Yanavah didn't learn of Shamael's successful battle for the position until two weeks after it ended.

"How is it," Jenot said, "that nobody in the caves knows about these creatures?"

The other Warlock stared at him. Understanding of what Jenot insinuated dawned in Yanavah's blue eyes. The man didn't look at all like other

Warlocks. He could pass for a southern noble or even an Azur-Lore user with his naturally good-looking and trustworthy face—an asset the Warlock often used to gain alliances and access where others had failed.

"Somebody has been hiding this from us," Yanavah said.

"Somebody has *created* these things," Jenot said. "I haven't explored the fens in three or more decades, but I assure you, creatures like this did not roam here when I did."

"Yes." The other Warlock leered at him. "You of all people, Leather Snake, would know about beasts such as these. Your love for snakes is unnatural, Jenot. It's no wonder you didn't attack them."

"Shapeshifters, spread out," Jenot shouted. "Lucresia and Praether, you take the left flank. Merloden, Crystal, and Blacknor, you're on the right. The rest of you position yourselves at intervals in between. Yanavah and I will bring up the rear and join where we are needed most. The moment you see those things rise above the water, attack. Whoever is protecting them can't stop us if we attack from different positions simultaneously."

The Kirocs and Demon Dogs advanced more cautiously now. The fens were eerily silent. The Dogs raised their noses and sniffed at the scents on the light breeze and their handlers urged them forward. Jenot couldn't remember ever seeing Demon Dogs afraid. They obviously didn't want to be surprised by the snakes again.

Jenot scanned the pond from a bank on the left side. His force was divided on each bank of the pond. Once they made it to the far side, they could regroup and move forward as a single unit again. He didn't like being split up this way, but he liked the idea of wading through the pond less.

He saw the water roil an instant before the serpents' giant heads surfaced again. This time, their attack was coordinated with one on each side of the pond. Dogs and Kirocs were snatched from the shore before they could fall back. Jenot and the other lore users raised their bone implements and fired bursts of angry red power from all different angles at the creatures. A shield rose in front of the snake that attacked the north ridge of the pond, but the serpent nearest Jenot was left unshielded and took the full force of power from his and Yanavah's assault. The shriek let out by the creature was piercing.

Kirocs dropped their weapons and covered their ears. Demon Dogs scattered, but the serpent dropped, obviously injured, back into the water. The other serpent shrieked and hissed but dropped under the protection of the water, dragging two Dogs and three Kirocs with it.

"Quickly!" Yanavah shouted. "Get to the far side while the serpents are on the run."

Jenot did a rough count in his mind; a dozen of the Demon Dogs were already dead and at least twenty Kirocs. Their force was still large, but they were losing numbers at an alarming rate. Hopefully there were only two of those creatures.

On the opposite side of the swampy pond, a dozen narrow channels coursed, mazelike, through islands of reeds and mounds of vegetation.

"It would be easy to get lost and separated in that labyrinth." Yanavah said, standing beside Jenot. "I'm sure Kintara is counting on that."

"The Dogs are still moving toward the trees deeper in the fens." Jenot licked his lips. "The scent clearly leads that direction, so . . . who is raising shields and controlling those serpents?"

Before the other Warlock could reply, one of the massive snakes shot out of the water, but this time surfacing from one of the narrow channels. It moved rapidly over and under the islands of mud and reeds, swallowing tens of Kirocs with its mouth and taking out dozens more with its tail.

Bolts of red power shot toward the creature, but the way it wove over and under the reeds made it a difficult target. A single bolt of power did strike the end of its tail as it disappeared into the water and steam rose, making a sizzling sound in its wake.

Jenot didn't know how many they'd lost in this latest attack, but it was a lot. Several Kirocs, those who'd only been grazed by slippery serpent, drug themselves back out of the water and onto the nearest spot of dry ground, but they scattered and ran, splashing in and out of channels, toward the tree line as fast as they could.

"Stop!" Yanavah shouted, "It might be a trap!"

Hraldur, the gangly Kiroc lieutenant who carried a whip, jumped onto a lone boulder that protruded a few feet above the water and perched, looking like a spider crossed with a lion. "Our men and Dogs are getting butchered out here, my lord. Whatever awaits us in there can't be as bad as standing out in the open to become supper for that serpent."

As if to punctuate his statement, the snake shot from the water a hundred paces north of where it last disappeared. It surprised three Shapeshifters, swallowed them in a single gulp, and disappeared back into the channels as the other magic users scrambled to shoot bolts of magic at it. The crackle and sizzle of steam from the water and the scent of burning flesh suggested that a few of them had scored a hit. However, three more were now dead.

The other magic users ran as fast as they could for the cover of the trees, followed by Yanavah, who shouted orders that went unheeded.

Jenot watched them go and smiled. *By K'Thrak's dark heart*, that creature was amazingly beautiful. Jenot's body shimmered, his human form melted into that of a serpent, and he slid silently into the murky waters of the fen.

PREY NO MORE

Kintara stepped carefully out of the canoe and onto the somewhat dry ground. Tall, sickly conifers, elms, and aspen trees reached out of the marsh, grasping toward the sky. Ferns, thorny shrubs, and grasses grew in between, hiding mud holes and swampy meres.

It was cooler under the cover of the trees. Out in the reedy portion of the fens, the sun was unfettered, but here under the trees, there was more shadow than light. The occasional log or bolder that rose out of the muddy bog was spotted with moss and lichen. She motioned for Avaris, who had goose pimples on his skin, to pull the canoe out of the shallow water. He glared at her. She frowned back and folded her arms. It wasn't her fault he'd fallen into the water and lost his paddle.

Kintara surveyed their surroundings, blew a strand of dark hair out of her eyes and considered their circumstance. Hopefully, Esrath and his giant serpents would do their job of whittling down the Kirocs and Demon Dogs—at least enough to give her and Avaris a fighting chance.

The water wasn't deep enough for the serpents to maneuver smoothly here, but this was a good defensible position nonetheless. Trees surrounded them, and they were on slightly higher ground. She would be able to see the enemy coming.

"Bring the bag of skulls and thighbones—we're going to use up several before today is over."

Avaris picked up the bag they'd retrieved from Myrrah's cabin in the Mord Mountains and joined her.

"When the battle begins, attack hard and fast," she said. "When cracks appear in a bone you're using, drop it and get a new one. We have plenty, and we'll need to fight at full strength for a long time."

Kintara opened the bag she carried over her shoulder and took out a pouch with crushed leaves and two brass cups. She filled one with water from the murky swamp, and then used her shirt as a strainer to filter the water, which she poured into the other cup. She set the cup of water on a small rock and channeled energy into it until the liquid boiled.

"What are you doing?" Avaris asked.

"Purifying the water before I prepare my tea."

Avaris's eyebrows shot up. "You're going to drink that foul stuff now?"

She didn't mind his incredulity at a time like this. Enemies were nearly upon them, and it probably seemed odd to him that she would take time to make tea.

"It isn't just bitter tea, Avaris," she explained and poured the correct measure of powder into the hot water. "This will keep a person young and increase stamina." She channeled more energy into the liquid—this time to cool it enough for drinking—and took a few swallows of the sour elixir.

"Today, you need to drink as well." She handed the cup to him, and Avaris looked at it with trepidation. He smelled it and wrinkled his nose at the pungent odor. Kintara chuckled at his reaction. She'd been drinking this daily for nearly sixty years, and she still wasn't comfortable the smell or taste. She nodded for him to continue. He took a deep breath, tossed the liquid back, and finished it in two gulps. Kintara laughed again as he coughed and sputtered.

"I can't believe you drink this every day," he said and spit to the side. "I think I'd rather grow old and frail."

"Shh." She held up her hand and peered through the trees. From this location, they still had a good view of the reedy fens, and she thought she saw movement. There it was again. And then she saw them: Demon Dogs—nearly a dozen of them—bursting through the reeds and splashing through the standing water. They sniffed at the air and plants as they moved forward and then stopped at the tree line and barked as they peered into the shadows.

Three Kirocs, also pushing through the reeds and cautiously wading into and back out of the stagnant water, followed close behind. Avaris lifted the skull and thighbone, but Kintara placed her hand on his arm to stop him from drawing the power.

"Wait," she mouthed. "Not yet."

She wanted to get as many of the enemy in view as possible before giving away their position. With a well placed surprise attack, she would be able to kill everything in sight. Attacking too soon would only cause their predators to scatter, making the task at hand much more difficult.

Soon, the first three Kirocs were joined by others who were drawn by the bark of the Dogs. They came in clumps of three or four, but each group was spread apart as they made their way toward the tree line.

The Dogs' barking turned into howling, and they ran anxiously back and forth along the tree line—impatient to rush in and attack. The Kirocs handling the Dogs, however, waited until more reinforcements arrived. Perfect.

Ryglunk, the massive Kiroc captain, pushed through the reeds and surveyed the situation. He was famous for his brutality and efficiency in battle. Well, he wouldn't be fighting against swords and humans today; his battle-axe wouldn't be able to parry blows of raw Aven power.

At least fifty Kirocs were in view now, but they were spread out. Kintara was sure Ryglunk would signal them to rush into the shadows of the trees to find her and Avaris soon. She tapped Avaris on the arm and gestured for him to start his attack on the right and move left. He nodded once, and they both raised a skull and thighbone. Kintara mouthed, "One . . . two . . . three!"

The surge of crimson power she forced into the bones was intoxicating as always, and she pushed the power out with all her strength, sending it directly toward Ryglunk. If she could take him out, the others would be easier to pick off. But the captain's senses were acute, and he dove to the side and under a channel of murky water an instant before the killing energy hit him. The two Kiroc warriors standing behind him weren't as fortunate. They took the full brunt of the impact, sending them flying backward through the air.

"*Ba Aven's Breath!*" she cursed. For the briefest of moments, she considered waiting for the massive Kiroc to surface so she could try again but instead continued her attack in a sweeping movement to the right before the others could scatter.

She couldn't tell how many they'd killed with this first assault, but bodies, mud, and water flew in every direction and chaos erupted among the enemy ranks.

The Demon Dog handlers shouted a command, and the animals charged, splashing through mud and water, jumping over fallen logs and around trees as they rushed forward. They were close enough now that Kintara could see their red eyes and rabid saliva dripping from their fangs.

Kintara killed the closest with a powerful blast of Aven power. A smoking hole the size of a large melon was all that remained of the animal's gut as it flew backward, slamming into and snapping the trunk of a small elm.

She dispatched two more in similar fashion, but as she was about to kill another, a red stream of power cracked into the tree just above her head, and she was forced to change the energy she intended for attack into a shield of protection.

"Avaris, create a shield and protect us from those Necromancers while I attack!" She looked at her Apprentice, and her mouth dropped open. His body glowed with the crimson power of the Aven-Lore and a massive river of power shot toward four charging Demon Dogs, reducing them all to ash within mere moments. He looked at her, and she could tell he was drunk with the raw excitement of so much power flowing through his body. She could never wield so much power at one time.

"Never mind," she shouted, "I'll keep the shield in place, you keep atta—" The skull in his hand glowed brightly and then shattered into a hundred shards, its capability for channeling the energy exhausted. Kintara shielded her face in her cloak just before the bone fragments shot out in every direction.

She reset the shield protecting them and tossed the bag of extra bones next to Avaris.

"Keep this next to you. You'll need them more than me." She nodded toward the growing number of Kirocs and magic users entering the wooded part of the fens. They were coming forward in a controlled march, letting the magic users lead the way with streams of power blasting Kintara's shield. If Avaris didn't hurry, this would be over soon. She could keep the magic attacks at bay, but as soon as the Kirocs were close enough to throw stones and spears through the barrier, it would be over fast.

"Rush forward, you fools!" a man's voice boomed through the swamp. On a knoll out in the grassy fens, still several hundred paces away, a Warlock stood with an aristocratic red cloak cascading down his back. Kintara didn't need to see his face to recognize Yanavah. She'd known him for more than half a century. She didn't realize he was part of the hunting party. That wasn't good.

A large swath of acrid power shot from the thighbone and skull Avaris held in front of them. He swept them in an arc from right to left, throwing Kirocs backward and blasting the trees in half. In the aftermath, it looked like a giant had swung a massive axe through the section where his magic had cut. Dozens of Kirocs died in his assault. But with the trees knocked over, Kintara and Avaris were exposed.

As Avaris prepared to send another surge of devastation, the muddy water in front of Kintara erupted and the enormous Kiroc, Captain Ryglunk, shot up and rushed forward. Avaris pointed the thighbone at Ryglunk as he leaped at her, but before the boy could summon the power, a long-legged, red-skinned Kiroc dropped from the tree behind him—Hraldur, Ryglunk's lieutenant.

Kintara saw Hraldur backhand Avaris at the same time that Ryglunk slammed into her. Her head hit the ground, and her bone implements flew from her hands. The impact knocked the wind out of her, but the ground was muddy, so at least the fall didn't knock her unconscious. Still, she dropped her Aven shield and could do nothing to help Avaris.

The massive Kiroc snarled, raised a fist and punched her in the face. Light flashed in front of her eyes as the bones in her nose broke, and she tasted warm, salty blood as it ran into her mouth. Anger welled up inside her, and she forced the aeon myriad into her body and out through her hands and eyes, blasting the surprised Kiroc ten feet into the air. The grunt he made as he slammed against a fallen log was most gratifying.

"It will take a lot more than filthy demon spawn like you to keep me down." She stood and raised her hands to deliver a killing blast of power at him, but changed her target in the last moment as a dozen Kirocs ran forward, leaping over logs and through mud. She killed several of them before one hit her cheek with a rock, sending her sprawling to the ground. Nausea and vertigo threatened to overwhelm her, but she drew strength from the energy she forced back into her body. She saw the thighbone that had been knocked from her hand when Ryglunk crashed into her sticking out of the mud. Grabbing it, she rolled over and sent a powerful blast of red power at the Kiroc warriors now hovering above her with raised swords and spears. Those who weren't directly hit and killed, dove to the side to avoid obliteration, and Kintara rose back to her feet.

She saw a snake slither out of the water next to her—finally, Esrath had sent her some help—and she took aim at the remaining misshapen beasts. She saw a red shimmering flash from the corner of her eye and then something occurred to her—Jenot Lexton could transform into a snake. Something hard hit her head and the world went black.

Avaris changed the direction of his next attack and pointed the thighbone at the huge, gray-skinned Kiroc who had just jumped out of the water in front of Kintara. But before he could send forth the power, a lanky red Kiroc landed next to him, kicked the bone out of his hand, and hit him hard enough across his cheek to knock Avaris backward several feet.

He landed hard on the wet ground and looked up as the tall Kiroc raised a barbed whip over its head, preparing to strike. The Kiroc's eyes were gold and deep set behind a stretched, pointed nose and nearly covered by long gray eyebrows. Its greedy smile revealed a row of sharp, pointed teeth, but that smile turned to a look of frustration as the end of the whip became tangled in branches above him.

Avaris rolled over but as he struggled to stand the Kiroc kicked him in the ribs, sending him flailing sideways through the air and knocking the wind out of him.

Pushing himself to one elbow, he struggled to regain his breath. He looked up and saw three Aven-Lore users on the far side of a shallow, muddy rivulet. They held skulls in one hand and leg bones in the other that were pointed at him and glowing with angry red power. He had no bones to aid his focus of the aeon myriad so he pulled the life energy around him into his body. He felt a strange sensation as power flowed into his elbow resting in the mud—like the strength of the aeon myriad was flooding into him in a torrent of life. When the attack came from the Necromancers, Avaris pushed the energy out into a shield the way Kintara taught him for the past few weeks.

He was engulfed in a dome of green energy as streaks of red power shot toward him. The strikes deflected off his shield and the tall, skinny Kiroc attacking him stopped advancing and shielded his gold eyes from the collision of energies. Avaris saw that the Kiroc now held a curved dagger in his hand that dripped a black, oily liquid from its tip.

The attack from the magic users stopped long enough for Avaris to send a burst of green energy at the red Kiroc, but the creature was so fast, it jumped to the side before Avaris's strike landed. However, the tip of his curved knife was hit by the attack and flew out of the creature's hand.

Before Avaris could mount another assault, the spindly legged Kiroc leaped in front of him, grabbed him by the hair and arm, and threw him more than twenty paces through the air. Avaris landed with a splash in cold, murky waters. He was a good distance away from the wooded area and back in the fens now. He stood, relieved that the water was only chest deep. His relief was short lived, because six magic users, several dozen Kirocs, and two Demon Dogs faced him on the opposite bank, which was less than a stone's throw away. Now that their prey was so close, they came at him with reckless abandonment. Kirocs howled and shouted as they splashed into the water and several streams of red power shot at him simultaneously. He reflexively put his hands up to block the attacks, but knew he wouldn't be able to build a shield fast enough this time.

"Devour those trespassing demon-spawn maggots!" Esrath shouted.

The magic attacks sent toward Avaris dispersed against a red shield that suddenly surrounded him. He turned and saw Esrath's muddy face screwed up in anger and concentration as he maintained the shield protecting Avaris. He felt something massive and slippery slide past him in the water, and then one of the giant serpents burst through the surface, scooping up a Dog and five Kirocs in his maw and killing as many more as it whipped its enormous tail across the water and over the bank.

Two of the magic users fell to the beasts' tail, and the others dropped their attack on Avaris in order to dive for safety. As the snake burst through the water again, the magic users turned their red streams of death toward the serpent, and it screeched in pain. Several Kirocs hacked at the thing with swords, clubs, and battle-axes. As it retreated into the swamp, Avaris was hit on the back of the head and shoved under the dark waters by the red-skinned Kiroc. Avaris had only been distracted for a moment by the battle; he couldn't believe that his assailant had closed the distance so quickly.

He struggled and managed to raise his head above the water, coughing and sputtering as he tried to clear his lungs. He swung his fists as fast and hard as he could in the direction he thought his attacker's face would be, and was rewarded with a solid collision and a grunt of pain from the Kiroc. He heard Esrath shouting, and in his periphery vision, saw the man disappear into a stand of tall reeds to follow the injured serpent. Several Kirocs and magic users chased after them, apparently anxious to put an end to the giant creature that had killed so many of their comrades.

He didn't understand what Esrath was shouting because he was forced back under the water by long, abnormally thin hands. He kicked and grabbed, trying to twist free, but the Kiroc's grip was unrelenting. The burning desire for breath seized Avaris's lungs as he fought, still the red-skinned creature pushed him farther down.

Avaris's right hand pressed against the loamy bottom, and he pushed with all his might in an attempt to gain some purchase, but instead his hand sunk into the earth past his wrist. Panic clutched at his mind like a wolf's jaw clamping onto a stag's throat. But then Avaris noticed and felt things he'd never experienced before. The soil where his hand was buried overflowed with incredible life. The energy from the aeon myriad within the earth practically forced itself into his body in response to his desperate need. He felt he would burst with the power that saturated every fiber of his being. The dark and deathly water now teemed with sparkling life like a billion stars on a clear night.

He released a small amount of the power that coursed through his veins, but it was enough to shoot him out of the water in an explosion of green energy—the Kiroc screamed and flew head over heels more than a hundred paces through the air. Avaris wasn't sure if the beast was dead, but it didn't immediately rise again to fight.

He didn't have time to pursue the red Kiroc, because three magic users attacked him with flows of crimson power. Still filled with aeon myriad, he lifted his arms, received the energy into one hand, and sent it out the other like a slingshot toward his enemies. As the power exited his body, he realized it had changed from red to green, and the force and size of the energy stream was significantly larger than what his attackers originally threw at him. He saw a look of shock and fear on their faces just before they, and all the Kirocs in the line of his fire were annihilated under the power of his counterattack.

He looked around for the next battle and realized he was alone. Had he killed them all? He looked toward the wooded quagmire where he and Kintara had made their stand, but she was nowhere to be seen. Then he heard shouts and cries coming from the direction Esrath ran moments ago.

He charged recklessly through waterways and reeds, rushing toward the sound. He wasn't sure if the massive amounts of power still coursing through his body had healed his wounds, but he felt no pain as he practically flew across the terrain to the noise of fighting.

The shouting and thrashing sounds of battle grew louder, but Avaris became disoriented and couldn't place the exact direction of the commotion. He stopped to listen and nearly fell over when the thicket of reeds he was standing on moved. He looked down and saw the head of a massive turtle-like creature. It turned and looked at Avaris with eyes that pooled with obvious intelligence. The creature wanted to help him.

In his experience, turtles were slow and languid. But, in water, this creature was at home and moved with surprising agility through the various fingers and channels of murky water. The turtle made turns and passed through swampy floating plants without hesitation. Several sections of grassy shoreline opened and allowed them to pass through to waterways beyond—more of the giant grassy-back turtles.

"I'll send you maggots back to Ba Aven!" Esrath shouted, his eyes red and bulging. Two Necromancers and seven Kirocs surrounded him. He was standing in front of one of the massive black serpents, trying to protect it from the blades of the Kirocs and the magical assaults of the lore users. Esrath had erected a red shield in front of them both, but as Avaris rounded the corner he saw the Kirocs charging through to attack the fens hermit with physical weapons. As the first raised a thick curved blade, Esrath swung the thighbone upward, hitting the Kiroc on the side of its skull. The strike was amplified by the magic flowing through the bone, and Avaris heard the crushing skull of the Kiroc and it sailed backward through the air.

The bone in Esrath's hand shattered, and the shield dropped. He held up the skull and shot a bolt of red power through its eyes at another Kiroc, but then two more jumped on top of him and beat him with clubs. The other Kirocs and Aven-Lore users turned their attention to the snake, striking it with axes and jets of red flame-like power. The air stank with a mixture of burning flesh and angry Aven energy.

Avaris felt indignation well up inside of him. He feared for the life of this man whom he'd never met before today, but was sacrificing everything to protect him and Kintara. Avaris pointed his hand at the creatures attacking Esrath and green energy crashed into them—the power smelled fresh and alive. The screeching and howling of dying Kirocs lasted only a moment as the assault ripped through their misshapen bodies and blasted them off the green-haired, mud-covered Esrath. The barbarian of the fens picked up the skull that had been knocked from his hands by the Kiroc attack and erected a shield around the massive snake just as the serpent's attackers turned to face Avaris.

The Necromancers pointed their glowing implements at Avaris but before they could summon the magic, they, too, were obliterated in a burst of green energy flowing from his hands. The remaining Kirocs turned and ran, stumbling through reeds and bushes as they tried to flee the certain death of Avaris's power. He let them go, feeling no desire to kill needlessly. They would keep running until they were halfway back to the caves.

"Leera!" Esrath cried, his voice thick with emotion. "Oh, my precious girl, where did they hurt you?"

The heavyset man dropped the skull and limped to the serpent, whose massive head rested on the grassy bank. Dark liquid oozed from deep gashes near her eye and along her sleek body. Avaris watched as the man gently caressed the beast and looked into its enormous yellow eyes. Leera's black scales reflected a hint of purple in the late afternoon light.

"Rish is dead?" Esrath asked as though repeating something he'd just been told. He then embraced the snake he called Leera and sobbed.

"Esrath." Avaris tentatively stepped forward. He didn't want to be insensitive to the man's sorrow, but they couldn't rest now. "Where is Kintara?"

His shoulders quaked, and he looked up at Avaris. Tears streaked the dried mud on his face, and he shook his head. "I thought she was with you." He looked around, scanning the surrounding reeds and cattails. "Are you telling me you killed all these by yourself?"

Avaris didn't answer. The man nodded. "Of course." His voice was tired. "The magic was green. I was so distraught I didn't pay attention—"

Whatever else he was going to say was cut off by otters, badgers, and other small animals that crashed through the reeds and twittered at the mud-covered lore user in a cacophony of high-pitched voices. Esrath listened intently and then looked deeper in the fens toward the wooded sections.

"Kintara's in trouble," he said, and Avaris could tell from his wide eyes that he was genuinely scared. "We need to hurry." He stood to follow the critters, but after taking two steps he fell to the ground and clutched at his leg. Avaris looked where the man grasped and saw bone sticking through the skin.

"Can you tell these animals to take me to Kintara?" Avaris asked. "You can stay here and protect Leera. She needs you." Esrath nodded in pain, rivulets of sweat now streaked the mud on his forehead. He didn't say anything, but Avaris felt him push and pull on the aeon myriad until the animals understood what he wanted them to do. They looked at Avaris, chattered at him as though they wanted him to follow, then turned and headed deeper into the fens.

As he fought his way through the muck and muddy ground of the marshy fens, Avaris grew tired. His head, ribs, and cheek were hurting from where the Kiroc had hit him earlier. The power he'd absorbed earlier was now spent.

They soon reached the area where he had battled the red Kiroc, but the creature was gone. Maybe Avaris wasn't looking in the right spot. After all, the reeds, mud, and water all looked the same—not to mention the grassy-backed giant turtles constantly altered the waterways. He climbed onto a boulder and looked around. Otters rose above the water and chittered anxiously at him. He took a deep breath and followed.

As he approached the place where he and Kintara had made their stand, he saw the bag of bones the Kiroc threw from his reach earlier, and he grabbed a skull and thighbone. The animals of the fens led him deeper into the wooded marsh and then stopped—apparently afraid to continue forward. He looked at them questioningly; the absurdity of it all was almost amusing. He actually thought the things might speak to him. One beaver looked meaningfully into his eyes and then nodded a direction with his head, like he was telling Avaris the way to go.

"Thank you," he said. Then as quickly and as silently as was possible in this terrain, he continued forward. It wasn't long before he could hear voices. Not the voices of battle or anger—these voices were jeering and laughing. He crept toward the sound, peering around trees and parting bushes as he neared the voices.

"The wench is almost pretty." The voice sounded familiar—it had an oily, snakelike quality about it. "You think you're so much better than me . . . so much better than everyone else," the man continued.

Avaris pulled aside the leaves of a tall fern and clenched his jaw in anger at what he saw.

Kintara lay unmoving on a hill. Her eyes stared straight ahead and held a look of panic. The person speaking was the Warlock Jenot, who had tried to kill them in the mountains several weeks ago—the night Kintara had saved him, his sister, and his friends.

A woman with dark hair parted in the middle hovered angrily next to Jenot. Another man in a richly embroidered red cloak, with neatly combed blond hair and a well-groomed light brown beard and mustache, stood a few paces away, looking particularly bored as he watched the scene. But more than ten large Kirocs circled her, laughing and jeering as the Warlock in tight brown leather taunted her—including the massive Kiroc with purple veins spider-webbing beneath his muscled gray skin, the same one who had jumped out of the water in front of Avaris and Kintara when the fighting first began.

"I think it's fitting that my friends and I should teach you a lesson in humility and pain—a lesson you'll remember for the rest of your life!" He rubbed his hands together, raised his head back, and laughed maniacally. "Don't worry. That won't be too much longer."

The Kirocs jumped up and down, shouting and thumping their chests with their fists.

"Stop playing with her and get on with it," the noble-looking man said, clearly annoyed. "We need to make sure Hraldur and the others killed the boy."

"Move aside, Jenot." The woman shoved the Warlock out of the way and slapped Kintara as hard as she could across her face.

"That's for killing my brother, you filthy whore!"

Jenot spun the woman around and held a finger to her nose. "Don't you ever touch me like that again, Suro," he hissed. "Remember your place. I could kill you as easy as a snake kills a mouse."

"I'll teach her the meaning of pain," the massive gray Kiroc rumbled. "She's been ordering me around like a slave my entire life." He moved forward and reached toward Kintara, but the reptilian Warlock shot his hand out and threw the Kiroc back with a small bolt of red power.

"*I* will be the one to bring her pain, you *fool*. You're so clumsy you'd kill her with a single blow. I want her to feel the pain, not be knocked senseless."

The Kiroc stood back up, glaring at Jenot, but stayed silent. The Warlock grinned, looked down at Kintara and ran a long finger down her cheek.

"I've made a lifelong study of torture, Kintara," he said. "Don't worry. I won't be gentle!" He slapped her cheek as if to punctuate his statement. She didn't cry out or move to stop him, but Avaris could see the pain in her eyes and the red welt rise on her face from where Jenot struck her.

"Stop playing with her!"

"Make her bleed!"

Why didn't she fight back? There was nothing binding her arms or feet. Her eyes darted back and forth, but other than that she remained perfectly still.

As the Kirocs shouted disgusting suggestions to the Warlock, he licked his lips, rubbed his hands together and then pulled out a long, thin knife.

"Relax Kintara." Jenot ran his thumb along the blade. He pulled a glass vial from under his cloak and poured dark liquid onto the steel blade. "You won't miss any of the excitement. The poison I gave you will ensure you stay conscious, and this lovely elixir will cause the wounds from the knife to burn like hot coals for hours."

The man in the red cape no longer acted bored; he wore a twisted look of anticipation on his face as he watched. The woman called Suro also watched with a depraved eagerness as Jenot dragged the blade across Kintara's left cheek and a thin line of blood appeared to drip down her face. Her eyes widened with pain but she didn't scream or try to stop her attackers.

Loathing and anger welled up inside of Avaris. He was sick of being prey to the followers of Ba Aven. His mother and brother had been killed and his tribe enslaved by Kahn. His sister had been treated worse than a dog in the caves. Avaris and his companions were attacked and nearly killed on the mountain when they escaped, and now he'd been hunted for weeks across the plains of Lemuria. He would run no more. He would put an end to the abuse. Regardless of what it took, he would force magic users to stop taking advantage of the vulnerable and weak.

"I AM AVARIS MORDRAHN!" His voice thundered through the fens, and the actors of the torturous scene turned to look for the source. "I AM NO LONGER YOUR PREY!" The skull and bone in his hands blazed to life with angry crimson power. "YOU ARE MINE!"

He sent a wide torrent of red energy at the knife-wielding Warlock and Kirocs who surrounded Kintara. He kept the flows high enough to avoid hitting the dark-haired Warlock lying in pain on the ground. Suro managed to raise a shield before the blast slammed into her and Jenot. The force of impact still brought them to their knees, but the Kirocs in the path of Avaris's attack weren't so fortunate. The large gray Kiroc dove to the side, but the others took the full force of Avaris's wrath. Kiroc body parts—half human, half animal—exploded and flew hundreds of paces in every direction. Avaris raised a shield of his own as the aristocratic man launched his own magical assault. He let his shield absorb the power of his enemies' assault, made it circle through his body, and come out of the thighbone back toward the man with ten times the force at which it hit Avaris. The blond magic user raised a shield but was thrown backward several feet by the force of the colliding energies.

Avaris turned back to the Warlock who'd been assaulting Kintara, but he was gone. While he was distracted by that, the blond man shifted into a golden eagle and flew away. But Suro shouted in rage and ran toward Avaris as she sent a stream of power toward him. The massive gray Kiroc ran and jumped toward him, raising a huge battle-axe over his head as he prepared to split Avaris in two like a log. Avaris held his shield in place with the skull but threw the thighbone at the beast as it fell toward him, sending the glowing red bone hard into its chest. The ensuing blast ripped a gaping hole through the screaming Kiroc's midsection and sent him careening through the air.

The eyes of the woman running at him changed from crazed rage to fear in a split second when Avaris pointed the skull directly at her and smiled. She dropped her attack and turned to flee. She began shimmering to transfigure at the same time that Avaris let the crimson energy escape from the eye sockets of the skull. The woman called Suro collapsed in a satisfying pile of burned flesh.

NEFARION'S CRYSTAL

The rude wood and mud shack had been warmer and larger than Avaris thought it would be when he dragged Kintara to here the night before. Esrath wasn't able to help him carry the paralyzed Warlock because he had a broken leg and was beside himself with grief at the loss of one of his pets—the giant serpent he called Rish.

The sky was growing light from the imminent rising of the sun, and the air was crisp. Soon it would grow muggy and mosquitos and gnats would mar the clear sky like swarms of wandering, annoying black clouds.

Avaris stood on the porch of Esrath's hut, wrapped in a dirty wool blanket, and stared into the marshy fens. The two Warlocks who had been with the attacking army had escaped. A human skull and three thighbones rested on a table made of gnarled wood next to him. He wasn't going to be caught unprepared if the Warlocks returned.

Avaris heard Esrath returning before the man rounded a tall stand of reeds. He limped, using a thick stick as a crutch. Avaris winced at the memory of the man screaming in agony as he had set his own bone. Avaris had wrapped it for him once the bone was in place.

"It was Jenot Lexington," Esrath said wearily, his voice still thick with grief.

"What?" Avaris was as tall as the squat man, and they locked eyes. The mud was mostly washed from Esrath's body now, but his hair was still a mess of green matted clumps.

"Jenot Lexington. He's the only Warlock I know of who takes the form of a snake. That's how he was able to sneak past my defenses. That's how he escaped." He sat down on a rickety, homemade rocker and rested his walking stick against the shack.

"Has she said anything yet?" Esrath asked, referring to Kintara. Avaris shook his head but kept looking over the fens, watching for anything suspicious.

"What did they do to her?" he asked. Kintara was awake—at least, her eyes looked awake—but she couldn't move or speak.

"A diluted preparation of Sarundran Asp venom," Esrath answered. "It's one of Jenot's favorite toxins. A bite from the snake will kill you in seconds, but when diluted and prepared properly, the venom causes temporary paralysis—the victim stays conscious and aware of what is happening around them, but cannot move. She'll be fine once the poison wears off."

Avaris nodded.

"What are you doing?" Esrath asked, and Avaris looked down at the dirty Necromancer and cocked an eyebrow.

"Somebody needs to keep watch to make sure they don't return," he answered. He thought it should be pretty obvious what he was doing.

"You're wasting your time." The Necromancer took hold of his walking stick and pushed himself to his feet with a grunt. "They won't return—at least not until they have reinforcements, and that will take a long time."

"How can you be sure? If I were them, I'd mount a surprise attack while we're still weak."

Esrath looked at him like he was a dolt and then laughed, shaking his head.

"You have no idea what you just did, do you?"

Avaris didn't like being spoken to like he was an idiot, so he didn't answer. He'd spent the previous day fighting creatures and magic users. Of course he knew what he had done.

"You've had little training and yet you just destroyed an army of Kirocs and a host of magic users, Avaris. If Kintara and I fought without you, we would have been easily overtaken and killed, even with the aid of Leera and

. . . and Rish." He nearly cried when he mentioned Rish. Then he grabbed Avaris's chin with a rough hand and looked into his eyes. "You *are* a Child of the Blessing, Avaris." He let go of his chin and reached for the door of his shack. "Those who escaped are halfway across Lemuria by now, and the last thing they want is another confrontation with you. Now, let's get you a cup of tea and some rest."

It was late into the next evening before Kintara moved her head and spoke. She whispered a single word, "Water." Avaris had tried giving her water before, but Esrath stopped him, afraid she would choke.

After a few hours, Kintara was able to speak and eat. She told them what had happened and how Jenot poisoned her, confirming what Esrath had already concluded. She hadn't been able to sleep during the paralysis, and so she was mentally exhausted. She was unsteady on her feet, so they helped her shuffle to the shack's lone sleeping pallet and laid her on the blankets.

"Come with me, Avaris," Esrath said once he was certain Kintara was asleep. "I have something to show you."

It was growing dark as they left the shack. Esrath's humble home was built where the reeds of the fens transitioned into a wooded swamp, a good hour north of where the battle had taken place.

The hermit led Avaris eastward, farther into the wooded section of the Andrus Fens. Trees blocked out the stars, and the erratic path turned Avaris around. Esrath, on the other hand, never hesitated as he led the way. Avaris kept close to the man. If they became separated, he didn't think he'd ever find his way back. Keeping up was easy because Esrath had to stop frequently and rest. The terrain here was difficult, even with good legs.

Esrath led Avaris into a tight and twisted grove of thin, black trees. Once they had pushed through several steps of tree trunks knit close together, they stepped into a clearing filled with dark, stagnant water, and entirely surrounded by the kind of trees they had just passed through. In the center of the dark waters was a neatly crafted shack with river stone walls and a thatch roof—it was considerably better than the shack where they had left Kintara. A small wooden bridge led across the pond to the entrance.

"Don't step there." Esrath pointed as they walked over the bridge. "Or there. I've set traps to keep out unwanted guests."

The man was breathing heavily and sweating profusely by the time they reached the entrance, and he rested on his wooden crutch before pulling a thighbone from beneath a fern growing next to the outer wall. The bone glowed as he drew power from the aeon myriad and muttered a few words. He traced a pattern in the air, and the door swung open with an audible click.

"What is this place?" Avaris asked

"This is where I spend most of my time." He sent a small stream of energy at a glass orb hanging from the ceiling. The orb came to life with a gentle crimson glow that lit the single room.

"No other human has ever seen this, Avaris," he said. "I'd appreciate it if you don't tell anyone about this place, not even Kintara."

A table in the center of the room was covered with papers and a book that reminded Avaris of Myrrah's grimoire. Earthen and glass jars cluttered shelves that lined two of the walls. Animal organs and body parts floated in foul-smelling liquid in several of them. Cages were stacked on other shelves and scattered around the floor—some with small animals Avaris had never seen and others held eggs bathed in light from small, red glowing orbs fixed to the top of each cage.

Avaris took in all of these oddities in a moment, but what caught his attention and sent familiarity shooting through his veins like a bolt of lightning was a painting on the far wall. It depicted a beautiful flying beast. Everything else in the room went out of focus as Avaris made his way through cages, jars, and papers to stand in front of the painting. He reached his hand toward the canvas but didn't touch the material. He slowly traced his fingers along the outline of the amazing creature. The serpentlike beast had strong legs, a crown of horns that shot backward off its head, and sleek batlike wings. Its long, pointed tail was spiked with sharp horns running down its ridge. It was solid black with yellow eyes that glowed with ancient intelligence.

"That's Roskva," Esrath said reverently over Avaris's shoulder.

"I've never seen such a creature, but . . . it feels familiar." Avaris pulled his eyes from the painting and looked back to Esrath. "What is it?"

"*She* is a dragon," he said reverently. "But not just any dragon. The mother of all dragons."

"I've never heard of dragons," Avaris said.

"Never heard of dragons?" Esrath said as though it was the most blasphemous thing imaginable. "How is that even possible? Didn't your parents tell you bedtime stories or your siblings ever sit around the fire at night and try to scare you with tales of dragons?"

Avaris felt a stab of pain. "My father abandoned me when I was a small child and . . . and I was raised alone in the mountains by a Necromancer named Myrrah."

"I see," Esrath said. "That's unfortunate."

"Where do the dragons live?"

"The question is where *did* they live?" Esrath said. "Most of the dragons died long before the Wizard Greyfel's time. Roskva"—he stepped closer and gazed sadly at the painting—"was caught up in the binding with the demons."

"Why?"

"Roskva, like Monguinir and the demons, was created by K'Thrak during the god wars. He rode on her back, fighting the children of El Azur. K'Thrak's sister Necrosys was jealous of K'Thrak, and so she created a dragon of her own—a male named Turoth. She made him smaller and more maneuverable, and he became her mount in battle. When Ba Aven and El Azur banished their children, Roskva and Turoth remained—just like the demons and the Avalian. Roskva and Turoth eventually bonded, and at their peak, the dragon populace reached nearly two hundred. To answer your first question, they spread out and lived all over Lemuria. Roskva ruled the skies in the north, Turoth ruled in the south, and their children roamed from the Drbal Divide to the Lemurian Sea."

"What happened to them?"

"About five hundred years before the binding, a great Warlock named Nefarion Drakkas became the first Grand Warlock, and he tamed Roskva.

She was his greatest weapon and closest friend. Nefarion had powers and creatures aligned with his cause whose names and descriptions have long been lost to history and legend. But he despised the constant battles between the demons and the Avalian. Humans were constantly caught in the middle, and so many innocent lives were destroyed."

"But if he was the Grand Warlock, wasn't he on the side of the demons?" Avaris asked.

Esrath sat down on a stool, lifted his leg, and rested it on a wooden crate. He took a deep breath and studied Avaris's face.

"Avaris, as you go through life, you're going to be told a lot of different things. Kintara, Shamael, Kahn Devin, even me—we all had our reasons for why we chose to study the Aven-Lore instead of the Azur-Lore. The truth is, the power for both comes from the same source: the aeon myriad. It's ultimately your beliefs and goals that will lead you to choose the path you are going to take. I thought you had already made the choice. After all, you've aligned yourself with Kintara, who is a Warlock. But when you use the power, it is green at times and red at other times. I've never heard of such a phenomenon, so I can only guess at what it means: you haven't fully committed to either lore. Sometimes you use the power the way a Wizard would, and other times you draw on it like a Warlock.

"I've made a life out of studying Nefarion Drakkas and the dragons. All these experiments you see in the room are part of my attempts to bring dragons back into the world." He smiled sadly. "My best attempts so far resulted in Leera and Rish . . . but now Rish is dead."

"So . . . what happened with the dragons and this Grand Warlock?" Avaris asked.

"Nefarion chose the Aven-Lore because he wanted to force order upon the world. I imagine that he realized he couldn't force people into his ideal society by using the Azur-Lore—it's too gentle for that. Those of us who choose to follow the path of Ba Aven don't normally share Ba Aven's ultimate goal. Ba Aven wants the destruction of all life and a return to complete chaos. If that happened, we would all cease to exist. Lord Monguinir is the son of K'Thrak, which makes him the grandson of Ba Aven, and he *does* share the burning desire to destroy all life. It is what he was created to do."

"Then why would any of us follow Ba Aven? I don't want to destroy all life," Avaris said.

"I don't think any of us wants to help Ba Aven reach his goal. I don't think any of us believe he will ever achieve his goal of total annihilation, so it makes no difference. If you follow the path of the Azur-Lore, you must *allow* the power to work through you with persuasion and compassion. If you follow the Aven path, you can force the power to achieve the specific thing *you* want. It's more powerful and less constrained."

"What does this have to do with Roskva and the dragons?" This was all interesting, but Avaris didn't see the connection.

"Nefarion wanted to force the people of Lemuria to live in peace. To do that, he had to force the aeon myriad to do his bidding, which meant he had to follow Ba Aven. But he didn't want to help Monguinir break and destroy the world. With the dragons on his side, he believed he was powerful enough to kill or banish the demons and rule the world himself. He nearly succeeded, but he was murdered just before his certain victory at the side of the well of sacrifice, and his body fell into that deep abyss. After that, the dragons were hunted by Monguinir and his minions. Humans also hunted the dragons for their commercial value and to stop them from killing livestock and destroying villages. After two centuries, Roskva was the only surviving dragon. When the Wizard Greyfel bound the demons, Roskva was also bound."

"Why was she bound with the demons?"

"Because she is a child of K'Thrak, just as the demons are. Greyfel bound all the children of Ba Aven's children. The Kirocs remained because they are a crossbreed."

Avaris turned back to the painting, considering the story as he looked at the beautiful black dragon. He felt a deep sadness and was surprised to find a tear running down his cheek.

"So you've spent your life trying to bring the dragons back." Avaris could understand that, but it posed a serious problem. "But if you release Roskva, won't it also release the demons?"

"I'm not trying to release Roskva," the Necromancer said. "I'm trying to use the lore and experiment with existing animals to recreate dragons."

Avaris turned back to the painting. "So why did you want to show me this?"

"We have all lived a thousand lives, Avaris," Esrath explained. "Maybe more. We live, we die, we contemplate our lives while resting in Valhasgar, and then return to learn more."

He picked up his wooden crutch and pushed himself back to his feet, then limped to an iron bound wooden chest. He drew power into a thigh-bone, traced a pattern in the air, and the chest clicked open. He reached in and retrieved an old leather pouch. Avaris looked over his shoulder and saw that the chest was empty other than this single pouch.

"Here." Esrath stood and handed the pouch to Avaris. "I found this years ago while searching the cave archives for information on the dragons and Nefarion. Open this and tell me what you think."

Avaris studied the pouch. The leather was brittle and dark. He looked back to Esrath who nodded for him to continue. Avaris untied the cinch, reached into the pouch and pulled out the contents—a beautiful pendant with a long dark crystal clutched by a silver dragon claw attached to a leather cord. Like the painting of the dragon, this artifact had a ring of familiarity about it.

"Put it on," Esrath whispered.

Avaris considered the man, whose dirty face and eyes were alight with barely checked anticipation. He wondered if this was a trick of some kind, but Esrath looked genuinely excited. Avaris put the leather cord around his neck and let the pendent rest against his chest.

The moment the crystal touched his skin, it came to life. A line of twisting red fluid undulated within the dark, translucent crystal and then a torrent of crimson light flooded the room. Avaris became transfixed as a thousand scenes played out in his mind, like memories of distant, dreamlike events.

He saw the ground racing beneath him as he soared through the skies on the back of a massive black dragon. Battles between people and horrifying creatures played out on the land below. His mount dove toward a band of Kirocs and massive creatures he could only assume were demons. They had molten red and black skin that smoked and hissed as they swung weapons of fire and twisted steel. Horns and wings protruded from their muscular bodies. Several looked up to see the dragon diving toward them, and they took to the sky to meet them in battle. An intense burst of white hot flame shot from the dragon's maw burning five demons as quickly as they left the ground. A shot of crimson energy as wide as a raging river burst from Avaris's outstretched hand, and another dozen denizens of the Aven army were incinerated on the battlefield. Then the dragon and Avaris shot up into the sky, wheeling around for another pass.

The scene in his mind shifted violently, and now he was walking through dark, rocky corridors. The crystal amulet around his neck released a gentle red light, allowing him to see. He passed through rooms filled with scrolls, bottles, jars, and down dark passageways until he reached a thick, black door set in the solid rock wall. The door exploded inward as he used the power to blast it away. A young man with dark hair and a Wizard's staff looked up, surprised, and drew upon the aeon myriad. Before the young Wizard could complete a spell, crimson energy blasted him against the wall, and he fell to the earth.

Once again, the scene shifted. This time, he was marching through a large city with twelve black-robed servants trailing behind. He walked past soldiers standing at attention and came to the doors of a beautiful palace. A man and woman, both wearing crowns and fine clothing, dropped to their knees when he approached.

Another scene flashed before his eyes. He was in a cave on a high mountain. Snow and wind whipped all around him. As he peered into the storm, he used the power to enhance his vision. He could see through the blizzard, down the steep mountain slopes to the sea below. Dozens of warships were being tossed by the waves. He smiled at the sight of soldiers fighting to keep their flotilla from being lost to the storm. He knew they would soon lose this battle. He climbed onto the dragon's back, shot into the white gale, and dove toward the ships below. The men on deck screamed in panic as their ships caught fire, knowing they would soon meet a cold, watery grave.

Avaris couldn't control the visions. Scene after scene, memory after memory blasted through his mind and took him wherever they would. He grabbed his head and dropped to his knees. He had to push the visions away, had to protect his mind before he was lost to the visions forever. He saw a memory of shielding his mind from intrusion by Lord Monguinir. The demon lord had been searching for him for weeks, and he was cornered. The demon probed with his thoughts, and Avaris placed a shield around his mind that looked identical to the rock walls around him. He could feel Monguinir touch and press against the shield like an avalanche crashing down a mountain, but the shield held and the demon lord passed him by.

Avaris raised the same shield around his mind now, and the visions vanished. He was back in the shack in the Andrus Fens, and the crystal amulet around his neck calmed to a gentle, pulsing force against his skin.

"Wha . . . What happened?" His voice shook, and his brow dripped with sweat.

"It is my belief that this crystal once belonged to Nefarion Drakkas," Esrath said breathlessly. "Now, I think it belongs to you."

MIDSUMMER'S AZUR-AVEN— 1248 AB

"I'm tired of looking at that stupid lock day after day," Tellio said to Gustov. The central lock of the Tiarak River was identical in design to the one farther north. The river wasn't as wide here, but it was deeper. Since arriving a few weeks ago, all they could do was watch as the Valdivarian soldiers took turns guarding the locks.

Ever since their successful sortie at the locks in the north, the Valdivarian army had been on high alert. Tellio considered it a miracle that he and his men hadn't already been captured. More than once, he thought they might be.

"I'm an engineer, Tellio," Gustov said. "We'd need an army to take down these lock gates—that or a dragon."

Tellio sighed and wiped the sweat from his forehead, and considered the plan he'd been discussing with his men for the past week. It was risky, but he couldn't think of anything else to do. Fortunately, only a few small supply ships had passed through here since Tellio's little band arrived. Their failure to disrupt the shipping lane wasn't hurting the alliance of the three cities too badly, but he was certain it would only be a matter of time before King Reollyn sent massive troops and supply reinforcements north.

"It's midsummer's Azur-Aven," Tellio said, making his decision. "We go in with our backup plan . . . tonight."

"It's risky, Tellio." Gustov had voiced his concerns every time Tellio discussed his plan. "If those soldiers don't believe your ruse, it'll break out into fighting for sure."

"It's *midsummer's Azur-Aven*," Tellio repeated. "Their guard will be down. Besides, Gustov, we all accepted risk the moment we crossed enemy lines."

Tellio put away the scope he'd been looking through, and Gustov followed him into the trees and their camp located several hundred steps away. He heard a whistle from the lookout hiding in the branches and returned an answering whistle so they would know it was him. Once they walked into camp, he gathered his men.

"We move tonight, boys." He saw the glint of nervous excitement in their eyes and understood how they felt. They were all tired of waiting, but they also understood the risks. The loss of Tynoveo during their last raid was still fresh on their minds. "They'll want to celebrate tonight, and with no moon, it'll be easier for our rear flank to move unseen."

"Who's in the wagon and who's torching the locks?" Donelvan asked.

"Me, Konir, Fish, and Gustov will be in the wagon," Tellio said. Then with genuine sadness, added, "Konir and I will have to shave off our mustaches—we have to look and sound like traveling peddlers and not men of Anytos. The rest of you will get into position and strike once we have the soldiers dancing and singing."

Danu had mixed feelings as he, Kivas, and Durham rode through Leedsdale. A line of people followed them through the street, cheering, and singing. The festival of midsummer's Azur-Aven was in full swing, and people had gathered from miles around to join in the three-day celebration. This was a time of feasting and joy, but Danu couldn't help thinking about Ehrlich and Artio. So much had happened here, and so much would never be the same. Still, he smiled, waved, and even climbed off his horse to talk with small boys who wanted to shake his hand.

The road from the village square to the Azur temple was so crowded that Danu had difficulty navigating it on horseback. South of the temple, the festival grounds were filled with merchant booths, games, rides for children, and tents where performers would be doing comedies, singing, and all sorts of entertainment for the masses.

Danu and his men dismounted in front of the stone stairs that led to the polished wooden doors of the temple and gave the reins of their mounts to a young, gray-robed priest.

"Lord Danu, your arrival is quite timely." Japhet, the high priest of the temple, stood on the landing with his arms folded such that his hands were hidden inside the sleeves of his robes. "The people will be pleased to hear from you tonight before the babes are blessed."

Japhet was a thin, middle-aged man with a large gap between his front teeth. Danu, Kivas, and Durham joined him on the landing and followed him into the dark and cool temple. It felt amazing to get out of the hot Boranica sun.

"We're glad to be home, Japhet, and I appreciate your hospitality," Danu said, removing his riding gloves. "It's nice to see some things don't change. We can always count on the priests of your order."

Japhet smiled and bowed his head.

"Do you have room for my men and me?" Danu asked. "I'm certain the inns are full."

"I always keep a room available in case you or your father requires lodging, Lord Danu, and I insist you join us and our other guests for dinner this evening."

"Although, please do take advantage of the baths before we dine," a familiar voice said from the shadows, and Lynmaria walked into the dim light.

"Lynmaria, what a pleasant surprise," Danu said. "I didn't see you there."

"I didn't see you and your men, either, but I could certainly smell you." She smiled and gave them each a quick embrace. Durham's face reddened when she hugged him. She wrinkled her nose and said, "Honestly, you men really do need to freshen up."

Japhet laughed. "As you know, Danu, I don't have private baths in the rooms, but you and your men are welcome to use the baths below the temple. Lynmaria reminds me and the other priests so much that we have natural spring baths fairly often."

"I've learned over the years," the Mage said lightheartedly, "that unless a woman is around to remind them, men forget the basic arts of cleanliness. For the life of me, I can't understand why you will go for days covered in grime and sweat when there are such nice bathing facilities at hand."

"Japhet, I see you have met our new Meskhoni, Lynmaria," Danu said, smiling. "We traveled with her across the plains, and I have learned it's best to follow her advice."

"I've had the pleasure of her company during these past few weeks and have already learned the same lesson, Lord Danu."

"Are you planning to live here at the temple then, my lady?" Danu asked Lynmaria.

"No, only until I find a proper cottage."

"Have you considered Artio's old home?"

"I went there just last week." The brown-haired Mage nodded. "The area is beautiful and quaint, but it needs a lot of work. I could clean it up, but I don't think I can fix that massive hole in the wall."

"That's one of my favorite things Renn did." Kivas's booming voice echoed through the open chamber of the temple's main room. "I wish I could've been there to watch when he blasted that Kiroc through the wall."

"Yes, I'm sure it was quite a sight," Lynmaria agreed, "but it rendered the cottage unlivable."

"I've got it!" Danu snapped his fingers and grinned. "Durham has been on assignment with me for nine months and has earned at least two months' leave. He would be more than happy to fix Artio's cottage and help you get settled."

"I would?" Durham scrunched his brow momentarily, but then his eyes lit up and an embarrassed smile touched his lips. "I would, Lady Lynmaria. That is, if you will have me. I mean, of course, if you would have my help."

Kivas, Danu, and even Japhet couldn't help but laugh at Durham's awkward offer to assist the pretty Mage, but Lynmaria smiled gracefully and nodded toward him.

"I would be grateful for your assistance, good man Durham."

An hour later, Danu, Kivas, and Durham settled into the hot baths below the temple. Danu let out a deep, relaxing breath and leaned his head back against the cool rock floor. Torches lit the chamber and caused flickering shadows to dance across the rough rock walls of the room. He wasn't sure how the priests heated these pools, and he didn't care. It felt like ages since he'd been able to relax. He felt his stress and cares melt away with the steam.

"It's the midsummer festival. Our task is over. Everything just feels . . . good."

"Aye, Danu," Durham said with a broad smile. "That it does."

Demaris looked beyond the balustrade that surrounded the gallery of the school's outdoor courtyard and out to the Oraima Mountains on the south side of the castle. The warm air smelled of pine and mountain berry blossoms, but snow still capped the peaks of the mountains. It was beautiful, but with only one eye the landscape lacked the depth he remembered before his accident.

His head pulsated with a light, but ever-present dull throb around his right eye. Master Daria had done her best to minimize the scar and his pain, but she couldn't save his eye. He knew he should be thankful to be alive, but it was difficult not to feel sorry for himself. Simple things like walking up a flight of stairs were hard now. He'd tripped many times during the past week as he tried to get used to this new perspective.

"Your move, Renn."

"Demaris," he corrected Genea with an absent mindedly. He looked down at the light and dark squares on the table and the blue and red tiles—even the game board had a different perspective. He moved his red tile, then looked northward in the direction of the meadow. Although not visible, he knew that the Sentry Cliffs dropped a thousand feet into the Lemurian sea beyond. Same thing—it was beautiful, but different now.

"You're not even trying, Renn," Genea said with exasperation, taking three of his pieces in a single play. "It's midsummer's Azur-Aven. We have the day off. They're preparing games and feasts. Try to enjoy the celebrations."

"That's easy for you to say," Demaris snapped. "You don't have a constant headache, and you're not missing an eye." He regretted the words as soon as they'd left his mouth. Genea had been with him almost every hour since the accident. She'd done everything she could to make him comfortable and cheer him up. Harlow also visited every day, but Estilla had only come to see him one time. He still remembered the look she gave him when she saw his vacant eye socket and the red scar on his face. She tried to cover up her revulsion, but he saw it. He was ugly now. He would always have an eye patch and a scar marring his face.

"You're not the only person in this world to suffer, you know," Genea said, her face turning red. "You still have a mother who loves you, an older brother and a little sister who adore you. It could be much worse." She held back the tears, but Demaris felt a stab of guilt. Genea lost everyone in her family. And she nearly died at the hands of her own father to protect Renn.

"I . . . I'm sorry, Genea," he said lamely. "I just . . . I wish things were different."

"Well, they aren't. You have a choice, Renn." She sounded like she was his instructor or something. "You can be miserable wishing for things to be different, or you can decide to be happy and take joy in the beauty that surrounds you in each moment."

He twisted his lips and stared at her. Platitudes—happy words that meant nothing. He had killed a Grand Warlock. He had commanded wind to blow a ship across the sea. He had saved Raven from the edge of death, *for the love of Azur*!

"What good is all my power, Genea?" He pushed his chair back and threw his hands in the air, which caused his head to pound even harder. "If I can't make things better, what good is it to have all this power?"

"Then heal yourself," she said as though it were the most obvious solution in the world.

Demaris stood, walked to the balustrade, and looked down at the large circle of dead ground in the meadow below—the place where he'd performed his "miracle." Nothing would ever grow there again. Genea joined him at the parapet wall and followed his gaze. He was afraid she might try to hold his hand or something, but she didn't. She just stood next to him and waited.

"I've thought about it," he said sadly. "I've even searched the memories of Greyfel's staff to see how it could be done. But . . ." He swallowed to cover up his emotions. How much life would he have to steal in order to heal himself? It might even be more costly than when he healed Raven. He couldn't take that chance. He was so lost in his own thoughts that he didn't pull back when Genea placed her hand over his.

"You're a good person, Renn," she said. "Maybe that's why the gods trusted you with so much power. They knew you would value other life above your own."

They stood in silence, looking over the meadow and the forest beyond. Demaris's eyes kept returning to the dead spot below.

"Enough of this self-pity," Genea said in a bubbly voice. "Today is midsummer's Azur-Aven, and we are going celebrate like we did back home. I don't care if you have a headache or not." And with that, she dragged him away from the wall and down the stairs to the celebrations just beginning to take place in the courtyard below.

"Ah, Halbert, you're just in time." King Reollyn sounded in high spirits. He'd slept in until late in the morning—something that had aggravated the merchants' guild master who'd been waiting several days for an audience with the king. The man had been promised one this morning, but Reollyn didn't attend.

Halbert had been sincere in offering apologies for the king and did what he could to grant the man's petition. He sent the man away happy and with clear instructions not to tell anybody the king was worthless and were it not for Halbert the kingdom would be a complete disaster. Those weren't the words Halbert had used, of course, but the merchants' guild master would come to that conclusion, which was certain to translate into him telling every other merchant about his experiences at the palace.

"Tell me," the king said. "Which doublet should I wear tonight?"

Reollyn's servant held out two doublets, one purple with gold embroidery and the other gold with silver embroidery.

"Tonight is midsummer's Azur-Aven, my king," Halbert said with flair. "You will be entertaining the most important nobles of the kingdom, and so you should wear purple—the color of royalty."

"Of course! I knew I could count on your judgment," Reollyn said cheerfully. He held out his arm for the servant to put the tight coat on him.

"Will you be attending court after lunch today, Your Majesty?" Halbert asked.

"It's a holiday, Halbert," Reollyn complained. "Don't these people have feasts or dances or something to prepare for?"

"It is a light schedule today, my king, only an hour or two of business," Halbert assured him.

"You will have to take care of it for me today, Halbert—you and Desmantor." He waved toward the court Wizard, who had just entered the room. "I simply have too much to do before tonight's guests arrive—a manicure, my hair . . . and I'm still not positive about this wardrobe. I may need to start over with an entirely different outfit."

Halbert smiled and bowed to the king. Times like this confirmed to him that his plan was not only best for him personally, but would serve the people of Valdivar better as well. Reollyn was simply not fit to rule.

"Of course, Your Majesty," Halbert said in his most respectful tone, "but what of your traditional appearances and speeches at the feasts of the commoners?"

Reollyn looked back and forth between Halbert and Desmantor, frustration written all over his face. "Must I *really* attend all of those tedious gatherings? I'll be out half the evening. Not to mention, it's only been a few weeks since these same commoners rioted against me. I don't think it's safe for me to go out in public."

Desmantor, Wizard and court Meskhoni, was about to interject, but Halbert forestalled him with a raised hand.

"I couldn't agree more, Your Majesty. Desmantor and I will make the speeches and appearances for you. You have far too many important guests coming to bother with such things."

"See . . . that's why Halbert is my favorite, Desmantor." The king removed the purple doublet and signaled for his servant to bring a different selection of clothing for him to consider, then said, "he always knows what's best."

The two men bowed as the king dismissed them, and left the room.

"What game are you playing at, Halbert?" the Wizard hissed as they walked down the hallway. Desmantor wore a white robe with a rich green mantle. His face, including his lips, were painted white, although he did have a small bright red line of color on the center of his lips, and he wore a green and white headdress. In his right hand he held a tall, white staff that clicked against the tile floor as they walked.

Halbert looked over his shoulder and down the hall; guards were stationed periodically and in strategic locations. He signaled for the Wizard to follow him into a small room—one he was certain had no secret passageways or areas for spies to hide and listen in on the conversation.

"You are a wise man, Desmantor," Halbert whispered, "and you have seen a lot more in your lifetime than I ever will."

"Don't patronize me, Halbert. I know your kind."

"Of course you do," Halbert agreed with a smile. "I know I can't deceive you, and that's why I won't insult you by lying or pretending to be something other than what I am."

"And what is that?"

"I am an opportunist." Halbert confirmed what he knew the Wizard already suspected. "I want power and riches. But that doesn't mean I don't also want what is best for the kingdom."

"And you think *you* know what is best." The Wizard said it as an accusation, not a question.

"I know that men like you and me need to take action when the times dictate it," he said. "I've been out among the people, Desmantor, and they have no love for the king. They despise his lifestyle, and they don't support his war with the three cities."

"So you ingratiate yourself to the masses and, when their pain is sufficient, you will step in and be their savior." Desmantor sounded curious, almost approving. "And what becomes of the king when this all plays out?"

"If the people choose to depose him, we need to be ready to offer an alternative, and we must be seen as the natural choice."

"You and I *already* have the power, Halbert," the Wizard said. "We *already* have luxury and wealth. An uprising among the people is dangerous for us. It may not turn out how you plan."

"We are at the whims of an imbecile!" Halbert shot back. "He's as likely to dismiss us from the court tomorrow as he is to decide to change into different shoes." He took a steadying deep breath and stepped closer to the Wizard. "If you and I work together, we can restore stability to Valdivar and gain permanent power and wealth for both of us. Everybody wins."

"Everybody, that is, except for the king."

Halbert didn't respond to that; he just waited while the Wizard considered his words.

"What is your plan?" Desmantor sat down and smiled. "Perhaps we *should* consider what is best for the kingdom."

Shamael was glad he hadn't attempted this climb in the winter with his soon-to-be vitiate magic users. Today was midsummer's Azur-Aven, the first new moon after summer solstice, yet it was windy and cool here on the face of the island's tallest mountain. The tree line ended a good half mile back, and they still had another mile to climb. Fortunately, it wasn't raining, or the loose, slate rocks would be as slippery as a Valdivarian merchant.

Shamael had flown to the rocky, uncovered plateau below the peak of the mountain where the black pool resided, so he knew where to lead his group. Unfortunately, none of them could shift into animals to make this journey faster, and so they had to make the arduous climb by foot—the journey had taken more than two days from the time the boat had landed on the island. The soldiers and engineers who'd made the journey with them waited on shore with the boat. With any luck, Shamael and his vitiate wouldn't need the boat for the return trip.

He turned and watched the line of young recruits. Most pulled their cloaks tight to ward against the cool wind. None of them had enough connection with the aeon myriad to learn to shape shift in this life. But once they became connected to him through the vitiate ritual, they would gain many lifetimes of knowledge and skill. If all went well they would fly away from this lore forsaken island.

As he climbed closer to their destination, Shamael worried that this entire trip might just be a big waste of time. When he flew over the black pool and scanned the plateau, he hadn't seen or sensed anybody else. There was no Guardian like Lord Monguinir said there would be. What was Shamael supposed to do once they arrived?

When they crested the last ridge and stood on the plateau, the flat ground left them exposed with no protection against the wind, which had picked up considerably. The plateau was rocky and large enough to hold a small village. On the east end, the land dropped several thousand feet to the ocean below. On the west side, the mountain peak continued to rise another thousand feet in the air where it ended at jagged points. Large boulders and a few gnarled bushes littered the otherwise barren tabletop bluff.

Shamael looked around and waited. No one appeared. The twenty-four students huddled in a small group, a short distance behind Shamael—close enough for him to call to them, but far enough that they wouldn't be in his way.

"Get something to eat," he shouted to them and walked toward the center of the plateau to where the black pool waited.

The pool was only ten paces across, but there was no telling how deep it was. Shamael bent down and looked more closely. The black material didn't bubble or ripple with the wind—but it had the appearance of liquid. As he stared into the blackness, he saw what appeared to be tiny, bright specks deep inside. The specks rotated and swirled through the black material like they were orbiting something. The longer he watched the more it felt like he was gazing at stars in the night sky.

"Aeon myriad," he whispered as sudden realization struck him like a blacksmith's hammer. "This is a pool of pure, liquid aeon myriad!" The possibilities of what a person could do with a physical concentration of the materials the gods used as the building blocks of creating life was stunning.

He looked around the barren plateau again; other than the vitiate, he was still alone. No Guardian to be seen. He pulled a thighbone from underneath his cloak and reached it toward the black pool. What kind of power could he draw upon if he submersed the bone into liquid aeon myriad?

The bone touched the dark, starry liquid, and Shamael was thrown violently backward, head over heels, away from the substance. Fortunately, he still held the bone and surrounded himself in a crimson shield just before he slammed into a massive boulder twenty paces from the pool.

A low, teeth-rattling, bell-like sound rang out, followed by a hissing screech that began soft, but built into an ear-piercing wall of noise. A gray-cloaked figure burst from the center of the black pool, but no liquid shot through the air or clung to his ratted, gossamer robes as he erupted from the dark earth.

The figure landed on the ground between Shamael and the treasure he guarded, and with a dusty, yet powerful voice said, "Who dares touch the Aeon Pool?"

Bony, liver-spotted wrists and hands extended from his dusty, tattered, gray robes as he pointed toward Shamael. A hood covered his head, but Shamael could see his dark circled eyes, and wrinkled skin that clung to his cheeks and face like overripe flesh on a rotting peach.

Shamael climbed to his feet and straightened his cloak with as much dignity as he could muster. He would not be cowed by this man, regardless of who he was.

"I am Shamael Daro, Grand Warlock of the Aven-Lore. I reached into the Aeon Pool to draw forth the Guardian."

"I am the Guardian of the Aeon Pool. What is it you seek, *Grand War-lock*?" The way he spat the words gave Shamael pause. This ancient being clearly wasn't impressed with his title.

"Lord Monguinir has authorized me to create twenty-four vitiate servants. I have come to ask your aid in accomplishing that task."

The old man's eyes widened and his mouth dropped open. His body shook as he slowly laughed. The wheezy and dusty sound grew louder and stronger with each passing cackle—until finally the Guardian looked up to the sky and his laughter boomed over the wind and echoed off the mountain peak behind Shamael and the cowering students.

"You are a fool, Warlock, and so is your master!" The Guardian finally stopped laughing, but Shamael saw something in the old man's eyes that wasn't there before—greed.

"Perhaps," Shamael said cautiously. "But you will grant my request, notwithstanding my foolishness?"

"Oh, yes." The old man wrung his dry hands and stepped closer to Shamael. "If you agree to the price."

"I am aware that there is a cost to this magic. What is it you require?"

"Ten years," the ancient man said, "for each vitiate." He licked his lips and continued rubbing his hands.

"I don't understand," Shamael admitted. He wasn't entirely sure he wanted to know what the Guardian meant.

"You will complete your miserable, mortal existence and then, rather than return to Valhasgar when you die, your soul will fly here to take my place—ten years for each vitiate."

Shamael considered the Guardian's words. He looked at the rocky plateau and its barren surroundings. Two hundred and forty years he would spend staring at that black pool. He looked back at the huddled group of candidates. Would it be worth the cost?

"Yes," the old man's voice sounded like dirt scraping across boulders. "Two hundred and forty years is a long time to a mortal, but compared to the eternities, it is a blink of an eye."

"Will it be worth the cost?"

"I'm not a fortune teller, Warlock," he wrinkled his nose and narrowed his eyes. "You will have incredible power with so many vitiate at your command, but only you can answer the question of worth."

The gray-robed man looked up at the sky and mumbled to himself before looking back to Shamael.

"I see that tonight is the first new moon after summer solstice—the event you mortals call midsummer's Azur-Aven. At least that simple-minded Monguinir sent you here at the right time to accomplish your task. Make your decision and return to the pool an hour before midnight if you wish to proceed with your quest. It is a dark thing we do, so it must be done when Lunaryn is at her weakest and K'Thrak at his strongest."

With that, the old man turned and walked back to the pool. Monguinir had said nothing of being here this night—it was just a lucky coincidence. Maybe the demon lord wasn't as knowledgeable as Shamael had believed.

"Wait," Shamael called and walked toward the man. "Which god do you serve, Ba Aven or El Azur?"

The man didn't turn around, but he looked over his shoulder and sneered. "Both . . . and neither." His voice dripped with anger. He took another step forward and melted back into the black, molten Aeon Pool.

STRONGEST MAN IN LEMURIA

The wagon bounced and creaked as Tellio and his small team rode down the dirt trail toward the lock. They had left camp several hours earlier, circled behind a village called Appledale, and then took the main road that led from the village toward the lock.

"I don't know why you had the men paint this thing with so many bright colors," Gustov said. "I can barely see the road five feet in front of me. Nobody will see the fancy designs on this thing."

Tellio stopped next to Gustov, who held the reins of the four-horse team. They'd found this old carriage a few weeks before at an abandoned farm house. His men had repaired the axle, tongue, and one of the wheels. Tellio had them paint the entire thing like a carnival wagon.

"Don't worry about that. Just focus on staying on the road," he said, and Gustov grunted. Tellio turned and slid open the wooden window so he could see the men and goods inside the carriage. He and his men had stolen spirits and weapons from villages and towns during their travels south over the past few weeks, and all of it was stockpiled inside with Konir and Fish.

"Get ready, men. We're nearly there."

Fish stopped playing his lute and frowned.

"Good," Konir said. "My legs are cramped and it smells horrible in here."

Tellio faced forward and peered through the darkness. He could tell they were close because the campfires of the Valdivarian soldiers had grown larger. Still, it startled him when a guard's voice called out from the dark.

"Halt! Who goes there?"

Gustov pulled on the reins, bringing the team to a stop. From up ahead, somebody struck flint and steel together, and a torch flared to life. Three soldiers stepped in front of the horses. The one carrying the torch raised it above his head and walked slowly forward.

"I'm Milo the merchant." Tellio dropped his lilting Anytos accent. "And this here is my Uncle Jack."

"What business you got at the locks at this time o' night?" The soldier peered at their faces and stretched the torch closer to get a better look. "And on midsummer's Azur-Aven, no less."

"Well, that's just it," Tellio said, trying to sound like a merchant from Divarlyn. "The folk back in Appledale didn't have no use for our spirits and entertainment skills—said they already had a celebration planned for the night. They suggested we come see if the soldiers here at the lock could use our services."

"And just what might your services be?"

"I specialize in spirits and swords," Tellio boasted with a flourish, "but my men and I also juggle, play lute, sing and dance, and help folk have a good time—for a price, of course."

"Of course," the man said tight-lipped.

"But seeing as how it's a holiday and you are men of the crown, I'll give you a special price." Tellio acted as though he were making a great sacrifice by offering a discount to the solider.

The man narrowed his eyes. "What's inside?"

"Like I said: swords and spirits," Tellio answered happily. "Also got two more of my crew riding in back. I'm sure you don't need more weapons, but if you do, I'll give you a special price on those, too."

"Open it up."

"Of course, of course." Tellio hopped down from the wagon and led the man to the back. The captain signaled the other soldiers to follow. When they opened the rear door, Fish strummed his lute, and Konir juggled three balls in the air with a wide grin splitting his face. The soldier with the torch stared at them and then regarded Tellio with an arched brow. He probably should've told the boys to wait to start performing until he gave the word. So he chuckled and pointed at them when he responded.

"Just a sample of the entertainment, Captain. They're merely trying to make a sale."

"I see." He held the torch inside and inspected the bottles of alcohol and box of swords and knives. Tellio gave a quick signal for Fish and Konir to quit performing.

"What kind of spirits you got?"

"Oh, the very best, sir," Tellio said. "Boranica red, Concordian whiskey, ales and meads—"

"Concordian whiskey, you say?" one of the other soldiers chimed in, and the captain gave him a withering look.

"Yes, as a matter o' fact. I have a bottle here what has aged for more than a hundred years." Tellio hated to part with this particular bottle, but he needed to get past these guards without incident for his plan to work. "I might be willing to, shall we say, part with it as a token of my thanks for allowing us to celebrate this special night with you and your men at the lock." He grinned and opened his arms as if offering them a gift. The captain pursed his lips and glanced at his men. They obviously wanted the whiskey. It had probably been weeks since they'd had a drop of liquor.

"Let me see it," the man said.

Tellio took out the bottle, unstopped it, and handed it to the man. The soldier gave the torch to one of the other guards and kept an eye on Tellio while he brought the bottle to his nose and sniffed the contents.

"You first," he said, handing it back to Tellio.

"I thought you'd never ask." Tellio winked, raised the bottle, and took a deep draft.

"Hey, now," the soldier said, grabbing the bottle. "Don't drink it all. I just wanted to make sure it wasn't poisoned." He raised the bottle to his lips, took a swallow, and grimaced. "Wow! That's good whiskey." He smiled and passed the bottle to one of the other guards.

"All right, what did you say your name was?"

"Milo, sir."

"Right then, Milo, you and your men can proceed."

Tellio bowed, shut the door of the carriage, and climbed into the seat next to Gustov. The gray-haired engineer clucked to the horses and flicked the reins. Tellio watched over his shoulder as they rode away. Soon, the guards were swallowed up in the darkness of the night. Tellio released a sigh of relief.

"Took you long enough," Gustov said.

Tellio raised his eyebrows and looked at him. "Just make sure you play your part right, old man."

They rolled up to the camp, just a hundred paces away from the locks. The west arm of the Tiarak River was close enough now that Tellio could hear its constant, gentle roar as it rolled southward on its journey to Valdivar and then out to the Drbal Divide.

"Who goes there?" a voice called as they approached.

"Here we go again," Gustov whispered and pulled up on the reins.

"It's Milo of Divarlyn." Tellio stood and threw his arms out with great flair, much as he'd seen the carnival leader of his old troupe do many times. "Merchant and entertainer extraordinaire accompanied by my humble assistants."

"How did you get past our guard, Milo?" Men in uniform walked forward to see what the commotion was about.

"I must commend you, sir, on the thoroughness of your soldiers. Your vanguard stopped us, questioned us, *and* searched our goods. They're a professional group of men—some of the best I've seen in all of my travels across this great land."

"Enough!" the man said, cutting Tellio off. "What business do you have here?"

"Business?" Tellio asked as though he were shocked. "It's midsummer's Azur-Aven my good man! Our business tonight is pleasure!"

"You got girls in that wagon?" a soldier from the back called out, and others burst out laughing and shouted for girls.

Tellio laughed with the men. "No, I wish I did, but I do have a juggler, a musician, and plenty of spirits!" The door to the wagon opened, and Konir stepped out and began juggling. Fish came behind him holding up his lute and smiling.

"Boring!" yelled someone in the crowd, and several others booed them.

"Well, did I forget to mention that you are looking at the strongest man in all of Lemuria?"

Again, the crowd erupted in jeers and laughter. Tellio smiled and bowed, acting as though they agreed with him. "And I'll prove it to you with a game."

"We're not children!" one man shouted.

"Go back to the village if you want to play games," another yelled.

"You'll like this particular game," Tellio assured them. "I have a fine bottle of Boranica red for the man who can best me in an arm wrestle."

"Wine is for women!" shouted a soldier in the back.

"Okay, it's your choice if you win—a bottle of red or a bottle of Blaylok vodka."

Men shouted their agreement and pressed forward, jockeying for who would arm wrestle first.

"Silence!" the man who first began questioning Tellio shouted, and the men quieted. "I am the captain in charge, and we are not—"

"Ah, yes, you should be first to challenge me, Captain." Tellio pretended the man thought his position as captain should give him first rights. "Your captain has challenged me," Tellio called out to the soldiers, "and I agree that he should have the first shot at a free bottle of fine spirits!"

"Smithson! Smithson! Smithson!" the men chanted their captain's name, egging him on to battle with Tellio. The man looked ready to protest but got carried along with the excitement of his men.

Gustov and Fish found a table and two chairs with the help of a couple of soldiers, and soon Tellio was gripping the hand of Captain Smithson. Soldiers surrounded the table, and when Gustov shouted, "Go," they erupted in shouts of encouragement.

Fish played a fast melody on his lute and started singing, Konir juggled and sang along with Fish. Gustov pulled out more bottles of spirits and found another table from which to serve drinks. Tellio let the match with Captain Smithson last long enough so the captain wouldn't be embarrassed, and then slammed the man's hand down to the table.

"You're a mighty strong man, Captain," Tellio said as he stood and offered his hand. "You didn't win the bottle, but my uncle over there will give you a shot of whiskey for being a good sport and the first man to try." The men cheered and pushed each other to get in line for a shot at Tellio.

"I'm not giving the rest of you men free drinks like the captain," Tellio shouted. "I am a merchant after all and need to make a little profit. But, for tonight only, the drinks are half price!"

Gustov was inundated with customers after that. Men bought drinks while they waited in line to arm wrestle Tellio. The old engineer only charged two copper valdins for each drink—most taverns would charge twice that—and he was liberal with the amounts he poured into their cups. Before long, soldiers were laughing and singing with Fish; others were taking turns juggling, trying to outperform Konir. Most tried to beat Tellio, some were on their second or third attempt.

Once each man had tried—and lost—several times, Tellio announced that the competition was over but suggested other drinking games.

"My Uncle Jack will set up the drinks," Tellio said as he slapped Gustov on the back, and he picked up a couple of bottles of whiskey. "Just make sure you pay for everything you drink," he said cheerfully. "I'm going off to relieve myself, and I expect there to still be plenty of spirits left when I return."

Tellio stumbled through the small crowd as though he'd had too much to drink, and walked toward the locks. As near as he could tell it was close to midnight and almost time for the others to sneak up to the rear of the locks. He needed to be sure that the four guards on duty there were distracted before that happened.

"Who goes there?" shouted a young soldier as Tellio approached the lower gate of the locks.

"Hello, son, the name is Milo." Tellio held out a bottle of whiskey. "The rest of the men are celebrating midsummer's Azur-Aven back in camp. I thought I'd come see if I could share some of the fun with you and the other guards."

"Sorry, sir, but we're on duty."

"But it's the biggest celebration of the year," Tellio said. "Even your captain is joining in the fun." Tellio looked around conspiratorially and then whispered, "I think he may pass out soon. Had a bit too much, if you know what I mean."

"Well, maybe we could have just a little," the soldier said, eyeing the bottles in Tellio's hand.

"Tell you what," Tellio said, "I'll just leave these bottles here, and if they happen to be consumed during the night . . ." He smiled and shrugged, set the bottles down, and whistled as he walked back toward the camp.

When Tellio walked back into the middle of the celebrations, he had to force a smile to his lips. These were his fellow countrymen. He genuinely *liked* these soldiers. They were just like Danu's regiment or even his own little special force. They didn't feel like enemies to Tellio. And yet there was a real chance he and his men would have to kill some of them before the night was over—all because the royals couldn't work things out. *I'd feed those kings to K'Thrak if I could,* he thought.

The celebrating and drinking continued for another half hour before Tellio saw the first signs of fire. It looked like flickering orange lights dancing on the river at first, but grew into a raging inferno. The locks were burning. As Tellio walked toward the wagon, men shouted and raised the alarm. Half of the soldiers were passed out, but the rest rushed toward the burning river.

"Let's get out of here before they come back," Tellio growled to his men. "Leave the liquor, Fish," he snapped at the younger man. Fish's short brown hair stuck out in all directions and he looked sorrowfully at the full bottles they would be leaving behind.

As they climbed in the wagon to leave, a pain filled scream sliced through the night, and Tellio glanced over his shoulder to the flames. A man fully engulfed in fire was running in circles screaming—the unlucky soldier must've gotten some of the naphtha spilled onto him. Once that happened, there was no quenching the flames. He would burn until there was nothing left to consume.

Tellio was about to signal for Gustov to head out when he heard the sharp clang of swords clashing. The shouts of men fighting confirmed his worst fear and validated Gustov's concern about this plan. Tellio's men didn't get away from the locks fast enough.

He peered through the dark, but there was no way of knowing who was fighting and how his men were faring.

"Come on, boys." He whispered encouragement to his men who were fighting near the locks. "Break through their ranks and get out of there."

He waited for the sounds to change. If they could just break through to the tree line and get to their horses, they would be able to escape. But sword continued to clash against sword, and men continued crying out.

"I've got to help them," Tellio said. "Stay here with the wagon and prepare for a quick escape.

"We're coming, too." Konir and Fish jumped out of the wagon, each with a sword in one hand and a knife in the other. Tellio nodded and grabbed two swords, and the three of them ran toward the fight.

By the light of the burning locks, Tellio saw that his men were surrounded. Only six remained on their feet, swinging their swords. The enemy had them outnumbered two to one.

Tellio yelled out a battle cry and crashed into the foray, swinging both swords; Konir and Fish followed close behind. The guards were disoriented by this sudden attack at the rear of their ranks. Four soldiers fell before the others scattered for safety.

"What's our damage?" Tellio asked Donelvan, whose red hair was matted with sweat, and blood ran down his forehead and into his eyes.

"I don't know. Some of our men got away, but Dale spilled naphtha on himself and . . ." He started counting the men on the ground but stopped and shook his head. "I can't tell who is who."

Tellio heard a familiar whistling sound and dove at Donelvan, sending them both crashing to the ground. Pain shot through his left shoulder and down his arm from the arrow now sticking out of him. They would be slaughtered if they didn't get out of here.

"Let's go," Tellio shouted. "Stick to the plan! Get to your horses and meet up where we agreed."

Donelvan nodded once, jumped up and shouted orders to his remaining team. Tellio ran back to the wagon calling for Fish and Konir to follow. As he ran, two soldiers attacked, but they were drunk, and Tellio blocked their thrusts and hit them in the head with the pommels of his swords, knocking them both unconscious.

"Gustov, let's go!" Tellio shouted as they ran up to the wagon. Konir and Fish jumped inside. As Tellio climbed next to Gustov, and the wagon lurched into motion, he heard another whistling sound and a second arrow struck him in the thigh. Gustov's eyes grew wide, but he shouted at the horses and whipped them into a run.

Tellio winced in pain as he looked over his shoulder. He could still see the flames—it looked as though a portion of the river itself was on fire. But no one was in pursuit. Hopefully the others had gotten away.

RISE OF THE VITIATE

The only part of the Aeon Pool that was visible in the dark night was the small, slowly rotating points of light within the inky blackness, which twinkled like stars in the sky. When Shamael gazed into the stuff of creation, his vision blurred, and his mind felt like it was being pulled into a sea of ancient memory. He wondered if he could use this like a scrying pool. If he could learn to harness this immense well of raw life, the possibilities would be incredible. Well, he would have two hundred and forty years to experiment with that.

"Drip your blood here," the Guardian instructed Shamael. The old man and the black amulet he held were barely visible in the night. He had formed the amulet by drawing out black liquid from the Aeon Pool and pressing it into a large circle as though it were clay. He used his thumb to make a small well in the center, and his fingernail to cut a spiraling channel that circled the center well but didn't breach its border. It was into this small center indentation that he told Shamael to drip his blood.

Once Shamael's blood filled the impression in the center of the amulet, the Guardian mumbled some words as he drew a rune in the air above it. White light trailed behind his fingers in the shape of the rune and hung in the air before falling onto the amulet with a hiss. The amulet now had a subtle crimson glow about the center where Shamael's blood had congealed into a deep red crystal. He looked closer and noticed that within the crystal, there was movement—like a miniature sea of blood gently churning.

"Bring forward the first vitiate," the Guardian said loud enough for the students who were standing in a circle around the two men to hear. Shamael saw the students share a furtive glance among themselves, and then a tall blond girl with determination set into her jaw took a deep breath and stepped forward. Shamael handed her the knife.

The Guardian reached his liver-spotted hand back into the Aeon Pool and drew out a smaller amount of liquid than last time.

"Let a few drops of your blood fall onto this," he told the girl. She placed the knife on her forearm, tightened her lips, and drew the blade across her skin. She let two drops of blood fall onto the liquid aeon myriad cupped in the old man's hand, and he pressed it into a small, circular pendant. He once again drew a rune of light in the air, which dropped onto the amulet with a burning hiss.

This amulet was smaller than the one he had made for Shamael and had no jewel in the center. It was a simple black amulet with crimson liquid undulating randomly, barely visible, beneath the surface.

"Place a single drop of your blood in the spiral channel that surrounds the blood jewel in the Grand Warlock's amulet," the Guardian said, and the girl did as he instructed.

The old man placed the smaller amulet in his hand with Shamael's amulet. "Now, rest your hand on the amulets, and Shamael, you rest your hand on top of hers."

They did as they were told, and the Guardian stretched forth a bony finger and once more drew a rune of white light in the air. This rune had an additional line crossing through its main line that wasn't there when he had made the blood jewel. Like before, the rune of light settled down toward the amulets, but this time it went through their hands before penetrating the pendants.

The blond girl sucked in a sharp breath and winced at the pain Shamael knew she was feeling. He felt it, too, as it burned into his hand, coursed up his arms, and flashed through his body and heart before it surged into his mind.

They pulled back their hands, and the Guardian threaded a leather cord through a hole at the top of each and then handed them their new pendants.

"Put these on," he said.

When the amulet touched his chest, Shamael heard a voice of fear and pain screaming in his head. He saw the girl's memories of growing up on a farm in southern Nortia, milking cows, shearing sheep, baking breads, dancing with village boys. Then he saw himself through another's eyes in the darkness. His face was twisted in concentration and confusion. He felt and heard himself screaming in the night, but it was a young woman's voice that pierced the air. He realized his mind was getting lost inside the mind of this girl. He was becoming part of her, or she was melding into him. A battle for control raged inside both of their heads.

Shamael raised a shield around his consciousness, placed it around the part of this girl that was within his mind, and locked it in place so she could never take it back.

"Why didn't you tell me that was going to happen?" Shamael was barely able to control his anger when he shouted at the Guardian.

"If you couldn't figure out how to control it on your own with a single vitiate, you wouldn't have the strength to control two dozen," the Guardian said. "Go on. See what you can do with this link."

Shamael looked at the girl. Her eyes, once blue, were a glossy black with a hint of swirling red inside. She wore a vacant stare. He focused on the shield that represented her mind and cautiously moved his awareness inside that shield. He saw the world through her eyes once more, but now he saw himself standing erect, in charge and powerful. She was waiting for him to command her.

Shamael pulled his awareness back to himself, reached into his cloak, and gave the girl a skull and thighbone. She took the implements and waited.

"Draw the aeon myriad into these bones and send fire into the night sky," he ordered. She looked at the bones and back to him with confusion. Then she grew frustrated and scared. He touched the portion of her mind he held in the shield, and could *feel* her frustration and fear. She was trying to obey, but frustrated because she didn't know how to carry out his order, and scared she would disappoint him and be punished for her failure.

He went further into her mind and showed her how it was done. He allowed her to feel the sensation of directing the power through his memories. All at once, the skull and thighbone sprang to life with red power, and a stream of fire shot from both into the night sky.

"Let's try something more difficult, shall we?" Shamael said, and the girl released the fire.

He entered her mind and showed her the concept of allowing her physical body to absorb the power and then melt with that power into another life-form—a black hawk. This took longer, and Shamael was careful to show her every detail with clarity. Doing this wrong could kill her.

Once he was satisfied she fully understood, he withdrew his mind from her and took a pouch from his belt that held twenty-four small pendants—each with a hawk carved from bone hanging from a leather thong—and placed one of them in her hand. "Use this to help you transform into a hawk and fly."

The vitiate placed the pendant around her neck, next to the one the Guardian just made, held the bone carved hawk in her hand, and drew on the power. Her body was surrounded with a crimson glow, and she transformed into a hawk. With a proud shriek, she launched herself into the night sky and flew.

Shamael smiled with satisfaction as the rest of the waiting students whispered excitedly to one another. This spell was beyond anything they would've been able to accomplish in this lifetime with the amount of talent they possessed.

"Amazing," Shamael said to the Guardian. "She's gone from being a Demonologist to having the abilities of a Shapeshifter in a matter of minutes. This would have easily taken her two lifetimes to accomplish in the normal way."

"And you owe me ten years, Grand Warlock. Shall we continue?"

Demaris grudgingly admitted to himself that he was glad Genea had forced him to enjoy the day. The entire castle-like school had been decorated with flowers, sun rune paintings and tapestries, and ribbons of all the colors of summer. Salas, the high lore master, created a massive, suspended solar system that rotated in the sky above the castle, complete with the earth, the moon, and the four wandering planets.

The kitchens served delicious foods the entire day, and students could stop by any time they wanted to feast on meats, pastries, fruit, and even cakes and puddings.

There were foot races, javelin tossing, and some of the older students had contests of magical skill. Demaris stopped to watch the magic contests, and students chanted his name to join the duels. When he tried to politely decline, they chanted and shouted louder. Genea rescued him by saying he had an appointment with Daria to check his eye, and she hurried him away—another thing he was grateful she'd done that day.

Now it was awful. Music and dancing—which he worked hard to avoid. They stopped the festivities at midnight, and since there were no babies to bless, the lore masters took turns shooting beautiful patterns of colored lights to swirl and race into the night sky.

Now, more than an hour later, the dancing and music had started again, and Demaris felt more awkward than before the magic display. Something was . . . wrong. Was it just his anxiety about dancing? So far, Demaris had been able to avoid dancing, but Genea kept making subtle hints.

"Look how easy this dance is, Renn," she said as the music sped up. The students just moved randomly with the rhythm. "You don't even have to know any dance steps."

No, the *wrong* sensation wasn't the dancing. It was a dark feeling in the pit of his stomach and was growing in intensity. Something *was* wrong— something far away . . . far to the west. He stood and walked away.

"Renn! Where are you going?"

He vaguely heard Genea's call, and he knew he should probably answer, but he had to find out what was happening. He walked out of the castle, across the courtyard, climbed the stairs to the gallery that surrounded the outer yard, and peered westward over the crenelated balustrade that encircled the castle.

With no moon in the sky, the stars dotted the night like a billion points of light. A gentle breeze blew in from the distant Sentry Cliffs. The night was beautiful, but it felt . . . dreary—*wrong*. He kept staring westward but saw nothing.

"You feel it, don't you?"

Without his right eye, he hadn't noticed High Master Salas walk up beside him. Demaris turned his body so he could see the man.

"What is it, Master Salas?"

The old man's long white beard blew gently against his chest with the incoming breeze. He also peered westward.

"Somebody is doing dark magic tonight."

"It's getting stronger," Demaris said. "At least, the darkness I feel is getting more . . ."

"Intense," Salas finished for him.

Lynmaria blessed the babies at midnight. Since it was midsummer's Azur-Aven, there were more babies to bless than she suspected there would be during other months. Parents often held over their babies who should've been blessed last month or even two months ago so they could be blessed on this night.

As she proceeded through the blessings, however, a sense of foreboding grew in the pit of her stomach. None of the babies had been marked with the gift of power this night, and at first she thought the dark feeling was just sadness that none of these children possessed the touch of magic. But by the time the blessings were over, the feeling in her gut was like a dark sickness that came from the north . . . far north.

The crowd dispersed, and Lynmaria ambled to a small hill at the edge of the fairgrounds, peering northward. What was happening up there?

"Is everything all right, my good lady?" The deep voice pulled her out of her thoughts, and she turned to see Durham walking toward her. He was a large man with a pleasant face, and his thinning blond hair blew lightly with the breeze. He was a calming presence, which was pleasantly surprising, considering he'd spent much of his life as a soldier. He joined her on the knoll, and she turned back to face the north.

"I fear that dark magic is being done tonight, Durham."

Avaris sat up with a start and was instantly awake. Sweat from nightmares had drenched his clothes and now that he was not sleeping, a sick and dark foreboding filled him at his core. He got up from his bed of reeds, grabbed a thighbone and skull, and crept out of Esrath's shack. Maybe the strange hermit of the fens underestimated his enemies and they had already returned.

Avaris stepped into the night and peered into the darkness. He saw nothing unusual, but with no moon, it was difficult to see much. But the foreboding sense in his stomach grew stronger with each passing moment. Something was wrong. Something was . . . changing. But it wasn't close by. The feeling came from . . . the northwest. He turned that direction and stared into the dark night.

"What are you doing, Shamael?"

Avaris jumped at the sudden sound of Kintara's soft voice. He had been so intent on the danger that he didn't hear her follow him out of the shack.

"Shamael?" Avaris asked.

The pretty Warlock absently pushed a stray lock of black hair from her face and nodded. The cut on her left cheek was red and she was still weak from the poison, but growing stronger every day.

"Powerful magic is being performed tonight, and it comes from the northwest—the direction of the caves." She stepped next to Avaris and peered into the darkness. "We will have to leave this place . . . soon."

Dawn broke before Shamael had successfully wrestled and subdued the mind and will of the last vitiate. They truly *were* vitiate now; they belonged to him. They would do his bidding. He trembled with exhaustion and fatigue, and his mind felt like it was near the breaking point. He needed rest.

"What happens when I sleep?" Shamael asked the Guardian.

The ancient, liver-spotted man looked down his nose at Shamael. The look changed from disdain to amusement, and the Guardian broke out in laughter.

"That depends entirely on your strength, Grand Warlock. With any luck, you'll go crazy soon and die. I'm looking forward to my two-hundred-and-forty-year reprieve from this cursed duty!" The old man broke out once more in hysterical laughter, and then he held out his arms, lifted his head triumphantly, and with a loud swooshing rush, his old body was sucked back into the Aeon Pool.

Shamael watched the calm, black pool for a long time after the Guardian disappeared into its depths. What would it be like to exist that way for over two centuries? Perhaps he'd just made a grave mistake.

But what was done was done. He would control the vitiate, and he would *not* go insane learning to do so. They would be his servants, and he would become the most powerful Warlock of all time. But for now, he needed sleep. Tomorrow, with these soulless warriors at his side, his reign of chaos would begin with a vengeance.

THE END

Thank you for reading *Chaos Rising*. If you could take a moment to review my book on Amazon, I would appreciate it. Readers like you and me often decide what books to read based on the number and quality of reviews. Your review of my work would mean a great deal to me. Thanks again for spending your valuable time with Renn, Avaris, and the rest of the characters on the continent of Lemuria.

To learn the story of how Shamael won the battle to become the Grand Warlock and how Avaris helped Lekiah and Kalisha escape the caves, read *Shamael and the Battle at the Well of Sacrifice*.

ABOUT THE AUTHOR

Perry was born and raised in the greater Salt Lake City, Utah, area. He is very happily married and has seven wonderful children and two grandchildren. His first exposure to the great world of fantasy was, of course, J.R.R. Tolkien's Lord of the Rings trilogy when he was fourteen. After that, he read the books of Patricia A. McKillip, Terry Brooks, David Eddings, and Stephen R. Donaldson, among others. Currently, his favorite author is Brandon Sanderson. He loves the unique and interesting magic systems Brandon creates, the memorable characters, and interesting stories.

Perry actually began writing the Lemurian Chronicles in 1993 and, after more than two decades of rewrites, editing, and reediting, finally decided to take the plunge and publish his epic fantasy. Don't worry—each additional installment will be released no more than eighteen months to two years apart.

50140088R00215

Made in the USA
Middletown, DE
23 June 2019